What readers have said about *Spring till September*...

"Sarah Kincaid leads her reader on a journey through adventure, love, friendship, and 'taking a chance'. Her characters are diverse and yet comfortable in their West Virginia roots. *Spring till September* left me with a desire to read further and continue experiencing life with our new friends. I look forward to the sequel."

Becky Reynolds, Coordinator – Discover the Joy Conference

"Grab yourself a cup of hot chocolate, find a cozy blanket, and curl up for a great story. Set in the charming town of Williamson, West Virginia, *Spring till September* will capture your heart as you cheer for Caroline and her unique cast of townspeople. Through all the twists and turns life throws at her, discover Caroline's secret of maintaining inner peace that passes all human understanding."

Susan Knight, Cypress Church
Galloway, OH

"*Spring till September* allows the reader to become part of a truly beautiful love story that reminds us of a time where respect and friendship were important in forming relationships – a time that society needs today."

Libby Goff, Belfry High School
Belfry, KY

This is a gift for my mother, Vivian. Thank-you for being my very best friend and always encouraging me that I have stories to tell.

Mamaw,

Look for HABAKKUK moments. — they are everywhere!

Sarah Knox

12/18   *Habakkuk 1:5*

Though this book is set in real places, it is a work of fiction and any similarity to actual people or events is completely coincidental...*However*, it is dedicated to those who believe they find themselves hidden among the characters of my pages.

-SEK

*S*pring till *S*eptember

Book One

*S*arah *E. K*incaid

WESTBOW
P R E S S®
A DIVISION OF THOMAS NELSON
& ZONDERVAN

Scripture quotations marked (NIV) are taken from the Holy Bible, New International Version®, NIV®. Copyright © 1973, 1978, 1984, 2011 by Biblica, Inc.™ Used by permission of Zondervan. All rights reserved worldwide. www.zondervan.com The "NIV" and "New International Version" are trademarks registered in the United States Patent and Trademark Office by Biblica, Inc.™

Scripture quotations are taken from the Holy Bible, New Living Translation, copyright ©1996, 2004, 2007, 2013, 2015 by Tyndale House Foundation. Used by permission of Tyndale House Publishers, Inc., Carol Stream, Illinois 60188. All rights reserved.

Interior Image and Cover Design: Maria Arlene Blackburn

This is a work of fiction. All of the characters, names, incidents, organizations, and dialogue in this novel are either the products of the author's imagination or are used fictitiously.

WestBow Press books may be ordered through booksellers or by contacting:

WestBow Press
A Division of Thomas Nelson & Zondervan
1663 Liberty Drive
Bloomington, IN 47403
www.westbowpress.com
1 (866) 928-1240

Because of the dynamic nature of the Internet, any web addresses or links contained in this book may have changed since publication and may no longer be valid. The views expressed in this work are solely those of the author and do not necessarily reflect the views of the publisher, and the publisher hereby disclaims any responsibility for them.

Any people depicted in stock imagery provided by Thinkstock are models, and such images are being used for illustrative purposes only. Certain stock imagery © Thinkstock.

ISBN: 978-1-5127-7561-7 (sc)
ISBN: 978-1-5127-7562-4 (hc)
ISBN: 978-1-5127-7560-0 (e)

Library of Congress Control Number: 2017902226

Print information available on the last page.

WestBow Press rev. date: 02/22/2017

Prologue

Spring – Today

Caroline picks up the laundry basket as she hears the screen door to the back porch slam then bounce shut. She works her way through the kitchen and living room collecting forgotten items along the way that never seem to make it to the washer. She climbs the stairs and an icy breeze blows across her face from the open windows despite the April sun casting its golden glow.

With basket still resting comfortably on her hip, she walks into to her bedroom, strips the sheets from the bed, coming back to drop them over the railing grinning as they fall to the living room floor below. Moving on, Caroline stops in the loft picking up books off the floor placing them neatly back on the shelf. She tosses two throw pillows on the couch then sets the basket on her desk. She thinks about clearing off the bills, unfinished lesson plans, and a stack of tests that needs to be graded, but decides today is too beautiful to be cooped up inside.

She walks away ignoring the paperwork for another time to crank open the three windows at the far end of the loft that overlook the back yard and the pool. Dad called this morning saying he would be down after breakfast to help dip out the leaves and drain the water off the cover. She looks out the windows and doesn't see him, so she knows she has a few more minutes, before she needs to go out and help.

Smiling again, her thoughts drift to pool day as a child. It was always one of her favorite days of the year and still is. Saturday morning and Dad would tell them it was time to take off the cover. She, Alex, and Nick would be wild with excitement even though swimming was still a few weeks away. They would rush around getting changed after breakfast and be running down the hill to see if Gran and Poppy were awake long before Dad would join them. It never failed, one of them would get wet or they would start fussing at each other as to who would do what, then Dad would roar out to them settled down. Privately, he was just as excited as they were, so his temper would not flare for long. One of the saddest days of Caroline's year always took place several months later when the cover had to once again be put on the pool and it was closed for winter. Summer was over; definitely a day filled with melancholy.

Thinking back, she remembers…

When she was about eleven, Poppy bought a heater for the pool and they had warm water through the end of October. The week of Halloween was so warm that year Caroline had a pool party and invited her friends to go swimming. Unfortunately, it ended early with screams of fright and nine little girls couldn't get out of the water fast enough, when a few bats decided to stop by for a drink of water. The screams quickly faded to laughter and wrapped in colorful towels they walked the path through a short stretch of woods back up the hill to Caroline's house. Before they reached the clearing, four figures in horrible monster masks came out of the shadows and chased the girls the rest of the way to the safety of her parents.

Charging through the front door, the girls all started talking at once trying to explain to Caroline's parents everything that had happened: the bats, getting out of the pool, climbing the hill, and then being chased. Before anything could be explained clearly Alex, Will, Carter, and Nick stomp onto the porch and start shouting for the girls to come out; beating on the windows, ringing the doorbell. Amid delighted squeals, the girls run out to see them and bask in the glow of the "beautiful older brother" leaving Caroline in the kitchen crying to her mother that the boys had ruined her party. Soon Caroline would be consoled and wet bathing suits are traded for t-shirts and shorts. The boys would be forgiven and allowed to stay for games, food, and laughter. Sometime just before midnight, Dad reminds the boys of their campout and they leave to their "fort" while the girls swoon. Even Caroline is a little disappointed they had to go.

She collects her basket then walks from of the loft, pausing briefly to dust the glass of a few picture frames and the length of a narrow hall table with the hem of her oversized t-shirt. Carefully placing each frame back in its appropriate place, she starts to move on to finish her morning house work, but one of the frames catches her eye. She returns to the table and instead of adjusting its angle, she picks it up to study the picture and is quickly lost in thought.

Without realizing, Caroline allows the basket to slip to the floor spilling at her feet and wanders back into her room to sit on the edge of the unmade bed. Moments earlier she was excited about Spring's first warm day that is sunny enough to hang out sheets. She was glad to have a chance to spend most of the day outside and took a small joy in how she loves line-dried sheets. The sheets, the sunshine, and the overturned basket are forgotten and no longer important. She sits on the edge of the bed holding the frame staring almost without seeing.

The day is one of those perfect days that you looked forward to when the snow is falling in January and you think the cold will never end. The day asks for the blinds to be pulled all the way up. Windows are to be opened to let fresh breezes blow stirring up old dust removing any hint of the forgotten winter. The sun wants to create a warm happy dance driving away all shadows. But, the excitement of the finally arrived Spring is gone and Caroline has returned to the past.

She sits and she remembers.

How many times a day does she pass this very picture and it goes completely unnoticed? How often does she pick it up to dust, like she did moments before, and return it to its place with not so much as a second thought. She is unsure why today is any different or why there is a tightness gathering in her chest and smile on her face.

Memory...too often it will take you farther than you want to go and keep you longer than you want to stay. In a matter of heartbeats, Caroline's memory is reeling down a road to an almost forgotten time. She traces the edges of the wooden frame with a finger and lets out a sigh. Thoughts of yesterday come back in an overwhelming flood. A silent tear quickly gives way to sobbing. Caroline slides from the bed to a sad heap on the floor, knees to chest, clutching the picture frame. Her mind and body are completely overcome and she does not even try to stop it. She lets the waves of sorrow pass over and over her. Pain and sadness, she has had locked deep inside are released in a torrent. The sobs are uncontrolled and has her gasping for breath as old wounds burst open bleeding out unending thoughts of why.

And she remembers…

"For I know the plans I have for you," DECLARES the LORD.

Jeremiah 29:11

Chapter 1

"For I know the plans I have for you," declares
the Lord – Jeremiah 29:11 NIV

March 2006

H *is heart races and he can feel sweat running down his back as he*
silently presses his body against the garage. The wall is cinderblock
and warm against his skin. He can feel sharp little pieces of concrete
scratching his shoulder blades. The night air is thick and heavy and the heat
is oppressive even as the time nears midnight. He slowly begins to round the
corner as home base comes into view; Eric Tucker's back porch. He can feel the
wet grass lick his ankles as he stealthily moves toward the target. With every
step he takes, the light shining through the glass of the aluminum storm door
grows larger and brighter as if beckoning to him.

Still safely behind the garage, he quickly looks to see if the coast is clear
before he moves on. No one appears to be close and all is silent except for the
sounds of a summer night; the chirp of crickets, rustling of leaves signaling a
coming storm, and a car driving away at the far end of the street. Nervous,
yet excited adrenaline rushes through his veins. He is getting closer with
each step.

He sprints across the yard and reaches the gate on silent footsteps. In a few
precious seconds he will race onto the porch and be free. Lifting the latch, he
carefully opens the gate without the slightest creak. As he closes it, he can hear
the distant shouts of the others making their way to base. A few more steps......
Just a few more steps.

He starts to run, but loses his footing. Letting out a sharp squeal when his
knee lands on a rock, he finds himself on all fours attempting to crawl to the

1

steps. He can hear the distant pounding of feet as the others hurry down the sidewalk and are quickly approaching the yard. Getting back up, he grabs his knee and tries to rub out the pain, but his hand feels torn flesh and a sticky trickle of blood. Ignoring the wound, he starts again, but the pain from his knee shoots down his leg forcing him to limp.

It then becomes difficult to walk and he is struggling to make it through what seems like knee-high grass. He is sinking and stumbling; it takes great effort to keep moving. It feels like grass is no longer beneath his feet. He becomes lost in fog and can no longer see the porch. The light now is so intense; he is blinded and disoriented, groping to find his way

The wind picks up and throws a thousand needles in his face. Instantly night vanishes, but the light is still there only high above him. His body is very hot and his breathing labored. His back is bent as if carrying a heavy load, but he cannot figure out what it is, nor can he put it down. Suddenly, there is a loud screech above his head and as he looks up…he falls…

Seth Garrett tears himself from sleep. His heart is racing and his face wet with sweat. Panting, he flips onto his back and untangles from the sheets. He feels the beads of perspiration run rivers down his temple wetting his hairline. He lifts the sheet and scrubs his face dry. Seth opens his eyes and lies motionless staring at the ceiling. He can faintly see the blades of the fan as he watches them turn round and round and round, almost mesmerizing. He lies there for the briefest moment trying to decide where he is, still disoriented from restless sleep. The only light in the room is red and intense, but shines harmlessly from his bedside clock reading 5:18am. Catching his breath, he swings his feet to the floor and rests on the edge of the bed. The only sounds are coming from the soft whir of the ceiling fan and the brakes of a nearby *Norfolk and Southern* train screeching as it slows in preparation to enter the railyard.

He sits there, slumped over, forearms resting on thighs, for several moments. He becomes acutely aware of the tiny hairs on his back, a delicate almost annoying crawling sensation, as the fan dries his skin. He sits there and waits. He waits for his breathing to return to normal. He waits for his heart to stop racing. He waits for this gnawing feeling in his chest to subside. What is it - this *feeling*; a pressure that is very real, but seems more emotional than medical. Seth cannot call it fear, but it is by no means pleasant or comforting. It is more like…uneasy or unsure, though, it is definitely familiar for this is not the first night his sleep has been disturbed.

This dream has awakened him several times before. It is always similar scenes playing out in his subconscious; a mix of jumbled confusion, of heat and light and running; only tonight, somehow, it seemed a little different. His mind lingers for a moment as to what this all means, but he feels no cause for alarm. His frustration at losing sleep is the greatest concern. Thinking about the dream again, he recognizes; however, one detail is always the same. He never makes it to Eric's porch.

Eric Tucker. What would make him dream of Eric Tucker? It had been middle school when they had last played hide-n-seek and Seth has only seen him a few times since graduation. Their lives quickly went in different directions and neither of them lives in their small Pennsylvania town anymore. It was more than three years ago when Seth met up with Eric at their high school reunion. He had moved to Philadelphia to open a small robotics firm, and was quite successful living comfortably in suburbia with a wife and child on the way.

Seth lets out a short laugh, more like an amused snort, as he remembers his childhood friend. Eric always had the best toys; erector sets, remote control cars with racetrack including two loops, chemistry sets, *Walkman*, *Gameboy*, unfortunately, the "like new" condition never lasted long. Eric would take anything apart and put it back together in his own creation. Some things were cool, others junk. The junked experiments were catapulted off the trampoline in his backyard as they jumped onto it from the roof of the porch.

Eric's back porch…Seth comes back to reality and remembers why he is awake. He leans back and stretches reaching towards the ceiling releasing an exaggerated growling sigh.

What are you doing taking this little walk down memory lane? You are a thousand miles away from home and those memories are a lifetime ago!

It is now 5:26am, and Seth decides it is time to get out of bed. He rises and walks across the room stopping briefly by his desk to turn on his laptop on his way to the bathroom. The floor tiles are like ice and he winces as he clicks on the light waiting for his eyes to adjust. When he finishes his morning routine, he turns, leans both hands on the sink, and stares into the mirror. *Williamson, WV...* Letting out a deep, almost sad sigh, he slumps, slowly shakes his head, and lets it hang between his shoulders. Before he has time to think about what on earth he is doing here, he puts toothpaste on his brush and jumps in the shower.

———————◆————————

Caroline Hatfield's classroom phone rings as the bell sounds the end of the day. Twenty-seven seniors make a mad dash for the door as her final announcements fall on deaf ears. She picks up the phone as it rings a second time.

"Caroline Hatfield."

"Heaaay, Caro-line." She recognizes the slow Appalachian voice immediately. Martha, one of the office personnel, has a Southern drawl all her own that is likewise entertaining and endearing. She has worked at Belfry High School even before Caroline was a student. It is her perky nature and ready smile that make you love her immediately. "I have a parent on the other line who wants ta schedule a meetin' with you. Would tomarra durin' yer plannin' be ok?"

Before Caroline can respond, James Blackburn sticks his head in her door and says, "Remember, eleventh grade Career Assembly during first, second, and third period tomorrow morning."

Caroline motions with her finger for James to wait a moment and returns to the phone call. "Martha, the earliest I could meet with them is Friday or any day next week."

"All-rite, I'll tell em and then email yooou the details. Mr. Tackett will want to join ya."

"Thanks, Martha."

Hanging up the phone, Caroline returns her attention to the visitor at her door. "Aggghhh. James, I forgot about Career Assembly. I thought those were finished?" Caroline asks with an exasperated growl.

"Nope," he responds, almost curtly. "We have this one and one more the first week of May, a financial planner from Pikeville. I sent *you* and the rest of the department a reminder email and it has been on the faculty calendar since Opening Day...in August." He smiles at her teasingly.

James Blackburn is a man in his mid-fifties with graying temples, a slight potbelly, and kind smile. He is the picture of casual distinction. He always wears a tie, though they usually have fun, eye-catching prints, never forgets to wear red on Fridays to support school spirit, and he carries a sense of respect and authority quietly, but effectively. He is loved by students and staff alike and has challenged Caroline as a student and now is her inspiring mentor as chairman of the social studies department. In addition to being a great teacher, he is also a wonderful godly man, husband, and father. Caroline often looks to him for guidance that is beyond the scope of the classroom, trusting both his wisdom and his faith.

"James," adding extra whine and a pouting expression for effect, "Career Assembly? I have a test scheduled for first and second period tomorrow."

"All I can tell you is – reschedule."

Flopping down into her chair she changes gears almost immediately, "Who do we have coming this time? That last guy was soooo boring. Where was he from? The hospital?"

"No, the guy from the hospital was in December," James begins as he comes into her room perching on top of a student desk directly in front of Caroline. "and he was the one who answered his cell phone three times during his presentation as he continued to click through the slides. The last guy was the electrical mine inspector who was *sooooo* boring. He was the one who told the joke about never licking a light bulb." He finishes with a wry smile.

Caroline, at first, seems puzzled, but as the memory dawns on her who James is talking about, then remembers the light bulb joke, she begins to laugh covering her face with her hands and leaning her elbows on her desk. She asks again with muffled voice through her hands, "Who do we have this time?"

"Captain Bryce Tyler of the West Virginia National Guard."

Caroline peeks between spread fingers and asks skeptically, "Who?"

James unfolds the paper he is carrying and attempts to read the email. *"Mr. Blackburn, this is to confirm Thursday, March 23 –"*

"The National Guard? From where?" Confused, Caroline interrupts.

"Williamson. *March 23. We will arrive –,*"

"At West End?" Caroline continues to question.

"Yes. *We will arrive at 7:30 –,*"

"That doesn't look like an army base to me." She questions, still skeptical.

"It's not an army base, it's an armory. *We have a short presentation and then some prizes for the students.* " James goes on patiently.

"So is it just a warehouse for guns? That must be why they have that tank parked in the front yard!" Caroline giggles as she drops her hands to her desk and grins. James only smirks at her over the rims of his reading glasses.

Caroline continues, "Bryce Tyler. Do I know him? He sounds familiar." She again looks at James with a crinkled forehead and puzzled expression as if trying to locate Bryce Tyler in her memory.

"You might. Two of his children go to school here, Deaton and Kayla Tyler. His wife teaches at Southside—,"

"Yes, I had Deaton last year in World Civ and Kayla is with me for geography this year. He was a great kid, very smart. Kayla is too, just a little more reserved. She is really quiet, but a lovely girl." Jumping back to her original thought, "Did you say prizes? I never see much of anything going on down there. There are only a few cars in the parking lot when I drive by to class –,"

Now, it was James' turn to interrupt, "Why don't you write down all of these questions and you can have Cpt. Tyler clear up any confusion… tomorrow. And speaking of class," glancing at his watch, "aren't you going to be late?"

James gives her a questioning look then leans over to tap her on the forehead with the paper. This seems to jar her back to the present and she quickly gets up, locates her many items, all the while having a conversation with James, none of which he understands, and rushes out the door leaving him sitting on top of the desk chuckling at his funny friend.

It is after nine, before Caroline finally unlocks the back door and walks into her house. She clicks on the light then hangs her keys from a hook on a small frame just above the switch. The backdoor comes directly from the garage into the laundry room that leads to either a screened porch running the width of the back of the house to the left or the kitchen to the right. She walks into the kitchen and drops everything on the small butcher-block island, before going into the living room.

She notices the red light of the answering machine flashing and walks to a narrow table next to the stairway, turns on a lamp, and listens to the messages. The first is from her mother this afternoon, *"Caroline, if you get this message before class, please call me, otherwise I will see you tonight at Bible Study."* Caroline deletes the message having already spoken to her mother.

The next was from her cousin, Will, in a demanding tone, but playful spirit, "HELLO! I have sent you three text messages today and you never replied. Call me tonight before eight; I have safety checks."

Listening to the last message, Caroline goes back to the kitchen to retrieve her cell phone and respond to Will's texts. She never has any worry about *not* getting messages from him, because he will continue to aggravate you every few minutes until you finally answer.

Walking back into the living room she hears her grandmother's voice. *"Caroline, this is Gran. Just callin' to see if you had made it home. I didn't get out to Bible Study this evenin' cause I wasn't feelin' well. I was out at town with Nadine all day and I just think I'm a little tired and maybe getting' a cold. She insisted that I stay in and take something and said this was no time to get sick. I don't know what that's got to do with anything. This is just as good of a time as any to get sick! Then your Uncle Davis called and I didn't think it was nice to ask him to call back. You know he doesn't call enough as is. So, I thought I had better –,"* BEEP!

Caroline smiles as she deletes the message. Gran ran out of time. She thinks it is funny how Gran always leaves so many details. Rarely does she finish with all of her information, before the machine beeps and cuts her off. Caroline picks up the phone and makes her way to the couch to call Gran. She wearily sinks back into the cushions and props her feet on the low table in front of her. After two rings, Gran answers.

"Hel-lo."

The sweet, country voice is so familiar to Caroline. In it, you can always hear a smile. It is just one of the things Caroline loves most about her. She also loves how her mother's voice is subtly beginning to sound more like Gran's. There are times it is hard even for her to tell them apart over the phone.

"Hey, Gran it's me. How are ya, this evening?"

"Oh, I'm fine. Nadine was just makin' a fuss, but she will make an even bigger fuss if I do get sick and not want me to go with you next Saturday."

"Do you think you will be up to it?" Caroline asks with a silent smile.

"Will I be up to it? Shooooot!" Gran exclaims, sounding more than a little miffed, "Nadine is not my boss! I'm 81 years old, almost 82, not some child. I've taken care of myself this long, and I think I've done a perty good job. Nadine may think I *need* takin' care of, but I don't! We're drivin' into Charleston, not California. So, yes, I will be going with you!" And that was that.

Caroline laughs at Gran and continues, "You better not let Aunt Nadine hear you talk like that."

In a slightly weary tone, "I know...I love her and she means well, but so help me Hannah, she wears me out sometimes! Besides, I have things to do. I need a new dress for Easter Sunday and want to go to *The Purple Onion* and get hanging baskets for the front porch. They always have the nicest hanging baskets of Wandering Jew and Southern Ferns. The *Farmer's Nursery* downtown gets their plants in too close to Mother's Day and that's just too late, and they usually don't have what I want. By then, they've all been picked over. I know it's a little early, but I can keep them warm in the upstairs bathroom until it's time to put them out," stopping, suddenly. "I'm sorry, hun, you were the one needin' to go to Charleston, and I should be askin' you what we're goin' to do."

Caroline smiles again at Gran's sweetness, "No, that's ok. We can do whatever you want. I just have to get to *The Supply Closet* before they close at 2:00. It's in the same area of town as *The Purple Onion*, so that will be no problem. And we can leave as early as you like and take the whole day if you want."

"I can be ready early, because I'm already up."

"Ok. We'll plan on leaving around 7:30. Is that too early?"

"I'll be ready," Gran says with a sighing laugh.

"Hmm – how about 8:00? I may want to sleep in a little."

"That's fine, because I'm with you."

"Ok, 8:00 it is, but I am sure I will change my mind before next Saturday...Well, Gran, I need to go. We have a guest speaker tomorrow that I forgot about, so I have some rescheduling to do...I feel so tired this evening, but I think it's too early to start looking forward to summer vacation! I'm glad you're feeling ok. I'll talk to you tomorrow...You have a good night."

"You have a good night, too, sweetie. Love you."

"I love you, too, Gran."

A tender smile comes on Caroline's face; she loves her spunky grandmother. They have always been very close, but in recent years, since Poppy died, they have become great friends holding each other in the tightest of confidences. She lets her head roll back onto the cushions of the couch and closes her eyes recalling Gran's excitement over Nadine's *fussin'*.

Nadine and Gran get along quite well, but there are those times, as Gran said, Nadine can wear her out. Nadine and Charlotte, Caroline's mother and Gran's only daughter are so different that *dealing* with Nadine is a challenge for Gran at times, but she handles it gracefully. Charlotte is very much like Gran; sweet, kind, understanding, feisty and funny, and most of all easy. Aunt Nadine, on the other hand, has a tendency to be a little difficult, high strung, and definitely wound too tight. She is lacking in perky and positive, and rarely understands jokes or humor. She is somewhat melodramatic and can cry at the drop of a hat. If she had lived during Bible times, she would have been hired out as a professional mourner. She has a touch of hypochondria, but loves completely and would do anything to make you happy.

Caroline knows her aunt and *knows* she could make a fuss. The woman is convinced pills can fix anything, a cold can kill you, and there is no pain like a sore throat. Never fail, every year, she wears a *Vick's Salve* rag tired around her neck most of the time from when the leaves began to fall until they bloom again. As a child, Caroline was always fascinated how Aunt Nadine had the most unusual aroma. In fourth grade, her teacher read the class a story about the Egyptians that told how pharaohs were prepared for the afterlife before entering their tombs. She explained how the bodies were rubbed with oils and *salves* then wrapped in cloth. The pharaohs were so well preserved, that over time their skin became like leather.

That Sunday during family dinner at Gran's, Caroline is sitting at the *kids' table* in the kitchen with her brothers, Alex and Nick, and their cousin, Will. She is telling them what Ms. Staton had read that week about the Egyptians when she asks Will if Aunt Nadine is related to one of the pharaohs. He and Alex began to laugh and suggest that she go to the dining room and ask her. Nick, the youngest of the four speaks up and asks what is so funny, a little more confused than Caroline. Alex and Will ignore him as they inch over to the kitchen door and listen to for Caroline to ask her question. They had to clap their hands tightly over their mouths to keep from bursting out laughing and risk getting in trouble.

Caroline walks into the dining room and edges up to the head of the table between Gran and Poppy and innocently asks, "Aunt Nadine, are you related to a pharaoh?"

The words have no sooner left her mouth when she hears Alex and Will make a huge commotion in the kitchen. Quickly, her head snaps back around as Aunt Nadine begins to speak. With a very confused look on her face, she gives her usual response.

"*Ba-bawk! Gobble, gobble, gobble?*" Well, at least that's how it sounds. A short, loud squawk like a chicken, followed by a series of very quick turkey gobbles. "What!?!? I don't even know what you're talking about?" very flustered, because she is confused with cheeks flaming.

Caroline, sweetly with honest interest of a child goes on to explain, "Ms. Staton, taught us this week about the pharaohs of Egypt and how when they died they were rubbed with salve and wrapped in cloth. So, I was just wondering if you were related to one of the pharaohs or just trying to get your neck to turn into leather?"

It all happens at once. Her mother's brother and Nadine's husband, Martin, Marty for short, showers everyone at the table in ice tea as it spewed like a geyser from his mouth. Her mother gasps and instantly says Caroline owes her aunt an apology, though Caroline doesn't have any idea why. Poppy breaks out into a loud donkey laugh and her dad almost falls out of his chair trying to avoid the tea-spray. Gran, lovingly, puts her arm around Caroline's waist and pulls her close to her side softly patting her behind and rescues her, "No," she chides sweetly, "she's not related to a pharaoh. Now, help me clear the table then we'll get dessert."

Gran's answer is perfect. Caroline wanted a simple yes or no and she got it. It is not until years later that Caroline sees the humor in her question and confides in Gran that she had conveniently left out whether or not Nadine wanted her neck to turn into leather. With a feisty smile, Gran says, "Well, she's not dead yet," and winks.

There is a similar smile is on Caroline's face as she laboriously pulls herself up off the couch and goes back into the kitchen. She opens the pantry door and just stares. She hopes something will catch her eye that is delicious, quick, and easy, because she is in no mood to cook and did not take the time to get something while she was out. She sees a package of *Ramen Noodles*.

Great! The king's feast for the not so young and single.

The noodles are ready in a few minutes; she pours them into a large mug, turns off all the lights. She hears her cell phone chime – new text message. Will is reminding her, as if she would forget, dinner and game night is at his apartment at 6:00 – DON'T BE LATE! This will be the first of several messages from him before tomorrow evening arrives. She laughs at her cousin and his overly intense ways, but does not stop to imagine what life would be like without him – quiet and boring! She checks the front door lock out of habit knowing she did not unlock it since she came through the garage and quietly climbs the stairs for the last time of the evening.

The loft is directly above the kitchen and overlooks the living room below. Caroline has made this area into an office. It was a neat, little nook of a space that she has always loved. She remembers playing here as a child when her great-grandmother was alive and still living in the house. There is a tiny door in one corner that always made her think of *Alice in Wonderland*. It leads into a small storage space, and was the perfect setting for magical times of childhood imagination.

When she moved in a few years ago, she had general upgrades made to the house – fresh paint, new kitchen appliances, carpet removed and hardwood floors refinished, replacement windows, and a red tin roof with matching shutters. She did make one main change, installing three skylights, two looking down on the living room and one positioned in the sloping ceiling over her desk. She wanted to keep most everything the same, so it did not lose any of its "old house" feel. That's what she loves most; it is a home that has been and is *lived* in which only adds to its character.

Caroline sits down in front of her computer, carefully placing the steaming mug on the desk. In addition to forgetting Career Assembly today, her students were wild. Spring arrives, the weather finally breaks, and each passing day gets you closer to summer vacation, but this also means students, who are still restricted to the confines of the classroom, all develop *Spring Fever*. The day has been chaotic: the classroom phone rang constantly, department meeting during planning, a District report that needed filing though the email was never forwarded to her was requested at the last minute, a fight in the hall during break had two boys tumbling through her open door just as two teachers arrive to take them to Mr. Tackett's office. The end of seventh period could not arrive soon enough. Then her night class is preparing for their last lab practical, which they hate, and finals, so that just adds to the usual chaos of her day.

She lets out a long deep breath and looks up. During the day, light floods through the windows creating a natural glow in the house year round, but tonight the sky is overcast and dark, no stars are out. It is like she is staring into a black box, devoid of all light, nothing. Leaning back as the chair rocks and swivels, she closes her eyes and lets out another deep breath. She sits there basking in the silence waiting for the emotional storm of the day to finally subside. The subtle pounding in her head is almost gone. Several moments pass as she loses herself in listless contemplation. She gently bounces the chair with one foot barely touching the floor, rocking, rocking, rocking herself into complete relaxation so very close to sleep. For a moment, she has a twinge of loneliness touched by a glimpse of sadness. The sky is dark and offers neither comfort nor companionship.

Finally, she hears the click of the heat pump as it comes on and the chairs raises with a jerk bringing her back from her wandering. She eats her noodles, checks and sends a few emails, updates her schedule and lesson plans, then spends the next hour immersed in the warm, silent comfort of her claw foot tub and crawls into bed alone.

Chapter 11

"being confident of this, that He who began a good work in you will carry it on to completion until the day of Christ Jesus." - Philippians 1:6 NIV

James demands little from his department, and is usually very relaxed and flexible. He does, however, have one rule he never likes to see broken: be early and you will always be on time. So this morning when they are to meet a guest speaker at 7:30, Caroline is not quite following that rule since she has yet to make it inside the building.

The morning does not start as Caroline had planned. She turns off her alarm when she thinks she has hit snooze and now is running twenty minutes behind. She pulls her black Ford Explorer onto campus and buzzes around the student traffic making her way out back to the faculty parking lot. The clock on the dash reads twenty-five after seven. She has only had a few minutes to drop her stuff by her classroom before she is to meet James in the Commons to greet Cpt. Tyler. She flips down the visor and hurriedly applies lipstick, checks her hair, which she thinks, looks like a wild mess, and races for the door.

The doors from the faculty lot lead her through the stairwell and into the back hall. Looking to the left, she can see into the Commons; only a few students have arrived this early. Three doors downs, she struggles to get the key in the door while juggling her red, distressed leather messenger bag (a gift from her parents after she was hired), a black with white paisley *Vera Bradley* with her monogram stitched in bold red across the front, and a set of textbooks the department is considering to use next fall. Inside her classroom, she unceremoniously dumps everything on her desk and lets out an exasperated sigh. Caroline hopes she can steal a few minutes during homeroom to get a little more organized. She hates being in a disheveled rush, but too often finds she is running behind.

Caroline smooths her skirt and tugs the jacket into place of her favorite black suit trimmed in red satin cording, frowning that both fit a little more snuggly than the last time she wore them. She admires her bright red nails shining through her new peep-toes with the dainty bow on the heel. Fashionable, yet not too trendy; James will not fuss. She then rubs her front teeth with a finger to remove any traces of stray lipstick. As the door closes, she takes a deep breath poising herself with an air of thinly veiled confidence and walks down the hall ready to face the day.

The Commons is a huge three-story room in the center of the school and is the hub of action. To the right, is the main entrance to the building, which opens up to the office and Student Services. It is bisected in the middle connecting the classroom wing with the gym. There is also a large stairway that leads to the second floor with mezzanine that encircles the room giving it an imposing since of grandeur. The far end of the room, with floor- to-ceiling windows that appear opaque due to early morning fog, serves as the cafeteria. It is near empty this time of day save a few scattered students sitting at round, grey cafeteria tables. Some are eating breakfast and others finishing neglected homework from the night before while others attempt to sleep a few more minutes pillowed by book bags and hooded sweatshirts.

Caroline walks across the Commons looking for James. She spots him near the doors of the office talking with another teacher who is on morning hall duty. She casually scans the main entrance, but does not see Cpt. Tyler. Caroline silently rejoices breathing a sigh of relief knowing she is safe not leaving James or their guest waiting. She arrives on the end of the conversation as James and Mike are discussing state testing that is to begin the first week of April.

"James, I don't have enough calculators in my classroom set and if I am going to proctor the test to my homeroom, I need more. Do we have enough money left in the budget to buy a full set? I can take what I need and divide the rest among the department and I need at least six, because you can't depend on kids bringing their own." James has served on the Site Based Council for several years and most teachers know if you want something accomplished, you must have James on your side. Mike knows this and is not above whining that the needs of the math department should always take precedent over the requests of anyone else.

Mike Hensley is a banty rooster type of fellow who teaches calculus and trigonometry. He is beyond forty and acts as if he believes he is still twenty. He is thin and wiry, with a receding hairline (much to his disappointment), and has an unforgettable, thunderous laugh that seems to far outweigh his body. He is full of energy and has a sharp, witty tongue, which he unleashes on anyone. He is always impeccably dressed; staying right up with fashion and this morning is no different. He is effectively carrying his cool confidence in a tailored white button-down shirt with a tiny light green pin stripe and French cuffs in the same green, complemented by a silk tie in shades of lime and Kelly. His black, flat-front linen dress pants have a perfect crease running down the front and back of his leg to blunt-nosed black dress shoes polished to a perfect matte finish.

"The Site Based Council meets on Tuesday, so I can make a request for the purchase, then." James says calmly not wanting to immediately give in to Mike and his usual overeager, demanding self.

"James buddy, that may not be enough time," he says a little insistent. "I have to order them from the County Warehouse and the last time, they were out of stock and it took over two weeks for them to get shipped." Mike is pushing, but he can see he is getting his point across.

James is quiet for a few beats either processing what Mike is saying or actually trying to figure out how to make the purchase without a meeting of the Council. "Tell Mr. Stowers what you need and why and he can give you the purchase order. Have the other members of the Council sign off on it and then go to Nina for the PO number. This way you can send the order to the County before the end of the day and we will decide how to pay for it at Tuesday's meeting."

Mike gives James a congratulatory slap on the shoulder, "Thanks, James. I really appreciate this," not even trying to conceal the pleasure with himself on being such a good negotiator.

Mike is about to leave when James adds, "Check with rest of the math teachers and see how many they need. You don't want to place an order and still run short."

"Ok. I will." Mike turns to leave, but sees Caroline and waits. As she approaches, Mike taps his watch with a sarcastic smile. "Good morning

Ms. Hatfield. I do believe you are two minutes late." He is certain to emphasize the Mizz.

"I'm sorry *Mr. Hensley*, I wasn't aware you were promoted to official time keeper." Caroline responds with an icy stare.

"Well, you know not just anyone could handle such a responsibility," he claims puffing out his chest in feigned importance.

"You are so right. The job requirements must have been that you had to be the resident metrosexual with a fondness for pastel colors and an acid tongue," she agrees seriously, trying to hold in a smile.

"One can only assume you yourself are not a slave to fashion," giving her the once over as if he does not approve of her equally as tasteful clothing. "Besides, my wife loves me in bright colors. She says it adds to my cheerful nature."

"*Cheerful nature.* Is that what she likes to call it?"

"Ahhhh, Caroline, such salty words so early in the morning. What a way to start the day." Mike says flashing a devilish smile followed by his signature laugh.

"Always a pleasure, Michael," Caroline ends sweetly. She has come to look forward to this almost daily banter. There are some who do not appreciate Mike's unique combination of humor and harassment, but Caroline enjoys it. He does keep you on your toes, but it is fun and adds levity to the sometimes-monotonous days.

It is now that James interrupts. "As entertaining as I find you all to be, could you please put on your professional face, because Cpt. Tyler has arrived."

They both respond in an apologetic tone like two contrite children, "Yes, James," but snicker behind his back.

James and Caroline leave Mike to greet Cpt. Tyler and within seconds of meeting him, one could tell he was born to be in the military. He shakes James and Caroline's hands with a firm, confident grip and a very professional greeting. He and James exchange a few pleasantries, obviously knowing each other prior to this morning, giving Caroline time to study him.

He is about James' size only lacking any hint of a potbelly. He cannot be more than forty-five, if not younger. His complexion is fair, with clear-blue eyes, and Caroline guesses, if he had hair, it would probably be blonde, but instead his scalp is razored slick. He definitely looks the part in his digital camo and tan boots laced up tight over his ankles.

Tan boots? I thought combat boots were black and had to be polished?

This detail piques her interest to take notice of his complete uniform: several pockets, two across the front that seem to be sewn on crooked, patches of hook and loop just waiting for something to be stuck to them, two bars in the center of his chest that looks like a grey 11, a flag on his sleeve that she thinks is flying backwards, and a patch on his other sleeve that she cannot quite determine what it is. Her mind dances along and again she is confused.

I thought camouflage was green and black and brown and looked like ink blots? Like the ones Nick wears to mow grass in –

"Ms. Hatfield, it is very nice to meet you, ma'am. I believe you know my children, Deaton and Kayla."

Caroline cannot decide if it is Cpt. Tyler's direct gaze, the serious clip to his words, or the fact that he just called her ma'am, but the combination is rather intimidating and she hopes it does not show. She also hopes that he has not noticed she was very closely scrutinizing him and his uniform, not really paying attention to the fact she too is to be involved in the conversation.

"Uhh, yes, I do. I had Deaton last year in world civ and Kayla is with me for geography. You have two wonderful children and should be very proud." Caroline is able to say without too much of a nervous stumble.

At her words, Cpt. Tyler's face relaxes and takes on a tender smile. "It does not bother me at all when someone wants to brag on my children and yes ma'am, I am very proud of them."

Caroline is touched by such a small moment of sweetness and his continued use of calling her ma'am. The captain's face and few words convey so much that she finds a small hiccup of emotion in her throat.

Where did that come from? I talk to parents all the time about their children, my students, and I never get emotional.

She is always professional when relaying positive or negative information, but this morning a soft light quickly fades Cpt. Tyler's austerity, and Caroline thinks, perhaps, he is also born to be a dad.

Returning his attention to James, "My staff sergeant is also with me and I had him pull around to the auditorium doors. He has everything for our presentation and I thought we would just meet him there.'

"Yes, that will be just fine. Everything should be ready to go," James looks to Caroline as conformation of what he has just said.

Caroline, still a little mesmerized and again not really paying attention, responds, "Yes, the auditorium is ready and Ms. Cross said two students would be available for lights and sound."

With that settled, the trio leaves the Commons to go to the auditorium. They pass Mike and with a shake of his head, he gives Caroline an exaggerated wink and an "Ok" just to get her flustered, mocking her now professional behavior. She snarls at him, both of them again acting like children and completely out of James' view, and then she follows the men to far end of the building.

James talks about some of the previous speakers and explains to Cpt. Tyler there is little formality and each session is relaxed and it is up to him how he wants to conduct his time. Caroline walks beside them quietly allowing James to do what he does best: make someone feel welcome and put them at ease.

Before they turn to enter the hallway leading to the auditorium, they pass the back stairwell. Caroline glances at the doors seeing two faces pressed against the narrow windows. The instant she recognizes the students, she hears them pounding on the doors and waving for her to come and let them in. James and Cpt. Tyler come to an abrupt halt with James' face becoming stormy over the antics of these students. Coming to their rescue, Caroline quickly says, "I will take care of them and then meet you in the auditorium."

"Yes, please do that," James adds still giving the boys a look of disappointment before leading Cpt. Tyler down the hall.

Caroline moves into the stairwell and the boys began to pound harder and shout through the door. She gestures wildly for them to be quiet, but that only increases their volume. By the time she reaches the doors, she is fairly sure they can be heard all over the school.

"What's wrong with you two? You know you're not supposed to come through these doors," Caroline attempts anger as Josh and Caleb edge around her carrying large foam cups and paper bags labeled *Double Kwik*.

"We had ta come in this way," Josh informs.

"Why?"

"Cause Ms. Cross wants us ta run lights and sound for Career Assembly this mornin'," Caleb explains.

The two are first cousins, but could pass for twins. They have mousy brown hair that is as fine as a baby's, gapped teeth and a spray of freckles across their noses. Both of their faces still bear traces of the boys they used to be even though they are seniors. Josh is about a hand's width taller than Caleb and Caleb carries about twenty extra pounds of weight. Rarely, is the pair not together wearing bright smiles on their faces and laughter on their lips. They are pranksters, hilarious, and loud. They are best friends and proudly take claim as being good ole boys from the head of Pickle Bean Holler.

Caroline does have to assert some of her authority and continues to question the boys. "What does running lights and sound have to do with you parking in the faculty lot?"

"Well, ya see Miz Hatfield, we figured that would be a good way for you ta pay us for workin' during Career Assembly," Caleb rationalizes with a very serious face.

"Yeah, ya know we have'ta miss *all* our mornin' classes so as we could help ya. Parkin' back here's only fair," Josh concludes, equally as serious.

Caroline nods her head in agreement then frankly asks, "Alright, but what am I to tell Mr. Tackett when he finds you back here *and* sneaking food up to the sound booth?"

The boys burst out laughing. "Tackett? He's harpin' at us all the time. Why should today be any different?" Josh reasons.

It was true. Josh and Caleb had spent so much time in Assistant Principal Tackett's office over the course of their four years at Belfry, they should have moved in their desks. They are never involved in anything too serious, just two rascals who if they spent half as much time focused on learning as they do being ornery, they could possibly cure cancer or learn how to walk on water. Instead, they keep their toe on the line of possible disaster and sheer fun. Even though they can bring anyone to the boiling point of frustration, you cannot stay mad at them for long, because their good nature always wins you over. Caroline decides to laugh, as well, knowing Mr. Tackett is often too rigid and these two make it their personal quest to irritate him.

"Well, let's go. I need to get you into the sound booth, because Mr. Blackburn is waiting on me."

19

She leads the boys upstairs and unlocks the door out to the catwalk. The lights are on in the auditorium and they can see James sitting on the edge of the stage, but Cpt. Tyler is gone. Both boys shout down to James enjoying the sound as they hear their voices echo from the high ceiling.

"Mornin' Mr. Blackburn!"

"Hey! I got an extra chicken biscuit if ya want it."

"Morning, boys. No thanks on the biscuit. I had breakfast at the house," James shouts back. "Cpt. Tyler will be back in a moment and we are going to get his presentation set up. Get ready for a sound check."

"Aye-aye captain!" Caleb says, producing the desired effect from Josh: choked laughter and giggles.

No matter how old these two get; they will always be in 7th grade.

Caroline shushes and hurries them along to the sound booth.

After hearing them speak and witnessing their lazy foolish behavior, one would assume Josh and Caleb would not have any idea how to run the highly technical computerized system, but those assumptions would be wrong. Yes, Josh does have to lean into the house microphone and growl out his own rendition of, "*Luke, I am your father*," as Caleb makes the lights go berserk, but that will be their only lapse in judgment. They handle the rest of the morning with precision. Caroline feels safe in leaving them and goes back downstairs to rejoin James and Cpt. Tyler.

Caroline came back to school before going home last night and saw that the stage was cleared for today's presentation and after the morning she has had, she is glad she left nothing to the last minute. The screen is lowered and the lectern hooked up awaiting the captain's laptop. There is also a presentation table setup for anything else they may have. She has even remembered to place two bottles of water on the shelf of the podium with a copy of the bell schedule and a small digital clock discreetly placed next to the microphone.

This is one of her favorite aspects of the job: projects and she loves all the details. Whether it is working on the homecoming committee or organizing the Honor Society tutoring program, Caroline loves projects and planning. In her short years of experience, she has realized students like projects as well and it is rare that she does not have her kids involved in something. Her thought is, if she likes the activities and finds them interesting and enjoyable, students usually do, too and you get better work from the class.

James is still sitting on the edge of the stage when she returns from the sound booth, looking at a list on his clipboard; BLACKBURN written boldly across the back in black permanent maker, which has begun to fade. He is often teased that he is more attached to his clipboard than his children or his wife, because it is an unusual occasion that he is seen without it.

During their sophomore year, the clowns in the sound booth thought it would be a great joke if they hid it. Days went by and James never made any mention of his missing clipboard, but the next Monday he brings in a new one. The boys are shocked that he had not questioned anyone and did not seem to be the least mad. What was the most frustrating, they had not gotten caught. Part of the thrill was getting caught and then squirming their way out of trouble and being able to laugh at their victim. To rub it in James' face, Caleb comes in the next day carrying the clipboard they had stolen. Again, no comment from James. The boys were very puzzled and decide to confront him after class.

"Mr. Black-burn, here's yur clipboard. I don't think ya noticed it was gone," Caleb says shyly laying the board on James' desk.

"Thank-you, Caleb. I had noticed."

"Well, did ya know it wuz us?" Josh includes.

"Yes, I knew you two had taken it."

"Well, why didn't ya say something or send us to Tackett?" Josh was still confused.

This is where James never misses a teachable moment, instruction he is still giving Caroline reminding her you were to always teach the whole person. "Boys, I thought if you two went through all the trouble to *steal* something of mine, you *needed* it more than me."

"Shoot, Mr. Blackburn, we's just funnin' with ya."

"I know. Have a good afternoon, boys."

"You mean you ain't mad? Not goin' ta send us ta Tackett?" At that comment, Caleb elbows Josh in the ribs and he lets out a yelp.

"No. Good afternoon," James begins and ends his conversation simply and quietly, but he has made a greater impression on the boys than yelling and days in ISS would have. They quietly leave the room not quite understanding Mr. Blackburn. They never gave James any more problems after that day. In fact, the three become very close and James is often their ally when they discover friends are hard to find.

The lights are coming on and off and the mics squealing, but it is Josh and Caleb working to get things set for the assembly as Caroline enters the main floor of the auditorium and goes to the stage to join James. He is still studying his clipboard as if it holds a wealth of captivating information. Caroline smiles and has to look away to keep from laughing in James' face at the memory. She is about to ask him a question, but is cut short when the stage phone rings and James gets up to answer it.

After a short conversation, he hangs up the phone and walks off the stage as if preparing to leave and says, "Mr. Tackett needs to see me. He said to tell you he has your homeroom covered, so stay here until Cpt. Tyler returns. I should be back before the first session; if not, you go ahead and start without me."

Not allowing another comment, James walks to the back of the auditorium, and out the doors, leaving Caroline alone. This is not an unusual request and she has taken care of Career Assembling plenty of times without any help, however, today seems different. She feels out of her element and Cpt. Tyler with his ultimate military behavior is a little unnerving. She has little time for a personal pep talk, because she hears the doors on the far side of the auditorium open and in walks Cpt. Tyler followed by another soldier. Caroline can feel her face grow hot from chin to scalp and little flutter in her stomach.

You are such a girl! Every female in the Junior Class is going to be swooning over these two in less than ten minutes and you're going to be leading the pack! Get ahold of yourself! What's your problem this morning? You must not be getting enough sleep to feel this overwhelmed!

Caroline takes yet another one of her deep breaths of the morning and prepares to be the consummate professional in James' absence.

Cpt. Tyler walks onto the stage and over to the podium. He sets up his laptop and in moments has the projector running without a word to Caroline, all the while exuding a presence of complete comfort and familiarity even though she is sure he has never even been here before.

The other man, younger than Tyler, sets down the large cardboard box he is carrying then stretches his long limbs to easily mount the front of the stage. He picks up the table next to the podium, walks it to the edge of the stage, and effortlessly lowers it to the floor. With a short leap down, he begins unpacking the box arranging various items on the table. They both work in relative silence and Caroline finds she does not quite know what to do with herself.

Should I stand quietly? Should I offer to assist them? Should I chatter about Career Assembly, even though James has already informed Cpt. Tyler of all the details? I can't just stand here like a ninny watching them, though both are rather fascinating!

She decides standing quietly, trying not to fidget too much, is her best option. She definitely does not want to disturb what appears to be a well-practiced routine.

"Ms. Hatfield, this is my Staff Sargent, Garrett," Cpt. Tyler, catching her off-guard again, is standing in front of Caroline introducing her to the other man while she is scratching red nail polish off her cuticle with her thumb not noticing they have finished and he has left the stage. She nervously brushes the paint chips off her hands and from the front of her jacket as morning announcements begin and she does not quite hear what he is saying. The Pledge of Allegiance given by the President of FCA immediately follows announcements. Caroline tries to interject, but the men turn sharply on a heel toward the flag on the far end of the stage ignoring Caroline's now silent comment. She is chastised by her faux pas and feels the heat again rising to cheeks. Luckily, they have cooled by the time the men turn back to her. Again, Cpt. Tyler addresses her.

"Ms. Hatfield, this is my Staff Sargent, Garrett."

"Good morning, ma'am."

Whew! Ma'am, again!

"Good morning. It is nice to meet you." Another firm handshake, confidant, direct gaze, polite nod of the head.

Garrett what? Is that his first or last name? It's printed on his jacket on one of those patches. Am I to call him Garrett or Staff Sargent? I sure hope James gets back soon. These two are making me a wreck!

"Ms. Hatfield, how long have you taught at Belfry?" Cpt. Tyler is a commanding presence and for the next several minutes dominates the conversation, which has Caroline thinking she is being interrogated. However, his demeanor has significantly softened and she is put at ease knowing all she has to do is answer the many questions the captain fires at her.

"For almost five and half years."

"What classes do you teach?"

"Uhh, two American history, two world civ, a geography, and a senior seminar."

"Senior Seminar?" Cpt. Tyler asks with a questioning look.

"Yes. Senior Seminar is a class to get students ready to leave high school. Make sure they have enough credits, help them narrow down college choices, give them career options, help them to understand financial aid, and then a variety of life skills: personal finance, how to prepare for an interview. You know, all that stuff a student who is getting ready to graduate needs to know, but is never really covered in a class."

"And did you graduate from Belfry?"

"Yes."

"So, do you live nearby?"

"Yes – Forest Hills."

"Ah, that makes for an easy commute. Where did you go to college?"

"I got my teaching degree in social studies and biology from Alice Lloyd College and did my graduate work at University of Kentucky."

"UK – impressive. Deaton wants to go to UK, but it's such a large school for freshmen. I'm not sure he is quite ready for that. He and his boys think it will be just one big extended campout where they have to go to class occasionally. They've been together so long, they already dread possible separation. But, he still has some time before he decides. Did you get a Master's from UK, then?"

Caroline smiles at the thought of 'Deaton and his boys'. She knows them all very well. They are a great bunch of kids, good students, athletic, very popular, but not spoiled by any local fame or high school status. Continuing, she answers, "Yes, a Master's of Science in human biology."

"My wife, Shannon, you know, works at Southside. She finished her Rank-I last spring. Have you begun yours?"

"Not exactly; I am getting a second Masters, but it qualifies for the rank change and pay increase."

Continuing to probe, Cpt. Tyler asks, "That's the most important thing. And what is that in?"

"Adolescent psychology and family counseling from Asbury University. Fortunately, I am able to do most of it online and I will finish in December."

"Well, you can analyze both Garrett and I after our presentation. Our minds could benefit from a little investigation!" Cpt. Tyler gives Garrett a sly look and genuine laugh though he does not comment. He then returns his attention back to Caroline.

"And your husband is Coach Hatfield on the football team?"

Caroline was able to take a breath while smiling. A little embarrassed by his forward questioning, but politely corrects his mistake.

"No. Coach Hatfield is my brother, Nick. He works here, too. He's a Special Education teacher. I am not married, sir."

Sir? Five minutes with a captain and now you are all 'sirs' and proper? Caroline, you better hope the bell rings soon, before they realize your gracefulness only goes so far!

"No children, then?"

Caroline laughs this time; her feelings of nervousness beginning to subside. "Of course, I do! 172 every day, but unfortunately, I have none of my own."

Cpt. Tyler's head snaps up and his face holds an almost stern gaze.
Told ya! Here's the slip!

He stares at her a few seconds then his face changes and laughs again. He mentally checks himself realizing he was, in fact, asking this young lady several personal questions and he has only met her this morning. He does appreciate, however, that she has kept up right with him and answered every question quickly and clearly without appearing the slightest bit flustered.

When it registers what she has said, he roars out with laughter and responds, "172? The two I have are a handful at times. You have more than your work cut out for you with that many. I would say it is difficult at times," he gives her another questioning look.

Caroline pauses before responding; weighing her words, "I would say it is far less difficult than leading soldiers into battle, sir."

Before Caroline has time to decide if her remark is regarded as complimentary or arrogant, the bell signaling the end of homeroom and the beginning of first period sounds and Caroline feels rescued.

"Shew! Saved by the bell!" giving Cpt. Tyler her own confident gaze and winning smile, "I didn't think it would ever ring and you were going to just keep quizzing me. I would have ended up revealing all of my secrets!" Caroline laughs again, lightly touching his arm, completely comfortable for the first time this morning.

Finally gaining the opportunity to take control of the situation, Caroline instructs, "Gentlemen, if you would please sit here," motioning towards the front row of seats next to the stage steps, "the students will be arriving and I will get us started. Feel free to take the entire period. The class ends at 9:00 and we have a total of three sessions this morning." Caroline smiles at the captain and staff sergeant. She can hear them quietly speaking as they sit down, but cannot make out what is said. Poised and controlled, she walks off to meet the students.

Less than five minutes later the tardy bell rings, Caroline boldly, if not confidently, walks to the podium, turns on the mic, looks to the sound booth for any signals from the Pickle Bean Holler Boys, and moves to the front of the stage to address the students.

In her best grown-up voice, she shouts to the assembly, "Belfry High School!" There is a little laughter, some random applause, and a few whistles, but within seconds, the auditorium is silent.

Watch this, boys! I can be a commanding presence as well!

"Juniors! For this morning's Career Assembly, we are privileged to have Cpt. Bryce Tyler with the West Virginia National Guard from Williamson. Please give him your undivided attention and respect…Class, welcome Cpt. Tyler"

With military precision, a boy stands and gives three sharp claps followed by the entire assembly doing the same in response, then all are silent. Caroline meets Cpt. Tyler as he comes to the stage, shakes his hand again, and then moves to the back section of the auditorium to monitor the students. James enters quietly through the back doors and sits beside her. He is reading some paperwork obviously given to him by Mr. Tackett. Once finished, he secures it neatly on his clipboard leaning over to whisper, "Everything good so far?"

"Yes. I told Cpt. Tyler he could take the whole class."

"Good."

Conversation over. James does not comment again and begins to rifle through the pages on his clipboard finding something that holds his interest for the remainder of the morning. Occasionally, he looks up acknowledging something Cpt. Tyler says, but quickly returns his attention to his papers.

Caroline's plans of grading yesterday's test while sitting quietly has changed, because returning to her classroom would not please James. He would find it very rude for her to leave the auditorium now that Cpt. Tyler has begun speaking no matter how discreet. Instead, she flips up the small desktop, leans forward, and prepares to listen to her fifth Career Assembly.

Cpt. Tyler forgoes the use of the podium moving instead to the front of the stage and begins talking to the students. He asks questions and though they act timid at first, the students start to answer him. Quickly, most of the class begins to show genuine interest in his topic, as does Caroline. Facts, information, trivia should intrigue any good social studies teacher, but it is more than that. It is the manner in which he is presenting: clear and professional with the occasional bits of humor. Not overly dramatic in his movements and just enough emotion in his voice to not sound theatric or rehearsed. He then shows what can only be called a recruiting video with a heavy metal soundtrack. Something you would hear in a locker room before a team runs onto the field. It's quite moving, especially for a high school audience. Caroline also cannot deny the small surge of patriotism she feels from the film and the intensity it evokes.

Boy, he's good! Half of these kids in here will be ready to enlist with the National Guard by the end of the day!

He goes to the podium and begins his formal presentation occasionally clicking through slides. He speaks of the history of the National Guard and how the role of the citizen soldier has been real and present since colonists first came to America. He discusses what their role is on a local, state, and national level and how they are called to duty during disaster and war. In his closing statements, he emphasizes the importance of education and how most of his men have at least an Associate's degree and explains how the National Guard helps them pay for college.

Caroline is impressed that Cpt. Tyler does not sound like a recruiter trying to meet a quota or appears to be offering a sales pitch. He has not dazzled them with false bravado, but instead is honest in saying it is not a job for everyone and at times it is difficult, boring, or frustrating.

"Our lives have day-to-day normalcy like any other citizen with jobs and families. We are able to have our familiar routine. However, it is during those times when we are called to duty that we must react, sometimes suddenly, and that is where the physical and most definitely the emotional training comes into action. I never look forward to leaving my family and I don't pretend to have a constant flood of courage when I am faced with danger. What I do know is that I am part of something greater than myself and if I can help even in the smallest way to protect our people and defend our freedom, I want to do it," calmly, but with greater intensity, "because I am *blessed* to be an American and proud to be in the National Guard!"

Several students jump to their feet in spontaneous applause and cheers. Caroline too is stirred, by the captain's words; humble, honest, passionate. Speaking for the first time of the morning, Garrett moves to the table, orders everyone to settle down, and starts quizzing the students about points from the film and Cpt. Tyler's presentation. T-shirts, footballs, water bottles, and other loot bearing the National Guard logo sail through the air to the happy recipients as awards for correct answers. Once all of the prizes are given out, Cpt. Tyler announces that anyone who has questions is to come forward and in perfect timing the bell rings. Several students with eager and captivated faces stay after to speak with the men before the next session begins.

Caroline walks down the hall to her classroom and retrieves the papers she intends to grade. Closing and locking the door, a student yells her name and weaves though the human traffic that floods hall.

"Ms. Hatfield, I was coming by to make up my test." The small, anemic faced girl with gray-blond hair, disheveled clothing, and a huge backpack speaks with anxious intensity that only emphasizes her hobbit-like features.

"Meredith, I told you the make-ups would be given after school in the tutoring room. You can –"

"But I was hoping to take it now. I have band practice and then I need to go to Environmental Club. We are collecting the recycling bins today and Mr. Dillon said he needed everyone to be on time," her face is overcome by panic and Caroline is certain her eyes are welling with tears.

A little frustrated, but tender, Caroline reassures the pathetic creature, "Meredith, Mr. Dillon and Mrs. Cooper are aware of tutoring today. I have Career Assembly all morning, so I will not be in my room to give you the make-up."

"But couldn't I just come to the auditorium and take it there? I just hate to be late for practice and I have already missed Environmental Club twice this semester and Mrs. Buchannan was complaining last week her bin was already too full!" Meredith was now to the point of desperation and tears.

It would be like a day without orange juice if Mrs. Buchannan was not complaining about something!

Out of sympathy for this pitiful pest and a way to get Mrs. Buchannan to hush, Caroline concedes.

"Be to the auditorium at the beginning of third period, before the tardy bell rings. Get an admit slip so you are not turned in for skipping. I will have everything ready for you."

Meredith's entire demeanor changes; face brightens and there is evidence of sweetness and even a hint of pretty features.

"Oh, thank-you, Ms. Hatfield! I won't be late and Mr. Hager can just print my lecture notes."

As quickly as the words leave her mouth, Meredith turns, whacking Caroline with her oversized backpack, and begins to scurry away.

"Meredith! Please, pay attention!" Controlling her frustration, "If you are running behind this afternoon, be sure to empty Mrs. Buchannan's recycling bin, first. No one wants to hear her complain," Caroline gives her a conspiratorial wink and Meredith's face gets even brighter.

"Ok, Ms. Hatfield. We will!" and off she goes, running to beat the tardy bell.

Chapter III

"Commit everything to the Lord. Trust Him, and
He will help you." – Psalms 37:5 NLT

C aroline returns to the auditorium to find James has resumed his duties and is at the front speaking with the captain, so she quietly takes her seat in the back and begins grading the tests. The second session proceeds much as the first did and Caroline is able to tune out the presentation and focus on her grading. Before she knows it, second period has ended and she is more than halfway through the stack. She gives an allover stretch and rubs the back of her neck that is tired from bending over the papers. She sees Meredith burst through the side doors still disheveled and searching with panicked eyes for Caroline. She rises to meet her taking her to the back to get started on the test. After a few instructions, Meredith unzips the huge backpack and looks as if she is going to crawl inside in search of a pencil. Caroline is certain it will be an unsuccessful hunt as Meredith digs through books, binders, endless amounts of paper, spilling out an uneaten *Pop-tart*, green plastic ruler, and ear buds, only to retrieve a mechanical pencil she shakes at her ear checking for lead. Finally, she is ready for the test and begins without looking up.

Caroline settles back down to grade and finishes before Cpt. Tyler does. She again is captivated by his presentation watching the routine he and Sergeant Garrett have in almost perfect timing. She notices Meredith has stopped working and is resting her chin on a curled palm. She too is leaning forward hanging on Cpt. Tyler's every word then is startled back to reality when Garrett begins to throw t-shirts. She smiles at Caroline all crunched up face and shrugged shoulders acting as if she has gotten caught doing something naughty and hands her the test. Once Caroline is finished grading, Meredith leans over to her and whispers, "They're pretty cool. Where did they come from?"

Before Caroline can answer, the bell rings and Meredith acts as if she has not even asked a question and begins wrestling with the enormous backpack again and scurries away. The students begin filing out the auditorium doors on their way to lunch or fourth period as Caroline stands, glad yet another Career Assembly is over and pleased her tests are graded.

No homework for me tonight!

She shuffles the papers into a neat pile, tapping them on the desktop, and secures them with a large clip. The auditorium is almost clear and James makes his way to the front to again exchange pleasantries with the men where 'Deaton and his boys' have gathered to talk with his dad.

"Ms. Hatfield," a voice booms over the room.

Spinning around looking at the sound booth, Caleb continues, "We will tear down the stage and return everything for you and Ms. Cross. Don't ya worry about a thang!" He and Josh lean over the railing and give her a mocking salute. She first smirks, but it changes to a smile and she nods approvingly. Caroline appreciates the boys are being helpful, but also knows they are just figuring out a way to spend more time out of class. For a change, Caroline does not care and agrees.

James continues to talk with Cpt. Tyler and the boys and everyone is laughing good-naturedly. The tardy bell rings and Cpt. Tyler addresses his son, "You boys better head out or you'll be late for class."

"Nah, we're not late, because we have lunch right now," Cpt. Tyler gives him a look that indicates he wants no argument, and his son quickly adds, "but we're going. Hey, you going to be home early tonight?" Deaton asks as he and the boys turn to leave.

"No, I will have to stay a little late, because this morning has gotten me behind."

"Ok. I'll probably stop by."

"You don't have practice?" the captain shouts as the boys near the doors.

"No. Coach Hayes is not here today. He had to go to a funeral. I will see you this afternoon. Bye dad!"

"See ya Captain!" the group echoes and leaves for lunch.

Caroline slowly walks to the end of the aisle waiting for James to finish his conversation before she leaves the auditorium. She will bid the gentlemen good-day then go to her classroom for planning; hopefully an hour of uninterrupted quiet to get settled and ready for her afternoon. The men, however, do not seem ready to leave, so she makes her way to the stage to join them and make a polite exit. Sgt. Garrett returns a few items back to the box he brought in a few hours ago, takes the captain's laptop under his arm and walks out of the auditorium. James finishes by saying, "Thursday is team planning, then we have lunch together. Caroline, who is cooking today?"

Not quite sure, but she believes James is getting ready to invite the men to join them for lunch and her mind goes blank and with it her intentions to spend planning period in her classroom. James prompts, "Whose turn is it to make lunch?"

"Uhh...it's Nick and Nathan's turn. I'm not sure what they have planned." Fumbling, Caroline's uneasiness from this morning has returned.

"I have invited the captain and sergeant to join us for lunch, but I am sure we have nothing to worry about. Your mother has probably taken care of the boys again this week," James smiles teasingly unaware how he has thwarted her plans.

James! Lunch guests?!?! I wanted to spend the next hour working before I had to come to lunch. Now, I know you will want me to help entertain these two while we wait on Nick and Nate. Agh!

"I'm sure you're right," she responds with distracted, nervous laughter. Fortunately, James once again commandeers the situation and she becomes child-like only speaking when spoken to allowing her mind to wander hoping the boys are not late for planning.

"Caroline...Caroline! Are you listening?" James questions her almost perturbed. "Caroline, did you hear what I asked?"

Completely fumbling this time, since she drifted off mentally planning her afternoon. "I'm sorry. What did you say?" staring at James blankly lost to the conversation.

"I said, I will take Cpt. Tyler and Sgt. Garrett to the workroom. You call the boys and have them meet us there and we will have lunch before our meeting. Ok?"

With a lights are on, but no one is at home expression, Caroline responds, "Yes, that is a good idea. I will call them and we will meet you there," and she heads for the door.

Once in the hallway, Caroline snaps back to reality and realizes not only James, but Cpt. Tyler must think she is a real doofus. She sprints to her room as well as she can in heels and calls Nick.

"Nick! Is lunch ready? James has invited the guests from Career Assembly and wants to eat now!" she is more than a little breathless and in no mood for Nick's foolishness.

"Sure thang, Sissy! Momma stopped by and helped me set everything up this morning. Potato soup is cooking away in the crockpot. Why are you out of breath? What've you been doing?"

"Career Assembly and James invited the speakers!" with a greater note of panic than she had intended.

"So," Nick is unconcerned, "He invites them every month. Why do you think he plans these things on Thursday?" his tone adds a "DUH!" his words do not.

"Yeah, but these two are staying."

Again, "So." Nick, who is never flustered does not see any issue about having lunch with total strangers.

"Agghh!" in a very unladylike tone, "Get Nathan and come on. Don't leave me in there alone. You know how I hate to talk to new people."

Blythe as usual, "They're not new. You met them 3 hours ago and I am sure you had to talk with them at some point. Just consider them old friends!" he finishes with a chuckle goading his sister.

"Nicholas!"

Fully laughing, "No worries. We're coming," and hangs up the phone.

Caroline looks at the clock and estimates how long she needs to stall to give Nick and Nathan time to get to the workroom first, but not have James notice she is tardy. Two minutes of casual conversation is one thing, but spending an hour with strangers and having to eat with them is another. Fortunately, James always keeps up a good flow of conversation and Nick could chatter with the Devil himself. That leaves her to talk with Nathan, but his social skills have a tendency to be inadequate as well and the fact that he along with Ben are Nick's requisite lapdogs, he will have little to say unless it is to Nick.

Nicholas Robert Hatfield is Caroline's younger brother by two years, reading specialist for the high school, one of many assistant football coaches, and was promoted to head wrestling coach this year with no fanfare or glory, because Nick claims he lost a heated battle of Rock Paper Scissors with Nathan winning the position no one else wanted. He is a perfect example of homegrown talent who eagerly returned after college to live and work in their small coal mining community. He was a good athlete all through school playing football, basketball, and baseball. Once in high school, he dropped the last two and focused on football then ran track. He was wildly popular among students and teachers (and still is) and often times overshadowed Caroline who was happy being the "good girl" involved clubs and community service.

Nick is also a passionate teacher and an advocate for his students. During his second year at Belfry, he addressed the faculty during a meeting and gave them a list of 57 names. "They are discipline problems, they have habitual absences, they have all have had to repeat at least one class or go to summer school, and more than half fall into poverty guidelines. There is no reason to analyze or categorize these students. We need to call them what they are!" With that statement, he had everyone's attention. "They are nonreaders! 57 out of a student body of 712 are nonreaders. 39 of those students are not even identified as needing special education and 12 of them are seniors. 12 students will leave Belfry High School in a few short months and they cannot read!"

This speech was not the Special Ed Department update everyone was expecting. Over the course of that meeting, Nick proposed a change in curriculum to better accommodate the non-readers. He said and everyone agreed, if a student cannot read any other education they may attempt to gain from high school is pointless. He said they need to be pulled from at least five of their 7 classes and basically be forced to learn to read. He then got approval from Site Based Council to implement a program that was computer based learning with intense classroom instruction he had used in college and began by targeting the 12 seniors.

"We cannot fix every problem or difficulty our students face. We also cannot make decisions for them once they leave here, but we must better equip them and prepare them for what is ahead." By the end of that first year, all 12 seniors were reading at 8th grade level or higher and by the end of the second year, the Board had earmarked funding for three of the five high schools to start the program with the last two to follow. Nick is not one to let it be said he is the stereotypical teaching coach.

Nathan Anderson, on the other hand is a different story. He lacks Nick's dynamic personality and intensity at being a self-starter. He is much more cautious in his approach and sometimes struggles with establishing a real connection with his students. He is very methodical in his teaching and likes order, rules, and routine maybe a little too much. Nick encourages him to have structured flexibility so he and his students will be less stressed and encounter less confrontation. On the plus side, he has impeccable paperwork skills. Every student file is up to date, he can recall each IEP modification in his case load from memory, and he submits all reports for the department, never needing correction. As the Special Education teacher for social studies, he happily collaborates with Nick at implementing the reading program into his classes to assist an even greater scope of students. Also, as one of the newest and youngest members of the staff, he is a complete devotee of Nick's and has become his humble servant and assistant wrestling coach. Nick is a good mentor, but also loves having his own personal minion.

With the illusion of being busy, Caroline circles her desk, rearranging and straightening stacks until five minutes tick by.

That should be more than enough. By the time I walk down the hall, Nick will be there.

Arriving at the workroom, Caroline is almost angered by her miscalculation, because neither Nick nor Nathan has arrived. To add to her distress, James has also disappeared. She is all the way into the room, before she realizes she has entered alone and there is no way to make an escape without looking foolish. She smiles to keep the nervous look off her face and goes to the refrigerator to retrieve six bottles of water setting them down at the end of the long conference table. Neither of the men notices she has entered. Cpt. Tyler stands akimbo reading the information on the bulletin board on the far side of the room with his back to the door. Sgt. Garrett is next to the window on his cell phone talking quietly.

She goes to the counter to check the soup. Just like Nick said, Momma had definitely helped him. In a small cardboard box beside the crockpot, she had a stack of foam bowls, spoons individually wrapped in two napkins, three sleeves of saltine crackers, salt and pepper shakers, and plastic container of cookies with a note taped to the lid.

"Nick, don't forget there is cheese in the refrigerator to sprinkle on the soup and banana pudding. Here are extra vanilla wafers if anyone should want them. DO NOT leave my crockpot at school. Love, Mom."

Nick was well taken care of to say the least, but Caroline could not complain, because her mother was equally attentive to each of her children including Alex who was married with three children and lived in Pikeville. If asked, Charlotte Hatfield would have still packed each of her children's lunch every morning and with Nick still at home, she usually did for him.

My perfect mother!

That was not a passing thought. Caroline truly believes Charlotte is the perfect mother. Not a June Cleaver or Donna Reed type, but a modern spin on a traditional classic. Really, she is great and everyone thinks so.

"You should have waited seven minutes." The voice was so close to her ear, she can feel him as much as hear him catching her off guard causing a small gasp and ruby flush. Whirling around, Caroline is face to face with her brother and he continues his teasing at a volume only meant for her to hear.

"I waited your *usual* five minutes and then lingered an extra two, just so you would have to sweat it out a little," smiling devilishly and pretending to be helping her with the soup.

"Nick!"

"Shhhhh! The Colonel is watching!"

"Hush, he's a captain!"

"Aaaa, colonel captain, what's it matter? Do I need to salute?"

Before she can answer, Nick quickly turns away and approaches the men with confidence leaving Caroline to flounder.

"It is nice to meet you again, Captain. Nick Hatfield," extending his hand to a man he apparently already knows. Caroline's eyes shoot darts at her brother's back knowing she again has been a game for him.

"It's nice to see you as well. I was not sure you would remember," Cpt. Tyler smiles genuinely as he and Nick share comradery that is so easy for men, often difficult for women and almost foreign to Caroline.

"No good coach would forget the father of one of our rising stars," Nick adds with ease and sincerity. For a moment, Caroline is so jealous of Nick, and not for the first time, of how relaxed and comfortable he is. Immediately, striking up conversation and never once showing any hesitancy. Hesitant, cautious, guarded all words that are synonymous with Caroline and totally opposite of Nick.

"Well, I think he is a rising star, but I may be a little biased," Cpt. Tyler confesses with the pleased expression he gave Caroline earlier when speaking of his children.

In a more man-to-man tone, Nick continues, "No – he is a rising star and I look forward to him becoming a leader during summer practice. He will definitely be a key element this fall."

With a look that could be confused for skeptical or expectant, Cpt. Tyler asks, "So we are looking to go to Bowling Green?"

"There is no place I would rather be the first weekend in December," Nick states with a gleam in his eye.

"Ha ha ha!" that noise only men can make: combination laughter and growl in the face of competition. The allusive gauntlet had been thrown down, but they would have to wait until fall to pick it up. "Then I plan on seeing you there!"

"Agreed!"

"Nick, let me introduce you to my staff sergeant and basically right hand man. In fact, I am not really for sure how I got anything done before he got here."

The young man, a few years older than Nick, extends his hand delivering a firm handshake. "Seth Garrett. It's a pleasure to meet you."

"Thank-you and the same to you. Gentlemen, have a seat," motioning for them to join him at the table as Nathan walks in. "And this is not quite my right hand man, but our principal won't let me fire him, Nathan Anderson," Nick smiles and claps Nate on the back, ushering him to the table and there is an exchange of more handshakes and introductions and they quickly fall into male conversation trading war stories that took place on the playing field, not the battlefield.

Caroline is glad to have Nick as a diversion especially since James has still not returned and begins to bring everything to the table. On her second trip, Sgt. Garrett startles her being at her elbow and offering his assistance, "Ma'am, let me help you," Before she can object, he reaches for the tray with six bowls filled with soup and takes them carefully back to the table. He places a bowl in front of each of the men and the three unoccupied chairs and then picks up the bottles of water and does the same. By that time, Caroline is coming from the refrigerator with a plastic container of cheese and the vanilla wafers. Without comment, he takes those from her as well placing them on the table and removes the lids then goes to the box Charlotte packed finding the spoons and crackers. Caroline is then able to put the tray of nine individually portioned banana puddings in the middle of the table and is ready to take her seat beside Nick when she remembers the salt and pepper in the box. As she turns, James enters and sits beside Nick.

"Sorry to keep you waiting. I had to sign some paperwork in the office," pausing to look up, James says, "Thank-you, Caroline. Shall we begin?"

Fleeting panic overtakes her as the five men at the table look to her and wait until she is seated. With salt and pepper shakers still in hand, she is forced to take the only remaining seat, at the head of the table and again with Sgt. Garrett at her elbow. Perched on the edge of the seat and not ready to relax, she replies, "Yes, James."

He quietly prays, "Our Father, we thank-You for this day and this time we have together. Please bless this food and those we share it with. I pray special blessings on our new friends and all they may face in coming months. It is in the name of our Savior that we ask these things...AMEN."

Amen is the whispered unison around the table and Nick says, "Dig in!"

The first few bites have everyone quiet except for the tearing of the plastic off the crackers and Nick offering the cheese to everyone. James takes on a more relaxed posed and begins to speak to Cpt. Tyler occasionally gesturing with his spoon. His face is serious and questions him about readiness and mobilization, words Caroline does not quite understand, but she does hear Cpt. Tyler say, "We are basically at the end of the first phase, but there is never a definite timeline. I can't imagine complete mobilization taking place until sometime after the first of the year, maybe even later. Our orders have been issued, but it is still a waiting game and we are still receiving transfers in to fill all our squads."

His answer makes nothing any clearer to Caroline, so she gives the appearance of actively listening, but her mind is actually far away.

"Ma'am, please tell your mother everything is very good and it was nice for you to invite us to stay," an almost whispered voice that does not quite project the confidence or the volume his demeanor displays. Again, caught off guard, Caroline turns to face Sgt. Garrett whom she has almost forgotten is in the room.

"I didn't invite you; James did," Caroline responds with a slight scowl to her face. Automatically, Sgt. Garrett pulls back and retreats a little from his conversational pose.

"Yes, well I thank you anyway," curt words and military face. Caroline again recognizes her blunder.

What is your problem? Not only are you acting foolish, but now you are insulting! Get it together!

"I'm sorry that's not what I meant," scrambling to cover her mistake. "You...you are most welcome and I will tell my mother. She is always fixing Nick's lunch. I am not sure he can boil water and Nate has less talent than him. They follow each other around like puppy dogs. I am surprised they make it through the day."

Sgt. Garrett reaches down the table for a pudding as Caroline continues to chatter. "You can have my pudding as well. I don't like it, but it's really good. I mean, Mom makes it from scratch. The custard not the cookies. And there's extra cookies if you want them," face fully aflame, Nick glances her way, but does not pause mid-sentence with Cpt. Tyler. This prompts Caroline to abruptly stop speaking as Sgt. Garrett makes his final comment to her, "Yes, thank-you, ma'am." The *ma'am* does not quite have the appeal from earlier and his voice has a hint of cool reserve. He shovels a large spoonful of pudding into his mouth and physically turns away from her focusing his attention on the others at the table.

The remainder of the meal continues without incident and the men cover politics, football, and spring planting. Caroline stays more alert and even answers a few questions Cpt. Tyler directs to her, but does not contribute to the conversation. Sgt. Garrett says nothing else to her, but she notices he does look at her when she speaks. Cpt. Tyler ends the lunch by rising, "Gentlemen, Ms. Hatfield, we have taken up too much of your day, but we do appreciate your hospitality and the invitation to speak this morning."

"It was our pleasure and we appreciate you coming. If any students want to contact you, I have your information," James looks to his team, "Let's see the men out."

James leads Cpt. Tyler and Sgt. Garrett to the rear exit where they are parked with Caroline, Nick, and Nate obediently following. At the glass double-doors, Cpt. Tyler pauses for his good-bye, "Boys, I will see you at summer practice," with a smile and look of knowing in his eye, he then addresses Caroline, "Ms. Hatfield, it has been my pleasure."

It is then Sgt. Garrett speaks one last time holding her for just a moment with his intense gaze, slight nod of his head, and a simple, "Ma'am." Turning, he walks out holding the door for Cpt. Tyler and James and they head to their car.

A cold breeze swirls around their ankles as the door shuts. "Nate, go and get us another pudding and bring one for Ben," wordlessly Nate turns to do Nick's bidding and he shouts over his shoulder, "He'll need a spoon, too!"

Watching James and the men approach their car they stop for some final conversation. Nick is silent for a moment then speaks not looking at Caroline.

"What shocks me is that someone as educated and intelligent as you are and claims pride in her poise and decorum can so easily become rattled and spout nonsense acting like a buffoon... How do you do you respond to that, Prof. Hatfield?"

Releasing a heavy sigh, "Something has to be wrong with my brain."

"No kidding!" chuckling at his sister and puzzled by her struggle with social skills, Nick walks down the hall to class leaving her to look out the glass doors and ponder.

Caroline – stupid, stupid, stupid!

Fortunately, the rest of the day is smooth and Caroline is happy to hear the final bell. Sophie Cross steps into her room as the hall music still plays.

"Thursday. Game night. You ready?"

Caroline looks up from her cell phone as her friend comes in ready to chat. "Who do you think I am texting?"

"Hmm, let me guess….Will?"

"You got it."

"How many messages did he send?"

Caroline lays the phone down and wryly comments, "Just four. It must have been a busy day at work."

"I agree. He sent me only one this morning as I was getting ready, but it was in all caps. He yells at me even through text message!" Sophie huffs, but smiles at the playful attack she and Will Dotson share.

Sophie O'Hara Cross is Nick's age and has been their friend since grade school. She teaches choir and drama claiming it is the poor man's version of musical theater, but it will do for now. She is lean and bubbly and overly dramatic in her actions and speech (perfect characteristics for the job) with a flippy, pixie haircut that is constantly changing colors. Today, she is a platinum blonde with a few streaks of hot pink in her bangs. Her clothing is as colorful as her hair and personality usually mimicking the style or genre she is currently teaching.

She strolls in wearing a cropped denim jacket turned at the cuff showing off a stack of mismatched bracelets, over a bright yellow scoop-neck tee with a necklace that resembles a psychedelic doorknocker, and a bold print peasant skit almost covering the tops of her distressed not-quite cowboy boots. The only thing understated about Sophie are the delicate silver hoops hanging from her ears. She was one who never wanted to be caught over accessorizing!

Sitting in a student desk and rearranging her skirt as she bounces her booted foot in the air, Sophie starts with, "You look tired!" It is the rare friend that can quickly pull off the Band-Aid and let you know what they are thinking.

"Gee, thanks!"

"Well, I'm just saying," with a 'Who cares' look, "but you do look tired."

"I am. We had Career Assembly today and…"

"Oooo, yuck! Who did you all have this time? Somebody really interesting like a used car salesman or a tollbooth attendant?" Sophie laughs remembering some of the real winners that have come to speak in the past.

"It was Bryce Tyler, a captain from the National Guard in Williamson and his staff sergeant. They were actually pretty interesting."

"What?!? There were two soldiers in this building and I did not know about it. What did they look like?" sitting up in her chair eager and giddy like a 10th grader.

"What do you mean? They looked like soldiers. Camo and everything.

Besides, Cpt. Tyler is close to twenty years older than us, married, and the father of two of our students. So calm down."

"What about the other guy?"

"I'm not sure about him. Maybe Alex's age."

"You spent the morning with them and all you can tell me is he might be Alex's age!"

"Not just the morning, James had them stay for lunch."

Exasperated, Sophie stands and begins to pace in front of Caroline's desk. "What?!? Did it not occur to you to call me and tell me to send my students to third lunch so I could join you?"

"There was no need," her volume rising in defense of her actions. "We took first lunch," before Sophie can issue another complaint, Caroline goes on. "Yes, having my dazzling best friend joining us for lunch was just what I needed so you could suck all of the air out of the room. They made me so nervous, I was struggling enough as is. Anyway, I think I offended the sergeant."

"Caroline!" Sophie's excitement would not be tamed without the whole story so every detail tumbled out.

"I was so cool right up to the point when James invites them to lunch. I got so nervous, I thought a swarm of bees was in my stomach. And then when they left, I don't think Sgt. Garrett was mad, but he definitely thought I was rude," puffing and rolling her eyes.

"Cool? Icy more like it – cold and then you break apart under tension. I am CERTAIN you are crazy. If I had the opportunity to eat lunch with an attractive soldier, I would never act like…What did Nick call you? A buffoon? So that's the end? Nothing else?" Sophie questions assuming Caroline is leaving out a juicy detail.

Caroline gives her a look displeasure and confesses, "There is nothing else to tell. I have one more Career Assembly and eight weeks of school. I think I can handle it…How did you know he was attractive? You didn't even see him?"

Sophie laughs in victory, "I knew it! I knew you thought he was attractive! That's why you had one of your typical *Maalox* moments. But no worries – I will let you have him. Strong, rugged, hero-types aren't really my thing. I prefer witty intellectuals that love museums… Anyway, the only reason I came by was to tell you I will meet you at

Will and Carter's. I want to go home and freshen up before dinner so I can dazzle and suck the air out of the room," winking, Tinkerbell flies out of the room.

Caroline closes down for the day to go home and get ready for game night mentally bracing herself for Nick and Sophie to rehash the events of the morning. GREAT!

Chapter IV

"Look at the nations and watch – and be utterly amazed. For I am going to do something in your days that you would not believe, even if you were told." – Habakkuk 1:5 NIV

S eth and Cpt. Tyler are back at the Amory within minutes of leaving the high school: perks of a small town. Seth removes the box and all of the items for their presentation from the car and the two enter the building. Cpt. Tyler goes to his office and is quickly immersed into his work while Seth goes to the supply closet to restock the box of merchandise. This time of year gets busy with campus visits, so he always has everything ready for when they have to go.

The supply closet is long and narrow with metal shelving on either side in dull 1950s army green. To his right, are office supplies: reams of paper, manila folders and envelopes, boxes of ink pens stamped in red – NOT FOR RESALE, containers of paperclips, staples, rubber bands, and endless cardboard boxes labeled FORM followed by a clerical code and identification sticker. Forms – there is not a move made without a form filled out. Very quickly, Seth learned that the military is equal parts action and paperwork. More often than not, it is paperwork and no action making him sometimes feel like a highly trained secretary.

On his right are clear plastic totes each with an inventory list and item description attached to the front in a plastic sleeve. Each description also has a full-color picture of the item from two opposing views. Seth walks to the end of the room and sets the box on top of a desk, also metal and also dull green, facing a windowless wall. Above the desk is a dry-erase three month calendar with most of the dates filled with information in a very precise color code: red – reorder office supplies, blue – merchandise shipments,

44

green – campus visits. There are eight high schools in their territory, nine if you include Belfry, but this morning was not an official recruiting visit since Belfry is in Kentucky. Today's visit fell under Community Relations, because they were invited to speak as part of Career Assembly since the Williamson Area spills over on either side of the Tug River and Cpt. Tyler's children attend Belfry. So it was an allowed visit, even though their jurisdiction is confined to the West Virginia.

The Greater Williamson Area! What a metropolis!

Seth laughs to himself for a second time today about Williamson. Again not taking time to analyze this brilliant move to "further" his career, proceeds with repacking the merchandise box. Next week, they will visit Chapmanville High School followed by Tug Valley High School. The week after that, they will be at the Regional Career Fair at Southern College's Logan Campus. He decides to go ahead and pack separate boxes for each trip, checks the requisition allotment for the amount of merchandise based on the number of students, counts out each item from the various boxes, marks the change in inventory on the lists along with the date and his initials, labels each box with event and date, gets a Merchandise Request Form to reorder items that are running low in stock, fills out the Inter-Departmental Mail envelope tucking the request form inside, double checks to make sure each box and tote is closed, turns out the light, and shuts the door.

Glorified secretary, maybe not, but Seth finds something soothing about the meticulous order and structure of his work. He has come to appreciate and even love routine and discipline.

Walking into the main office, Seth drops the envelope in the tray for the currier. Cpt. Tyler's door is open, and he can hear him talking on the phone, so he decides to proceed with a normal afternoon of work until the captain has any specific instructions for him. He checks and responds to a few emails, updates the captain's schedule which is electronically linked to each of their computers and cell phones, gets an alert for immunizations that are expiring for some of the men and have to be completed before deployment, tagging their personal file. Seth checks the fax machine for any announcements and clears the calendar.

A three month, dry-erase calendar like the one in the supply closet, though much bigger, occupies the wall between Cpt. Tyler's private office and the main office where Seth works. With just a week remaining in the month, Seth assigns the next quarter. Again, everything is color coded and meticulously written. There is a fourth panel – ANNOUNCEMENTS – where he lists the men and their expiring immunizations, upcoming events, and trainings. At 4:02 he snaps the lid on the marker, dropping it in a coffee mug with the others and Uncle Sam on the front.

And in walks Cleat.

Cleat's actual name is John Smith, but no one ever calls him that. He has a very youthful, though unattractive face. His cheeks are hollow, almost sunken exaggerating the features of his prominent chin and overly full lips. Even though he is approaching thirty, his skin is not clear of acne and bears many scars that would make one think his nickname is because his face looks like it has be walked on with cleats, but no. It is simply a term his grandfather began using when he was very young and like many things from childhood, it stuck. His hair and eyes are pale and unremarkable adding to his "just average" appearance. He could easily blend into the background and go unnoticed if not for his personality – it was larger than life and often dominated the room he was in. Always laughing and ready with a joke, teasing though not insulting, eager to tell you how happy he is with his many blessings, and never encountering a stranger. He always has on a well-worn baseball cap, today Cincinnati Reds, settled back on his head giving him the look of a classic redneck, but it suits him well.

Pushing through the double doors and announcing his arrival with plenty of noise, Cleat finds Seth still standing in front of the calendar.

"Workin' hard, Sar-Gent?" Cleat asks as he comes closer to Seth mocking as if he would wrestle him to the floor.

"That's the only way I know how to work!" Seth responds pushing back continuing their spar. "What are you doing here so early?" giving him one last jab, Seth walks his desk to sit down as Cleat takes a seat along the wall, leaning his head back.

"Some of the equipment was down and would not be back up until the after my shift ended, so I was able to cut out early. I thought I would come see my bestie!" Cleat winks at Seth and gives him an air kiss.

Looking away and emotionless in his response, "Well, the captain is busy right now, but he should be out in a few minutes."

With exaggerated pouting face, "Sar-Gent, you break my heart!"

"Shut-up!" Seth growls at him, knowing he will be Cleat's next victim of ridicule.

"So, what did you and the captain do today? Play checkers then get a Happy Meal?" Cleat teasing again. He loves to pick at Seth and badger him that he was the captain's secretary and personal assistant.

"Unlike you, we actually work every day!" Seth casting a looking-down-my-nose face at Cleat.

"Ha! Ain't that the truth! Really, what did you two do?"

Turning to give Cleat his full attention, because his work for the day was complete, "Captain Tyler was invited to speak at Career Assembly at Belfry."

"Are they still having those? I remember them when I was in school. Some of them things were so boring!"

Seth again taking on a stern face, "But, I'm sure that wasn't you two at all!" Cleat covers though smirking.

"No one appeared to be bored," Seth remarks with feigned offense.

"I can imagine…You two were probably riveting!" Cleat makes no attempt to hide his laughter. "Did they clap for you?"

"Yeah, they did. I hadn't seen that before. It was pretty cool."

With a little pride, Cleat explains, "That's the Belfry Clap. It's been going on for years. I was Clap Leader my senior year."

Rolling his eyes, Seth adds in a very sarcastic tone, "Sounds like an important job!"

Mildly defensive, "It was! Only the brightest and best were chosen," Cleat nodding his head and rubbing a hand down his puffed chest.

"And still, they chose you?" Seth's face was questioning and teasing.

"Not quite as important as being a secretary…but close!" Cleat is serious at first then throws his head back laughing at his friend.

"Hey! Do you want to hear what we did today or do you want laugh?" Seth barks at his friend trying to focus the conversation.

"Sure. Sure. I'm just teasin'. Please, tell me all about Career Assembly," Cleat settles back to listen with a foolish display of poise.

"We had three sessions in the auditorium and Captain gave a presentation to juniors. We saw Deaton and the boys, then Mr. Blackburn invited us to lunch."

"James Blackburn?"

"Yes. A man about 55."

"He's a great guy. Was my favorite teacher. I had 'im for World Civ and Economics. I hated that class! In the spring, he let us play the Stock Market Game and my team won and he bought each of us ten dollars in penny stocks as a prize. I still have them, too! He always did cool stuff like that…So, you had to eat school food?"

"No. We ate with Mr. Blackburn's team in the –"

"His team? Whatta ya mean? Who's on his team?" interrupting, though finally interested in the conversation.

"Nick Hatfield and Nate something. They were both in special education and another history teacher."

"Nick Hatfield!?!?" rising to his feet, Cleat walks across the room with a look of disbelief, but a wide smile on his face. "He was one of my best friends in high school. Such a great guy!"

Questioning, Seth looks up at Cleat who is now in front of him, "Then what happened?"

"Ahhh, life!" Cleat walks back across the room and leans against the table in front of the calendar, fiddling with the mug of markers. "He went to college and I went to work. You know – time passes and things change."

Nodding his head in agreement, Seth quietly answers, "Yeah, things change."

"Who was the other teacher?"

Seth has drifted and Cleat's comment pulls him back in.

"Who?"

"The other teacher? Who was it?"

"Nate, something. Another special ed teacher. I can't remember his name."

"I don't know Nate, but I'm talkin' about the guy? The history teacher. Who was he?"

"Uhh, her name was –"

"Her! It was a *girl*?!!!" extra wide smile and beaming eyes, Cleat begins to probe. Seth will have to guard his words, as his friend begins his interrogation.

"Yes! She was a *girl*! Girls can be teachers," replying with his own 7th Grade tone. "It was Caroline Hatfield, Nick's sister."

"CAROLINE!?!?" Cleat looks at Seth in shock. "I had the biggest crush on her in school!" smiling and shaking his head as his mind begins to recall sweet memories.

Forcing himself to sound casual, Seth leans back slightly in his chair and asks, "So, why didn't you ask her out?"

"Caroline Hatfield? Are you kiddin'?" seeing Seth's face is a little blank, Cleat explains, "I was a moron from River Road that only came to school so I could play ball. Football from July to December and baseball from January to May... and my grades were juuuuust high enough to keep me eligible for the team. Caroline was two years ahead of me and a top student. She was in all that smart people's stuff and clubs for good girls. You know – helpin' the homeless and savin' the planet. We weren't quite in the same league."

"Where was she from?" asking though he already knows.

In his best Robin Leach voice, "*Forest Hills*. I thinks she still lives there. The whole family does, maybe."

"What's that got to do with anything?" Seth knows he is trapping Cleat, but it will only serve to confirm his suspicions.

"Buddy! River Road is a LONG way from Forest Hills," raising his eyebrows with a wry smile, "That would have never worked."

Seth digging a little deeper, "But you said Nick was one of your best friends?" looking at Cleat as if he really did not understand.

"Yeah, but being friends with a guy is one thing and then tryin' to date his sister, especially if she is Caroline Hatfield, that's a horse of a different color!"

Seth's face becomes a confused scowl, so Cleat continues. "She was best friends with our assistant principal's daughter who owned a little, white convertible. Those two were everywhere in it and just looked so cool. They had the plaid skirts and designer backpacks and me, I wore *Mossy Oak* most days, usually with holes in it and the paint on my tailgate didn't match the rest of my beater truck."

"So, they were snobs?" Seth's brow furrowing deeper.

Cleat's face reads – 'What are you talking about?' – "No. They weren't snobs at all. Actually, they're really nice. Sort of like, they had it all, but weren't spoiled by it. You know what I mean?"

Seth, still playing his cards very carefully, "Not exactly."

"Agghh, I don't know how to better describe 'em. They were just good girls that people liked. What's the word? Genuine! When so many others were fake or wannabes. Why? Whattda you think of her?" Cleat's face and tone change, only slightly not quite knowing where his friend is headed with this.

Leaning forward and taking a more serious pose, Seth asks, "Do you want me to be honest?"

"Sure! Cause I ain't a fan of lies!" Cleat winking and laughing at his own joke.

"Ok...I thought she was arrogant," Seth honestly admits with his own touch of arrogance.

"ARROGANT?!?! Are you sure we're talkin' about the same person? Caroline Hatfield? Blonde, messy-curly hair? Nick's sister?" Cleat begins his probe.

"Yes! Caroline Hatfield," it is Seth's turn to rise to his feet and prepare to defend his opinion. "I thought she was arrogant and her confidence was almost contrived. She seemed a little...uh...a little haughty, even," realizing that sounded bad as soon as he said it.

"*Contrived? Haughty?* What is this – Masterpiece Theater? Who are you, Mr. Darcy?" Cleat looks at Seth with his face all scrunched truly shocked by his friend.

Seth is surprised Cleat knows Masterpiece Theater or Mr. Darcy, but continues. "And she was almost rude at lunch. Very socially awkward," again Seth knows this sounds bad.

"Caroline Hatfield?" Cleat puzzled by his friend's completely wrong analysis of her. "I have known her for years, and I have never heard anyone describe her that way!"

"Who?" Deaton Tyler enters the room from school at such a perfect moment. Seth gives Cleat a look of warning, which he completely ignores, and invites Deaton into the conversation.

"Caroline Hatfield," Cleat calmly answers.

"Ms. Hatfield from school?" Deaton glances back and forth from Cleat to Seth.

"Yes. What do you think of her?" without even looking at Seth, Cleat seeks out 17-year old wisdom.

"She's really nice and so funny. Everybody loves her classes. Why?"

"Oh, no reason. Seth and I were just talkin' about her. He met her today at Career Assembly and then they had lunch," Cleat is so innocent, Deaton does not detect his undertone.

Equally as innocent and very naïve, Deaton asks, "Why Seth? Didn't you like her?"

Staring him full in the face, Seth starts to squirm and it does not go unnoticed by Cleat. "No. I mean, yes! I…I just met her this morning. I don't even know her," with his face pinking slightly, he returns to his desk hoping to change the subject. Fortunately, Deaton rescues him.

"Oh – ok! Where's Dad?" and before they can respond, Deaton walks into Cpt. Tyler's office.

With only a hint of a devilish smile, Cleat drags his chair right up next to Seth's desk, and begins to quietly question him again. "When did you meet Caroline?"

"She came and spoke with Captain and I right before his presentation, then introduced us to the assembly."

"So, you didn't talk to her again until lunch?"

"No." Now, Seth feels like Cleat is going to trap him, but not sure how.

"What'd ya'll eat?" Cleat narrows his lids and scratches his chin like Sherlock Holmes pouring over evidence.

"Potato soup and banana pudding."

"Did Caroline make it?"

"No, her mother did and she started rattling about how everything from was from scratch and she didn't like pudding and how *she* didn't invite us to stay for lunch," the scowl returns to Seth's face remembering how he felt singed this morning by her remarks.

"So, you sat next to her?"

"Yes. We were at one end of a long table."

"I see…And what kind of shoes was she wearing?"

"Black peep-toes."

"Ah-ha! I knew it!" Cleat pounds his fist on the desk like a gavel causing Seth to flinch. Cleat is overjoyed at cracking his case. "You like her!" smile so wide his face is liable to crack.

"What? You're crazy! I just told you I thought she was arrogant? Aren't you listening?" Seth's frustration with his friend is clear.

"Buddy, I'm hearin' every word and you're the one that's not listenin'," giving him another smirking glance as he lays out his case. "First, you're basing your opinion entirely on a very brief encounter. Second, you said she was confident, almost haughty, but then at lunch was rattling and awkward. And third, I'm not sure I even know what peep-toes are, but you took the time to notice that very specific detail…So, there you go." Cleat leans back and with flourish of his hands, he suggests the case is closed.

"There you go what? You haven't said anything!" Seth's cheeks have a full flush and he feels the faintest of hummingbird wings in his chest.

"Call her!"

"I'm not going to call her!" Seth looks at Cleat as if he has lost his mind and they have somehow entered a John Cusack romantic comedy. "Besides, I don't have her number."

"Ok. Call the school," Nonplussed, Cleat calmly suggests, ready to deflect any of Seth's refusals.

"You're crazy! I'm not calling the school! What would I say, 'Uhhh, can I talk to Caroline?'" in a dumb voice and rolling his eyes.

"Yeah, that's what I would say," Cleat looking at him as if that was a perfectly rational suggestion. "Fine then. Email her. You were the one who had to make the arrangements for Captain to be there. So, send her an email."

"I emailed Mr. Blackburn," Seth is also ready with his own rebuttals.

Releasing a growling sigh, Cleat leans over to three low filing cabinets adjacent to Seth's desk. On top sits a large printer, the fax machine, and a series of trays holding National Guard stationary.

"Ok. Write her," slapping down a few sheets of paper and envelop on his desk in front of him. Cleat reaches for a pen, but pauses, "Or would you prefer quill and ink on this ahh, ahh. What's the word? *Auspicious* occasion," giving his friend a toothy smile knowing his resolve is cracking.

"Write her! I'm not going to write her! That's the stupidest thing I've heard," Seth leaps to his feet trying to retreat, but his desk and Cleat have him penned in. Instead, he turns and faces the wall lacing his hands behind his head.

"Ok, I'll do it, but your handwriting is much better than mine. 'Ms. Car-o-line, roses are red, violets are blu –' Cleat stops abruptly when Seth yanks the paper from his hand and tears it up.

"Hey! What's the big idea? I'm just tryin' to help," Cleat pretends shock.

"NO! You're trying to make me look foolish!" crossing his arms over his chest, Seth continues to crush the paper in his hand.

"Urnt! Wrong answer!" his buzzer noise startles Seth and he almost smiles. "I'm *trying* to help," giving his friend a knowing glance. "This is how I picture it: you were pretty impressed with Ms. Caroline when you first saw her, because you commented on her confidence and took time to analyze what she was wearin'. Then, you had three hours to think about it, about her. Soooo, when the opportunity came around to talk to her, you were more than ready, but didn't take the time to realize," with more emphasis and volume, "that she's a teacher and still at school! And your normal tactics proved to be, hmmmmm, INEFFECTIVE! Thus, flusterin' the young lady and makin' her feel all squirrelly resultin' in you barkin'."

Seth's head jerks up and looks at Cleat for the first time with an angry frown. "Yes dear. You're a barker. You bark when you're angry, when things don't go your way, or when you feel attacked. I would guess, sometime around lunch, ya' barked!" Cleat again gives him a toothy grin, rests his palms on his belly, one gently patting the other, waiting for Seth's reaction.

A few beats go by and Cleat adds, "What frustrates you is that all of your *charming* ways did not impress Ms. Caroline, but instead got her all rattled. Which tells me, she, too, was impressed, but caught off guard."

Cleat looks at Seth, surprised by his own wisdom and continues. He almost has Seth reeled in. "Caroline Hatfield is not the kind of girl you pick up in a bar or take to some place smoky and seedy. I knew in tenth grade she was a Thoroughbred; a real Kentucky Derby Winner – and I couldn't compete. What made you mad today, is that you were ready to run and she didn't even invite you to the race!" laughing, but pressing on before Seth has time to get angry, "Write her and ya won't have'ta see or talk to her and it will be completely up to her – if she gives ya a second chance. This way, it also lets ya do a little chasing. Girls loved to be chased...So, Sar-Gent! Whatta'll it be?"

Eyes dilated and nostrils flared, Seth's face begins to soften, mutters a possible curse, and growls as his hand covers his face; thumb and ring finger massaging his temples. Looking at Cleat, he releases an exaggerated sigh and says, "Give me the pen."

"Ha ha ha! That's my boy!" rubbing his palms and springing into action, Cleat is more than happy to oblige.

Seth sits down and squares the paper, tapping the pen on the edge of his desk mat. "So, what should I say?" an almost grin touches his lips and now he feels a whole flock of hummingbirds in his chest.

Leaning back as if he was truly pondering the situation, Cleat suggests, "Well, I wouldn't start with 'Hi, I'm a punk who struggles in social situations' cause I'm pretty sure she already knows that!" followed by a silent laugh that takes up his entire face.

Barking at his friend, Seth's angry face returns and the hummingbirds are going wild. "Be serious! What should I say?" punching Cleat in the chest.

After twenty-five minutes, a rough draft, followed by some editing, a well worded note is folded, placed in an envelope, and ready for Ms. Hatfield.

Seth turns the envelope over and tapes the flap, opening his desk drawer.

"What are you looking for?" Cleat questions.

Seth doesn't even look up, "A stamp."

Cleat quickly snatches the envelope and states, "You don't need a stamp," pulling away as Seth reaches.

Pushing him off with his hand, Cleat repeats more forcefully, "You don't need a stamp!" and begins to explain his reasoning. 'Tomorrow is Friday, so if you drop this in the mail, it will be at least Monday, before she gets it and that will be too late," still playing keep-away, Cleat goes on, "That will be too much time and look sort of stalker-ish if she gets mail from you. It needs to be hand delivered, tomorrow."

Another bark, "What?!? You said this way I wouldn't have to see her or talk to her."

Cleat smiling so sweetly, yells, "DEATON!" a moment later the boy comes out of his dad's office.

"Yeah, whatta you need?"

Cleat gets up and moves to Deaton quickly before Seth realizes what he is doing. "What time does school start in the morning?"

"First period bell rings at 7:56. Why?"

"And what class do you have first?"

"Chemistry. Why?"

"And is that class very far from Ms. Hatfield's room?"

Seth roars out, "CLEAT!" once he realizes what is planned.

Cleat just looks at him as Deaton answers, "No, just down the hall. She's the first classroom after the Science Department. Why?"

Pleased that his master plan is coming together, Cleat asks, "Do you think you could deliver this to Ms. Hatfield, *before* first period?" looking past Deaton at Seth as he hands the boy the envelope. Cleat can't decide if that is fear or pain on Seth's face, but does not care.

"Sure. That's no problem. What is it? Something to do with Career Assembly?" Deaton is unsuspicious, but looks back and forth between the two men.

Cleat lets out an amused snort and answers honestly, "It has everything to do with Career Assembly. Now, you won't forget or lose it will you?"

"No. I'll put it in my backpack as soon as I get to the car."

Seth finally speaks and his voice trembles a little, "I will text you in the morning to remind you…And don't open it."

"Nah, I won't…Hey, I'll see you guys later," turning, Deaton shouts to his father's open door, "Love you, dad. See you at home!"

"Love you too, son. I'll be home by 6:00. Drive safe!"

"I will! Bye guys," at the door he turns and holds up the envelope and says, "Seth, I won't forget," and leaves.

Cleat looks at Seth, so proud with himself, "Alright, that's done. Now, take me to dinner. Leanna has to work tonight, and you know I starve when she's not at home."

Seth makes no move to leave sitting on the edge of his desk, arms crossed protectively over his chest again.

"Come on. Let's go. It's already after 5:00," Cleat tugging on Seth's sleeve, hopping around ready to spar again.

Seth's hands drop to the edge of his desk, pushing off, he sighs: disgust, fear, anticipation all rolled into one. He walks to Cpt. Tyler's door to tell him he is leaving and the captain nods as he leaves already immersed in the weekly conference call.

"I'll buy you dinner, if you promise to buy me a drink," Seth says shaking his head and rolling his eyes. The hummingbirds have calmed, but he is now uncertain if writing Ms. Hatfield was a good idea.

Why did you let him talk you into this? Are you 17?

Cleat gives him a disapproving look, "Nah, you have the wrong idea!

55

Sarah E. Kincaid

Remember – THOROUGHBRED!" and slaps his friend on the back leaving the armory.

Sleep that night is restless for Seth, to say the least and he arrives at work early to watch the clock. At 7:54, he sends a text. Deaton responds in seconds, "Already delivered."

His heart rises then sinks. Now, Seth has to wait…it will be a long day.

We can make
our plans, but
the LORD
determines our
steps. Proverbs
16:9

Chapter V

"We can make our plans, but the Lord determines our steps." – Proverbs 16:9 NLT

Friday…Caroline is so happy to see it. She should be tired this morning since it was close to 12:00am before she got home from Game Night. With Will's new schedule, he has Friday's off, so having a *Trivial Pursuit* challenge until almost midnight knowing all of his friends have to work the next day does not bother him in the least. The evening went much better than Caroline expected. She was prepared for a full on attack of harassment from Nick and Sophie with Will and Carter serving as reinforcements. Surprisingly, they were very mild.

Sophie pulls up moments after Caroline arrives. She has changed clothes claiming she wants to be casual and comfortable, but all the while looking like a page from a magazine in perfect slim-fit jeans pegged at the ankle, vintage letterman's sweater Sophie probably bought at the Salvation Army, with a floral tank that does not look like it should work with her outfit, but does, and a bandana tied in her hair very Rosie the Riveter. Caroline is equally as casual in jeans and a long-sleeved Kentucky blue v-neck, exchanging her peep toes for strappy sandals since the evening is so warm for spring, but she does not believe she pulls off the look quite a well as Sophie. Caroline is quietly proud, however, that she trumps Sophie in at least one area. Sophie's chest has remained very prepubescent while Caroline's developed nicely; not extreme, but enough to occasionally turn heads. Otherwise, Caroline feels in all ways, she comes in a very distant second, third, tenth to anyone, including Sophie.

Walking down the sidewalk towards her, Sophie takes a huge breath. "Just practicing on sucking all the air out the room!" and mimicking as if she were preparing for a marathon.

"Ha! Ha! We both know you need no practice. You perfected that skill long ago!" Caroline gives her friend a wry smile and an exaggerated roll of the eyes as they round the corner to the boys' private entrance.

Will and Carter live in an apartment in the newly christened 'Downtown'. The building, along with several more, is part of MacGuire Holdings a company started by Carter's grandfather and now Carter has a significant interest. This was the first in a series of projects adopted by the Tug Valley Revitalization Authority of which Carter's mother, Sylvia, is a board member. Businesses and companies that once thrived in Williamson during its heyday in the previous century have long since moved out or became defunct leaving large, empty commercial space behind. The Revitalization Authority is attempting to capitalize on tourism and lure commerce with culture and history as many other small towns have done. Sylvia is tireless in her efforts and some would speculate her motives are more financial than altruistic, but no one openly complains, because thus far the Authority has been fairly successful.

The building is the former home to the Persinger Supply Company where Warren MacGuire worked when he first arrived in Williamson. Over the years, he accumulated stock and held a sizable interest in the company. After he left, he purchased the building from the company and leased it back to them for years, then it sat empty when Persinger moved and was later bought out by a larger competitor. This became a project for War to play with in his retirement and before Carter even finished college, War began teaching him the business of commercial real estate quickly becoming even more proud of his favorite grandson by the speed at which he picked up and how effortless and natural his knack was for the business.

So, the *Downtown* has undergone a variety of transitions, with the *Persinger* as the focal point. The first floor has been converted to a series of small shops, bakery, women's boutique, and a studio gallery featuring local talent and artisans. The second floor is office space including the Revitalization Authority along with its own conference room. The third is a series of two-bedroom apartments that stay full and has a long waiting list to be considered for occupancy.

Then, there is the fourth floor. Sylvia insists on calling it the Penthouse, but War and Carter refuse claiming that sounds pretentious reminding her this *is* Williamson and only four stories high. To Sylvia's credit, it is grand by anyone's standards and she was so proud of her contributions to design and decorating, she was able to get it featured in a copy of *West Virginia Magazine*. On that point, War did not fuss – he saw it as another opportunity to capitalize.

The fourth floor has a private secured entrance and is only accessible by freight elevator at the far end of the building. Access is almost hidden and easily overlooked allowing for extra privacy and a feeling of being far removed from all other tenants. At the door, Caroline enters her personal code. Carter had a new system recently installed that he is considering to add to more of his properties; using his home as the test. The code is constantly changing and sends code holders a text message periodically with the new codes. Caroline is on the list so Carter can monitor the system's performance. Just as expected, the door unlocks and the key screen reads, "Hello Caroline."

Once the door closes behind them, the lights gradually rise from dim to full light illuminating an interesting space. The room is just wider than the freight elevator and about the same length. To the right, the wall is exposed brick with large black and white matted prints in aged wood frames of various landmarks from Williamson's bygone era. The left wall is pale sandy grey sheet rock the exact color of the mortar between the bricks with very aged wood as baseboards and crown molding – original to the building. The doors to the elevator are well worn and still has remnants of paint advertising – *Persinger Supply Company: In the Heart of the Billion Dollar Coalfields since 1911*. This door is also coded which Caroline enters, releasing the huge latch. She tugs the leather strap, sending the doors in opposite vertical directions, and the girls walk in. After a few moments of grinding and lurching, the doors again open to the fourth floor, smells of dinner, and Will shouting.

Just as Sylvia described – GRAND. All indications that this apartment once served as a warehouse is very clear with much of the original features remaining. The wide plank wood floors are bowed and marred though refinished keeping the worn oiled look. Sylvia wanted to remove the nonfunctioning ventilation system, but eventually agreed with War and Carter to keep it in place even though new units were installed throughout the building. They believed as much of the old needed to be salvaged or repurposed in order to maintain the antiquated theme. She had everything painted flat black so it would fade into the background, noticed though not taking your attention away from the rest of the space, and adding to the sense of height throughout the room. Additional industrial features – wheels, pulleys, rigging for loading and unloading – now serve as an art installation and homage to the place Williamson used to be. Carter and War wanted everything to look like it had been there forever, untouched by time and they were simply taking their turn in the building.

To the left of the elevator is small sitting area merely for decoration and never sat in. Two black leather club chairs sit on a large rug, more geometric than Persian, in shades of reds, golds, blacks, and traces of other colors that set the tone and are reflected throughout the entire apartment. An aged steamer trunk is in the middle holding the perfect arrangement of bowls, books, and whatnots. Behind the chairs is more exposed brick and matted prints. Nondescript lighting projects from the wall highlighting the art and shines through a huge potted plant casting shadows on the wall.

Three extra-long leather couches in burnt red frame the living room right of the elevator. They are tufted with grommets, but not the least feminine or look like something that would be at home in a fraternity. A rug similar to the other, but much larger is in the center of the area with a low coffee table made of reclaimed wood the exact height and distance from each couch for propping your feet on while watching the flat screen television. A huge antique fireplace was removed from a property War was having demolished and placed on a brick hearth just under the television. The six foot mantle is a little Victorian in style, but is not out of place in the room.

Along the far wall of exposed brick beyond the living room and running the length of the space is a double bank of industrial windows with black framing. The top row is exposed allowing a constant wash of light. The bottom row has rolled blackout shades mounted to the top of the frame that are electrically lowered each night for privacy, but for now are up letting in just a faint glow of the remaining spring sunshine.

The dining room is just behind the living room and adjacent to the kitchen sectioning the space into four specific areas. The reds, golds, and blacks continue here with the sandy grey walls and aged wood trim. The table has seating for eight with a matching buffet and two additional chairs on either side. All pieces are large of dark wood and the only modern elements in the room. A darkened hall faces the elevator and serves as a dividing line between dining and the open kitchen with craftsman table and lamp in front of another large window at its far end.

From this angle, the doors to the large bedrooms are unseen and is the only part of the apartment considered 'new construction'. Each has a walk-in closet, complimentary bathroom with stained concrete and tumbled stone, and enough room for a king-sized bed. They also have small wood burners that were taken from the original offices. Both are fully functional, with Sylvia bringing them in to add a connection to the old in these new rooms and to be an option for more heat. The boys have had them lit only once.

Carter's room shares a common wall with the dining room and includes an office space and vanity area outside his closet. The concrete mimics the colors of the rugs, the stone is grays and tans, very similar to the walls, and the granite at the vanity and the sink is the same as Will's bathroom and the kitchen. The floor of the two person shower runs seamless with the rest of the room and has a series of heads on either end with an oversized rain head in the middle. When designing this room, Carter teased, though completely serious, "Men don't take baths…At least not alone," and opted for no tub.

Will's room is not as large as Carter's, but still impressive as the smaller replica with his own bathroom and walk-in closet, though no vanity nor office space. Between his room and the kitchen is a powder room that is entered from the hall. Also, there is a combination laundry room-pantry accessed from the kitchen. A pocket door is at the near end of the hall, so the private areas of the apartment can be closed off, though it is rarely shut.

Will looks up from his work at the large island that sits at an angle facing the rest of the room. Glancing up, he continues to bellow.

"Where have you two been?" he shouts as soon as the girls walk off the elevator.

"It may surprise you, Will Dotson, you are not the only person in this town who has a job!" Sophie lashes back beginning their usual cutting banter joining him in the kitchen to nosey around as to what they are going to eat.

"Ha! You hang out at that school *singing* for less than seven hours a day with a lunch and a planning period included, every weekend off, plus holidays and snow days, and SUMMER!" Will accuses then stares her down ready for an attacking reply, but is disappointed when she responds sweetly, "No one told you not to be a teacher," as she lifts the lid off something cooking on the stove.

"Leave everything alone!" Will roars and playfully swats Sophie's backside with the wooden spoon he is about to use.

"OUCH!" Sophie squeals as she rubs her wounded bottom and glares at Will maliciously with a glimmer of challenge to her eye.

"Set the table," is Will's low-growled reply and Sophie does his bidding without any complaint. Caroline moves to assist her shaking her head at their behavior – equal parts fighting and flirting. It is often, however, that one part heavily outweighs the other, but it always seems to work for them.

"Where's Carter?" Caroline calls to Will from the dining room.

"He just got home and is taking a shower. Nick and Darby should be here any minute. You can go ahead and put ice in the glasses."

Will, Sophie, and Caroline finish their tasks while the others arrive in perfect time. Nick begins to shout that he is hungry having Will shout back as they have some good natured wrestling. Darby gives quick hugs to the girls then is handed something to carry to the table. Carter comes out of his bedroom pulling a t-shirt on over his head and they all make their way to their seats as if each has a preassigned placement. They each pause and Will nodding says quietly, "Nick."

Nick and the others bow their heads as six friends take one another's hands. He offers, "Father, we come to You this evening with Thanksgiving in our hearts that You allowed us another day, a meal to be shared together, a school year that is winding down, and a summer that is upon us. We continue to seek Your guidance and may we be forever faithful to the call on our lives. It is in the name of Jesus Christ we ask these things... AMEN."

Instant chatter begins: talking to each other, talking over one another, passing of bowls, the clink of forks and plates and glasses, talking with mouths full, laughing at jokes that never grow old, and sharing a secret story written in a language they all understand: friendship.

"How much longer do you all have?" Carter directs towards Nick in between passing and chewing.

"40 days! I don't start any countdown until we get to 25, but this time of year gets so hectic, you run out of time before you know it."

"So, when is your last day?" Will asks stabbing another bite, but still looking at Nick.

"May 25th with students. Closing Day is Friday with graduation that night," Nick finishes crossing his fork and knife on his plate. He takes the last gulp of his sweet tea and silently hands the glass to Darby. Without comment, she knows what he wants handing the glass back to him full.

Carter, who is also finished and pushes a little away from the table, remarks, "Isn't that early?"

"YES!" all heads snap up as Caroline and Sophie almost shout in unison. The girls have a little laugh and Sophie finishes, "It is the first time we have been out before Memorial Day in years. Woot-woot!"

"My car will be packed and I plan on leaving to the Cabin as soon as graduation is over!" Caroline adds and dances, excited at the approaching summer. She begins to clear the table, Sophie and Darby following suit, continuing her silent cha-cha as she enters the kitchen.

Will bellows as he and the boys get everything else off the table and six clean up, "You threaten to stay at the Cabin all summer every year and you *never* do. You always find some excuse to come home." Handing her a platter as he enters the kitchen with a mockingly judgmental look.

Caroline quickly fires back, "I have two days of meetings at the Board the last week in June, otherwise, I will be on South Holston." Cutting Will off before he can give her any other arguments, she says, "Alex and Megan want to spend their vacation on the lake. Mom and Dad agree and I have no other plans."

"Will Gran be going with you?" Darby asks as she grabs a towel hanging from the oven door drying the dishes Sophie is washing.

"Yes. She won't come until the first part of June, even though I have already asked her to come with me. She said she knows we will all be there and she doesn't want to crowd us," Caroline answers with a disappointed frown.

"We are still going, right?" Caroline asks the group as she places something in the refrigerator closing the door.

"I have the days off!"

"It is circled on my calendar!"

"Where else would I go?"

"I have already started to mentally pack."

"Well, I will have to see..." Nick says casually getting the response he was looking for.

All activity coming to a halt, five voices yell NICK!

"I'm just kidding. I am more than ready to be on the water..." Stepping a little closer to Caroline, Nick adds, "But plans can *change*, Big Sister!" in an almost sadistic voice insinuating their earlier conversation and mocking her behavior, with a huge smile and wink.

Caroline scoffs feeling like she must defend herself as she always does when her brother and cousin question and doubt her; sometimes unmercifully. She stops abruptly in the middle of the kitchen and responds with her own calculating words, "I'm sorry that I am not answering correctly. It is my intention to spend the entire summer at the Cabin. Yes, plans could *change*, but it is not my *plan* that they do." Hoping she has won this discussion and Nick will not laugh at her again, she closes her lips tightly and shakes her head at him in subtle challenge.

"But they could change," pausing for effect and whispering to his sister as they crisscross the kitchen putting things away, "When you least expect it!" and nothing else is mentioned by neither Nick nor Sophie, because she has resumed her own banter with Will. Carter has returned to the dining room setting up the Trivia board, so Caroline is free from any further harassment or interrogation.

"Are we playing guys against girls tonight? Or can you boys not handle another display of our intellectual feats of strength?" Sophie laughs teasingly as she folds her pixie self up on one of the dining room chairs; Carter's snorted laugh is his only response as he finishes setting up the game board.

"I'm always ready to thrash you all! But, to make things fair, I will check," Will retrieves a notebook from the top drawer of the buffet. Leafing through the pages, Will discusses their recent play and gives them options for the evening. "We can have a final match of Boys vs. Girls since we have each won two or we can go ahead and start two person teams. I vote we boys hurry and beat you, then we can start the next series," smiling at Sophie without a hint of arrogance in his confidence, though it is Darby who quickly challenges him.

"What makes you think *you boys* will win? I say, we girls hurry and beat you all, *then* we can start the new series."

With that said, everyone takes their appropriate places and little over an hour later, the boys come out victorious in a very heated battle of knowledge, well-placed insults and goading. It is now the boys' turn to dance and taunt with the girls hiding their laughter behind vicious faces. A quick break is taken during half-time with Caroline and Darby getting dessert from the kitchen and Will sets up the next game. Everyone returns and Caroline carries in a tray with turtle brownies, three glasses filled with ice and milk, and pot of hot tea ready for honey and lemon. Nick immediately reaches for one of the mugs and the tea pot.

"You are such a pansy to drink hot tea!" Will teases Nick watching him drop a lemon slice and drizzling honey into his mug before carefully pouring the steaming hot tea.

"And YOU are so wrong…First, it is full of antioxidants and vitamin C. Second, it is good for my allergies this time of year. And third, coffee gives you trash breath!" Nick says so sweetly, delicately placing the pot back on the tray in such poised fashion as if he has high tea regularly with the Queen. "So, you should consider drinking it!" pinky and eyebrows raised in Will's direction.

"Shut up and roll!" Will barks handing Nick the die to determine who would be partners for the next series. Nick casually tosses it on the board and between sips states, "Odds." Everyone rolls in turn putting Nick and Sophie, Will and Darby, and Carter and Caroline on teams. As the hour approaches midnight, each team has successfully won a match with Will claiming they have time for one more round, but he is quickly out voted by everyone who has an early morning ahead.

Hugs and goodnights then everyone makes their way to the elevator. Just before they descend, Caroline shouts to the boys, "Sunday dinner is at my house this week, if you all would like to come."

Will shouts back, "I'm there!" Carter just smiles and Caroline smiles as the doors close. On the street, everyone scurries to their cars reminded Spring has yet to arrive as the night is cold. "Good night, Darby!" followed by three "See you in the morning!" and they each drive home.

Now, Friday morning, Caroline has made it to school early, all of the tests she was supposed to give yesterday during Career Assembly are ready, her afternoon lessons are in place, she has responded to all her emails, and with twelve minutes until the bell, she finally looks through the textbooks and curriculum maps James asked her to review.

At 7:50, a knock on her open door, "Ms. Hatfield?" Deaton Tyler sticks only his head through the doorway, hesitant as if he is worried he is going to disturb her.

Caroline smiles closing the books and pushing them to the edge of her desk ready to give Deaton her attention. "Deaton, come in…What can I do for you?"

A little more relaxed, Deaton walks to the front of her desk sliding an envelope between his hands. "Good morning, Ms. Hatfield. I have something for you. Seth said it was about Career Assembly."

Looking up, Caroline asks with a puzzled look on her face, "Seth?"

In those short moments, Deaton takes time to examine Caroline. He never thought she looked the part of a teacher and this morning is no different. She is wearing jeans and a dark heather-grey tee that looks like an old baseball has been skinned and somehow attached to the front of her shirt, stitches and all, in the shape of a large heart. He has always believed she had to be younger than anyone else on staff, proving it this morning with her messy bun tied with a red polka dot ribbon, earrings of dangling baseballs, and finishing her look with bright red Chuck Taylors. He is brought from his thoughts when Caroline asks again a little more firm, "Deaton! Who is Seth?"

"Sorry, Ms. Hatfield! Uhhh, Seth Garrett. Staff Sargent Garrett. From the Armory. He was here yesterday, with my dad. Remember?"

Remembering all too well, Caroline gets a curious flutter through her chest at the mention of his name and touch of a flush to her cheeks she hopes Deaton does not notice, "Yes, Deaton. I remember. What do you need?"

"He said I was to bring this to you, first thing this morning. He said it was about Career Assembly," handing her the envelope he has been tapping nervously on his palm.

Without looking at it, she takes it from him rising from her desk, "Thank-you, I will take it to Mr. Blackburn right now," walking with Deaton to the door.

"No!" he says a little too determined. "I mean, it's not for Mr. Blackburn.

Seth said it was for you and I was to bring it to you this morning before the bell," Deaton stops as if his feet are glued to the floor needing to make it clear that the envelope was not for Mr. Blackburn and emphasize the importance of his mission.

Flipping it over and looking at the envelope for the first time, Caroline sees '*Ms. Caroline Hatfield*' written in very bold hand across its front. "Deaton, what is this?" asking with a slight stern look on her face and a hummingbird flying inside her chest.

"I don't know. Honest! I didn't read it," panic rising in his voice like he is about to be chastised by a teacher, Deaton confesses, "I stopped by the Armory after school to see Dad. Seth and Cleat were there and before I left, Seth told me to bring this to you. I promise; I don't know what it is. I left it in my passenger seat since yesterday and remembered this morning I was to bring it to you. Honest!" Now, Deaton was almost worried he was going to be in trouble and should have asked Seth what this was about.

Caroline's stern look has turned to a deep scowl as she continues to question the boy, "Cleat? Do you mean John Smith? He's about my age?"

"Your age? Nah, he has to be older!" Deaton honestly asks laughing at the thought.

"John Smith? Actually, he is two years younger!" smirking at Deaton, she asks again, "Are you sure this is not for Mr. Blackburn?" attempting to maintain a good teacher voice.

"Seth said I was to give it to you…Ok, then," Deaton makes a break for the door before she has a chance to asks more questions to which he does not have answers removing his buzzing cell phone from his pocket. Glancing at the text, he smiles at Caroline, "You have a good day, Ms. Hatfield," head down, he begins to type his response walking out the door.

"You too!" she hollers after he is gone.

Caroline looks at her name again on the envelope. The return address is preprinted in the upper left-hand corner:

West Virginia National Guard
Williamson Post
1603 Armory Drive
Williamson, WV 25661

Looking at the back, it has been sealed and taped – not tampered with, so Deaton was telling the truth, not that she doubted him. Nervously, she breaks the seal and removes the tri-folded paper. It is official letterhead with the same address from the envelope centered across the top and same bold hand has written a page long letter. Color leaps to her face as she leans against the doorframe and begins to read.

Good Morning Ms. Caroline,

>*I want to thank-you for your kind hospitality yesterday. Belfry and her students are quite impressive and lunch was the best I have had in a long time. It is very clear to see why so many are proud to be part of this community.*
>
>*If you are interested, I would very much like to take to you dinner this weekend and you can show me the sights of the Big City, because I have not lived here long.*
>
>*I'm a soldier, a poet, and a dedicated fan of the Oak Ridge Boys. I enjoy picnics and long walks and rollercoasters. I'm not a fan of chocolate, allergic to cats, and hate onions. I am up for anything and look forward to hearing from you.*
>
>*Below is my contact information.*
>
>*Seth Garrett*

His signature is followed by his email, cell phone number, and office hours with a smiley face by his name.

What is this? A joke?

Looking up and down the hall to make sure no one was watching and laughing that she is in fact part of a joke, Caroline is stunned reading the letter several more times as the morning bell rings. Stuffing it back into the envelope and rushing to her desk, she puts it in the middle drawer and returns to the hall for morning duty. She pastes a smile on her face, greets students as they walk by, answers a few as they file inside that they are having their test, and remarks to her colleague across the hall, "I got it from Custom Print on Central Avenue," when she comments that she likes her shirt. The bell rings and she closes the door behind her and sits at her desk to take attendance and wait for the announcements.

The FCA president begins to speak on the intercom. "Good Friday morning, Belfry High School! There will be a home baseball game tonight against Mingo Central. Everyone come out at 7:00 to support the Pirates. Players need to report to the field by 5:00 wearing red pinstripe... There will be no after school tutoring today...Anyone wanting to go white water rafting with the Hiking and Camping Club needs to pick up permission slips from Mr. Gilmore by the end of the day...The band and choir will have their Spring Concert in the Auditorium on Sunday at 4:30. Admission is $2 with proceeds to help pay for new performance uniforms.

And for the Thought for the Day – It has been said, it does not matter how you start, but how you finish. Students with the school year coming to a close and the weather getting warm, remember to be focused in your studies and behave in your activities. Have a great day!"

As he concludes, all the students of her class stand as the National Anthem plays. Once the music ends, Caroline sits back down, dumbly unaware of how to proceed with the day forgetting she was so organized just minutes ago. Staring at her desk, she is brought back to the morning by someone saying her name.

"Ms. Hatfield...Ms. Hatfield! Are we having the test?" Maria, a bubbly, beautiful girl with long, dark hair and large, dark eyes sits in the front of the third row asking with a bright smile on her face.

"What??? Yes! I must have been asleep for a moment!" Caroline jumps to her feet as a few students giggle at her comment. Shuffling books and papers, a few moans, and the squeak of a desk, the students get ready for the test.

"You know we have a big game tonight, Ms. Hatfield...You could move this to Monday," Jeremy Urps, a member of the baseball team calls from the last seat in the row laughing and punching the guy beside him. He is wearing his game day shirt, but upon looking at him, you would have no other indication he is suited to play baseball; defensive tackle is more like it.

"Mr. Urps," Caroline likes to say that, because she thinks it is a funny word, too bad Jeremy's humor does not match his name, for Caroline – and many others – find him infuriating at times. "I could, but since it was already scheduled for yesterday, I would hate to disappoint you and let all that studying go to waste," she answers sweet as candy, so only to insult him a little.

"Why do you care, Urps? The only thing you'll have to do at the game is run from the dugout to the concession stand to get Coach Hayes his *Dr. Pepper* when he starts yelling because you all are losing!" his face serious, though the comment is meant to completely irritate.

"Shut up, Elkins! We're not going to lose to Central!" Urps settles in his seat choosing not spar with Elkins this morning.

Scott Elkins is the picture opposite of Jeremy Urps – tall and lean, well defined muscles, perfect athletic style, and just enough arrogant confidence to make girls swoon and guys curse. Fortunately for him and much to the disappointment of Jeremy Urps and others like him, Scott Elkins has a tremendous amount of talent at his disposal and is happy to show it off at middle linebacker, 220 wrestling weight class, and the 440 hurdles he says he runs just for fun.

He throws his head back in roaring laughter in answer to Urps' comment, winks at Maria who sits to his left and who has stopped being impressed by him since grade school, turns and takes his test from Caroline, saying no more.

Caroline also chooses not to comment not wanting to start a war between the two that is always simmering. Instead, she finishes passing out the tests, gives some basic directions, reminds the class of test protocol, and returns to her desk, because the letter she stashed in her drawer is screaming at her. She opens the drawer slowly, trying to act casual so none of her students will notice she is about to fall apart. She reads it again deciding this is no joke, but is uncertain how to proceed. Glancing at her students, seeing they are all absorbed in the test, she opens her email and sends a quick message to Sophie. She types a string of exclamation points in the subject line then says, "I have something to show you! I will be over during homeroom."

Now, she must wait until the end of class willing her heart to slow down.

Her students all finish with a few minutes remaining and when the bell sounds, she jets out the door ahead of all of them. Rounding the corner and heading down the back hall to the choir room, Caroline has to weave through the flood students some who are already carrying their breakfast bags to homeroom. A student stops her to ask about the test, exasperated,

71

Caroline responds, "YES! We are having the test!" Arriving at the door to the fine arts department, Caroline is panting as Mr. Tackett almost knocks into her as he rushes out the door.

"Excuse me, Ms. Hatfield! I didn't see you there!" Moving to the side holding the door open for her.

"You weren't looking!" Noting his frown, "I mean, I wasn't looking. Sorry!" giving him a cheesy smile, she edges around him not allowing further comment and thwarting her plans of speaking to Sophie.

Only glancing in her office, Caroline see she is not there and walks into the choir room where Sophie's homeroom meets. There are three students chatting and munching digging breakfast from white paper bags while a boy attempts 'Heart and Soul' on the piano. Nearly shrieking, Caroline asks, "Where's Ms. Cross?" the three eating only shrug and boy at the piano, yells, "Office!"

Aggravated the kids are soooo being kids this morning and absolutely not helpful and that Sophie went to the office when she wanted to see her, Caroline returns to her room amid questions and complaints and seemingly hundreds shouting her name.

Seth Garrett would have to wait.

Chapter VI

"Farmers who wait for perfect weather never plant. If
they watch every cloud, they never harvest."
– Ecclesiastes 11:4 NLT

Second and third period goes by without incident and Caroline is able to focus her mind and get some work done, so she has almost forgotten she emailed Sophie when her friend bursts through the door at the beginning of her planning.

"I'm so sorry! I just read your email. I have had a crazy morning!" Sophie is a whirlwind as usual setting her neon paisley print lunchbox on the desk in front of Caroline, flopping down, releasing an exaggerated sigh. "I don't think I have sat down all day! Fridays are just as crazy as any other day of the week!" sucking on the straw of the oversized insulated cup that matches her lunchbox.

"Is everything ready for Sunday's concert?"

Recovering slightly from her weariness, Sophie opens one of several plastic bowls and starts munching on cucumber slices. "YES! But, I am to the point that I really don't care. I have every detail marked off my list and during 6th and 7th, we will get the stage set and the auditorium ready. My goal is NOT to come here tomorrow and I will show up early on Sunday for any last-minute touches. If everything is not to perfection, the only one to notice will be me. I've also decided that I will *not* choke any student who fails to show up!" grinning wickedly, Sophie teases.

All the while, Caroline knows she will be in a ridiculous panic until moments before the performance begins, then she will muster a shocking level of calm and the concert will be perfect. As always.

"Why am I jabbering on? What's this email about? What's going on?"

Sophie changes channels quickly, stuffing more cucumbers in her mouth staring wide-eyed at Caroline.

Caroline hesitates and exhales deeply pulling the envelope from the drawer. Nervously tapping just like Deaton has done earlier, Caroline hands it to Sophie and explains, "Deaton Tyler brought this to me before 1st period. He said it was about Career Assembly."

Sophie takes her time reading, flipping the page and the envelope over examining it like Caroline. When she finally looks up, she fires several repeated questions.

"Is this the guy?"

"Yes."

"The one from yesterday?"

"Yes."

"The dude with the National Guard?"

"Yes. Yes! YES!" Caroline yells nervously frustrated as her best friend keeps asking the same thing – either unbelieving or painfully confused.

Sophie reads the letter again. "Did you see he likes the *Oak Ridge Boys*?" smiling excitedly trying to encourage her friend, "You LOVE them!"

"Sophie! Everyone loves them. They are the perfect combination of gospel, pop, and country!" disgusted she would even make the connection, because it is so obvious to Caroline.

"Why did Deaton bring it to you?" Sophie continues her questioning trying to organize everything whizzing through her mind and solve this mystery which Caroline has had over three hours to ponder.

Caroline begins to lay out the facts as she knows them. "He said he went to see his dad and Seth and Cleat were ther –" Sophie cuts her off.

"CLEAT!?!? I haven't seen him in forever! I loved him in high school. He has to be the funniest guy I have ever met! I forgot he was in the National Guard!" smiling brightly, Sophie changes tracks again.

"SOPHIE! Focus!" not waiting for her to apologize, Caroline proceeds. "He said before he leaves, Seth gives him this envelope and asks if he could give it to me. When I question him why, he repeats it is about Career Assembly. He leaves the room before I open it, so I couldn't ask him anything else. He said he had not read it and it sat in his car all night. It was sealed and taped, so Deaton did not open it."

"Maybe it wasn't sealed when he got and Deaton taped it shut."

"Uggghhh, I hadn't thought of that." Fear creeps onto Caroline's face at the possibility of Deaton reading the letter.

"Are you sure Deaton didn't write it?" Sophie picks up the letter scanning it for evidence.

"No. I'm not a hundred percent, but if it is from Deaton, someone else wrote it for him, because his handwriting is terrible."

Sophie works her mouth side to side in deep thought. "Deaton is a great kid and I can't imagine him playing a prank on you...Sooooo, call him!"

"No! If Deaton hasn't written the letter and doesn't know what it is, I'm not telling him," reaching across her desk as Sophie hands it back to her.

"Not Deaton...Seth. His number is at the bottom," Sophie proceeds with her lunch as if that is the obvious and most sensible answer.

"SOPHIE!!! Are you crazy?!?!? I'm not calling him! I'm not in tenth grade!" Caroline flops back in her chair face flaming shocked Sophie would make such a suggestion.

"Why not? He obviously wants to talk to you," continuing to chew nonplussed by the idea.

Calming, Caroline rationalizes, "Sophie, I was a buffoon yesterday and I am sure he left here mad."

"Apparently, he's not mad now," countering her argument.

"What would I say, 'Hey, this is Caroline. I am usually not a moron and I would love to go to dinner!" scowling at her friend at how absurd that sounds.

"Yeah, that's a great place to start!" Caroline angrily gasps and before she can comment, Sophie goes on, "He knows you're not a moron and probably got back to his office and realized he may have been a little bit of a punk. So, he seems pretty classy to take the time to write you a letter. I would be swooning all over the place if a guy did that for me!" continuing to plead her case, "Besides, you have nothing important going on and when was the last time someone asked you out?" smirking with a very accusatory face, both knowing it was too long.

Sophie eats and Caroline sits quietly – deciding her course. Biting her lip, she confesses, "I cannot call him," before Sophie can argue, Caroline explains. "I will be too nervous to call him and I'm afraid everything will just tumble out all wrong like yesterday."

"Say no more!" Sophie shoots up and is going through Caroline's desk in an instant. "This is so romantic! Writing letters! Ahhh, I believe I am going to swoon!" panting and fanning, Sophie finds pastel paper and several *Sharpie* pens holding them out to Caroline, returning to her seat ready for this adventure to begin. "Use several colors. It will make it more girly!"

"I'm not writing him either! Sophie, have you lost your mind? You probably expect me to have Deaton deliver it to him this afternoon!"

"Ah! I hadn't thought of that, but it's a great idea!"

Caroline's eyes look like they are about to pop out as she yells at her friend again, "Sophie!"

"SHOOSH! You know you like the idea…Who is that guy you love so much in history that wrote his wife?" Sophie watches her practical, cautious friend knowing she is luring her over to her way of thinking.

Not wanting to answer, Caroline responds quietly, "Stonewall Jackson."

Sophie's face and voice are full of glee, "Even better! He's a soldier, too!"

"Yes, a soldier who was shot by his own men, got his arm amputated, and died before 40!" Caroline still wears an angry face.

"Wonderfully romantic! Then when he marches off to war, you can tie a yellow ribbon round the ole oak tree!" Flapping her hand at Caroline, Sophie disregards this last tidbit no less delighted. "Caroline, please! Don't spoil it with a history lesson!" Sophie becomes more tender, but honestly voices what they both know. "I don't know when it happened, but somewhere along the way you decided to marry Belfry High and now most of your life revolves around this school! You are just as excited as I am, probably more, but you think you have to hide it, like you are too refined and mature for fun," knowing her friend too well, always wishing she were more of a free spirit, she gives her a more comfortable alternative, "Call him. Write him. Send him a text or email. Just contact him. You have nothing to lose and he has taken the initiative, so there is no worry… And if nothing else, you get a free dinner." Packing up her lunch, Sophie prepares to leave Caroline to mull all this over.

Walking with her to the door as the bell ending first lunch rings, Caroline agrees, "Ok."

Sophie looks at her, "Ok?"

"Ok."

"Ok..."

Sophie's grin is childlike and the little pixie flutters out of the room with Caroline locking the door behind her. She walks to her desk, opens the letter, smoothing the paper still doubtful this is true and really happening to her. After a few moments, she makes a snap decision to email him, not waiting to change her mind. She is pleased with the clever and witty lines, types her name followed by a smiley face (just like he did), and hits send. Excitement outweighs the dread in her stomach and the hummingbird quiets, but she can occasionally feel his wings beating inside her chest.

Again, she must wait...

At 3:17, just minutes after the bell, Sophie is again in her room ready to leave for the weekend. "Well..."

"Well, what?" coyly, Caroline baits Sophie with her answer.

"You know what! What did you decide about Seth?" waiting by the door, because Caroline is on her way out, too.

"I emailed him during planning," slinging her bag and purse over her shoulder.

"And..."

"And nothing. He didn't respond," clicking off the lights, they begin to walk down the now vacant hall.

"Oh..." followed by a disappointed frown. "Well, how about dinner, then we come back to the game?" Sophie offers as a poor substitute.

Caroline laughs, but does not remind her they are both married to Belfry High School, "Sure, that sounds great," and they walk to their cars ready for another *exciting* weekend to begin.

Dinner, complete with hashing and rehashing the last two days, discussing the complexities of the male mind, dredging up memories of loves from the past and laughing, the girls are in the stands with legs outstretched thrilled with the warm Spring weather waiting for the game to start.

"I just can't understand why he didn't respond," Sophie asks for the umpteenth time frowning and puzzled.

Caroline's first thought is, 'Because he's a *guy*!' but decides to answer, "Maybe he was busy or out of the office?"

"Yeah, maybe, but why would he send the letter this morning and say he wants to see you this weekend, if he knew he would not be able to be reached today? It just doesn't make sense."

This time Caroline says what is on her mind, "Because he's a *guy!*" adding a hint of disgust for effect.

Turning and giving her full attention, "What exactly did you say to him?"

Caroline gives Sophie more than an aggravated look, because she has told her at least three times already and again has to defend herself, "I said, *'Hello Mr. Garrett, Are you aware students are recklessly handing out your personal information? Yes, I agree we should meet and discuss this.'* And then I put a smiley face at the end, just like he did. I thought it was teasing and funny just like his."

Looking sheepish and giving her an odd smile full of teeth and eyebrows, "Well, maybe he didn't understand your humor? Maybe you should have said you hate cats or some other personal detail or ended with an exclamation point?"

"What? What do you mean, 'He may not understand your humor.'?" Caroline asks almost growling at her friend.

Sophie quickly explains herself, not wanting to hurt Caroline's feelings, "Don't get me wrong…I think you are hilarious – everybody does! But, your humor is sometimes…uhhh…a little…mmm…INTELLECTUAL!" noticing Caroline's frown deepens, Sophie scrambles for more words. "I mean – you are smart and witty, which is totally…uhhh…hilarious!" laughing awkwardly that she used the same word to describe her twice, "But, that *type* of humor sometimes can be misinterpreted, especially through an email, for example," ending with the same odd smile – more teeth and eyebrows.

Caroline leans back with a closed mouth frown nodding her head in agreement. "So, you don't think I should quit teaching and join the comedy tour?" raising one brow in Sophie's direction.

Huge, toothy grin and pointing with both hands, "See! That's it right there! Funny, but sarcastic! And I know that, but I've known you since we were nine. Seth just met you, so he may think it sounds a little…uhhh?" lips pursed and eyes squinted, Caroline watches and waits for Sophie to locate the perfect descriptor. "ARROGANT!" she almost shouts and Caroline flinches.

"Arrogant," Caroline echoes.

"Not actually arrogant, just the perception of arrogance," speaking slowly and gesturing like she is conjuring a spell.

"Arrogant," Caroline nods again appearing to agree.

Sophie continues knowing she has dug her grave and might as well pull the dirt in. "And arrogant can be intimidating…and guys don't want to be intimidated, especially by a girl, especially the soldier – alpha male – tough guy type."

Shaking her head in further agreement. Caroline relinquishes her casual pose turning more towards Sophie: feet down, hands resting on thighs – a subtly defensive position ready to strike her own offense. "Arrogant and intimidating…but hilarious!" her smile indicates menacing far more than mirth while Sophie continues to shovel.

"SEE! There's more of it! And a little frosty. You know – cold and sort of emotionless."

"And I thought I was just coming to the baseball game! Never realizing I would get a free character analysis to boot! Sophie, since you started this little therapy session and we are both laying on the couch, why don't you tell me how you really feel?!?!" Caroline wants to attack her friend, but much of what Sophie is saying, to her chagrin, Caroline has heard before.

Sophie softens her tone and gives Caroline honest advice, "All I'm saying is, I know you *and* I know you are not arrogant or cold, but Seth doesn't. Instead of you being intimidated by him and guarding yourself with sarcasm and wit, second guessing EVERYTHING, why don't you decide to relax – before it goes any further – and show him immediately the person I know; the person I love and he will be dazzled," Sophie squeezes the hand of her oldest and dearest friend, knowing that despite all of her knowledge and education and attempts at grace and poise, Caroline struggles in new social situations, usually retreating before either side sounds the attack.

Taking a deep breath and blowing it out her lips, Caroline honestly answers, "I'll try."

Friday has been crazy for Seth Garrett as well. First thing, two guys came in needing vaccination papers complaining about renewal and did Seth know if they would be in trouble if they didn't get them. Then, a call from Knoxville wanted to know if processing was complete for a transfer of one of their men to fill a squadron in Williamson's unit. Seth explained there was one form that had yet to be received from the man, then Tennessee and West Virginia, both, had to approve the transfer since he was not a resident.

"Son, isn't there any way you can get this taken care of faster? I need him out of my command, so I can fill his spot. I mean we are the ones doing you the favor!" his tone demanding Seth to disregard proper procedure to make his life easier.

"Yes, sir. I am aware of that. I will do everything I can. We appreciate your assistance, sir. Have a good day!" Seth maintains his calm and respectable behavior throughout the conversation, but slams the phone down when he hears a click then the dial tone realizing the colonel has hung up. Seth fumes and mutters a few curses directed at the man who far outranks him, though lacks the polish of his bestowed brass.

A fax comes in announcing the date for the vehicle requisition has changed and is two weeks sooner, so Seth's report will need to be to Charleston – with all necessary adjustments – by 5:00. On his way out of the restroom, he steps in a sticky mouse trap that he must pry off his boot with a screwdriver leaving behind a gooey mess. He goes to the garage finding only gasoline to clean it off and he smells like a tanker spill the rest of the day. Just after noon, Cpt. Tyler walks through the office carrying his executive military binder under his arm and hat in hand ordering Seth, "Let's go," leaving the building. He has forgotten the monthly battalion meeting in Logan. Fortunately, everything he needs was ready on Tuesday and he can easily grab his backpack following the Captain.

The meeting was a repeat of the last three. They should be called 'Hurry Up and Wait Sessions' instead of battalion meetings. It is like they are a pot that needs to boil and has only warmed up to a simmer. Since their battalion is in the preliminary stage of readiness, boiling will be slow coming.

They return to the armory and Seth makes the adjustments to the unit memo that were issued during the meeting, checks the instructions seeing they are ready to receive the first shipment of the weapons load on Monday, syncs his and the Captain's calendar, and begins to check emails that have piled up while he was out.

Seth has read all the emails and made the necessary replies. Scrolling through his inbox, he hopes to leave early, because Cpt. Tyler has already left for the weekend. Seth sees an unread message from this morning; subject line – Career Assembly??? – and an address he does not recognize – ceh.bhs@kyschools.us.

CEH? Who's that?

Seth opens the email and realizes it is from Caroline and thrill passes through him…until he reads the message and rereads it. He sees she sent it before noon and it is now almost 5:00. As he reads the message a third time, he picks up his cell phone.

"Hello, Friennnnd!"

Wasting no time on explanations, Seth instructs Cleat, "On your way home, stop by the Armory."

"I'll be there in a few minutes."

Seth reads Caroline's email several more times with fear and dread slowly rippling through him. Cleat walks in with his usual noise and commotion finding Seth on his hands and knees digging through the recycling bin.

Noticing the almost panicked expression on Seth's face, Cleat genuinely asks, "Bud, what's wrong? What did you lose?" coming to hover over him.

"Help me look!" Seth growls pulling out page after page from the bin only glancing then tossing them aside.

Kneeling on the other side, Cleat digs through the papers, "Ok… Uhhh, what are we looking for?" cautious, because Seth looks like he is about erupt – so unlike him. Seth is always so calm and collected, quite nearly cold and emotionless. He rarely is relaxed and playful, at work, and is above board in professionalism. He is also extremely organized and efficient, completing any task in advance and paperwork almost never needs correction. So, today's behavior is unusual.

"The first copies of the letter!" Seth barks at him.

"The letter?" puzzled, Cleat stops looking resting back on his heels.

"YES! The first ones we wrote to Caroline! I need to read them!" panic was on his face and in his voice.

"Ok…" still puzzled, but he begins to slowly sort through the papers, "Uhhh, why do you need to read them?"

Seth ignores his question stopping suddenly with a page in his hand. Smoothing the edges on his thigh, he stomps to his desk looking at the page then at his computer screen. Cleat chooses not to question him anymore and cleans up the paper mess in the floor that looks like the copier exploded. When he is finished, he drags a chair to edge of Seth's desk as he has done the day before, though his friend's attitude is much changed. Cleat sits quietly and waits as Seth barks again.

"Read this!" shoving the paper in Cleat's face and continuing to bark. "Did we say anything else in the final copy we sent to her?"

Cleat scans the page, setting it down in front of Seth and responds quietly, "No."

Seth leans his elbows on the desk and rests his forehead on the butts of his palms. Speaking, he talks to himself more than to Cleat. "What was I thinking sending something to a teacher, while she was at school? Stupid! STUPID!"

"Hey!" Cleat grabs Seth's arm giving him a firm, but gentle shake. Never seeing his friend like this, he begins to get a little worried as well. "What's going on?"

Seth looks up, releases a deep breath, and reads Caroline's email. "…'students are recklessly handing out your personal information? Yes, I agree we should meet and discuss this.' Can you believe that? What was I thinking?" his face pleading for his friend to give him reassurance. Unfortunately, Cleat offers none.

"Ok…Uhhh, maybe I'm missing something, but I don't see the problem?" Cleat looks at him with a confused smile.

"You don't see the problem!" Seth's bark has changed to a full roar, increasing in intensity with each word. "She is obviously – MAD!"

"MAD?!?! She wrote you two sentences and from that you decided she's mad?" Cleat's face changes from one of confusion to thinking his friend may be crazy.

"YES! But look how she said it!" roughly rolling his chair back so Cleat can have a clear view of his screen. Seth crosses his arms over his chest breath rushing through flared nostrils.

Gingerly, Cleat rises and leans over the desk reading the email, looking at Seth, reading it again. As he sits down, he begins his humorous questioning of Seth. "Again – she writes TWO sentences and from those TWO sentences, you have decided that she's mad?"

"YES!" Seth roars again maintaining his self-protective pose, breath coming faster. "I used a *kid* to take a letter to a *teacher* while she was at *school*! That was so stupid! Why did I agree to do this?" looking at Cleat expecting him to take at least part of the blame.

Cleat shouts back, "Stop sounding so military! You're acting like we were trying to sell drugs or start human trafficking! You didn't use a *kid*. You used Deaton, so that doesn't count. And Caroline is not just some *teacher*. You've already met her, so that doesn't make it too weird. Anyway, she said she wants to meet you, too! And! She put a smiley face at the end. That doesn't sound like angry to me!"

Gritting his teeth and closing his eyes, Seth cannot believe Cleat does not understand and see what a STUPID move this was. "It is the way she said it!"

"Yeah! She talks just like you, my over-educated friend! You're making a big deal out of nothing!" Seth opens his mouth, but quickly closes it. "Did you email her back?"

"No!" Seth roars again like that is the most ridiculous idea.

"What time did she send it?"

Without moving, Seth glances back at the screen, "11:37."

Cleat scratches his chin, leans back in his chair, lacing his hands on his middle, once again laying out his case to Seth, "You write this girl a letter claiming you want to go out with her *this* weekend and have it hand-delivered *this* morning. She replies with an email, I'm sure the first chance she gets. Now, approaching seven hours later, you have chosen NOT to respond...Oh yeah! You are completely right! She is MAD! Probably furious!"

Cleat gives way to uncontrolled laughter. "Now, you don't stand a chance! I bet, she and her friends have cut you into little pieces and are ready to feed you to the sharks! She is DEFINITELY mad AND probably thinks you were making fun of her!" Cleat continues to laugh. "You wrote a letter...to a teacher..." gasping for air "and had a *student* deliver it to her! AT SCHOOL!" laughing even harder, Cleat can barely speak as he doubles over and smacks the edge of the desk. "You're right! That was pretty stupid!

And now, you don't even have her phone number to call and offer some lame excuse!" wiping his eyes, he sits back silently laughing at his friend.

Seth slumps and rubs both hands across his face, "AAGGHH! What am I supposed to do now?" looking at his accomplice in this moronic 10th grade scheme.

"Well," Cleat begins by offering, "There's a home baseball game tonight. We could go and hope to run into her," Seth's angry face negates that suggestion. "Ok...We could go to her house; I've been there before. I mean, her parents' house. We'll just knock on their door and ask if they know where she is," Seth's face does not improve and Cleat gives one more option. "You could do something really crazy to get her attention," and he walks over to the phone beside the fax machine picking it up off the stack of phonebooks. Pulling out one from the middle, he tosses it on Seth's desk with a loud thud. "Look up her number and call her," Cleat walks towards the door as if he is going to leave Seth to decide, but turns back and offers his friend very good advice.

"Remember – Thoroughbred! Caroline Hatfield comes from the best of stock and you are going to have to treat her differently...better than anyone before. But...you just may end up winning the Derby!" Cleat smiles, but before leaving makes one final suggestion. "Oh, and honesty really helps, too! Remember – THOROUGHBRED!" Cleat acts like he is running and makes his quietest exit ever.

Seth looks at the cover of the phonebook with a picture of what he thinks is the Levisa River running through Pikeville, KY. In the yellow frame across the top, Big Sandy Region is written in bold type – '*Serving Mingo, Logan, Wayne, and McDowell Counties in West Virginia and Pike, Martin, Floyd, Johnson, and Lawrence Counties in Kentucky*'. Several moments pass before he decides to open it to Pike County which is subdivided into districts then communities: *South Williamson, Turkey Creek, Forest Hills, Hardy, Blackberry, Stone, and Belfry*. Now, all he must do is turn to the H's and find her name.

There has to be over 200 Hatfield's! I wonder if they're all related to Devil Anse?

Chuckling, Seth traces his finger over the columns of names until he arrives at *Caroline E. Hatfield – 38 Sunlit Cove, Forest Hills*. Without thinking of how this could be perceived as an invasion of privacy or seems a touch stalker-ish, he plugs her address into *Google Earth* and within seconds is looking at her house and pool and garage and large backyard. She is the second branch of a private drive with two others on each side with the road ending at the third house. The trees have been cleared all around each home, but they still appear to be nestled in their own area of privacy. He can determine little else about her house other than it is probably two-story with a red tin roof and there is a black SUV in the driveway.

Pulling an index card from the stack on his desk, he writes down her name, address, and telephone number folding it in his pocket. Seth leaves for the day ignoring the questions in his head and goes home.

Chapter VII

"Blessed is she who has believed that the Lord would
fulfill His promises to her." – Luke 1:45 NIV

The Pirates pull off the win over the Miners. Caroline does notice, however, Jeremy Urps making at least two trips to concessions returning with bottles of *Dr. Pepper* for Coach Hayes. Just before leaving, Sophie says, "Caroline…Nothing," and gets in her car. She does not make any more comments. She knows Caroline's head is buzzing. She also knows, that before Monday, she will make some decision about Seth and since they are not 17, Sophie lets Caroline make that decision on her own.

Caroline starts her car and leaves campus making the short trip to her house. Seven minutes from driveway to parking space, if she times it just right. She comes through the back door, hanging her keys, and dropping everything else on the kitchen counter. Her answering machine is not blinking, so she grabs a bottle of juice from the refrigerator, fishes her cell phone and Seth's letter from her purse, and heads upstairs to her bedroom.

Tossing the phone and letter on her bed, Caroline tries to act casual.
What does it matter? I'm alone and no one is here to watch me?

Still, she acts as if nothing has changed, she walks into the bathroom and brushes her teeth. Putting her brush back in its holder, she glances at her bed and it feels like the phone is calling to her. She tries to ignore it for about three seconds and walks to her bed.

There is no message blinking, because you did not give him your number. Moron!

Refusing to pick it up, she takes off her jewelry and removes the ribbon from her hair. Kicking off her shoes, she takes them to her closet. Never has Caroline been this neat and organized to get in the shower. Walking back to her bed, she opens the letter and picks up her phone. Looking that the time is after 10:00, she hurriedly writes a text message.

"Soldier, poet, Oak Ridge Boys? Picnics, long walks, and rollercoasters? Did you just copy and paste your online profile and send it to me? ;-)"

Winky-face, smiling again at her humor, she checks the time and drops the phone back on her bed. Still debating whether to hit send, she goes for the shower. Once out, she picks up the phone, pacing her room.

You've already wasted four more minutes! Hit send before midnight!
And she does.

Placing her phone on the nightstand, she returns for the last time to bathroom to take out her contacts, then she gets into bed.

I will not pick up my phone fifty times to check when I sent the text and add up how many minutes have passed!

So, she picks up a book and begins to read. On her third attempt of the same page, her resolve cracks and she checks her phone.

7 minutes! What am I doing?

Caroline decides on this rare occasion to be a total girl and double-texts, *"Is that your best pick up line or were you being coached?"* Again, phone on nightstand. Less than a minute later, her phone sounds and she almost hits the ceiling. Her heart pounds and a hot wave courses through her chest. The hummingbird that she thought was asleep has about a thousand friends joining him, their wings attacking her ribs.

She does not think her hands will work to pick up the phone and read the message, but she manages and her face flames.

Seth – *Nope. I was just being honest.*

Without hesitation she responds, trying her best to remember Sophie's advice.

Caroline – *So, you weren't being coached?*

Seth – *I didn't say that. ;-)*

Caroline – *Fortunately, I like picnics and rollercoasters (the bigger the better), the Oaks are always on my playlist, and I would pick a dog 100 times over a cat any day. ;-)*

Double-text again!

Caroline – *Anything else I should kn-*

Her phone rings. As the tune begins to play through a second time, she accepts the call and he does not even let her say hello.

"We could text back and forth for the next hour, but I decided to kamikaze and just call you. That was a good choice, right?"

Caroline is smiling so hard, she is sure her face is going to crack. She wants to laugh, but decides to play it cool; just not cold.

"Well, that was a pretty bold move...but I think it was the best!" certain he can hear her smile on the other end.

"I was nervous, especially since you have already given me one heart attack today!"

"What?!?!" Caroline gasps, enjoying their conversation already. "How did I give you a heart attack?" smirking at his comment and reaching for more pillows to prop herself up.

Smiling wide on his end, Seth accuses, "That email!"

Defensive, but laughing, "I didn't say anything bad in *that* email! As I recall, I only sent you two sentences! You must be mistaken."

Focus, Caroline! Don't start sounding all Amy Vanderbilt! Relax and just talk!

"Oh yes you did! I was expecting your principal and the State Police to show up at any minute. I was convinced I had breached a safety protocol. I left early, so no one could find me!" Seth hopes his teasing softens her and he gets the response he wants. Caroline starts to laugh and his nervous heart begins to calm.

Seth was in the shower when he thinks he hears he got a text message. Jumping out, he slides across the bathroom floor as his phone sounds again. Picking it up and not recognizing the number, he reads the message and says, "She must not be mad after all!" smiling, he prances like a proud peacock; swagger, a touch of arrogance, brimming with confidence – only achieved by the males of any species. Women love to hate it or hate to love it, but whatever you call it, it gets the job done and as Sophie would say, causes women to swoon.

Toweling dry, Seth settles onto his bed to talk to the young lady he also finds to possess her own brand of arrogance, but is also too intriguing to pass up. A few messages later, he decides that method is wasting too much time and calls her. She has had the upper hand all day and he needs to get some of it back.

"No worries. He wouldn't bring the State Police...A deputy would work just as well!"

He knows she is teasing and likes it. Banter is so rare with a woman, Seth appreciates her wit already. "Ha! Ha! I will keep an eye on the door from now on! Seriously, I was in a panic. I wasn't thinking when I sent the letter with Deaton. I just couldn't think of any other way to contact you. So, when I got your email, I was certain you thought I was a stalker or something!" Seth is able to laugh now, but he remembers how he was on the verge of sickness just a few hours ago.

"A stalker! Don't be silly!" Caroline's face is glowing at his honest admission. She would have never guessed this was the same guy from yesterday. "I thought it was cute...I may have even swooned a little...once I decided someone wasn't playing a prank on me."

Seth's face is also glowing at her honesty, surprised as well that Cleat's description is more accurate than his own. "This is the South and every Southern Belle is supposed to know how to swoon properly before they complete finishing school, aren't they?"

Caroline enjoys his teasing and makes a mental note to tell Sophie that Seth's humor could also be considered 'intellectual'. "You are correct – this is the South, but I did not go to finishing school and I doubt I am much of *belle* by any standards.

"Nope. I doubt that! Besides, I have already seen you in action and different ones have praised you!" remembering how impressed he was by the way she handled the assembly and she did wear great shoes.

"Who has praised me? You just met me yesterday?" worried his sincerity is about to vanish and he will again become such a *guy* – full of himself and empty flattery.

Hearing the doubt in her voice, Seth plays along, "Various people... mainly Cleat!"

Scoffing, Caroline protests, "Cleat! I don't know if he can be trusted! He has known me too long and I haven't seen him in forever. How is he?"

"I'm sure the same Cleat!" and they both laugh.

Much of the next hour is spent discussing Cleat and few more topics with which they are both familiar – very safe and neutral territory, but the conversation flows easily and with lots of laughter.

His tone taking on a more serious note, "So...I was thinking it would be really nice to see you tomorrow??? Maybe around 11:00?" even though their present conversation has been one of the best Seth has had in a long time AND she already agreed to meet him in her email, there was still that cloud of uncertainty hanging over them. That nervous possibility that she may say no and laugh in his face. He is silent waiting for her reply. Two, three seconds tick by, feeling like an eternity, his hand begins to fidget with the sheets – folding and smoothing, folding and smoothing. After what he thinks is a prolonged pause, Caroline answers, "I think that is a great idea!" Seth can hear the smile in her voice, moves the phone away from his face, and releases a deep breath he did not realize he was holding repeating some of the peacock dance.

Caroline has snuggled into her pillows feeling warm and giddy – suddenly jumping up like a gun has been fired to start a race. "WAIT! I can't!" disappointed she has to say that and doubtful he will understand.

Seth practically leaps out of bed, anger and embarrassment running neck and neck at the sound of the gun, as red works its way across his chest aiming for his face. Shocked at her sudden change, he questions, "What?"

"Oh Seth, I'm sorry!" Caroline is near frantic again thinking MORON!

A lilt passes through him when she says his name. Clearing his throat so as not to sound angry or disappointed, "Umm, ok. I understand…"

Caroline tries to clean up yet another mess she has made, "It's not that I don't want to see you. I just forgot I have to give the ACT in the morning!" gritting her teeth and taking the side of fist to pound her forehead. She has proctored the ACT one other time and tomorrow just *had* to be her turn!

Stupid! Stupid! STUPID!

Seth ceases his death march around his room sitting on the corner of his bed. The anger and disappointment flees from his chest and he asks Caroline, "Are you talking on your cell phone or landline?"

Caroline doesn't quite understand the question nor why Seth has changed gears so quickly. "Uhh, my cell phone?"

"Ok. Call the paramedics on your landline, because we have a man down and I'm bleeding all over the place!"

She is silent trying to process what he has just said and decides, "You are not!" but still thinking there is the slightest possibility she may have to rescue him.

"Yes I am!" changing his tone and fully teasing, "You gave me a heart attack this morning, now you shoot me down. I'm certain not to survive and we just met…yesterday."

Pleading, yet flirtatious, "I PROMISE, I'm not trying to kill you!... You would know it, if I were!"

For the first time, Seth detects a hint of seduction wrapped in playfulness and sinister laughter. He loves the thrill it sends through him and responds low and gravelly, "Well, Ms. Hatfield, I will be sure to stay on guard!" maniacal chuckle only slightly suggesting the possibility of things to come. Returning to the moment, "What time is the ACT over?"

Forgetting all about the test and thinking how she likes that he jumps from one topic to another, forcing her to pay attention, "Umm, it will end around 11:00 and then I will have a little paperwork when I turn everything in. But I know I will be totally finished no later than noon," with fingers crossed, she hopes that works for him.

"Great! I will be to the school by 11:30, just in case you finish early."

"Ok. That sounds great!" enjoying his commanding tone and his now take-charge behavior.

"Well, it was nice talking to you and I will see you in the morning."

Smiling at the return of her shyness, "Yes, it was very nice talking to you as well."

"And Caroline," his voice is gentle and Caroline becomes giddy at the sound of her name.

"Yes?"

"Don't wear anything too nice. I don't want you to get upset if it gets dirty. Goodnight!"

"Goodnight..." conversation over.

Puzzled as to what he has in mind for them to do and a little stunned the call ended sort of abruptly.

What are we going to do?

Stretching her hands over her head and looking at the clock – 1:19am. Dismissing that she has to be up in a few hours, Caroline walks into her closet to decide what she is going to wear.

A first date and he says not to wear anything nice. Yeah, right!

Deciding it will possibly be something outdoorsy, she finds her favorite jeans and a long-sleeved scoop neck shirt in pale melon. Her mother says that color looks good with her skin and hair. Remembering the forecast said it is going to be cool, but sunny, she finds a plaid flannel button-up in olive, tan, and ivory with the tiniest line of melon. Pleased with her selection, she gets her brown ankle boots that are a little rugged, though very girlie and takes everything to her bed laying them out for examination. Finally, turning off her light, she is once again in bed though sleep is slow to arrive, she drifts off well after 2:00am with thoughts of Seth Garrett and what he has planned for tomorrow.

Chapter VIII

Caroline does not have to wait for her alarm. Hopping up, she feels completely rested though getting only about four hours of sleep. Making her bed, she lays her clothes out again, not changing her outfit and rushes to the bathroom. Scrubbing her teeth, she checks her face for blemishes and stray hairs. Knowing a magnifying mirror and tweezers can be your worst nightmare and best friend, she ends her examination and gets in the shower. Once out, she starts her normal routine of making several trips in and out of the bathroom, plugging in hot curlers, drying her hair, brushing her teeth again, rubbing lotion on her legs, moisturizing her face, putting six jumbo curlers in her hair, first spritz of perfume, flossing, makeup, underclothes, curlers come out, hair is pinned back, final spray of perfume – *Beautiful Day* – because she knows it is going to be, and finally her clothing. Lacing up her boots, she walks to her dresser and picks up plain thin gold bar earrings on threader hooks – simple, but dangly. Caroline is in her Explorer and heading towards school with just enough time.

At 7:20, about seventy-five sleepy students, some she does not recognize from other schools, gather in the Commons for the ACT. Caroline is to proctor the second group and leads 20 kids down the back hall to her room. Distribution of the materials complete, reading the rules and procedures they have all heard before, setting the timer, and making her rounds through the rows, Caroline sits down to wait. She realizes, she is nervous about seeing Seth, but calm and being at school this morning was better than flying around her house. She would have had too much time to second guess and worry. Here she must stay quiet and still for three hours. Plenty of time to get her game face on.

Each of the students have their heads down totally focused on the test, so Caroline opens one of her desk drawers and gets out a bottle of bright red nail polish and shiny topcoat. As she is about to finish and turn on her desk fan to dry her nails, the boy in front of her whom she has never had in class, looks up – snorts and smiles – then returns to his test. Caroline only smiles back, but doesn't care that he was watching. Seth may have told her to come casual, but she can still have red nails!

At 11:06, Caroline picks up the last test booklet, organizes her supplies as instructed, signs the seating chart, returns all the #2 pencils to the box, and heads for the Guidance Office. Turning everything in, she has enough time to run by the restroom. She brushes her teeth, adjusts her hair, blots powder across her nose and chin, and picks up her *Lilly Bloom* backpack purse. Walking out of the office, she meets Sophie coming off the elevator with a loaded cart on her way to the auditorium.

Scolding, she asks Sophie, "I thought you weren't going to be here to today?"

Laughing and rolling her eyes, "You know me? Hey, where are you headed? I'll finish up here and we can go to lunch. 34:Ate has raspberry waffles and fried chicken today!" smiling and licking her lips in pleasure.

"Mmm, I can't...I have a date!"

"Caroline!?!?!" Sophie's face is complete shock!

"Sorry, I gotta go!" beaming, Caroline pushes out the door leaving Sophie to draw her own conclusions. On the porch, she takes a short gasp followed by a delighted sigh.

She does not have to look far to find Seth. He is an inviting picture in a maroon washed out collarless knit shirt that his strong chest fills out like a 50lb sack of seed you can find at *Westcott's* this time of year. Five dark grey buttons trail down to the middle with the top two open revealing a grey t-shirt underneath. They both are tucked in at a stout waist below a flat abdomen and cinched with a dark brown leather belt and plain buckle. His jeans look like they are tailored for his long legs and fall to the perfect hem at his boots. His face is clean shaven and his short brown hair that glints in the sunlight is combed to the side in a hard part.

Seth looks exactly the way men are supposed to look – a natural, unpolished beauty. His teeth are a little crooked and his nose is a touch big, but it is these subtle imperfections that make him even more striking. Flaws making him more attractive. Shadowed steely blue eyes give him an air of mystery; a story that is rarely told – they can dance with laughter or ignite in rage. Yes…He is exactly the way a man is supposed to look: tan and athletic like he just returned from Spring Training. Lean yet brawny as if he was on his way to chop enough cords of wood to last through the winter keeping you warm every night. It is a rare woman who does not experience a hot shiver upon seeing him.

An Army Green Jeep Wrangler with its camel colored top rolled back is parked in front of the large porch at the school's main entrance. Seth leans against its side, arms crossed over his chest, and one foot propped up on the edge of the sidewalk. Hearing the door open, he turns his head from looking down campus to see Caroline and his smile is wide. She cannot help but feel like Molly Ringwald at the end of *Sixteen Candles* when Jake Ryan is waiting on her. Caroline almost skips as Seth pushes off the Jeep to meet her, taking the steps two at a time.

At the edge of the porch, they stop just in front of each other. Caroline has to look up in his face, because he is tall, very tall. Smiling, the worry there may be lipstick on her teeth zooms through her head, but she does not have time to think about it as Seth squeezes her upper arm and in a low, quiet voice says, "Good morning."

She is so glad his hand lingers on her arm, because she feels a swoon coming on and thinks she may collapse at his feet. "Good morning," knowing her smile is way too big, she cannot get it to soften.

Releasing her arm and stepping back only slightly, "You ready to go?"
"Yes!"

He lets her walk down the steps and she feels his hand resting gently on her spine when he reaches around her to open the door. Taking mental note so she can look back on this day again, and Sophie will demand play-by-play. She reaches over to make sure his door unlocked and he comes to the open window.

"Thanks!" he smiles and fondly notices the gesture.

"You're welcome!" smiling sweetly knowing she has scored a crucial point, she asks, "So, are the boots *and* Jeep army-issued?"

Buckling his seatbelt, he answers casually, "The boots are. I paid for the Jeep," leaning towards her as he puts the key in and starts the ignition, he whispers, "Smart aleck!" with a devilish smile completely enjoying her banter. She looks over her shoulder at him impishly as the Jeep jerks forward. He rounds the parking lot and heads off campus turning left at the light. Caroline does not know what he has planned or where they are going and does not ask. She enjoys the sunshine and the thrill of the wind in her hair and face watching him change gears and maneuver around the other cars.

What is it about a man and how he drives? How he controls the machine – confident or reckless? And the car he owns tells so much about his personality – the side he shows and the side he keeps hidden.

The wind occasionally picks up the scent of his cologne and teases Caroline – clean and masculine, no dark, musky notes; very *Ralph Lauren*. She enjoys this time to study him, but he demands her attention all too soon by asking, "How did the test go?"

"It was fine. You have kids in three different camps: the ones who are a nervous wreck, the ones who will not be awake until long after it is over, and the ones who really don't care."

Looking over at her as he changes lanes, "And which camp were you?" thinking she has probably been a *school teacher* for a long time.

Answering honestly and surprisingly feeling quite relaxed to talk with him, "Hmmm, somewhere in the middle. I knew it was something I had to do. I mean it's just a test and they let you take it again, so no big deal."

Nodding and looking back at the road, "That's how I felt both times I took it."

"You only took it twice?" Caroline remembers she spent many more Saturdays than two trying to get to her desired score.

"Yeah. After I got a 29 for the second time, I decided that was enough." There was not the slightest indication of boasting or even pride. He was simply answering questions. "Why? How many times did you take it?"

Raising her eyebrows, she admits, "Well, more than two and I only reached 27."

Looking at her like it was no big deal, "Huh…Ok."

They continue to chatter about nothing of substance as they make their way up the highway. Just before they begin to climb Coeburn Mountain, Seth slows, gearing down, and cuts off to the left down what is locally called 'the Proach'. The road is very narrow with the creek on one side weaving its way through the coal camps. The mines have long since moved out, but the houses remain – some converted to single family homes while others deserted and dilapidated; an artifact of a time never to be again.

Caroline sits quietly watching the passing scenery, because she has not been here in years and impressed Seth seems so comfortable and familiar with the area even though he has said he has not lived here long. Serval minutes go by and they arrive at Runyon Elementary and he keeps driving.

"I've just entered new territory."

"What?" Seth also was absorbed in silence enjoying the ride.

"Yeah. I've only been as far as Pinsonfork, where the school was and that was years ago."

Disbelief creeps onto his face, "Really? I've lived here less than a year and half and I've been all over the place. That's just hard to believe."

"Believe it! You are taking me to somewhere I have never been," and she smiles, scrunching up her nose like a child.

His immediate thought is to make a comment laced with innuendo and obvious suggestion – *'where I have never been'* – but Cleat's words come back to him "Thoroughbred…and you just may win the Derby!" so he remains silent and smiles at the thought of winning.

When Caroline thinks the road cannot get any narrower, Seth comes to an almost complete stop and turns right through a large gate bearing the sign

Grants Branch Park
Stone, KY
Park Hours: Sunrise-Sunset
Operated by the Pike County Fiscal Court
www.TourPikeCounty.com

Reading it as they pass, Caroline turns to Seth and asks, "This is Grants Branch? My students talk about it all the time!" smiling, her face shows she is excited to be here. Seth is pleased he has made the right choice. Whipping her head from one side of the Jeep to the other, taking it all in, Caroline asks him so many questions assuming he will know the answers as they weave back and forth across the face of the mountain on their way to the park at the summit.

Making the final climb, it is as if the world has opened up, leaving the tight, narrow valley below. She looks back down from where they have come; the land sectioned off in terraced meadows before rolling back to the entrance gate. On their left is a large two-story log cabin with wrap around porch nestled at an angle against the mountain. Looking at it as they pass, Seth informs, "We will check that out in a bit," and pulls into a huge parking lot with a picnic shelter and playground at the end. Seth parks facing the lake, steps away from the ramp that leads to the dock. Caroline leans forward with her hands on the dash like she is trying to get closer.

Seth looks at her and smiles, "You wanna get out?"

Giddy, and again looking like a child, she wastes no time and gets out. He reaches behind his seat for his backpack and hurries to catch up with her. Caroline rounds the fence and rushes all the way to the water's edge with Seth trailing behind her. Once there she just stands and stares watching a bird glide just above the water, flapping its wings soaring higher and higher then entering the darkened woods disappearing. Looking up at him as if to say, "Did you see that?".

Caroline turns back to the lake and says, "I've known this was here… But I never realized it would be so beautiful…" Again, looking at Seth, completely serious and completely grownup, but with an unfamiliar innocence about her, "Thank-you for bringing me."

Seth has an odd sensation move through his heart and for the first time in years, he feels awkward and out place, but also safe and comfortable. The moment passes quickly and changes direction like smoke in the wind. He shuffles his feet and tugs at the strap on his backpack, "You hungry? I thought we would eat before we go exploring."

"Yes! I didn't have breakfast," they turn and make their way to the concrete path that leads to the shelter. Stepping over some rocks, their knuckles brush and Seth feels a lightning bolt go through his arm. Caroline obviously has not been affected by the casual touch and keeps walking. The path winds up the bank to the shelter or down to the dock. Seth starts towards the shelter though Caroline stops and calls after him.

"Seth, can we eat down there?" Caroline points to the tables on the dock. He hesitates and Caroline adds, "It's so nice and sunny and on the water. Please?"

He does not know if it is her smile or her childlike ways, but his heart gets that unfamiliar feeling again and he is happy to accommodate her.

The ramp and the dock are metal with railing all the way around. At each end, the dock widens creating a large 'I' adding more space for fishermen with two square tables on opposite sides. The tables are metal and bolted to the dock with a bench, also bolted, big enough for two on each of three sides. Caroline picks the table closest to the water and asks, "Is this alright?"

Seth responds, "It works for me, but you may get a little dirty," setting his backpack on one of the benches.

Frowning cutely, she reminds him, "You told me last night not to worry about getting dirty. I don't mind if you don't!" Without hesitating, Caroline uses her palm to dust off where they will sit and asks, "Do you have any napkins or paper towels?"

Seth digs into his backpack and brings out several sheets of paper towel he pulled off the roll this morning when he packed their lunch. Caroline takes two leaving the rest in his hand, walks to the edge of the dock, and gets down on all fours. Wiggling her hand under the railing, she dips the towels in the water, and pulls herself up. Seth watches as she squeezes the water onto the table then wipes it off her red nails sparkling in the sunlight

"I think that's clean enough. Besides, we've both had our shots!" smiling she sits down ready to be served.

Seth is a little confused. The person who was almost a mess and borderline rude the last time they had lunch together is nowhere to be seen. She is replaced by someone who is completely a girl – childlike, innocent, playful – yet undeniably a woman – blonde, curvy, confident. Who did not ask where they were going and came dressed just as he suggested. Climbed in his Jeep not concerned her hair would get windblown. Has nearly run around excited about the day, and nothing has happened yet. And is now sitting poised at a dirty table at Grants Branch Park ready to eat ham sandwiches like it is the State Dinner.

Tucking these thoughts in his mind to consider later, he puts the towels down he was dumbly holding, slings his leg over the bench, and sits down adjacent to her. She spreads one towel out in front of each of them as he unpacks their lunch.

Hands folded on the paper towel in front of her, she pipes up, "What are we having?"

She is just chattering and seems happy to be here, but it is making him so nervous. Cleat keeps echoing in his ears and he begins to doubt his choices for the day. He finishes unpacking and she does not seem to mind.

"I hope you like ham sandwiches...Uhhh, I should have asked first in case you're picky or allergic."

That sounded so dumb? Relax! What's wrong with you? You were fine ten minutes ago.

"Nope. No allergies and I'm not picky. I can eat just about anything... Except radishes. YUCK!" disgusted child face.

Fumbling with his words and the lids on the plastic bowls, "Yeah, uhhh, I hate radishes, too." Digging deeper in his backpack, he cannot find what he is looking for. Dejected, he looks at Caroline. "I forgot plates."

Caroline thinks his face, the change in behavior, and the lack of plates means they must pack up and go home. She tries to keep things light getting the feeling he is nervous all of a sudden. "No worries. We can just eat out of the bowls. Unless you're worried I have cooties?"

He knows she is teasing him again and laughs nervously, "I don't think you have cooties." Handing her a sandwich and sliding all the bowls closer to her, he continues to fumble in his backpack wishing he could crawl in and hide. He notices she is not eating and says, "Go ahead."

"I will. I was just waiting for you, because you seem unsettled," crinkling her brow, because his face is frowning.

Dropping his backpack to the floor, he rests both forearms on either side of his sandwich. It is like his brain is filled with mud and he has forgotten how to eat. Caroline places her hand on his arm and instead of a lightning bolt, a cool calm washes over him. With an almost smile, she closes her eyes and says, "Jesus, we thank-you for Spring time and picnics and new friends...AMEN"

Childlike and beautiful, Seth is unaccustomed to prayer, but is confident the Almighty listens to everything this girl has to say.

Caroline unwraps her sandwich and reaches for some grapes in one of the bowls. Popping one in her mouth, she asks, "Well, I know you're in the National Guard and you've not lived here long. Seth Garrett, what else do I need to know?"

Her tone and manner are not prying, but she seems genuinely interested. Feeling much more settled, he returns with a question, "What do you want to hear?" He, too begins to eat and the combination of the food and company, relaxes his mind and tongue as he answers her series of questions.

"Hmm, how old are you?"

"32. I'll be 33 on the 21st of July...How old are you?"

"I am 30 and will be 31 on October 4th," mocking him. "What's your middle name?"

"Charles. What's yours?"

"Elizabeth."

"Caroline Elizabeth Hatfield..." enjoying her name on his lips. "That's huge! Were you in like 6th grade before you learned how to spell it?"

He's teasing me, now. Maybe he will finally relax!

"Ha ha ha! NO! But, you're right. 25 letters long!...Where did you go to school?"

"WVU."

"Really? Will and Carter went to West Virginia and they're about your age. I bet you all were there at the same time," smiling at the coincidence.

Giving her a confused look, "Who is Will and Carter?"

"Oh sorry! I forgot you don't know them. Will is my first cousin and Carter is his best friend. They are roommates and live downtown in the Persinger Building...So, where are you from?"

"Mmm, a few places."

Sensing his resistance to talk, but wanting him to feel comfortable, she suggests, "How about you tell me your life story. As much or as little as you want and I will save the rest of my questions until the end," again noticing his hesitation. "I'm a great talker, but I'm a good listener as well." Chomping on a carrot, Caroline settles in to hear what he is going to say.

Washing down the mouthful of sandwich that seems to be stuck, Seth clears his throat and begins "Well, I was born in Freedom, PA northwest of Pittsburg right on the Ohio border, but I'm from Holidaysburg in central Pennsylvania just south of Altoona. My parents were high school sweethearts and were married by the time they were 21 and I arrived not long after." Seth looks at Caroline a little embarrassed by the admission, but she appears unfazed, so he continues.

"My parents are both from Holidaysburg – born and raised. My mom's parents still live there. They went right to work out of school and didn't go to college. My dad worked a string of different jobs never quite finding a good 'fit'. The last one he got when they were still in Holidaysburg was with a traveling sawmill, but it was only temporary, because once the job was finished, the crew moved to the next site and picked up new local workers. He worked it until they moved out of state. They offered him a job with the permanent traveling crew, but that was right after they married and mom didn't want to leave.

"My dad was the restless type. He was happy...well, maybe not happy, but at least used to temporary things and changes. His mother died when he was young and his dad never remarried. He always provided, but at times it was the bare minimum. He also shifted from job to job, and uhh...was not the best at parenting." Looking up, he needs to clarify. "My grandfather was an alcoholic and not very nice to my dad, but they always got by..." Seth tries to find the right words as how to explain family history that he has only heard, "I guess you could say they were estranged by the time my parents married. He and my dad had a nasty fight and not long after that, they moved to Freedom." Seth looks at Caroline and she is engaged in his story. Her eyes almost pin him down waiting for his next comments, so he continues.

"Dad had a buddy who told him there were great jobs at an oil refinery in Freedom. He got one almost immediately. I think two days after they moved to town, unfortunately, about six months later, he was laid off. That was about the time I was born. So, he took a job in a factory, Ohio-Penn Casket Company."

Caroline interrupts forgetting she promised to save her questions until the end, "Did you say *gasket* or *casket*?"

"Casket, like a coffin."

"Agghhh! Are you serious?" looking at him like he has just told her something icky.

"I'm serious! It was a locally owned factory; a small assembly line operation and he advanced pretty quickly, but he always hoped he would return to the refinery. When I was about two, he thought he got passed over for a promotion and had this ridiculous blowup on the owners. So, they fired him. He tried to go back to the refinery, but they wouldn't have him. Freedom is a small town, smaller than Williamson, so news spread quickly why he got fired." Again, pausing to formulate the right words. Seth wants to paint an accurate picture, but not give her wrong ideas. "My dad's temper has been known to be a little more than volatile at times." He gives her a sheepish look and Caroline does not know if she is to question what he means or just draw her own conclusions.

I wonder if he was mean or violent? Did he have an abusive childhood?

Quieting her thoughts, she relaxes and lets Seth keep talking as much as he would like.

"When he realized a good position was not going to open up, mom wanted to go work, but he refused. So, he did odd jobs for a while, but nothing too prosperous; mainly small time carpentry." His tone and demeanor change quickly, "My dad can build anything. He is great with his hands. He can just see things and figure them out. He doesn't need a pattern or blueprints. It's just all in his head and he does it. Some of the things he has built are very functional, but attractive as well." Pride was so evident in is his voice, though he hesitates.

Caroline knows there is more to that story, decides not to question him, but asks, "Do you like to build things?"

"Yes!" Seth realizes his eagerness and quiets. "I'm not as good as my dad, but I really enjoy it. I've made a few things: tables, benches, stuff my mom wanted – I'm sure she likes them more because I made them, not because they are that good," a faint smile is on his lips as he returns to thinking.

"So, would like to be a builder one day?" Caroline asks reaching for a bite-sized iced cookies she allows herself to get only occasionally from the bakery.

"Maybe…One day, I guess. I've been busy with the Guard since college and I have never been quite settled. The main thing I want to build is my own home. I mean with help, but be all part of the planning and the construction. Taking my time to get it just the way I want it. Nothing grand or elaborate, but mine," his smile is much bigger and Caroline can tell he has very clear plans in his head.

"I know what you mean. My house was a remodel. Don't get me

wrong, I love it, but there is nothing like new construction and the smell of sawdust."

Seth nods and smiles knowingly. He considers commenting that he has never heard a girl speak fondly of sawdust, but silently agrees. Knowing she wants to hear more of his story and for once, he feels relaxed and almost eager to tell her.

"After several weeks, when money started getting tight, my mom suggests they return to Holidaysburg. She never wanted to leave in the first place, but they were married and at that time, she would have followed him anywhere," looking back for only a moment before adding, "I don't remember this, but she says they had a horrible fight and he was gone for three days. She knew he drank some before they were married, but nothing since. He would always tell her, 'I'm not my dad. I will never be like him.' She said that was when the drinking started, but she didn't realize it until much later."

"When he comes back, it's like nothing has happened. He's happy and has a plan. FLORIDA!" Seth's eyes widen and gives a mocking flourish sarcastically speaking of the amazing idea. "My mom was dazzled by my dad's enthusiasm and excitement and his determination to work hard. That's some of why she first fell in love with him. She says, anyone could get easily caught up in one of his ideas, because they sounded so sure. When they never quite materialized or came to a bust, he was always so… so wounded." Pausing again, she can tell he is trying to decide how much he should share.

"So, we moved to Florida. He said, 'It's always sunny in Florida and warm in Florida and the beach is in Florida.' He was always looking to get rich quick with many failed attempts." Holding up his hand, he begins to count. "Hand-wash Carwash. Grass Mowing and Lawn Care. Hotdog vendor at the beach. And somehow he always seemed to pick up jobs working at the airport in shuttle service no matter what town we lived in."

Interrupting again, "What towns did you live in?"

"Agghh – Clearwater, Jacksonville, Kissimmee, Boynton Beach, some other places. During moves or while he was cooking up his next scheme, Mom and I would return to Holidaysburg and live with her parents. The last few moves, he started working in maintenance at resorts. Sometimes, that was pretty good money, but he would soon quit," holding up two sets of fingers making air quotes, "so he could get his business off the ground." Chuckling, he shakes his head seemingly more humored than disgusted by his story.

"After each move, the resorts got less resort-like and we were living in some shabby places. When I was 7, I remember this one the best, because I turned 8 a few weeks later. Dad sent us back to Pennsylvania one last time. He and a friend had gone in as partners early that Spring to be fishing guides on Lake Okeechobee. What was so crazy, is I don't think my dad had ever caught a fish in his life! They had saved some money and bought a john boat and were living in a camper. One would guide during the day and the other at night. They were actually making good money and getting ready to buy another camper they could also rent to fishermen. But what they didn't plan for was summer. People don't come to Florida to fish in the summer and by May, most of the snowbirds have returned north."

"So, they worked all summer anyway, as much as they could. He didn't come home that whole time. As a kid, I thought this time it was going to work, so I didn't really pay attention. A few weeks before school started, he shows up for my birthday and we had the best day. We went to a carnival and I got my face painted and he bought me a goldfish. That night, mom and dad tuck me into bed and I remember thinking again how this was the best day and they were both so happy."

He rarely even looks at Caroline shifting his eyes to some far-off place and he just keeps talking. Seth drifts a little and grows quiet. After a long pause, she thinks he is going to say no more, but starts again.

"My room was on the second floor and faced the front yard and the driveway. I woke up a few hours later and I heard them talking – fighting on the porch. The window beside my bed was open, but I couldn't quite hear what they were saying...I don't even know what made me think to do this, but it was like I knew what I was going to hear. I get out of bed and crawl out the window to sit on the roof." Looking at her for the first time, he says with a sad smile, "Dad tells her Billy has left with all the money. I remember my mom acting like she didn't hear. She wasn't disappointed or angry that our lives were again being upended. Towards the end, neither of them hid their behavior from me. Fights were common and whomever remained in the room after a battle did not hesitate to give me their side. Even then, I would think, 'I'm a kid. Why are you telling me this?'. That night they are both silent for a few moments and I can hear my mom sitting in the rocker going back and forth across the floorboard. Dad is leaning against the railing just below me. I can still see his shadow as he moves in and out of the light. She is calm and aloof saying, 'Seth needs to start school.' and all he says is, 'Ok.' I couldn't hear what else they talk about, but a while later, he walks down the steps. Just before he gets in the car, he looks back, right at me, like he knew I was sitting there the whole time…He almost smiles, but he doesn't wave or say anything and then drives off…" Seth is again looking down the road as he drives off, "I didn't say anything or wave…I just sat there watching him, wondering why I didn't move." Looking to Caroline, he exhales and his voice changes, "She files for divorce, it goes uncontested and is finalized in three months. It was a little over a year before I saw him again at his dad's funeral. After that, our visits were sporadic."

Seth stops talking. Caroline knows there is much more to his story, but she does not press him. "Where are your parents now?"

"My mom is still in Holidaysburg and my dad lives just south of Kissimmee…Woo! I hadn't planned on telling all that. I'm sure your story is way different?" looking at her, he comes back to the present and wants to change topics.

Looking at him with a kind, gentle face, "It is, but you can hear it some other time." Placing her hand again on his arm and giving it a firm squeeze, she reassures him. "Seth, I'm glad you told me your story. One day, I hope you tell me the rest."

"One day, I will." At that moment, he feels foolish, because the thought that races through his head is, "I would love to hug you!" tight in his arms and she would just hold him and not let go. Neither of them would have to say anything, they would just know and understand and be in the moment together. Before he has time to ponder that idea, Caroline stands up and says, "Let's take a walk!"

Glad the air has cleared, Seth packs everything away and drops it off in the back of his Jeep. Caroline takes off her flannel, because the day has warmed tossing it on her seat.

"How did you find this place?" happy to put him on different conversation.

"Cleat brought me here fishing right after I moved to town. Some days, I come here to run the trail. Running through town gets boring."

"Do you run every day?" she asks trying to remember when the last time she ran was.

"Sometimes, but not always, but at least three times a week."

She laughs and says, "Seriously? I only run when chased!" putting her hand to her forehead, shading her eyes looking for where the trail starts.

"Oh really?" challenge is in his eyes and her heart flip-flops. Pushing him in the chest and knocking him off balance, she tries to take the lead, but is quickly outmatched. She hears his feet stomping up behind her and his hands and arms are around her waist swinging her feet in the air before she can get away. Squealing, he puts her down, but does not release her.

"Oh please! I will die out here in the woods, if make me run!" she pleads, out of breath from laughter and excitement.

Husky and close to her neck, "I would never let you die." Removing his hands, "Come on! I won't make you run.

Pushing him away, she growls, pretending to not appreciate the spar and giggles when he tries to grab her again. They walk to where the trail starts leading them into the woods. It is cool and shaded, but the sun's beams make their way to the forest floor.

"We picked a good time to come. In a few weeks, the trees will be full of leaves and we would not have as good of view." Turning to look at her, she is very cautious when the path narrows and is paying very close attention to her baby steps across roots and rocks. "Are you ok?"

"Yes. I just have an extreme fear of falling."

Seth stops and she almost runs into him, because her eyes are on the trail. "You mean like off cliffs?"

"No. Just falling down. In front of people, on bleachers, an icy sidewalk sliding into oncoming traffic and I'm killed. You know – just falling, in general."

"That sounds like a phobia," he looks at her skeptical and mocking.

"Nope. You're wrong. I wouldn't be out here if it were a phobia!" looking up at his grin with a hateful face, she taps him on his chest. "Keep walking." Obedient, he leads on.

At the halfway point, they reach a clearing that looks across the lake opposite from the dock. The path is beaten down in front of some exposed rocks making a natural bench. Seth sits down and Caroline joins him. They chat relaxed and easy. Nothing heavy and emotional or too silly and pointless.

Seth picks a long blade of grass. Holding it between his thumbs, he tries to whistle. After several failed attempts, Caroline laughs at him picking her own blade. She makes a loud, clear noise on her first try, but is unable to repeat it. They continue to ask each other idle questions as Seth concentrates on weaving several blades into a wreath. Pleased with his work, he proudly places it on her head like a laurel, sweeping her hair from her cheek with gentle fingers.

Caroline lies back in the grass, with one hand behind her head and the other to her side, watching the passing clouds in the cornflower sky. Seth joins her in the same position and they lay there in silence listening to the sounds of the forest watching the sky. Seth shifts, their knuckles brush, and his heart pounds, but Caroline does not move. He moves again and their fingers touch and she is unresponsive. He traces his thumb across the back of her hand and she turns her palm up and laces their fingers. They stay this way for several moments falling under each other's spell and he lifts her hand drawing it near him. She turns on her side to face him as her hand reaches his mouth, kissing her knuckles. They just lay there not daring to come any closer, then she says, "Show me the rest," and sits up. Irritated she has spoiled the moment, Seth doesn't move, pride singed. Standing in front of him, she offers her hands to haul him up and reluctantly, he takes them. Back on the path, she quickly laces their hands leaning her cheek against his arm. His heart pounds and anger vanishes.

Chapter IX

"Let your roots grow down into Him, and let your lives be built on him..." – Colossians 2:7 NLT

The trail on this side of the lake is wider and more open. Caroline chatters up a storm, asking him lots of questions, though nothing personal. She flits around like a butterfly looking at things, veering off the path, but always returning to him, taking his hand.

The trail dips low creating a small 'beach' – sandy and close to the water. Evidence fishermen are here often litters the ground – cut line, a forgotten bobber, a candy bar wrapper, and an empty *Skoal* can. Caroline squats down and picks up a rock, tossing it in the water with a 'PLOP!' Dusting her hands on her jeans, she duck walks looking for another stone.

Seth watches her and after her second toss asks, "Is that as good as you can do?"

Looking up with no emotion in her face, "You think you can do better?"

Stepping by her, he nudges her knee with his shin knocking her back on her rump and digs at the bank with the toe of his boot. Caroline huffs and scrambles to her feet; arms crossed and sassy watching him. Bending at the waist, he picks up a flat stone and rubs it between his palms then sends it skimming across the water skipping one, Two, THREE – plop! Looking back at her with a wink, he says, "Top that!"

Trying hard to hide her smile behind a sullen face, Caroline moves next to him and repeats everything he did – boot digging up the rock, sliding it in her hands, and skimming across the water skipping one, PLOP! Seth watches with arms crossed, brings his fist to his mouth to hide his laughter. She glares at him and picks up another rock – skipping one...PLOP! Five more attempts and Caroline's rocks only have one skip. Frustrated and winded, Caroline glares at him again with hands on her hips.

Seth moves forward silently, picks up a stone, and with half the effort she used skims the rock – skipping one, two, three, four, FIVE! Delighted by her angry face, Seth roars with laughter – all chest and throat, loud and masculine. With his head tossed back he doesn't see Caroline coming for him and she shoves him hard sending him tumbling backward, but he remains upright. Recovering his footing, he sees she has disappeared, but can hear her running up the trail and he chases after her.

The trail leads him out of the woods and he jogs to the top of the knoll. At the edge of the playground, he expects to see Caroline waiting on him, but she is not there. He scans the whole area – shelter, dock, parking lot, seeing only his Jeep. Going back to the trail, he calls, "Caroline?" Hearing nothing, he walks the path all the way back to where they were skipping stones and she is not there. His excitement from just moments before is quickly fading to fear.

Has she fallen? We weren't a hundred yards from the playground. Where did she go?

Turning to look back down the trail, scanning the lake to make sure she has not fallen in, looking up the hillside deeper into the woods thinking maybe she had gotten off the path. As he completes the rotation, his mind quickly deciding what he should do next, anxiety is about to give way to panic and turn on rescue mode where he is not thinking just reacting, and a pinecone hits him in the face followed by three more pelting his neck and chest. He hears Caroline laughing and running towards the end of the trail.

This time he is quicker to react racing down the path as if the Devil were on his heels. He reaches the clearing and sprints passed the playground running into the shelter pausing just a moment and then to his Jeep. He looks inside and all around knowing she is hiding, because she has again disappeared. Looking around, he does not want to make too much of an avid search, because he knows she is somewhere watching and laughing. He hears a dog bark near the log cabin and starts in that direction. He makes it just beyond his Jeep and he hears clunking behind him. He whirls around and runs for the playground. By the time he arrives, Caroline is swinging, pumping her legs back and forth like it was recess. He stands in front of her, grabbing her ankles and jerking her to a stop mid-air causing her to shriek.

"I guess you think you are funny. Don't 'cha?"

"Not always, but sometimes." Winking at him.

"For someone who says they don't run and *claims* to be afraid of falling, you have sure been acting pretty reckless," he squeezes her ankles hard until she tries to pull away.

"Where have you been?" shaking her feet like he was really scolding her.

She snickers and points to the crow's nest on top of the play set. Realizing she has come down the slide and gotten on the swings without his noticing. When his head is turned, she wriggles free.

"Why don't you grab a swing and join me. I'm sure you could use the rest." Laughing and scrunching her face up again.

Growling, he lunges for her, grabbing the chains like he is going to shake her off her seat. She laughs and squeals, "DON'T!"

He takes the swing beside her and they both pump their legs saying nothing.

Reek...Eek...Reek...Eek...The chains create a monotonous yet soothing song. They look out over the water and see the sun is headed for its evening descent. Their swings slow and their feet drag through the worn-out pits below rocking up on their toes. He leans forward, elbows bent still holding the chain.

"You ready to go?"

Her smile is soft and sleepy. She waggles her head 'no', but responds, "Yes."

He takes her hand and leads her back to the Jeep. Hand on spine, he opens her door. The engine starts and they make their way back down the mountain. Their exit is a much slower than their drive earlier. In shared silence, neither wants this day to end. Leaning her head back, he begins to whistle softly through his teeth and she can detect notes from *Y'all Come Back Saloon* and her heart smiles if her face does not. Unfortunately, not nearly enough minutes later, they find themselves turning onto the school's driveway, but they are greeted by a closed and locked gate. Caroline's mouth opens in an irritated frown, "Agghh!"

"Don't you have a key?" Seth looks at her trying to figure out what do.

"No." forgetting it was Saturday and the gate would be locked when they return.

"Is there another way in?" he tries to be helpful, but is glad to have a few more minutes with her.

"There's the North Gate near the soccer field, but it is always closed on weekends." Trying to decide what to do about her imprisoned car, Caroline asks, "Do you think you could drive me home?"

Smiling, eager to see her house, though he has already completed some initial reconnaissance, he agrees, "Just show me the way!"

Shifting into reverse, Seth turns in the driveway and comes to the traffic light looking to her for instructions. "Just go through the light. I live in Forest Hills," pointing to the entrance of the community across from the school.

Acting like this is new information, Seth comments, "That sure is convenient." She nods and takes her home.

They pass a typical subdivision with the streets named for different trees. The road winds past the row of houses and the lots are bigger. Some homes are modest, but others quite large: brick, Tudor, modern, Georgian, Victorian farmhouse, and one stately Southern – white columns and everything. All of them have manicured lawns with nice landscaping. The weather is cool for azaleas that are ready to burst, but brightly colored pansies are still showing their painted faces after the winter. Many of the homes have pools and few even tennis courts and circle driveways. Seth notes the difference between here and where they spent the morning and Cleat is again in his ears, *'Forest Hills'* and his uneasiness returns.

Not quite a mile beyond a large Baptist Church, Caroline tells him to turn left crossing the creek. This is a long private drive that branches off the main road that continues ahead of them. A stone flowerbed overflowing with pansies has a sign in the middle:

Sunlit Cove
Established: 1916
'I lift up my eyes to the hills!' – Psalm 121:1

Seth's uneasiness intensifies, but he does not comment. Forest Hills, Forest Hills, Forest Hills chants in his brain.

No wonder she said she would wait to tell me her story! Mine made me sound like the stray dog that I am! And she nearly panicked when we couldn't get in the gate and had to ask me to drive her home!

Convincing himself that Caroline is part of small town royalty, they drive in strained silence. The first house they come to is on the right with the yard reaching the road. "My gran lives there." Seth is surprised expecting something much larger and grander. This craftsman house is almost small and compared to the homes they have just passed, it is modest and practical by any standards. It looks to have one story with attic rooms and dormer windows. White siding with stone accents on the foundation, wide steps, and a porch that he can see wraps around the front and down the side. Black trim, black shingles, black front door, and black shutters. A porch swing is left of the door and painted red. Just like all the others, the lawn is manicured and the landscaping is perfect.

His nerves calm, slightly.

About five hundred yards further, Caroline tells him to turn right and says, "My parents live on up there with my younger brother, Nick," pointing ahead at the road that turns back to the left and begins to incline. You cannot see Caroline's house from the road and the trees are heavy on either side of her driveway that curves back towards Gran for a few hundred yards. They reach a clearing and much like she has experienced earlier, Seth believes the world has opened up and he is surprised and pleased.

"This is your house?" but it wasn't just the house he was seeing, but the yard and the lack of trees, and how the sun was spilling in from everywhere even this late in the day. He comes to an abrupt stop and just takes everything in.

The trees have been cleared in a wide perimeter around the house. The personal driveway makes a lowercase 'b' with the stem extending to the garage that is attached to the house, but stepped back like it was added on later. The belly passes in front of the porch and extra wide steps before curving back to them.

The house is two-story cut limestone the same color as the flowerbed at the entrance to Sunlit Village. It is a combination of craftsman, Victorian, and modern with each element complementing the other, not competing. The roof is red tin, red trim, red shutters, and also a red swing. The porch is off center with a mission style door in dark oak to the left edge and the red swing on the right. Three large windows left of the porch are dark and he cannot see inside through gauzy drawn sheers.

"Just pull in front of the garage," watching him take inventory of her property, she suggests, "Why don't you get out and I will show you around."

Moments ago, Seth had decided just to drop her off like a teenage, believing she was out of his league, then go home and debate if he should contact her again. But he could not resist the invitation to explore this magical place. Coming around the back of his Jeep, he honestly admits, "Caroline, this is beautiful."

"Thank-you. I love it, too." Agreeing, she is proud, but not boastful. "My great-grandparents built the original house and the first two of three additions. So, you can imagine, it was fairly small to begin with. They moved from Wise County, VA at the turn of the century with some of the first waves of people into the coal industry. Grandad was a miner, but also a stone mason and bricklayer. Coal and limestone often times run together, so the limestone was put to use in framing or buildings and that's where Grandad did most of his work. The coal was shipped out and any surplus of the limestone was sold to the general public or ground into gravel, because as my Gran says 'Mud was everywhere'. So, Grandad bought the limestone for cheap and built his house."

Coming to the side, Carter notices the fine detail and artistic accents; subtle, but skillful. The yard is large and empty on this cooler side of the house as the woods curve around the edges. Caroline could tell him of family dinners and reunions, badminton and croquet, church Easter egg hunts, and campouts, but he directs her attention and asks, "Was he always a coal miner?"

"No. He stayed on through World War II and just after, but the industry was changing and becoming more mechanized. So, he started *Robinette Block and Stone* with Poppie, he was Gran's husband, eventually joining him. They still worked extensively for various coalmines, just as contract labor. They also did commercial work and some residential"

Seth remembers seeing similar stonework on Gran's house and *Robinette* chiseled in the rise of Caroline's top step. Guessing they both had already passed, he asks, "What happened to the business?"

"My mom's brother, Marty runs it now. Her oldest brother, Davis, started there first," rolling her eyes and not giving any details about him. "Davis is a story all his own! My dad even worked there some when the coal market dropped in the '80s. Marty is primarily residential now. He has three crews that work for him now: one for brick and stone, one for concrete, and one for tile. He prefers concrete and is a real artist of his trade, but mainly sticks to running the business."

"And your dad?" realizing he is asking her several questions, but interested in the story she is so freely sharing.

"He was laid off for about three years and worked with Poppie and Marty, but he also finished his Associates Degree during that time in Business Management of the Coal Industry from Southern."

Cutting her off, "The school down by the armory?"

"Yeah – the community college. Now, he's the superintendent at Big Mountain #2 which used to be part of King Coal Mining, but it was bought out several years ago by North American Fossil Fuels…This leads to Gran's. I can walk there faster than I can drive." Caroline stops in front of a proper English gate and trellis that opens to a wide rock-lined path back through the woods. Hansel and Gretel come to mind as Seth looks at yet another aspect of this magical place.

Caroline keeps walking bringing him to the back of the house that has a large screened porch that runs the width facing west. The porch leads down a patio the same width surrounding an in-ground pool that has yet to be opened for the season. A three-span clothesline is behind the garage and does not interfere with the view from the backyard. Angled from the garage and about 100 feet away is a stone building with double crosshatch doors. The way it is positioned, it serves as the end of the yard and beginning of at least two acres of field with an ancient barn in the distance. Everything glowing and dreamlike in the setting sun.

"Wow! This is just beautiful! And huge! How much land do you have?"

Smiling again at his admiration, "Well, sort of, but not really. The complete property is about 165 acres and I own less than five. Mom and Dad have twelve and Gran owns the rest."

Looking at her he blurts out realizing too late how rude he sounds, "Then you are rich."

Caroline notices that is more of statement than a question, and responds honestly. "Yes! But money is the thing we have the least of." Liking her answer and appreciating its meaning, Caroline says, "Let's go inside," and she walks on ahead leaving him to steal a few more glances, seeing another English gate leading to the woods on the north side of her property. He enters a side door into the garage as she clicks on the lights revealing two *Waverunners* on a double trailer. One black, charcoal and electric blue, the other black, silver and red metal flake.

"You own two *Waverunners*?" his face is now giddy like a child walking over to examine each.

Caroline was touched he was so impressed with her house and property and is not the least disappointed when she sees the little boy in him completely dazzled by the two machines and answers casually hoping to tempt him more, "No. Those are Will and Carter's. I own a boat, but it's at the lake," walking to the door.

"A boat!" he whispers. "This girl is amazing!" then something sparkly catches his eye and the puppy inside him is excited again. It is a paintball gun – flat black with high gloss accents, dual-trigger and double handgrips, with an extra-large bottle magazine. Seth lifts it off the hooks from the wall, "Thoomp, thoomp, thoomp," Caroline screams, "Thoomp, thoomp," and she screams again.

It all happens so fast that he does not even realize what is going on until it is over. Caroline is on the top step, splatters of neon green on her neck, chest, and the door behind her. He puts the gun back and rushes to her. He has fired five rounds and all connected – with Caroline. He feels extremely awkward and foolish trying to wipe the paint off, but he is just smearing it further and she winces when his hand touches her neck.

"Caroline, I'm so sorry. I didn't realize the safety wasn't on," the puppy is now whimpering.

"Well, it's supposed to be!" shouting at him, "Are you sure the Army trusts you with a real gun!?!?"

He finds her keys on the floor, handing them to her, he reaches to help her up. Shaking her head as if to clear her mind, "I can't believe you just shot me!"

He feels overgrown and stupid, unsure if she is hurt and if he should treat her delicately. She opens the door and they enter through her laundry room. She hangs her keys and says, "The bathroom's in there," pointing to a door, he remembers he has paint on his hands. She walks into the kitchen, clicking two switches. The kitchen brightens and two lamps in the living room come on. She drops her bag at the bottom of the steps and runs upstairs.

In her bathroom, she gently takes off her shirt knowing the paint will not come out and does not want to get it anywhere else. She turns to look in the mirror, seeing her back has three large welts. She grabs some toilet paper and blots the paint off her neck and chest then washes off the rest careful not to rub too hard. Pulling the arm of her magnifying mirror closer to her, she examines where both paintballs hit her neck. Each has broken the skin and is starting to bruise around the edges with a white knot in the middle ringed in red.

That's going to look awesome on Monday!

She notices the grass halo Seth made is still on her head and any annoyance from being shot disappears. She gently pulls it from her hair and walks it to her nightstand.

I'm going to want to keep that.

Caroline returns to the bathroom and shakes down her hair only to pile it all back up again pining it away from her neck. She reaches in the drawer for some *Vaseline* and gingerly dabs some on her neck. She puts a t-shirt on and goes back downstairs to Seth.

Seth quickly scrubs his hands clean making sure no paint is left in the sink and goes to the kitchen looking for paper towels. Pulling several off and wetting a few, he goes back to the garage to clean the splatters off the door and wall. Searching for the garbage can, he finds it inside the pantry. He feels nervous waiting on her and doesn't know if he should sit or stand. The living room is dimly lit, so he thinks that means he is not allowed in there. He decides to sit at the counter on a stool. He can hear her moving upstairs and tries not to fidget. When she returns he is very contrite and apologetic.

"Caroline, I am so sorry. I should have been more careful."

"Seth, I'm fine. It's my gun and I've been shot before…Just never in my own home." He wilts and she swats his arm. "Seriously, no big deal. I'm fine. Say, are you hungry?"

Still a little panicked, his uneasiness has returned, "No, you don't have to make me anything. I should probably go?"

She looks at him noting the change, "Why? I'm going to eat something. No reason you shouldn't join me. What would you like?"

"Umm, do you have any toast?"

"I can make some."

"And peanut butter?"

"Yes."

"And syrup?"

"All in the pantry," gesturing with her head, "You can grab it."

Finding both, he places them on the counter and sits back down. She puts two plates and forks in front of him, a butter knife, and two glasses. Going to the refrigerator for milk, the toast pops and she grabs it and tosses them on the plates with burnt fingers.

"Could I have ice in mine, please?"

Smiling she picks up the glasses walking back to the refrigerator, "I thought I was the only one who liked ice in their milk?" She brings back the glasses and pours the milk as he slathers peanut butter on the toast for each of them, commenting off handedly, "My mom used to make this for me all of the time when I was a kid. It is still one of my favorite snacks."

He stacks both pieces up, cuts them into bite sized squares, and drowns them in syrup relishing each bite. Caroline leans against the counter, holding her plate, she cuts each bite with her fork. They eat in silence until he asks, pointing with his fork to a picture on the phone table, "Is that your dog?"

Putting her plate in the sink and taking a drink of milk, she walks to the table and brings the picture over for him to look at. "My dad said he thought she was part Australian shepherd and part Border collie. My brothers always teased me she was just a mutt, because she was small and one of her ears was sort of crooked, but I didn't care, because I thought she was great."

"I had a Border collie. My stepdad got her for me right after he and my mom got married. I was around ten. Sophomore year of college, Mom calls and says 'Feather has had a stroke and the vet doesn't think she is going to make it.' I drove home and missed three days of class to be with her. The last night, she and I were in bed and I was curled up beside her petting her belly. She'd been really struggling, but had calmed...and then she was quiet. When I realized she was gone, I just laid there next to her and cried. I finally fell asleep and Mom found us the next morning. We buried her out back and I spent the rest of the day in my room crying." Pausing as if he were remembering the tender memory, "I loved her. She was the best dog, EVER!"

Reaching in his wallet, he holds out a picture to Caroline. She takes it and sees Feather leaning over with one white paw raised like she is waving. Her belly is white with three black feet and her right eye is stamped white. The rest of her is shiny black.

"She looks like she's smiling," handing the picture back, he tucks it away.

"She was. She smiled at me all the time and she loved to sing," he answers like it was not unusual for a dog to smile or sing and Caroline's heart is again touched.

"Why did you name her Feather?"

"She was so small and fuzzy when I got her and I said she was as soft as feathers. Dad...uhh, Tim thought that was good name and I agreed. What was her name?"

"Lemon."

He acts like he is going to ask her why, but reaches back in his pocket for his buzzing phone. Frowning, he looks at the text then smiles. He stands up and says, "I'm sorry, but I have to go."

Bruised by his abruptness, but still disappointed he is leaving, she says with hints of frost he does not notice, "Let me walk you out." Taking him through the front door and out on the porch.

He clomps down the steps and turns back to her and says, "I had a really great day and you have a wonderful place."

At the top of the steps, again laced with frost, "Yes. Thank-you."

He turns and looks at his Jeep, hesitates and second guesses. Coming back up the steps, twilight has him almost completely shadowed, but she can still see his striking eyes. Lifting her chin, low and husky, so close she can feel his breath on her skin, "I'm sorry I shot you," kissing both her wounds, "We'll talk soon." And he is back down the steps and gone before Caroline's head stops spinning.

119

Chapter X

"A friend loves at all times…" – Proverbs 17:17 NIV

Watching the glow of his taillights fade around the curve, Caroline does not have time to contemplate the fascinating, confusing, and extremely attractive Seth Garrett, because her phone rings. Running into the house, she picks up, "If I'm interrupting, we can talk in code!" giggling at the first of many military references.

"You're fine. I'm here alone," puffing her cheeks, Caroline thought she would have at least a few minutes to reflect before Sophie demanded details.

"Great! Because I just passed the church and I will be there in a few minutes."

Caroline hangs up the phone knowing the interrogation is about to begin. She washes the plates and glasses she and Seth have used and wipes down the counter. She gets two more glasses out and Sophie comes through the door already talking.

"Please tell me, that beautiful hunk of man in the green Jeep that just drove by me was SETH GARRETT!"

"It was," Caroline responds dryly.

Sophie instantly recognizes her tone. "Ohhh…Ok. I brought pizza to eat while you tell me everything that happened today. And, if it was bad, I brought *Moose Tracks*, and we can down the entire container why we systematically psychoanalyze the male animal," huge grin – all teeth and eyebrows. "WOWZERS! What's wrong with your neck? Caroline Elizabeth! I'm shocked! This must have been some date!"

Exasperated already with Sophie, "It's not what you think!"

"Yeah! But it sure does look like it!" in slow motion to emphasize her point.

Sophie drops the box on the counter and takes the ice cream to the freezer. Caroline fills their glasses and gets plates. Sophie noses through the pantry finding chips and joins Caroline on the other couch – casual dining at its best. Sophie opens the bag sniffing with her eyes closed, "Mmm, I love sour cream and onion. And since there is no chance of *me* getting any kisses tonight, dragon breath will not be a problem," angling the bag in Caroline's direction, "What about you?" if she had a moustache and cigar in hand, Sophie could almost pass for Groucho Marx with her manner of questioning.

Caroline is evasive and refuses to give Sophie too many details. Anything she wants to know, she must ask. "I love sour cream and onion, too. That's why I bought them!" grabbing a handful and dropping them on her plate and delicately placing one in her mouth.

"So! That's the way it's going to be! Play it cagey. I've got nothing but time!" Sophie acts offended and begins to eat as if she is going to ask no more questions.

They munch in silence. After less than two minutes, Sophie nearly explodes, "Are you seriously not going to tell me what happened?!?!"

Primly wiping her mouth, Caroline asks, "What would you like to know?"

"For starters, where did he take you?" ready to gobble up Caroline's story with more enjoyment than the pizza.

Answering as if she were on the witness stand – give as little information as possible. "Grants Branch."

"Grants Branch!" disgust at his choice of setting for what she hopes to be a simply romantic interlude. "What did you all do there?" not appreciating this location as an option for a first date at all.

"We played mostly," taking another bite of pizza knowing Sophie's head is not quite wrapping around the day.

Frowning and snarling, "Played? Like ball?" already deciding all of the *Moose Tracks* will be gone before the evening is over.

"No!" giving in, because she knows Sophie will not quite 'get it' and this could last hours, she details the day.

"He picks me up after the ACT. He didn't tell me where we were going just to not wear anything that I wouldn't mind getting dirty."

"You looked great, what I saw…When did he tell you this?" going to get another piece of pizza.

"On Friday, when he called…" cagey again, but smiling, remembering their conversation.

Skeptical, "He didn't have your number. How did he call you?" Sophie is liking the story a little better.

"Well," exhaling deeply, "I decided to take your advice – relax and be myself. So, I sent him a text when I got home from the game. Actually, I sent two before he responded," knowing she would like this.

"Caroline! A double-text? Sooo unlike you!" folding her feet up under her, Sophie is eager to hear more. "What did he say? What did you say?"

"Mmm, I just teased him a little, we bantered around, and he called me. He said he decided to kamikaze and just take the risk!"

Holding up her hands so she will stop speaking, Sophie pleads, "Just answer me this, but I still want all the details…Was it worth the risk?" Hands steepled to her mouth, eager for the words she wants to hear.

Caroline sucks her teeth, smacking her lips, "Weeelll, I would like to think YES!"

Squeals of delight come from Sophie accompanied by her hands pounding a drumroll on the coffee table and begging, "Tell me the rest! Tell me the rest!" settling back in the cushions ready for another helping.

Finally giving in to her own schoolgirl excitement, Caroline eats up the moment and relishes it with Sophie. "We talked about nothing and it was so easy and relaxed. He is very funny and witty," giving her friend a smirking glance, "And he has a great vocabulary. I mean – not overly wordy or chatty, but what he says it has substance and what he says he says it well. He's just really easy to talk to. He asks good questions. You know, like he's interested and wants to keep the conversation going. And really… Uhh, we just talked," unable to take the smile off her face, but not caring, because she is happy to tell her best friend.

Sophie continues to probe, "So, Friday night he told you what to wear, but not where you were going? And you weren't suspicious? Let me rephrase that – you weren't nervous?"

"I know what you're thinking – sooo out of character for me. But, I felt totally relaxed…Ok, maybe 85%, but that's pretty close. He just made me feel, uhh… comfortable."

Sophie nods her head approvingly, "Comfortable…That's way better than awkward! So, he picks you up Saturday…"

"That is the best part!" Caroline sits up and becomes dramatically animated. "I don't have words to describe what he looked like when I stepped out the door. If he would not have thought I was completely crazy, I would have taken his picture leaned up against that Jeep," surprising even herself, Caroline swoons. She goes into detail about his stance and Molly Ringwald and Spring Training and his arms crossed over his chest. "In fact, I don't want you to meet him, that is how nice looking he is!" laughing, but giving Sophie a stern look.

Serious face herself, "I'll give you about three more dates, then I will insist on meeting him. BECAUSE no man is going to fall in love with my best friend without my stamp of approval!"

Tossing a pillow at her, "LOVE!!! Sophie, I don't know if we are going to even have a second date!"

"Yes, you will! Why would say that?"

"I don't know," making a lightning fast mental review of the day, "Everything went really well – fun and playful, but still nervous and squirrely enough to be exciting for a first date. Then he drives me back to school and the gate's locked and he sort of gets all weird," remembering his sudden change was evident.

"Weird? How?" Sophie asks ready to cut him into pieces if necessary.

"I ask him if he could drive me home and he agrees, like it's no big deal, but then he gets all quiet. Like this was not in his plans at all. He didn't say anything until we got here. But then he was ok again, so I don't know."

"Hmm, that is a little weird. Maybe he was just nervous. Doorstep goodbyes are nerve-racking. Maybe he's a second-date-for-a-first-kiss kind of guy and that's why he was happy to meet you at school instead of at your house. Guys are very linear and he's in the military, so that makes it worse. He had the day planned like a mission in his head. So, when plans changed suddenly, his mind had to catch up," Sophie reasons practically giving Seth the benefit of the doubt.

"Yeah, you're probably right…But," deciding to add another detail. "We were here and he was relaxed again and talking. He asks me about Lemon and tells me about his Border collie, Feather – when he got her, why he named her Feather, and how she died. He even had a picture of her in his wallet."

"He has a picture of his dead dog in his wallet? Oh, my goodness!

MARRY HIM!!!" it would be hard for Caroline to say anything now that would convince Sophie that Seth wasn't perfect.

"Sophie, please! Then he gets a text message and says he has to go and practically runs out the door!" voicing her annoyance and though Sophie is objective, she silently agrees this would be confusing and hurtful.

"Well, maybe something came up or there was an emergency or maybe the day just lasted longer than expected and he had something else planned. You all were together a long time." Rational, sensible Sophie is worse than zany, crazy Sophie.

"I know…He told me, we would talk later, but he didn't say we would go out again," Caroline pouts a little hating that she has had a Best Day, but now that it is over is sad and a little confused.

"Sooo, you goina call him?" knowing what she will say before she answers.

"No! I called him first!" flaming and nervous, Caroline refuses.

"Ah, ah, ah!" Sophie waves a finger at her, "Technically, *he* called *you* first. You sent him a text, but that really doesn't count. Text him later that you had a good time; something small and encouraging. Guys are fragile and need confidence not to be intimidated. Maybe he's just waiting for the greenlight," Caroline wonders where Sophie has gained all of her psycho-social knowledge and Sophie is impressed she is making such good sense.

"I think I have given him several greenlights!"

"Yes! I would agree. And me or you or any number of *girls* would agree – Greenlights Garlore…BUT – we are talking about a *guy*. A single guy who is not 17. A well-educated and highly trained guy. One who has been taught to always have a contingency plan. So, he is not going to charge in without having prior knowledge that he will be successful. No guy wants to be rejected and they all hate to lose. He wants to take the lead, but it is going to have to be mapped out for him, before he proceeds. GREENLIGHT!"

Growling and falling over to her side on the couch hugging a pillow. "This is what hate! All these games, when you should just be honest."

"No you don't! Where's the fun in that? This isn't a math problem; it's art and you must look at it from all angles. Games, intrigue, all the Cat and Mouse uncertainty mingled with excitement and fear. That's why it's the best game and we all love to play it!" Sophie's tone is scolding, but she has a glint in her eye. "Ok, so tell me…What's going on with your neck or am I just going to have to assume Seth Garrett caused it?"

Clearing the coffee table and taking their plates to the sink, Caroline answers, "Seth Garrett did cause it."

Sophie's shock and delight is clear, "Caroline Elizabeth! On a first date? You teenager!" coming to sit on one of the stools.

"Sophie! You know better than that!" fussing at Sophie, but Caroline cannot deny, she would not mind too much if Seth had caused the marks on her neck. "We came in through the garage and he was like a kid in a toy store when he saw the *Waverunners*. He was examining them like a fine piece of art. I no sooner tell him they are not mine that he takes my paintball gun off the wall. I'm trying to unlock the door and he fires three shots in my back, I scream and turn towards him, and he fires two more times hitting me in the neck. Paint was all over the wall and door, ruined one of my favorite shirts, not to mention it hurt like crazy!"

No laughter or any signs of amusement come from Sophie, "He shot you? In your own home? That just awful! But, a great story to tell the grandkids!"

"It wasn't awful, but it was shocking! I had no idea what was going on and it happened so fast. He was scared to death and apologetic trying to helping me up. He tried to wipe the paint off, but just smeared it all over me," she remembers his whimpering and fumbling.

"So, he left after that?" Sophie inquires hoping this is not the end of the story.

"No. We come inside and have a snack – more reason I should not have enjoyed the pizza so much, but thank-you for bringing it – and talk for a while about the dogs. Then – TEXT MESSAGE – and he practically runs out the door!" Seth's departure once again irritates Caroline.

Sophie puzzles over the information, "So, he just gets up and walks out?"

"Well no. He reads the text and tells me he had a good time, but has to leave and I walk him out to the porch. He goes down the steps, but comes back and tells me he is sorry he shot me then kisses my neck. Then he says 'We'll talk soon.' So nothing definite!"

"CAROLINE! That is altogether different!" Sophie shouts at her pessimistic friend. "How can somebody as perky and positive as you, be so negative?!?! He was clear he had a good time, said you would talk later, and kisses you. Do you need gilded invitation?" shaking her head in disbelief. "Do you not know what linear means? He was probably rattled and nervous – just like you – but hides it well after years of practice – just like you! Then, when the day is coming to a close and all the expectations collide with good sense and intimidation – he shoots you with a paintball gun not just once, but FIVE TIMES! His mind was so all over the place that he probably needed an aspirin," taking the bowl of ice cream from Caroline, Sophie returns to her post on the couch. "If you truly want my opinion, you two had a great time – better than either of you expected. And two people, who are pros at self-protecting, didn't really know how to respond to something – someone who made them feel so…What word did you use? Comfortable?" knowing that is what Caroline said, Sophie pins her down with her own words, gesturing wildly as if she were conducting an orchestra. "You didn't feel nervous, but you behaved awkwardly. Thus, the date just stopped and now, you are flooded with questions and doubts. Seth is most likely feeling the same way," taking a bite of Moose Tracks then thrusting her arm, spoon in hand skyward as a true victor, "GREENLIGHT!"

Caroline has no response and sits down to think washing her worries away with ice cream. One movie and several bowls of *Moose Tracks* later, Sophie announces, "Jeremy Piven is the best Best Friend, ever!"

"I would have to agree. He is the perfect funny yet calming counterpart." Caroline says as she stretches her legs onto the coffee table.

"New York!" Sophie fantasizes. "Ice skating and Bloomingdale's and Christmas and then a wonderful adventure in search of your true love; your destiny…Ahhh, romance! It would be nice to have a story like that to tell," walking her bowl to the sink Sophie picks up Caroline's laptop off the counter returning to the couch. "Seth…What was his last name?"

"Garrett," looking over her shoulder, Caroline answers placing the DVD back in its case.

"Seth Garrett. Holidaysburg, PA?" Sophie announces as Caroline sits back down.

"Yeah, but I didn't tell you where he was from," wondering how Sophie knows this.

"No, you didn't, but Facebook tells me! Seth Garrett. FROM

– Holidaysburg, PA. LIVES IN – Williamson, WV. WENT TO – Blair Independence High School. STUDIED – Political Science and Comparative Literature at West Virginia University. Staff Sergeant United States Army, West Virginia National Guard," looking at Caroline with glee like she has just uncovered their next clue in this mystery.

"Sophie!" Caroline shrieks. "Stop creeping!" but wanting to know all the information.

Sophie scoffs, "This isn't creeping! I'm just using all my resources to find out more about the delightful Mr. Garrett," making room for Caroline to squirm in beside her. "Rats! His page is private, so I can only see two of his pictures. I wonder why his profile pic is not of him? It's an American flag in front of a castle."

"A castle? America is not known for her castles," Caroline adds sarcastically not believing Sophie.

"Well, it looks like a castle to me, but it's too close to tell," moving the screen to give Caroline a better view.

"Hmm, that does look like a castle. Click to the next one," Sophie obeys. "What is that?" Caroline asks as her head automatically tilts trying to figure out what she is looking at.

"I'm not sure. It's so dark," Sophie also tilts and squints. "I think it's a *Batman* mask."

Caroline looking more closely, "I believe it is. I wonder why he has that?"

Sophie again using her rational tone, "Naturally, he is a *Batman* fan. And everyone knows he is by far the best hero."

"Well, that's true," her analytical tone sounds like they are Comic-Con devotees. "He depends on his brain and ability. Others use gimmicks or have some superhuman skills. *Batman* is awesome all on his own," Caroline agrees further studying yet another fascinating mystery behind Seth Garrett.

"Look! Mutual friends – 3. Send him a friend request and we can learn more," Sophie concentrates scrolling through Seth's page reading his posts and Caroline snaps the lid shut whisking it from her grasp.

"Sophie, enough! Up, up, up! You are too much in my head and I need time to think! Go home!" Caroline collects all of Sophie's belongings and begins to escort her to the door.

Sophie begins to laugh, but listens surprised by her friend. "Are you seriously throwing me out?"

Not wanting to justify her reasons, Caroline answers, "I'm not throwing you out. I just need to decide what to do next. With you here, it will be 10th grade all over and my stomach will not be able to handle it. You will have me in knots and there will be no way I could ever talk to him again. So! You're going to leave and I'm going to decide," shooing her to the door.

Laughing and wanting to tease her friend, Sophie allows herself to be ushered out and as she offers one last appeal, Caroline shuts the door in her face and promptly goes upstairs hoping to find a few moments of solitude to clear her head and decide what to do next.

Cleat sends Seth a fourth text and wants to know if he should organize a search and rescue mission. Knowing he is teasing, but also knowing he will be more than persistent until Seth responds, he replies as he makes it to the end of Caroline's driveway and beyond the view of her house.

"Rescue mission unnecessary. Will be there in a few minutes," he hits send and makes his way out of Forest Hills headed to the armory. As Seth comes to the door, he braces himself, because he knows the harassment is about to start. Cleat and three others are in the gym having a shoot around apparently waiting on Seth. Once they see him, the questions start to fly.

"Where have you been? We've been waiting almost a half hour!" Cleat fusses as he shoots then gets his own rebound and throws to the next guy who makes his basket and prepares for his next shot.

"Out," is Seth's simple reply and steps in for the rebound.

Cpl. Jared Stanley and Pfc. George Jones, whom the entire unit teases without shame, stop to investigate Seth as Cleat's brother-in-law, Lucas, continues to shoot.

"Out?" this first questions.

"Yeah. Out."

"You're not dressed to play basketball," the other comments, face filled with speculation.

"Nope. I'm not."

Cleat notices how Seth is dressed and how his answers are telling, but evasive. "Where have you been? And don't tell me 'out'. I wanna know."

Shifting and nervous, Seth knows they won't stop until he confesses, so there is no use trying to hide it. By this time, Lucas has joined the group with the ball propped on his hip under a wrist.

"I had a date," Seth moves quickly, stealing the ball from Lucas, leaping to make the shot – SWISH. The four others have lost interest in the game and want to know about Seth's day.

"A date? Who with?" Cleat asks hatefully, disappointed this is the first news he is hearing of it.

Seth rebounds, dribbles out to the key, and shoots again – SWISH. "Caroline Hatfield," getting his rebound, he takes position for his next shot.

"CAROLINE HATFIELD!?!? You didn't tell me that!" offended he has been left out of the loop. Jared, George, and Lucas do not know who Caroline is, but are eager to find out.

"Sorry, bud. I don't tell you everything," Seth winks – SWISH.

Cleat charges over and forcibly removes the ball from Seth's grasp determined to know what's going on. "You've been on a date with Caroline Hatfield and you didn't tell me! What's going on?" If Cleat had begun to tap his foot following his last statement, he would not have appeared more amusing.

Seth's answer is casual and not nearly as informative as his listeners hope. "Well, we talked last night and I took her to Grants Branch."

The group's response is too similar to Sophie's, "Grants Branch!" Cleat asks what the rest are wondering, "You took a girl on a first date to Grants Branch? What did you all do?"

Again, casual, "We played mostly."

"Like ball or something?" George is confused and needs Seth to explain.

"No. We hiked the trail and just…played," gently smiling at the memory of the day.

"Did you have a good time?" Jared wonders thinking 'playing' sounds like a great first date and the girl who would enjoy it sounds like someone he would like to meet.

Crossing his arms over his chest and smiling proudly, his response only hints at suggestion, "I think we both had a really good time."

Lucas sees the traces of boyish wickedness in Seth's smile, "And what did you do after Grants Branch?"

Chuckling, if only to send their thoughts and questions in the wrong direction, "We came back to her house."

The group squeals like a bunch of school girls and break into mildly ribald talk not quite locker room language, but entertaining including lots of teasing, hoots, and laughter. "So, when are you going out again?" Cleat questions when they remember they are adults bouncing the ball between his feet.

Seth comes close to blushing and decides to include the disaster anyway. "Well, I'm not sure," and four heads snap to attention. "See, when we were coming in her house, we walked through her garage and she has two sweet *Waverunners* in there. I go to look at them and hanging on the wall beside them is a paintball gun." George interjects wanting details about the gun and they sidebar in a short discussion and how they need to go paintballing and there is this great place in Scott Depot – all before Seth informs them he shot her. Silence, wide eyes, shifting glances, followed by a collective, "Ooooo!"

"Fat chance on that one," Jared laughs, taking the ball from Cleat ready to start the game.

"Dude, sorry about your luck," and George joins him.

Shaking his head in disbelief, "You shot her? In her own house? On a first date?" Lucas laughs and slaps him on the back, entering the game.

Cleat shrugs his shoulders and Seth takes off his shirt. The five play with no more discussion about the date, but they want to hear more about the *Waverunners*. Two hours later, the others have gone home and Seth and Cleat are resting against the grill of his Jeep.

"So...You had a good time?" Cleat has waited patiently to hear what Seth would not be willing to share with the others.

Wanting to be honest and share his own school girl excitement, "I had a great day. It was just so relaxed and comfortable. She was so easy to talk to. Like I could have said anything and she would have just taken it all in – not judging, just learning...And she was fun...I will admit, Grants Branch was a little test," Cleat gives him a speculative look. "I had already met her and no matter what you said, I still think – thought – she might be a high dollar and high maintenance. When we talked on Friday, it was so...so, comfortable and we laughed a lot. When I told her I would pick her up the next day after she gave the ACT and said not to wear anything she minded to get dirty, there were no questions. She just said, 'Ok.' She didn't even ask what we were doing. She was so impressed when we got there and was running around like a kid and asked if we could sit at the tables on the dock when we picnicked even though they were dirty. Then she asks for my life story and I tell her," another glance comes from Cleat. "Well, I don't tell her my whole life story, but most of it. When I'm finished, she puts her hand on my arm and says she was glad I had told her and looks forward to hearing the rest," debating if he should be completely honest with Cleat and proceeds. "I thought my arm was going to catch on fire and when I looked at her..." struggling to find the right words, "I felt... peaceful and thought she was beautiful," the last word comes at a whisper.

Shouldering him, Cleat completely appreciates Seth's admission and is touched by his friend's apparent happiness. "Told ya...Thoroughbred."

Seth's smile and voice are filled with tenderness, "Nah, she's a breed all her own."

Cleat's heart is touched again, because it is so rare that Seth is this sensitive and vulnerable, "Well, then what makes you think you may not see her again? It sounds like you had a great time and so did she, even if you did shoot her!" teasing only slightly to lift Seth's spirits.

"I know. We both did, but...I don't know!" pushing off the Jeep, pacing in front him, Seth runs his fingers through his hair hoping his brain underneath will be able to explain. "Did you know she owns her own house and five acres of land and a boat?"

Cleat sees where this is headed and in his own way knows the battle of insecurity and unworthiness Seth is fighting. "I guess I did. Her boat is probably at the *Cabin*?"

Confused and frustrated, Seth keeps his hands on his head and with his first bark, "The *Cabin*?"

Cleat brings him up to speed and for once, Seth is glad Williamson is such a small town and Cleat knows everything and everyone. "Well, it's more like a house. A lake house. It's in Virginia, not far from the racetrack at Bristol on..." scouring his memory for the answer, "South Holston! They took me several times when we were in high school. It's nice."

That last detail does nothing to encourage Seth and he releases a deep sigh, dropping his hands. "They have a lake house?"

Trying to act like this was commonplace and reassure Seth, "Yeah.

Cabin. Lake house. Summer home. Whatever you want to call it…So, you goina call her when you get home?"

Seth returns to leaning beside Cleat and his shoulders slump. The strong confidence Cleat has come to admire and respect is deflating. "Agghh, I don't know."

Giving his buddy the boost he needs and helping him find the greenlight, "Why not? Did you struggle to find things in common? Did you ask about her personal debt or how much money she has in savings? Did you ask her a string of political questions? Or did you give her your very cloudy and misguided opinions on religion?" not waiting for Seth to respond, "Then I see no reason why you shouldn't call her…Look, I can imagine the stuff that is flying through your head," eyes closed and hands up, Cleat does not want to hear it. "I can imagine, because I have been there, too. You've already decided you don't fit in her world and it would be best if you just bow out gracefully. Now is not the time to be noble."

Honest, yet again, "I don't know what to do?"

Reacting quickly, Cleat grabs Seth's arms, shaking him, and in his best Sicilian accent says, "You can act like a man!" playfully slapping Seth on the cheek bringing him back to reality and Seth spars back. They both laugh and Cleat gives one more comment before leaving, "Triple Crown," and walks to his car.

A few minutes later, Seth is sitting on his couch with his wrists resting on his knees staring at his phone. He smiles at Cleat's *Godfather* and remembers Caroline's golden honey hair and shiny red nails and her 'Thank-you'. Taking a deep breath, he dials her number.

Chapter XI

"Take delight in the Lord, and He will give you the desires of your heart." – Psalms 34:7 NIV

Caroline goes upstairs and occupies herself with unnecessary tasks to avoid thinking about Seth and Sophie's guidance. Knowing the paint will not come out of her shirt, she picks it up off the bathroom floor and puts it in the trash. She takes off her jeans and holds them to the light to make sure there is no paint on them. Glad to see they are free of stains, she tosses them in the hamper. Walking to her office, Caroline makes a note of something she remembered while at school about prom committee. Lingering in front of her desk, she hopes something will catch her attention and allow her to be useful for a few moments as a means of distraction. Nothing comes to mind and she considers calling her mom under the pretense of questioning her about Sunday Dinner. Remembering, they are at Alex and Megan's and probably not home, she drags her feet back to her bedroom. Looking at the clock, it has been almost four hours since Seth's departure, and still it is not even 10:00. Caroline knows it is not too late to call, but her usual self – filled with insecurity and doubt and fear and anxiety and all kinds of other emotions that do not have names – returns, so she hesitates.

She goes to the bathroom, flossing and brushing, examines her teeth and face, straightens her make-up drawer, clips her toenails, and prepares them for polish, opens the linen closet looking for nothing and sees a bath bomb, but shuts the door before grabbing it. She walks to her bed where she tossed her phone earlier trying to ignore it. Flipping it over, she sees there are no messages, takes note of the time – 10:06pm – and goes to the bathroom removing her clothing on the way. Everything makes its way to the hamper and Caroline gets in the shower having a conversation with herself.

> *You know Sophie is right. Give him a call.*
> *NO!*
> *FINE! Then send him a text!*
> *A text is safer…*
> *Safer? What is there to worry about?*
> *I don't know? You know I am no good at this! My stomach is already hurting…*
> *Don't be such a wimp! You had a good time, so you should let him know it!*
> *HEY! I need a greenlight as much as he does!*
> *He already gave you one…Two actually! He kissed you twice!*
> *Those don't count!*
> *Why not? Did his lips not land on your skin at some point?*
> *Yes…After he shot me!*
> *With a paintball gun…You will survive!*
> *I did have a great day…*
> *And he was striking leaning against that Jeep!*
> *He smelled delicious!*
> *And he packed a picnic…*
> *Grants Branch was beautiful…*
> *And you played all day! When have you had that much fun?*
> *I wish he would call first…*
> *Give him the confidence to take the lead.*
> *Ok…but I will send a text…*
> *Agh! Ok – that will work!*

Mind made up, Caroline gets out of the shower and marches confidently to her phone to send the text…before she chickens out!

"Seth, I had a great time today and I really look forward to seeing you again. Next time, I am going to hide all my weapons!" Winky face – SEND.

RING!!!

Caroline's heart almost stops and she drops the phone. Her text has not even completed sending when the music indicates an incoming call. Nervously, she picks up the phone as the music plays through a second time. SETH GARRETT is identified on the screen. She steadies her breathing, not wanting to sound like Mickey Mouse, and answers the call.

"I just sent you a text!"

"Hello to you, too!" Seth's already familiar voice says on the other end of the line sending a thrill through Caroline.

Face flaming, Caroline apologizes, "Seth, I'm sorry...Hello! I was meaning that I sent a text at the exact moment the phone rang...I guess I got a little startled," she makes it almost all the way through without nervous laughter, but some comes at the end in spite of herself. There is a long pause and she is afraid he hung up.

"You feel that threatened by me? How many more weapons do you have?" his voice is low and almost frosty, hinting at defensive and suggestive.

Caroline decides to head towards playful and avoid seductive, "Hmm, a few. No worries, my arsenal is very limited."

Sinister laugh, he nearly growls out his words, "Oh...I seriously doubt that!"

She can sense his invitingly wicked smile through the phone and is again red to the scalp. Caroline is proud and confident of her verbal banter – usually – enjoying her quick wit and appreciating it in others, but Seth Garrett leaves her fumbling and stumbling over her words with a response hard to find. Fortunately, her silence is not too awkward and he changes topics.

"I know I should have waited a few days before I called...You know – make you wait it out, really start to sweat wondering if there will be a second date..." again in a teasing tone.

"I would never think that and I *rarely* let people see me sweat! I try my best to keep it together...Even if I am falling apart inside!" her honest admission puts a smile on his face and leads him into more teasing.

"I would *never* think you would allow yourself to get flustered!" silently laughing about their first encounter and how he had judged her so right and so wrong. "Well, I decided to break with convention – I mean we're not 17 – and call you anyway. Besides, I had to check on you. Or have you forgotten about your wound?" Seth's voice is teasing, but his mind is nervous, maybe even a little worried.

"No worry there! I haven't forgotten!"

Great! She's mad! Stupid! Stupid! Stupid!

Hesitant and contrite, Seth does not even hint at playfulness and is yet again apologetic, "Caroline, I'm really sorry…I should have been more careful…How's your neck?"

Hearing her name as well as what sounds like a sincere apology, Caroline's heart flip-flops again and she would have probably forgiven him of anything. "Weeelll, it will look really good by morning," walking into the bathroom to inspect the red welts that have doubled in size forming a large red patch and purple broken skin.

Still speaking gently and worried, "So it looks that bad?"

Reassuring him, "It's already started to bruise, but no big deal. I can cover it up with make-up or just have a great story to tell!" her laughter is lighthearted wanting to dismiss his fears.

She hears him sigh, repeats his apology, and begins to scold himself, "Caroline, I really am sorry…I should have been more careful! You always check the safety! How many times have I gone through weapons training?!? Enough to know that you don't shoot a pretty girl on a first date in her own home!"

He said I was pretty! Swoon!

"No worries! You kissed it and made it all better! It will just look rough for a few days," Caroline scrunches her face and shoulders giggling at her silly remark even though Seth cannot see her.

"Did it help?" his voice deep and male; tenderness wrapped in strength.

Caroline's heart trips and she has to shake herself to stay focused.

You cannot fall head over heels for this guy in one date!

"Hmm, it definitely didn't hurt."

Responding with his own low chuckle, "I just hope I haven't ruined my chances for a second date?" Seth waits for Caroline's response and nothing – CRICKETS. Not quite pleading, but close, Seth makes sure she is still on the phone, "Caroline?"

Pausing before she answers, "I think your chances are still pretty good," she smiles hearing a more labored sigh.

"Oh good! You had me worried there for a minute. I thought you had hung up again!"

"Nope! Just making you sweat a little bit!" followed by delighted laughter.

"Aren't you funny! Should I be prepared for constant teasing or does this just come occasionally?" Seth is accusing, though not the least irritated.

Enjoying him more by the minute and pleased his banter is quick and witty, "Hmm, not constant, but often! Can you not handle that, *Sergeant?*" coy and teasing, Caroline silently admits she does love *playing the game*.

His male response is more challenge than coy, equally thrilled with the game, "No worries – I can handle it! You just need to be prepared for more of the same. I may show no mercy!" Stretching out the length of the couch, Seth settles in for another round of conversation with Caroline finding that to be just as attractive as she is.

"Well, I was going to be kind, but since you have thrown down the gauntlet, I guess I will have to report that little misfire in the garage to your superior officer!"

"Go right ahead, but just remember..." Seth waits for her to think and then promises, "Snitches get stitches!" followed by a maniacal laugh.

"*Snitches get stitches?* What is that? Grade school playground threats?" Caroline challenges back laughing all the while.

Voice cool and honest, "Not at all. I am just giving you fair warning... Besides, Cleat already knows. So, I'm sure he's going to be more than excited to tell the Captain the first chance he gets and announce it to the entire unit. So, I'm not afraid of your threats either!" He changes gears again before Caroline has time to fire back. "I wanted to tell you, I had a really nice time today and apologize I left so suddenly."

Thrilled and shocked, Caroline plays it cool, "Me too and I didn't notice."

"LIAR!" he shouts at her laughing knowing he is making her squirm. "You did too! When I said, I had to go, you practically threw me out!"

A wave of anxiety runs through Caroline's chest.

Was I that obvious?

"I did not!" she tries to defend, but knows it is useless.

"You did too! When I drove down the road, I knew you were mad and would probably not answer when I called," thinking back to earlier, Seth knows he made the wrong move.

Pleased and flustered that he already has her pegged, Caroline explains, "First of all, Mr. Garrett, I am rarely mad, but when I am, you will most *definitely* know it…Secondly, I did not throw you out, but I was not about to keep you when you so *obviously* wanted to leave!"

Quiet and emotionless, "I didn't want to leave…"

All evidence of teacher voice gone, Caroline swallows down her heart that jumped into her throat and answers equally as quiet, "I didn't want you to leave…"

The boy and girl on either end of the line no longer hold their breath and silently rejoice over getting a GREENLIGHT! Realizing a moment of intimacy has been shared, Caroline does not want to lose it, but remembers something he said, "What do you mean Cleat already knows?"

Wedging his hand behind his head, Seth's heart and body relaxes still eager to talk to Caroline. "That's where I went – to meet Cleat. He and some of the other guys had a basketball game planned at the Armory. I was late, so he decided to bombard me with messages. He didn't know I was with you and I knew he would keep sending texts if I didn't show up."

"Oh," a touch of disappointment returns knowing he left her for Cleat.

"I didn't plan on being late, but I was having such a good day, I wasn't ready for it to end."

"Really?" Caroline is afraid he is going to yell PSYCH and all her disappointment will come flooding back.

Seth's smile is wide as he hears her childlike voice again. He reassures the little girl, "Really."

"Agh! Hold on a second!" Seth is a little ruffled by her abruptness, but can hear her fumbling around. "Sorry, I dropped my towel."

"Your towel? Where are you?" wondering what she is doing.

"Walking around my bedroom. I just got out the shower when you called."

Caroline's comment is innocent, but the boy in Seth takes it in a different direction. "Really? So, you've been in nothing but a towel the whole time we've been talking?"

"Yes, I was getting ready to dry my hair and paint my toenails when you called," Caroline responds, thinking nothing of her answers.

Seth continues to pry and finally gets the reaction he is hoping for. "So, you're in *nothing*, but a towel?"

"Yes, I –" Innocence interrupted by shock. She doesn't finish before she hears laughter begin – all junior high and foolish.

"Seth! I'm hanging up now!" Caroline is embarrassed and needs to retreat.

"Fine by me! I've been playing basketball for two hours and some crazy girl had me running all over the place today. I'm beat!"

"Yeah, me too," she covers wanting to say no more.

"Good night, Caroline. I'll talk to you tomorrow."

"Goodnight, Seth...I'll be waiting."

They both smile, pleased with that promise.

"And Caroline, one more thing..." his voice is silky smooth and tender.

"Yes," Caroline has already decided she could get way too used to bedtime conversations with Seth.

"What color's your towel?"

"Seth!" Caroline shrieks and she hears him roar with laughter just as she ends the call. She tosses the phone on her bed and immediately her mouth is hidden behind nervous hands. In a matter of seconds, she begins to attempt to compartmentalize the gamut of emotions she has experienced over the last few days, when Sophie's voice is shouting in her ears.

"Don't over analyze! Just enjoy it!"

Forging new ground, Caroline blows out a deep breath and decides to listen her friend. Standing in front of her vanity, she is surprised to see her face is a normal color as she reaches for the hair dryer. Tossing her hair from side-to-side, the dryer almost drowns out the noise in her head as images of Seth race through her mind – his head thrown back in laughter, his repeated squirrelly behavior from someone so confident, his quiet tenderness as he shares emotional pieces of his past, his clean, masculine scent, and the feel of his lips on her skin. Nails painted, she gives each toe a quick blast of drying spray and prepares for bed. Her normal routine of back and forth before she settles in to make her nest. Clicking off her lights, Caroline's heart and mind are not at odds and she quickly drifts to sleep without Seth Garrett entering any of her dreams.

Seth on the other hand is much more restless after his eventful day. He sits up on the edge of the couch, wide smile still on his face. He considers sending Caroline one final teasing text, but decides not to press his luck. Admitting he is tired after the long day, a shower and in bed earlier than usual sounds very appealing.

Clicking on the light in his closet, he removes his boots and they are neatly placed alongside all his other shoes. Mentally preparing for next week, Seth runs his hand over the hangers counting ACUs – shirts, pants, jackets – washed, pressed, and organized as neatly as his shoes and everything else in his closet, his drawers, his life. Everything has a place and is in its place. He goes to his long dresser and takes out black shorts, a gray t-shirt with 1/150th Armored Reconnaissance Squadron across the chest also in black, and black socks. Placing them in a row on top, he returns to the closet for a pair of running shoes sitting them in the floor in front of the dresser. He is ready for his morning run, even on Sunday – there are no off days. Removing his belt, it is placed on a hook next to others on the back of the closet door and he shuts it for the night.

His shirts come off and he folds them as precisely as if they were being placed back in the drawers and are stacked in the bottom of the hamper followed by his jeans. As he bends to take of his socks, Seth glances at the calendar over his desk. He does not have the large 3-month dry erase calendars like in the office at the Armory. Instead, he has taken apart two regular calendars and has all twelve months tacked to the wall with his entire year mapped out in military clarity. Dates requiring him to do something are boxed in green. Dates when he must be out of town for training or assignments are red; his annual physical, eye exam, the dentist in blue; every sixty days are orange reminding him to donate to his blood storage. Details of the days written in small, clear hand; times and instructions included.

Yellow highlighter is reserved for personal days. Days when he has plans that have nothing to do with forms or requisitions or training or meetings. Days when he is not thinking of the Army or rank changes or personnel issues or emails. Days when he is not Staff Sergeant, not the Captain's clerical assistant, not the highly trained secretary. Days when he is Seth...like today.

Picking up the highlighter, Seth completely fills in Saturday, March 25, 2006. Then with a black pen, he writes *Caroline* in large letters and gives into impulse adding a smile in the corner. He is pleased with his work and scanning the coming months, he is already looking forward to yellow boxes that have yet to be placed, but will fill up the empty spaces. That pleasant and unexpected feeling of sweet anticipation fades quickly and words like readiness and deployment and combat come to his mind.

He knows the red and green boxes will increase in number as the end of the year approaches. Seth has no feelings of dread or anxiety or fear, though fingers of sadness begin to clutch his heart at the thought of leaving Caroline.

What are you thinking? You've just had one date! Readiness has just begun and deployment is months, maybe a year or more away. Get it together, Garrett!

Seth shakes his head returning his thoughts to the present knowing there is no need to look too far ahead, because life can change in an instant, though he is always prepared. He gets in the shower and washes images of red and green boxes from his mind, focusing only on yellow and the golden strands of Caroline's hair all windblown and dancing around her face. Her red nails that sparkled in the sunlight continually grabbing his attention while she talked and gestured. Green eyes that were wide with shock after being pelted with paintballs. Seth thinks how most girls would have been so angry, some would have cried from pain and embarrassment, and all would be yelling and complaining, but Caroline barley flinched. She did not need to be coddled or soothed and told him repeatedly apologies were unnecessary. She did not pout or nag him that her clothes were ruined. Instead, she recovered her cool confidence and was ready to attentively listen to any of his story he chose tell.

Out of the shower and pacing around his room in nothing but a towel, Seth analyzes the day second, third, and fourth guessing himself as if to decide if it did go well.

I took a girl to Grants Branch on a first date!
Caroline Hatfield is no girl; she's a lady – good and fine!
I stuffed ham sandwiches in a backpack that probably smells like diesel!
She said she liked ham sandwiches and asked to sit at the dirty tables.
How many times did I touch her? Groping teenager!
She wasn't complaining for you to keep your hands off.
And I shot her…I shot her in her own home!
HA! Yes, you did!
I think she almost laughed.
Maybe, but it was probably shock!

I told her about Dad and Feather all on the first date!
You talked all day…Did you even ask her any questions?
I don't know.
She said she wanted to hear the rest of your story.
My Story…
You don't share that often. Maybe she really wants to know.
Yeah, she just thinks she does…
Cleat said she was different. Don't you agree?
Umm…yes.
Are you going to call her tomorrow?
I want to.
She sent you a text first.
I'll call.
I knew you would.

Crawling into bed, Seth's thoughts do not quiet and his sleep is fitful. His dreams are all over the place – swing sets and the lake, the dog barking and Feather runs across the parking lot to meet him. He reaches down hugging and kissing her telling her how much he has missed her and she is the best dog ever. Feather whimpers and paws at him sniffing him all over and Seth starts to cry; his heart is bursting.

Still holding Feather, he turns on his heels to look for Caroline so they can meet and she is not there, but he can see Eric Tucker's back porch in the distance and he starts to run. Feather matches his steps as they get closer and the light gets brighter.

He hears the shriek of the train whistle as it comes out of the tunnel across from the Armory. Seth is on his morning run, but is on the tracks instead of the road. He turns away from the train and tries to run, but stumbles over the ties and falls – hands and knees pound onto the ballast. Trying to get his footing, he places a hand on the rail, but his palm is bloody and he slips going down face first knocking the wind out of him. Clawing his way up, he runs, but the train is closer as he looks over his shoulder and hears the whistle. Ahead of him, another train is coming. He forgets about the pain, because his mind cannot decide which way to run. Suddenly, the trains are upon him. The whistles are loud and constant. He is confused and can't understand why he just doesn't step off the tracks, but his feet are buried deep in the ballast and his legs will not move. Seth is panicked and frozen. His hands cover his ears and he closes his eyes. Just before the two angry beasts collide, all goes black and silent.

Seth wakes up sweating and panting – chest heaving and his sheets are soaked. He is not afraid, but at the same time overwhelmed by fear. His hand drapes over the edge of the mattress hoping he can entice Feather to join him in his bed so he can feel safe and not alone, but she is not there. With a mind still blurred by sleep and dreams, Seth is not aware he rolls to his side and cries himself to sleep.

Chapter XII

"I want you to understand this mystery, dear brothers..." – Romans 11:25 NLT

The morning sunlight peaks its way around the edges of the blinds in Caroline's bedroom. She rolls over and looks at the clock, fully rested, but unwilling to get up. Watching the light spill onto the floor and dust particles rising in the beams, she is reminded of Seth and how his hair held glints of honey and gold. Smiling and flushing, her mind is filled with new memories of yesterday. Such an enticing man, who is still very much a boy, making him all the more attractive.

Caroline wants to lie in bed all morning letting her mind wander all over yesterday, analyze all details of Seth Garrett, anticipate the next time she is to see him, playing out endless girly ideas and scenes in her head. How many hours will it be before she can talk to him? How many days will she have to wait to see him again? Disappointment meets expectation. How we want to savor every moment, but insist the moments quickly arrive.

She nearly shouts as she bolts upright in bed. It finally dawns on her that it is Sunday and her turn to cook family dinner. In all the excitement of yesterday and Seth, she forgot to make any plans. Rushing downstairs, Caroline scours her pantry and deep freeze to see what she has that does not look like she threw everything together at the last minute.

Grabbing two bags of frozen chicken, she fills the sink with warm water, plunging the bags, and weighting them with a platter. She goes to her refrigerator looking for buttermilk she knows is not there and gets the gallon of 2% and lemon juice.

I've seen Gran do this dozens of times and she doesn't even measure!

Caroline does not risk it and carefully pours two cups of milk in a bowl and adds two tablespoons of lemon juice. Setting it to the side to allow that little chemical reaction to take place, she returns to the pantry for potatoes. Scrubbing, peeling, cubing, the potatoes go into a pot and she makes room for them in the refrigerator. The chicken is thawed and the milk has clabbered. She whisks in some cayenne, because she knows Dad and Will like a little kick, dumps the chicken in the bowl with the milk, covers it, and puts it next to the potatoes. Caroline goes back to the pantry coming out, her arms loaded with self-rising flour, a can of shortening, shifter, and her *biscuit bowl*.

Gran told her years ago, the secret to good biscuits was the bowl and use it only for biscuits. Her bowl is creamy white stoneware with a row of painted strawberries with leaves and flowers banding the middle that she and Gran found at the flea market in Abingdon. It was one of her first purchases when she moved in her house. Gran has a similar bowl – creamy white stoneware with a thin black stripe and two red stripes around the top – that she got as a wedding present when she and Poppie were married. Caroline loves Gran's bowl and was always eager to watch when she made biscuits – never measuring, sifting the flour which was always *Martha White* by tapping the sifter on the heel of her hand, raking the shortening, always *Crisco*, with her fingers to grease the pan and plop just the right amount into the flour, kneading everything by hand slowly adding the milk until the dough was to the right consistency. No measuring – everything was done by feel and turned out perfect each time. Caroline smiles at her favorite memories placing the items on the counter and very pleased that she is going to use *her* bowl in *her* house to make *her* biscuits.

Back to the pantry, she retrieves two quarts of greasy beans she helped Gran can last summer placing them beside the biscuit preparations. Looking at the time, she decides to cut salad after church, removes plates, bowls, glasses, and silverware from the cabinets, putting them on the counter next to everything else, and rushes back upstairs to get ready for church.

> *My Jesus, I love thee, I know Thou art mine;*
> *For Thee all the follies of sin I resign;*
> *My gracious Redeemer, my Savior art Thou;*
> *If ever I loved Thee, my Jesus, 'tis now.*

The final hymn is sung and the repeated line speaks to Caroline's heart. *"If ever I loved Thee, my Jesus, 'tis now."* Now. Not only when prayers are answered. Not only when I feel blessed. Not when the struggles of life are over. NOW – is the time to love Jesus.

Her smile is bright and there is a skip to her step, because her heart feels a little fuller this morning. Caroline's heart is never empty, but alone and lonely can make you feel not as full. Sometimes it takes a friend like Sophie to point out that you are becoming too good at being alone or new friends like Seth that you did not even know existed, but realized you have been missing them for so long once they finally arrive.

"What's for dinner? I'm starved!" Nick bumps Caroline knocking her hip into the side of the pew causing her to stumble and lose the well-controlled poise he is always teasing her about. Glaring at him, Nick takes her arm leading her down the aisle as if she were feeble and could not do it by herself. She jerks her arm away, not angry, because this is Nick's usual treatment and answers sweetly, "Fried chicken."

"Mmm…Are you making gravy and biscuits?" Nick asks gleefully rubbing his palms.

Caroline pushes her hair behind one ear as she answers Nick and he grabs her hand.

"Caroline! Who has been chewing on your neck?" not even considering the church sanctuary may not be the best place to begin quizzing his sister.

The welts of last night made serious bruises by morning that makeup barely covered. She has worn her hair down to shield her neck from prying eyes, but has forgotten during services about the marks. Frowning at Nick's uncouth remark, she tries to divert his questions. "No one has and yes, I'm making gravy and biscuits," knowing Nick has no shame in making requests for what he wants to eat. If he was not pleased with what she has chosen, he would politely suggest something else and expect her to change the menu. What could she say, he was the baby! Nick, however, has forgotten about his hungry stomach and continues to probe Caroline, moving her chin aside to examine her further.

"What's going on with your neck? It looks terrible!"

Not ready to make complete explanations to Nick, she answers honestly, but vague. "I got shot by a paintball," and begins walking down the aisle with the rest of the congregation, Nick trailing and confused only to be intercepted by Will.

"Who got shot?"

Nervous frustration and panic floods Caroline, but she gets control of it quickly in order not to give too much away to the boys too soon answering in unison with Nick.

"No one!"

"Caroline!" grabbing her chin again showing Will.

"WHOA! What happened to you?" Will is like a wall preventing her escape from the sanctuary. Caroline must think fast otherwise these two will have her blurting out every detail of yesterday before she realizes what is happening just so they will stop asking questions. She expertly carries on a conversation with both of them.

"I got shot by a paintball—"

"Looks ten paintballs!"

"No, just two."

"And Darby's coming too."

"I know. She sent me a text yesterday," Nick says not quite sure of Caroline's answer and pretty confident there is more to this story, because he can detect her panic.

"Darby's coming where?" Will asks as he turns and starts walking towards the door.

"To dinner at Caroline's. FRIED CHICKEN!" Nick enthusiastically informs him.

"I'm so glad I'm coming. I've been craving fried chicken for weeks!" Will pats his none-too-flat belly for effect.

Caroline is glad Nick and Will have attention spans of a gnat and she avoids further questioning...for now. They each walk down the steps of Williamson Wesleyan and meet their parents in the church yard as they have done for years. Nadine is the first to approach the 'kids' directing her normal Turkey Talk towards Caroline.

"Ba-bawk! Gobble, gobble, gobble! Caroline! Marty and I are coming to dinner. I hope you have planned for us and have enough food!" Nadine could have never been with Jesus when He fed the multitudes, because she would have definitely discouraged Him that there simply was not enough food! Never, had Nadine believed at any meal there would be enough to feed everyone without running short.

"Yes, Nadine. I planned for you and Uncle Marty and it is not my plan to run out." If Nadine knew how humorous and entertaining Caroline thinks she is, she would be livid and hurt. Caroline loves her aunt and would never want to hurt her, so she answers nicely and tries to dispel her aunt's fears, but still must endure her attack of questions. "We are having fried chicken and I got everything in order before church."

"Are you soaking it in buttermilk? Gobble, gobble!"

"Yes, and cayenne. Just the way Gran does it."

"Gobble! You know buttermilk keeps it from drying out. And no one likes dry chicken!"

"Yes. We are also having potatoes, gravy, greasy beans, salad, and biscuits."

"Three quarts? Gobble! You are making three quarts, right? If you don't have enough, I can bring you some."

"No worries. I have enough for three quarts."

"Good!" conspiratorially taking hold of Caroline's arm, Nadine leans in to inform her, "I'm glad you're making biscuits. They're delicious! Maybe even better than Ruby's. GOBBLE!" Nadine laughs loud and turkey-like, as if she and Caroline are sharing a hilarious secret.

It was no secret. Nadine has questioned and examined Ruby's biscuits, among other things, for years claiming, "These are not quite the way my mother made them, rest her soul," and announced on more than one occasion that Caroline's biscuits were superior. It embarrassed both Caroline and Ruby at first with Caroline coming to Ruby's defense. Privately, they would tease Nadine and Gran would say, "That silly Nadine! She doesn't realize we use the same recipe and I taught you everything I know!" Leaning in closer and with her own conspiring voice, Gran confided, "I'll never tell her, but your biscuits are better, because you make them in a much prettier bowl!" Gran would then wink and squeeze Caroline's hand. This was the extent of Gran's wickedness and Caroline loved her even more for it.

"Well, anyway. I have a beef roast with onions and carrots that I pressured last week and put in the freezer. I will bring that, just in case. Gobble!"

"Thank-you, Nadine. I'm sure it will be eaten," which was the truth, but Caroline was thinking how she would not be eating any of it, because Nadine's beef roast always tasted like she had boiled all the flavor out of it leaving behind a piece of meat swimming in brown water that never had enough salt.

Everyone continues chatting, speaking to other members of the congregation, and the crowd begins to disperse. Clayton has pulled the car down front and gives Ruby his arm like a gentleman, not like Nick who tried to wrestle Caroline to the ground, leading her to the front seat. Charlotte and Nick get in the backseat as Caroline walks towards her Explorer.

Shutting the door, Caroline is encapsulated in a few moments of silence. She knows she has only ended Nick's questions for the moment. He will figure out some way to get her to confess or go into his own private search for the answers she will not supply, so she braces herself for further interrogation. For now, sitting alone, driving home alone, to fix dinner alone, where afterwards everyone will leave and she will be alone again. Alone and with her thoughts. Sophie is right – she is getting too good at alone. Maybe Seth has arrived at just the right time. Thinking again of Seth and the warmth he has already brought into her life, Caroline's aloneness vanishes, if only temporarily, because she must make dinner and later expects a call from him…sometime.

Caroline gets home and knows she has about forty-five minutes before everyone arrives. Dinner will not be ready, but she wants it to be well underway before they get here. So, she scoots up the steps to change. Her shoes, dress, slip, pantyhose, and foundation garments that smooth and slenderize come off. She will pick them up in a moment after she scratches her belly and thighs.

Smooths and slenderizes – nothing! More like squeezes and suffocates and itches you to death! A man – no matter his size or weight – can put on a shirt and tie and look great while a woman will wear five different layers, can't breathe, and still feels fat!

She has no time to think about that as she goes to use the bathroom and wash off all the handshakes. A few minutes later, Caroline is dressed, her hair is up in its typical messy bun, careless of her purple neck.

Stick to the story about paintball, act like nothing is wrong, and maybe Nick will not ask any more questions...Maybe, but doubtful!

The clothes are out of her floor, and she is in the kitchen beginning her work when Gran walks through the front door and says, "Hel-lo! I thought you could use some help."

"I sure could!" Caroline tells her grandmother, fibbing just a little, because she has everything under control and really likes cooking for a crowd, but she wants to make sure Gran feels useful. Ruby still has family dinner at her house occasionally, but does only a little of the cooking, oftentimes, she and Caroline team up. She lets Caroline create new dishes and since they are served at Gran's house, there are few complaints when exotic and eclectic is not always enjoyed.

Coming up beside and kissing her cheek, Gran gasps, "Caroline! What happened to your neck?"

Knowing this would not be the only time this question was asked today, "Oh, it's nothing!" Caroline just laughs it off. "I got shot by a paintball."

"Honey, you should be more careful! Did you put liniment on it?" Gran's sad face shows that she hates her girl was wounded, but believes in the power of the smelly ointment she and Poppie have put on everything from burns to bullet holes over the years.

Smiling at Gran's tender concern and uncertain how she still has bottles of that stuff when Caroline is sure it was taken off the market years ago, "No. I didn't have any, but I covered it in *Vaseline* right after it happened," hoping this was an acceptable treatment.

"Well, that's good, but liniment is better."

Caroline is touched by her grandmother who is a perfect mix of yesteryear and gives her a task to help.

"You can set the table. I already put in the two leaves, because we are having a crowd today," Caroline says looking over her shoulder as she dredges the next piece of chicken then places it in the iron skillet.

"The whole gang will be here?" Gran asks as she picks up part of the stack of plates and walks to the dining room.

"Yep!" Caroline answers giving the complete rollcall. "You, me, Mom, Dad, Marty, Nadine, Will, Nick and Darby, Alex and Megan, Jackson, Jacob, and Sam. Fourteen total!"

Gran makes several trips from the kitchen counter to the dining room. Plate with salad bowl in the center, napkin folded to the edge with fork, knife, and spoon placed on top, glass at the corner. Caroline has a low vase of cut flowers and without asking, Gran picks them up and takes them to the table as well. Coming back to the kitchen ready for her next assignment, Gran comments, "Your Poppie always liked flowers on the table. He bought them for me often, but the ones he picked were the ones I loved the best."

There is a glimmer in Gran's eyes one that is always there when she speaks of Poppie. How wonderful to have such tender memories of someone and how awful to be forced to continue to live without your love; your best friend.

Caroline sooths Gran. "I remember. That is why I buy them for myself. I loved it when I saw them on your table and thought it was so sweet he got them for you. Most of the time, I buy them and take them to school. The kids like them and always ask who they are from and I will say, 'From me and I bought them for you!' They get all silly and squirrelly, but they like it."

Caroline finishes with the chicken covering it with a lid to cook slowly not to burn or dry out. Gran sits on one of the bar stools and talks as Caroline cuts salad.

"Someday, someone special is going to buy you flowers, too," Gran winks and Caroline blushes. "But you know, it was so much more than flowers and the hundreds of nice things John did for me…He was my best friend…I think we were best friends even before we got married and it just got stronger and deeper every day."

Ruby steps out of the County Clerk's Office after an interview Mr. Reynolds set up for her. Three of her girlfriends moved to Charleston right after graduation and had taken jobs in a branch office with the War Department. They tried to get Ruby to join them, but her parents refused. It would be so exciting actually contributing in some way to the war effort and living in the city. She had only been to Charleston once and it was so different from Williamson and the thought of living there was thrilling. When she suggested the idea to her parents at the dinner table one evening, her father calmly asked who was going, what were their jobs going to be, how much were they getting paid, and where were they going to live. Ruby could only answer the first of his questions, so he responded flatly, "Well, looks like you don't know much and I'm sure neither do those girls. I would suggest you look for a job in Williamson, first, and you can consider Charleston later."

Ruby made no further arguments, though privately complained how her father was no fun and he treated her like a child and there would never be a job as interesting as the War Department in Williamson. Now that September had arrived and Mr. Reynolds knew of a position with the County Clerk, and one of the girls had already moved home, because the other two had been almost immediately transferred to Richmond, Ruby was glad her father did not embrace her plans. Charleston may be exciting, but Richmond was much too far from home.

Coming down the hall, she is reading one of the papers she was given at the end of the interview and does not notice Mr. Reynolds round the corner with two young men she had never seen.

"I'm sorry, Mr. Reynolds. I wasn't paying attention." Ruby is flustered as she bumps into the older gentleman and he takes her arm to keep her from slipping.

"Whoa Ruby! Not to worry! I'm glad to see you! Did you have your interview this morning?"

"Yes. Thank-you sir. Mr. Potter said his secretary would contact me in a few days."

"Yes, that is good to hear. I will remind Potter what an excellent choice he would make in hiring you. But, no promises, mind you!" Mr. Reynolds was a jolly good-natured man who was liked and well respected by the whole town. Upon first seeing him, one would never guess he had any clout and when you got to know him and that he was no one of substance or wealth, the level of his influence surprised you. He knew everyone, was highly trusted, people valued his opinion, and he was a man who could get things done.

"Let me introduce you, Ruby, to two prospective citizens. This here is," gesturing to the first man allowing him to make his own introductions, "I'm Warren MacGuire. It is nice to meet you, Miss Ruby. My friends call me War," extending his hand for a firm, yet appropriate handshake.

"Yes. Very good. And Ruby, this here is," Mr. Reynolds moves aside with a flourish.

The second man removes his hat and is much quieter and seems to lack the confidence of the other. "John Robinette, ma'am. Honaker, VA." He does not extend a hand to Ruby and smooths the brim of his hat with both.

"I remember that day clearly as if it were yesterday. I was wearing a brown skirt and jacket with white polka dots, a brown tam trimmed in white with brown polka dots, and white gloves. I thought I looked so smart," Gran smiles at Caroline and shakes her head saucily. She enjoys retelling this story as much as Caroline loves hearing it. "War was more interesting at first glance, but John...well, I thought he was beautiful."

Gran would have gladly gone on to tell her that Poppie was wearing a navy shirt and brown pants tucked into dark brown riding boots and that he went back to Virginia for a time and it would not be until the next Spring that she saw him again, but the front door opens. With a finger to her lips, she shushes Caroline and the story ends, for now.

Organized chaos enters Caroline's house as the rest of her dinner guests arrive nearly one after another. Clayton, Alex, and Nick turn on the television and begin, as Poppie would have said, 'feisting' with the boys. Charlotte joins Caroline in the kitchen helping without being told what to do next, but leans in quietly to ask, "What's wrong with your neck?" to which Caroline responds, "Paintball," and that was all the answer she required. Darby takes a chair beside Gran cutting up cucumbers, peppers, and carrots that Caroline has not gotten to yet. Will yells from the door acting like a monster ready to attack the boys and they all squeal running to him latching onto his legs. Nadine comes in behind him with Marty in tow carrying a covered *Corelle* dish no doubt filled with watery beef instructing him to place it in the oven and gobbling to Caroline, "Is the oven on, gobble?"

Everything comes together as planned and is carried to the dining room. Three little boys squirm at a miniature card table in primary colors eager to eat and grabbing at each other's action hero sippy cups. The adults find their seats and Alex reaches over and snaps his fingers, a gesture Clayton directed towards him and Nick so many times and he is still amazed how effective it is with his own boys. There is a pause and near silence as everyone joins hands. Even though this is Caroline's house, Clayton speaks, "Ruby, would you pray for us, please."

Heads bow. "Our gracious Lord, You alone saw fit that we again have lived to see another Sabbath and are blessed to share our table with those we love. We ask now that You bless this food to our bodies and the hands of those who have prepared it. May our lives forever give You the glory and it is in the name Christ our Savior I ask these things…AMEN."

Followed by whispered *amens* and with the three at their own table adding a little louder in their response, but no less confident in the words. Bowls are passed and conversation begins amid chewing and compliments. The meal is about a third finished when Alex remarks,

"So, Caroline, who's been chewing on your neck?"

Caroline stops her fork mid-bite, Nick squeaks covering his full mouth shifting in his seat, Will snorts, coughs, and takes a drink while Alex pins her down with his stare as if this were a completely normal question, but the sounds coming from his accomplices, it is obvious he has been coached. Her slight hesitation to gather her composure causes the rest of the table to pause turning their attention to her also eager for an answer. Knowing Nick has been waiting for days to tease and laugh at her, she is ready with her cold Ice Queen voice to answer Alex's rapid fire questions with all heads at the table swinging back and forth between then two of them.

"No one. It's paintball."

"Paintball? When did you play paintball?"

Nick and Will add to his question digging the hole for her to fall into.

"Yeah, Caroline. When did you play paintball?"

"And didn't invite us?"

Ready to choke all three of them, because she is certain they are conspiring against her. She has to be careful of her steps, because she has fallen into their trap her whole life.

"I didn't play. I was in the garage." Each of them fire a question in unison.

"You were in the garage?"

"Is there paint on my *Waverunner*?"

"You shot yourself?"

Again, careful well-placed words, "I was in the garage and the safety was not on and it fired. There is no paint on your *Waverunner*." She finally places the chicken in her mouth, knowing this will not be enough of answer for them, but chewing buys her some time to think as Alex continues to question.

"It just randomly fired while you were in there?" Looking to Nick and Will he says, "We need to check her gun. It could have something wrong with it," his comment of concern only thinly veils his mockery and he, too, now believes his sister is being truthful yet hiding something.

Nick further probes, "Where were you yesterday?"

Ready for this question, Caroline answers as she continues to eat as if this is normal dinner conversation though the boys have all but forgotten their meal and are devouring and digesting her every word. "I gave the ACT," and before he can ask his next question, Caroline goes ahead and answers, "Then I saw Sophie. She was at school to get ready for the Spring Concert. She came up and we had pizza and watched a movie."

Nick is irritated she so cleverly has an alibi for the day. He takes a bite and regroups his thoughts. Fortunately, Alex is one step ahead of him.

"Was Sophie here when *you* shot yourself?" his sarcastic draw brings tenth grade snickers from Nick and Will.

Caroline's face ignites, but she does not fidget even though they are getting painfully close. Charlotte comes to her daughter's defense though throws her under the bus in the end.

"Boys! Why are you harassing your sister? She has said it was paintball and if there is anything else, she doesn't have to tell us. Now, hush and eat!" Charlotte scolds the boys as if they were the ones sitting at the kids' table.

Nick and Will mutter, "Yes, ma'am," and resume eating, but it is Alex who throws out one final challenge, "No worries, Mama…She'll tell us!" he picks up his fork and diverts his attention away from Caroline and begins to speak with their uncle about an upcoming contract they are both working on.

The meal proceeds without further incident and as the last dish is washed and put away, Caroline walks everyone to the door. The rowdy little boys have tired and are carried to their car seats by Alex, Will and Clayton. Marty, again carrying the *Corelle*, follows Nadine as she clucks and coos instructions to him. Nick takes his grandmother's arm having already offered to walk her home as she stops at the door.

"Caroline, give me just a few minutes and I will be ready to go with you."

"Ok, Gran. I will change and get Mom then we will pick you up." Caroline stands at the top of the steps as Nick and Gran make it to the sidewalk on their way to path leading to Gran's house.

Gran turns and says, "I'll hurry," and before she walks away, Nick fires one more question with no intention of letting Caroline answer.

"Caroline, you never did tell us why you were locked inside the gate at school and we had to pick up your car this morning…Especially, if Sophie was with you yesterday." He pauses to look at her and his face should be surrounded by floating cartoon question marks. His head turns in slight challenge and he says no more walking with Gran. Caroline's face does not flame, but her nervous stomach churns. She knows her brothers are onto her, but is thankful they know her so well that they must ease her into telling them what's going on. Both of them, including Will, are confident she will tell them.

Chapter XIII

*"These things happened as a warning to us, so
that we would not crave evil things..."*
– I Corinthians 10:6 NLT

Sophie is in her element as she comes to the stage of the auditorium to greet everyone to the Spring Concert. She explains to the audience, "This afternoon will be a tribute to our Appalachian heritage in music, word, and song. We will explore the worlds of folk, hymns, and bluegrass, both traditional and contemporary. We welcome you today, now sit back and enjoy our amazing students."

Applause spreads through the auditorium, the lights dim, and a quartet of students – banjo, mandolin, guitar, and violin – play a haunting rendition of *My Old Kentucky Home*. When the violin drags its final note across the strings, there is a momentary hush followed by the choir singing in round fashion increasing the number of singers and intensity with each line. The final words are a dynamic, though quiet solo from a senior girl Caroline has never had in class. Ninety minutes later following readings and music, Sophie and her students have delivered an impressive concert with the choir once again singing the state song and then the bluegrass quartet completing the evening with a touch of whimsical melancholy.

Gran and Charlotte are all smiles and applause as they look at Caroline who is so obviously impressed with the students and proud of her friend. The auditorium fills with conversation and the audience begins to make their ways to the exits. Not wanting to get caught in the flood of people, Gran stays seated and speaks with her girls.

"Caroline, I want to congratulate Sophie on a wonderful performance. When she is finished talking, run and get her. This was almost as wonderful as that recital of Carter's we went to years ago, at the Rose G. Do you all remember that?" They both did for very different reasons and flutter of melancholy not unlike the final decrescendo of the evening waffles through them. Gran's face is filled with pleasure and pride as she inquires, "Charlotte, did you say the boy playing the mandolin went to your preschool?"

"Yes, he did as well as his two sisters and a brother. He is the youngest of the four and they all play at least one instrument and some of them two. They were all so talented even when they were young," Charlotte answers referring back to the program noting that his sister was part of the choir. "Caroline, did his brother and sister graduate already?"

"Yes, remember they are Irish Twins. I had never heard that term before I met them. They went to Centre together and if you can believe it, they are more talented than these two. Everyone was shocked when they chose not to major in music."

"Really? You would have thought they would have with such natural skill," Charlotte is surprised thinking back on the two who had an other-world presence about them even as children. They were almost unordinarily close with the sister being very protective of her slightly younger brother. Their devotion to their music was evident even then though all other studies came easy as well.

"I know! To have such talent and not pursue it further. Skylar is majoring in computer science and Aden engineering. I asked him why he was not going into music or at least something associated with music. He answered very matter of fact, 'I've done that. I want to do something else now.' I thought that sounded so wise and mature for someone so young."

Charlotte nods in agreement again remembering the delightful children and Gran adds, "That's true, but look at Carter. He was so talented – nothing he could be taught. He has a gift, but he went in another direction. Lucinda and I have often spoken of the change that seemed so sudden in him. He loved to play and was so proud of his music. We think Jonas and Sylvia just pushed him too hard and he lost interest. It became a chore not a passion. They always wanted him to be so much more. Like he was never quite enough to please them," shaking her head in sadness at a topic she had discussed more than once with her dearest friend and Carter's grandmother. "So sad, really."

Charlotte does not comment, but slowly shakes her head, because she and Clayton have also had the same conversation. It is Caroline who voices what the three are thinking.

"Yes, Gran. I believe you are exactly right. So very sad."

Charlotte only glances at her daughter, but clearly notes her crestfallen tone.

Oh, Caroline. My dear girl!

The auditorium quickly empties and Sophie finishes speaking with some parents down front, and Caroline brings her to talk to Gran who is waiting with arms wide.

"Sophie! Your students were wonderful! I am so glad I came today!" Gran hugs Sophie like one of her own as she has treated her since they were children.

"Ah, Ruby, thank-you. They have me worried right up until the last minute, like something is just not quite going to come together, but it always does and I am so proud of them!" Sophie beams and gushes over her *children* like any proud parent. It is so easy to invest so much in a student or several students and feel like they are your own.

"Now, I have to get the stage back in order, because there is a meeting in here after school...Caroline, could you stay and help me?" giving Caroline a cheesy grin in hopes her friend will agree.

"Yeah, I don't mind. Mom, you can just take my car and you and Gran go on to church. I will stay and help Sophie," Caroline says fishing for her keys.

"That's ok. I told your dad to stop by on his way to church in case you couldn't leave when we were ready. I'm sure he is waiting outside."

Charlotte and Gran give Caroline a goodbye hug and congratulate Sophie again before heading towards the door. Sophie slips her arm into Caroline's leading her down the aisle of the near empty auditorium and says, "I won't say you didn't have to stay, because if you would have refused, I would have started crying in order to convince you. I will simply say thanks for the help and have you talked to Seth?"

Caroline pulls away and accuses Sophie, "You don't need my help, you just want to question me so more!"

Sophie's eyes dance with eager expectation and her smile is tenth grade excitement, "So you have talked with him! YAY!"

"Sophie, hush! But, yes I have!"

Over the next hour, the girls stack chairs on carts and return them to the choir room, collect random items students have left in the wings and the Green Room, pick up forgotten sheet music, and even locate a French laying in its open case backstage.

"That belongs to Cooper. He has a practice instrument he leaves at school and a performance instrument he has a home. He must have had both today and forgot to take this one back to the band room." Bending, Sophie snaps the case shut and she and Caroline walk out the stage door leading to her office connected to the band and choir rooms. She sets the case on her desk, picking up her purse, and the girls walk to rear parking lot.

"So, when are you going to see him again?" Sophie asks, not probing, as they each push through the doors on their way out.

"I don't know. He said he would call tonight. I guess we will decide then," glad to share this with Sophie, but Caroline is still very unfamiliar with talking about Seth. It is just all too new for her.

"I'll be honest, Caroline. I know I give you a hard time, but there is something about this guy, that I like and I think you do, too."

Caroline gives her a skeptical smirk, "Sophie, you haven't even met him yet."

Sophie is quick to challenge the rational, cautious Caroline. "I know, but that's what makes me so sure. It's more of a feeling," Sophie reasons with calm assurance. "Did you tell anyone you went out?"

Caroline's look is fearful, "No, but Nick is on to me and he had Alex and Will quizzing me about my neck during dinner. He will figure it out soon if I'm not careful. I will tell them; I just want to enjoy Seth all to myself for a while. We have only gone out once. It may become nothing. Who knows."

Sophie could easily criticize her lack of optimism, but she also knows her friend's heart and mind very well, so she decides to give her tender comfort.

"Then I will leave you to enjoy him. You keep him all to yourself and I will be patient until you decide to share him with the rest of us." Sophie squeezes Caroline's arm and kisses her cheek. "Thanks for the help, Friend."

"You're welcome. Thanks." Caroline appreciates that Sophie knows her so well and that she understands what she means. Caroline would have said more, but her phone rings. Pulling in out of her purse, Sophie sees Seth's name light up on the screen and releases her friend shooing her away with a flap of the hand.

"Go ahead. Enjoy your boy!" Sophie turns to her car with glee for Caroline and a whisper of her own loneliness which lingers so rarely, she decides to be happy for Caroline wondering when she will finally let her meet the fascinating Staff Sergeant Garrett.

Caroline turns away from Sophie before she answers, "Hello Sergeant."

His heart tripping a little and smile wide, Seth responds releasing hummingbirds in Caroline's chest.

"Hello, Pretty Girl…How are you this evening?"

Caroline is so unaccustomed to Seth's comments, but loves them just the same. "I'm good; better now. How are you?" asking as she slides into her SUV, turning on the engine and heated seats.

"Hmm…better now. What are you into?" genuinely interested in what she is doing.

"Well, I just walked out of the auditorium and got in my car."

Teasing, yet curious, "I thought good girls like you generally go to church on Sunday night."

Again, enjoying his banter, "I usually do, but there was a concert at school and my best friend is the band and choir teacher and she needed some help cleaning up. So, now it's too late to go." Out of habit, she pulls down the visor and looks in the mirror checking her face and teeth as if he can see her through the phone.

"So, you're not home?"

Running her tongue across her teeth, she flips the visor up and reaches for the knob on the heater. "Nope. Why?"

"Wanna meet me?" Seth is glad he called her before he got home. "I've been at Cleat's. How about we go to Dairy Queen and I'll buy you a sweet treat?"

"Mmm, that sounds good. I'll see you in a few minutes."

"Good."

Cleat. Meet. Sweet. Treat. Sounds like the Addams Family song.

The visor comes down again to check for bats in the cave and chives in her teeth. Digging through her purse, she finds her makeup bag, powdering her nose and chin, retouching her lipstick. She tosses several cinnamon *Tic-Tacs* in her mouth, crunching them up and believing her tongue is on fire as she shifts into reverse.

Second date – no nerves, no apprehension. Maybe the spontaneity does not give her time to worry, because Caroline feels completely comfortable to meet Seth. Besides, Dairy Queen is just a few minutes from school, and if she wants to second guess, she will be there before her mind has time to spin in a thousand directions. She has decided already, however, that the *sweet treat* will be Seth.

Pulling onto the parking lot, she sees he has already arrived and there is an empty spot next to him. Seth does not notice her at first and Caroline is again given a few moments opportunity to examine him by the glow of the dashboard lights. She gets out and walks to his door and he still does not realize she is there. Tapping on the window, he jerks, obviously startled, but smiles as he turns off the engine and joins Caroline ready with his teasing banter.

"Are you trying to give me a heart attack again tonight?" he fusses coming close to her face – inviting, not threatening.

Caroline retreats only as far as the door of her Explorer and offers no defense with her hands stuffed deep in her coat pockets.

"Not at all. You were just sitting there and I had to get your attention. If I knew you were so skittish, I would have started blowing my horn as soon as I got on the lot. I'll know better next time," Caroline raises her eyebrows and smiles, very Cheshire cat.

Seth's approach is menacing, but playful. "Smarty pants already! Let's not make a habit of that. Shall we?" as his hand makes a fake gun and taps the end of her nose.

With a confident, icy stare, Caroline informs him, "Sorry. No promises."

Hooking his arm through hers, he jerks her away from the car and growls as her feet pitter-patter and she giggles. He opens the door to the warm restaurant and it is like they have changed channels as he leads her to the counter and Caroline meets semi-disaster. A boy whom she had his freshman year is working the register. He was a good student and Caroline really liked him, but his major flaw was he thrived on gossip. Not exactly the person you want to meet on a second date in a small town. A touch of uneasiness surfaces in Caroline, but true to form, her poise wins out taking command of the conversation before he has a chance.

"Hey, Cam!"

"Hey, Ms. Hatfield! What can I get you?" Cameron Stewart is ready to take her order, but his eyes jump more than once between Caroline and Seth.

"I'll take an *Oreo Blizzard* and a *Cherry Coke*," Caroline answers with no tremor to her voice and moves over to let Seth order.

"And I'll take a strawberry-banana *Blizzard*, a medium fry, bottle of water," Cameron gives them the total and Seth reaches for his wallet.

They wait quietly for Cameron to turn their cups of ice cream upside down, then brings their drinks, and fries. The after-church crowd begins to file in with plenty of chatter and laughter. Seth picks up their tray and observes, "Looks like we got here just in time. Where would you like to sit?"

Before she can answer, Cameron yells, "Bye, Ms. Hatfield," giving her a very mischievous grin.

"Good night, Cam. See you at school," and Caroline turns leading Seth to a corner booth away from Cam's line of sight and the crowd that has suddenly joined them.

Sliding in across from Seth, Caroline stabs her straw through her lid and asks, "What – no *Cherry Coke* for you?" taking a sip and looking at him.

"Nah. I don't drink pop," he responds handing her a spoon and spreading a napkin in between them as a place for the fries intending on sharing with her.

"So, you prefer water?" scooping a bite of *Blizzard* in her mouth ready to casually question him.

Not hesitating with his words, "I prefer *Woodford Reserve*, but I save that for a treat now. I haven't drunk pop since high school – it can't be good for you. I mainly drink water and sweet tea. I love it," taking a big bite of strawberry-banana licking the spoon before diving in for another.

Skeptical and mocking, Caroline asks, "Pop's not good for you, but you toss back bourbon?" convinced his answer will be interesting.

Cool and honest, "I don't toss it back. I sip it. Slowly. But like I said, that's just a treat now," picking up two fries and dipping them in his ice cream.

Wanting to know why, Caroline pries, "A *treat*? Why *now*?" also taking some fries.

He swigs his water – not a sip and not slowly – and explains why.

"First, I'm not 19 wanting to go to a Frat Party and second, I got a little burnt last fall," unsure if he should tell her more, he leaves the story unfinished.

Caroline smiles at the Frat Party remark and knows he is intentionally being evasive, so she prods him to explain. "Burnt? I'm sure that's a good story. Tell me."

Seth looks at her and he cannot decide if she is baiting him nor can he decipher all the warnings screaming in his head as her mossy green eyes, with flecks of honey and traces of navy hold him intently. He goes with honest and waits for her reaction.

"A few guys and I from my unit had some training at Fort Campbell that ended Friday morning, so we decided to spend the weekend in Louisville and do part of the Bourbon Trail. We went to two distilleries on Friday and three more Saturday," seeing no judgment in her face, he continues. "By the time, we finished the tour at the second one on Saturday, it had gotten really hot and they brought us outside for the tasting. They had four different samples and with the third, they recommended you follow it by eating slices of orange to '*heighten the flavor and cleanse the palate.*' It was terrible, so I ate about five pieces to get the taste out of my mouth and the fourth sample. I was fine then. *Then.*" His face and eyes emphasize the *then.*

"It was several minutes' drive to the next place and I was feeling very relaxed and fell asleep in the car. When we got there, I was ready for the next tour and four more samples. At this place, it was different, though. Instead of at the end, the samples were given out through the tour and when we came outside the fourth was waiting on us. They called it an evening bourbon that was to be drunk after dessert. Then they gave us this chunk of dark chocolate to eat. I don't know why I took it, because I don't even like chocolate, but it was too late when the guide told us to suck on it, because I had already chewed it up. As soon as it hit my stomach, that chocolate went to war with those oranges and ALL that bourbon."

Caroline is laughing silently hiding behind her hand imagining where this story is going to go. Seth recognizes she is enjoying his tale and gets a little animated.

"I start pouring the sweat and the nasties rise up in the back of my throat. The guide tells us where the store is to buy bottles to take home and indicates where the restrooms are. He probably saw the panic in my face! I run as best I can, and by now, my head is spinning and I know it is about to get ugly!"

Caroline is laughing so hard her shoulders are shaking, completely enjoying his story.

"Fortunately, I make it to the handicapped stall, because I knew I was going to need plenty of room. I don't even lock the door and I am on my knees just in time for this violent flood to leave my body – again and again and again. It was so painful, I thought I was going to die! And once it was over, I just laid in the floor thinking I was going to have to crawl to the car, because there was no way I was going to be able to stand."

"GROSS! You were laying in a bathroom floor!" Caroline makes a totally disgusted face amid her laughter.

Seth shouts back in defense, "I didn't care! My buddies didn't even check on me and I was in there for more than thirty minutes!"

Only feeling slightly sorry for him, Caroline asks, "Where were they and where did they think you had gone?"

Gesturing wildly, "They were in the store getting t-shirts and bottles of that stuff to take back to the hotel! I started to feel better and sat up when the tour guide comes in and says, 'Sir, I am not allowed to help you up, but I can get your friends to come and check on you,' and he hands me a small tray with a mini can of *Sprite*, several packages of saltine crackers, and a cup of coffee with 'Always Drink Responsibly' written all over it. Apparently, I was not the first guest to be found in the bathroom floor!" Seth closes his eyes and shakes his head at the memories of that day.

"My hands are shaking when I take the tray, I set it in the floor, and he leaves me to my misery. I drink a little coffee, but almost immediately, the flood comes back and I puke and puke then start to heave. One of the guys finally come in to see if I am alright and laughs his head off. I am none too nice and he leaves. After nearly an hour, I am able to get up. The DD brought his minivan, the kind that the seats can be hidden in the floor. He folds down the last row and I crawl in the trunk and go to sleep."

Laughter subsided, Caroline asks, "Were you ok after that?"

Seth chooses not to tell her they load him on a luggage cart to get him to the room, because he was barely conscious when they get back to the hotel, and concludes his story.

"I slept until Sunday morning and only ate the crackers on the drive home. Plus, my head felt like it was going to crack open. I felt terrible until Monday!" Seth's is exasperated as if he has had to relive that horrible event.

"You must have been really drunk!" Caroline shows him an eek-face.

"That's just it. I didn't realize I was. It hit me all at once. Never again!" shaking his head again with eyes closed.

Caroline adds and Seth worries he has told too much of the story. "I've never been drunk, but to hear you tell, it sure does sound fun! Would you suggest I start drinking bourbon?" her eyes are wide and unblinking and her faces reads complete innocence that slowly gives way to a mocking grin with traces of hidden wickedness. Teasing again.

Seth is serious with a patronizing, older brother tone, "I wouldn't recommend it!"

"And you don't like chocolate?" after that whole story, confessing he is drawn to the evils of alcohol and does not always use good judgement, her greatest disappointment is about chocolate.

"Not really. And I hate peanut butter! I think it is the most disgusting invention!" Now, it is Seth's turn for a grossed face.

Shock and disbelief stun Caroline. "What?!?! You don't like peanut butter either? You have to be un-American! Are you an alien?" she scowls as him under the ruse of scrutiny.

Hands and shoulders up, "YUCK! Is all I will say." Ready to stop talking and wanting to turn the conversation towards her, he asks, "Why did you name your dog Lemon?" returning to his ice cream that he has ignored.

"Because of Stonewall Jackson," like that was the most obvious answer.

Seth lowers his forehead and looks at her over nonexistent spectacles, "Because of Stonewall Jackson? I'm sorry to be obtuse, but you are going to have to explain.

Obtuse, just reminds Caroline how well-spoken she thinks he is and his use of vocabulary is intellectual and likewise attractive.

"Well." Caroline prepares for a story she loves to tell. "I told you Dad brought her home to me and I thought she was beautiful! I was in fifth grade and we were studying the Civil War. There was this whole series of children's biographies in our library and four of them were about Civil War characters. I read them all, but my favorite was Stonewall Jackson! I was just fascinated with him. On Spring Break, we went to visit my mom's oldest brother. He lived in Buena Vista, VA at the time and I was telling him all about Stonewall Jackson. The next day, he takes us in to Lexington to visit his grave and we take a tour of VMI. I LOVED IT! But, I was so disappointed I did not bring lemons to leave on his grave," Caroline's tone changes as if she needs to take a moment and give him a small history lesson. "Jackson suffered from stomach problems and was always sucking on lemons, so visitors are to leave lemons on his grave instead of flowers and I didn't have any. A few weeks later, Dad brings me a puppy and I name her Lemon in honor of my beloved Stonewall!" Caroline smiles and swoons.

"VMI."

Caroline thinks he is questioning her so she further explains, "Yes, VMI – Virginia Military Institute. It was amazing! I even wrote my Defend-and-Debate paper on it in senior English class in high school," cheesing over the memory.

Seth appears stern and uncertain of this history lesson. "What was your paper about?"

Caroline forgetting for a moment that Seth is in the military and may have very opposing views, she hesitates on how she should safely word her statement deciding absolute honesty is best.

"I had read an article about military academies being forced to admit female students or lose State and Federal funding. I believed that VMI should be allowed to maintain their public-school status without being required to admit females. We had to defend our position then participate in a formal debate with at least one other student. The girl I was up against did not agree with me in the least and in her final statements she was shrieking at me saying I was a chauvinist and supported oppression of women and was opposed to suffrage to which I replied I was none of those things, that West Point had had female cadets for years, which I agreed with, but something is to be said for the value of some time-honored traditions. When our teacher said, I had won the debate, the girl was irate and said she could not believe our teacher agreed with me. I remember clearly her reply, 'I do not agree with Caroline, but her arguments were well-founded and she presented her opinion while maintaining control of her emotions.' Afterwards, the girl cried and that was just a bonus for me!" smiling and pleased at the memory.

Seth looks at her with almost an air of condescension, "So, it's safe to say you don't cry?"

Again, her honesty is on point, "Of course, I do…when appropriately moved. Never when I am angry and don't get my way. And I almost never pout."

Withdrawing from her from and asking with noticeable arrogance, "So, you are not like one of *those* girls, Ms. Hatfield?"

"Mr. Garrett, you will soon realize, I am not like *any* girl," filled with frost and her own level of arrogance.

Both are pleased with the other's answer, but their actions do not reflect those feelings. Conversation continues that is neutral and random. They stick to safer topics, though learning all kinds of tidbits about each and forming clearer opinions about the other.

The minutes pass and *Dairy Queen* empties. Seth stacks their trash on the tray and allows Caroline to lead them out. He is in no rush to get in his Jeep and has taken her hand as they come outside. Closing the space between them, Seth releases her hand. Caroline is again leaning against her door as he comes closer taking her face in his hands. His warm palms are a distinct contrast to the cold night air with Caroline becoming mesmerized by his touch. Coming just inches from her, his eyes rove all over her face as his thumbs stroke her cheekbones. In utter seriousness, he says, "Caroline, you are a beautiful portrait of contrasts," and he claims her mouth, long though not deep with tenderness and controlled passion. Caroline's eyes close drifting in a bliss she thought she has forgotten, but remembers so quickly. Pulling away slightly, she can feel his smile on her lips before he kisses her again – sweet, tender – bottom lip, top lip, bottom lip then whispers against her mouth, "Goodnight, Caroline."

Reaching behind her, Seth opens her door handing her inside as if her Explorer were a royal carriage. Smiling through the window, he gets in his Jeep. Their engines start and they leave in opposite directions. Caroline realizes she has said nothing to him, not even goodnight, but is comforted in knowing there are no words that were enough for those few moments.

He tasted like strawberries...

"Have you SEEN the one ➤my heart LOVES?"

Song of Soloman 3:3

Chapter XIV

"Have you seen the one my heart loves?" – Song of Solomon 3:3 NIV

C aroline is able to enjoy Seth Garrett all to herself for exactly two weeks.

They talk or see each other nearly every day, dates are low-key adventures; it is a well-paced time of *getting to know you*. Tuesday of the second week, Seth invites Caroline to his house for dinner. She is more than excited, because no boy – no man – has ever made her dinner.

When the afternoon announcements begin to sound over the intercom, she packs up her stuff faster than the students getting ready for the bell and is out ahead of a few of them, turning off the lights signaling to the evening custodian she is out for the day. In her Explorer before the buses are released out front, she is at the North Gate without getting jammed in parent pickup traffic.

Through the front door, all her school gear is dropped at the bottom step and she races upstairs to her room. She knew her time would be limited after school, so Caroline has everything laid out the night before. Kicking off shoes and stripping out of her clothing, she makes a cursory glance at her decisions just to make sure it is the perfect outfit and gets in the shower.

In record time, with several minutes to spare, she pushes in the last bobby pin her hair which looks carefree and tousled like she pinned it up without looking though she has taken meticulous care with every strand. Thankful the weather has turned warm; she slips into her gauzy ivory sundress with crocheted neckline. Not yet browned from the summer sun, rub-on tan works in a pinch to take that blue-white glow from her legs.

Stepping into caramel colored, strappy leather wedges, Caroline checks to make sure there are no stray marks on her toes from the navy blue polish she is wearing today, a bold contrast to her outfit.

Looking in her dresser mirror for some final touches, she puts on her earrings, turquoise teardrops trimmed in gold, an extra-long necklace of two gold chains with dainty, flat beads in gold and clear. She dons her tissue weight ivory sweater before placing on a hammered gold ring and three thin hammered gold bangles. A final spritz of perfume and walks down the stairs.

Checking the clock – 5:25 – Caroline has some time to kill, because Seth told her to be there around 6:00 and it only takes about 15 minutes to get to his house. Not wanting to get wrinkled, she stands in front of the television and surfs stopping when she hears the host say, "*We are visiting Blackbird Bakery in historic Bristol, VA. Located just off State Street where the city is divided between Virginia and Tennessee. This 24-hour bakery is a hit with locals and a fan favorite throughout the Tri-Cities serving up everything from brownies to baklava, cakes, pies, doughnuts, and ice cream made at a Virginia creamery.*"

Caroline watches the entire segment, until it breaks for a commercial noting she wants to visit the Blackbird on her next trip the Cabin and yelps when she realizes she has wasted too much time – 5:42.

Hurrying to the door, she takes the handrail to walk down the steps cautiously in her high shoes. She loves heels and with Seth towering over her, she can wear whatever she wants without coming close to matching his height. However, Caroline hates – no abhors is a more emphatic word – the thought of falling – not off a cliff or in front of a train, just falling down, crilling an ankle, getting dirty, being a spectacle in front of an unsuspecting audience. That totally out of control feeling as your body crashes to the ground with a thud and the pain of embarrassment exceeds physical pain though knees are scuffed, palms are burning, and you are completely disoriented as you try to figure out how seconds ago you were upright and now, you are a heap on the ground. There is NEVER a graceful way to fall!

Safely on the sidewalk, she does not see the small rock, and does some quick scatter steps to keep her balance. That tingling hot wave sweeps all over her and she blows out a "WHEW!" as she makes her way to the driveway unscathed. Safe and sound, she backs up and is on her way to Seth.

Seth lives in Fairview just outside West End of Williamson and she thinks how convenient it is for him since the Armory is just a few minutes away. He told her he sometimes will run to work to complete part of his PT early in the day. She first thought he meant physical therapy, but realized without having to ask, that he was talking about daily *physical training*. She is learning that she must always be thinking Army when speaking with him, so she is sure to keep up.

Seth's house is a small, cottage with a wide front porch. White with green metal awnings shade each window indicating it was probably built sometime in the 1950's though the prime siding has been updated to white vinyl and the roof is green aluminum. Situated close to the road, it still has a very private, even secluded feel with its large, flat yard rolling down to the edge of the Tug River. There is much less traffic in this neighborhood since US 119 was improved to a four-lane several years ago diverting everyone out of town more efficiently on their way north instead of through the twists and turns of narrow highways this part of the country is famous for. Now, you are more likely to hear a train on the tracks just beyond the road than you are a passing car.

Caroline parks behind Seth and gets out eager to see inside and how he lives. She can smell the scent of cooking as she reaches the top step. The front door is open behind a wooden screen door sectioned off in nine panels and painted white. Long, wooden shutters flank the door painted a green that does not quite match the roof or awnings. The shutter to the left is cracked and a spider is peeking its head out spinning the beginnings of a web from its hiding place.

Looking through the screen, Caroline sees the living room upon immediate entrance, a darkened hall apparently leading to bedrooms is directly across from the front door, the kitchen is in the back left corner with the dining room in the front open and connecting with the living room. Noticing the spider once again, she looks for a doorbell, but none is present so she raps on the door three times and waits. A few moments pass and she has her hand raised to knock again when light floods into the hall. Seth comes out of what she assumes is the bathroom in nothing but a towel walking away from her. A surge of excitement shoots through followed by terror. She jumps away from the door hiding as best she can hoping he has not seen her. Looking around, she is certain he would not have noticed her coming in the driveway if he was in the bathroom when she pulled up. Knowing she cannot hunker outside the door, Caroline is panicked she has arrived too early and is about to tumble in unexpectedly.

Stealthily glancing back through the door, she looks to see if Seth is still in his bedroom. The hall and the front rooms are empty. Debating whether she should knock again, she hears his cell phone ring and the buzzing vibrations are coming from just a few feet away from where she is standing. Caroline moves like the Devil is chasing her and makes it back to her Explorer before Seth gets to his phone. She is nearly panting as she sits there pretending she has just arrived.

I walk around my house with nothing on all the time! What if I would have seen him naked? I would have died of embarrassment! But, I don't think I have ever seen a nicer back! My face has got to cool down and my heart stop racing before I go back up those steps! AAAGGGHHH!

She waits exactly four minutes and gets out. She locks her doors so the security horn will sound and hopefully announce her presence to a possibly not prepared Seth. Gracefully, she walks up the steps and is fairly certain her heartrate is normal and not going to result in a stroke. Again, peering through screen door and feeling like a peeping Tom, Caroline knocks much harder. She can see the light from his bedroom darken as his impressive frame fills the doorway.

"Caroline! I didn't hear you drive up," Seth shouts from his room hustling down the hall to greet her; still not quite ready, but opening the door. "I'm sorry! I got in late from work and my mom just called, so I am running behind. Can you give me a few minutes?"

Caroline fumbles with her words unable to speak clearly, because Seth smells all shaved and shower clean in a classic blue and white striped *Ralph Lauren* shirt with the polo player stitched in red, completely unbuttoned revealing an equally as strong chest complimenting the back she saw earlier, "Uhh," unsure where to settle her eyes after they have inventoried his entire body – down the sharply ironed creases of his flat front khakis to his bare feet in just a few seconds. She decides his face is the best place to focus her attention. "Uhh...sure. No worries. I'll just wait here!"

Smiling and quickly squeezing her hand, "Thanks! I'll just be a minute," he races back to his room.

Of course, you will wait for him here! Where else would you go? Recline on the end of his bed like Belle Watling and watch him get dressed? Mmm, TEMPTING!

Caroline drops her purse in the floor next to a low, dark wood credenza. Smiling, the term 'Frat Party' comes to mind as she looks at his flat-screen television perched on top – at least 60 inches. On the far end of the credenza, three jarred candles of staggered heights are flickering. Scanning the room – long, brown leather couch and matching leather recliner, both facing the television at slight angles with an end table between and what she would almost call an artsy, if not art deco lamp. A plain square coffee table is in front of the couch with the latest *Sports Illustrated* and two remotes. Two wooden chairs are in the corner like they are only brought over when necessary. There is not much in the room, but it does not feel like an empty space.

Looking in the room behind her, the walls are a shade of khaki just lighter than Seth's pants with all the woodwork white. This seems to be the same throughout all the house that she can see as well as the tightly woven Berber carpet with flecks of brown, tan, beige. The dining table is wooden and as dark as the credenza, square with four chairs. Cloth placemats in shades of blue are in front of two chairs at right angles with plates, forks, knives, and glasses ready. Three jarred candles also flicker on the table. This room is also uncluttered with sparse furnishings and neither room has window treatments, just dark wooden blinds – masculine, clean lines, not frilly. It looks like Seth.

Uncertain where to sit, she reaches for her purse to take one last look at her hair and teeth before Seth comes back out, but the strap is caught on the door handle of the credenza and when she tugs on it, an avalanche of DVDs spills out. She tries to stop them, but to no avail and is on all fours scooping and stacking when Seth walks over to her. Standing with arms crossed, she looks up at him with a guilty face and begins to rattle her head off to the annoyed and confused giant, though he is nonetheless striking.

"I was just reaching for my purse, but the strap was caught and when I gave it a yank, the door opened and all the DVDs started falling out and

I tried to stop them, but they kept coming, so I decided to put them back before you caught me snooping! I'm not snooping! Really! Honest!"

Before she finishes, Seth is squatted down beside her, "Caroline, it is no big deal. I know you're not snooping. Besides, I have nothing to hide if you were," gently chiding.

Caroline sits back with her feet folded under her with several DVDs in her lap and all of a sudden, she feels overwhelmed, awkward, and foolish – like a child ready to cry. No matter how much care she takes with her hair or clothing or makeup, nothing will hide the fact she is a complete dunder riddled with insecurity. Poise and grace is a very thin and too often an ineffective disguise. She feels very embarrassed knowing she is out of her league.

Noticing she has stopped and her head is downcast, he asks, "Hey, what's the matter? It's just some movies."

Caroline lifts her face and is unable to answer his question, because she cannot quite explain it to herself and if she attempts, she will be a blubbering mess before the end of the first sentence. Seth notices that she is close to tears looking so young and completely vulnerable, very unlike most of the women he has known. Her hair is golden and wispy, framing her face at perfect angles. The girl who was proud to say she only cries when appropriate would be shocked to know her pouting mouth with burnt coral lips makes the most inviting picture. Seth must tread lightly knowing this is not a ploy; her usual tactics for seduction. He is realizing her innocence is genuine and her confidence stems from her virtue. Her teasing and sharp tongue is a direct result of her intelligence and wit, with which most people cannot keep up.

You are in new and unfamiliar waters, Big Man. You had better be very careful!

Gently, Seth's hand cups her cheek, his thumb lightly tracing her jaw, "Caroline, it's ok. You're ok." He could not have been more clear had he said, "I understand."

Caroline's hand covers his and her eyes close as she turns and kisses his palm. Dropping their hands to her lap, he takes the rest of the movie cases from her returning them to their spot, shutting the door. Rising to his feet, he pulls her up and soothes her further, "Now, that you have seen my entire movie library, it will be easy for you to decide what we will watch after dinner when I convince you to snuggle close for two hours on the couch." He does not know if his gentle teasing has worked or pushed her over the edge, because she lunges against him resting her head on his chest. Nothing has ever felt more right, more natural than to hold her. He breathes in her hair, her scent – fruity, flirty – the feel of her warmth as her arms circle his back and her hands clutch him in near desperation, but soon relax. His one forearm holds her close as his hand rubs her shoulder while his other arm is lower tracing her spine.

Speaking against the top of her head and giving her plenty of time to decide when they should let go, "It's ok if you're not ready to eat, but if we stay this way much longer, I warn you, I will not be responsible for where my hands choose to travel," chuckling softly to ease her heart.

She lingers for just a few more brief moments, then squeezes him tight. Lifting her face to his on tiptoe, she kisses him softly in three short pecks. Resting her chin between his collar bones, the confident, teasing girl has returned. Grinning she says, "Let's eat."

Seth leads her to the table, attending to her chair then goes to the kitchen for their meal. She can see he has everything already in bowls and platters keeping them warm in the oven. More than ready to eat so she can leave that scene in the living room behind, even though Seth never once seemed flustered or frustrated. He was kind and gentle; a real tenderness from someone who so evidently displays strength.

Watching as he hurriedly gets everything in order the way he wants it. Burning his hand, he shakes his fingers, quietly cursing, and Caroline giggles. She feels much better and says, "It smells wonderful and I'm hungry!"

Glancing at her, he smiles and returns to his work. "I hope you are hungry enough not to notice my novice cooking skills."

"I can't imagine any of your skills are novice. I would venture to say apprentice, proficient, even distinguished," laughing with her last word.

Seth comes to the table with the first set of dishes with a confused face asking, "What?"

Spouting the rote memorization of educational vernacular, "Novice, Apprentice, Proficient, and Distinguished. They're education terms. Scoring guides, we use to tell you what level of progress a student is making."

Returning to the kitchen, he says over his shoulder, "And I thought the military was the only place that uses ridiculous terms that tell you absolutely nothing."

"Ha! Education is filled with them! If you are lucky enough to coin a new term and brand it with your name, people just start printing you money and you become a messiah to the neo-religious world of education," before adding with extreme sarcasm, "That is until the next *new* idea gets published and its blasphemy and Hell for Certain if you do not jump on the bandwagon of excitement!" rolling her eyes in near exasperation. "There is one thing you can hold to in education." Seth sits down at the table with her as she finishes her mild rant with delightfully colorful language he is coming to enjoy. "Department, team, learning community. Chair, head, lead. We're all teachers and should be able to recognize a synonym – different words that mean the same thing wrapped in new packages. Policy, technique, strategy – whatever you want to call it, rarely stays around for much more than three years and something new comes along. The tide comes in, but it also goes out. So, you just have to learn to roll with it and not get stressed."

Contemplative, he asks, "So you're not one of those uber-teachers? Consumed, but climbing," again recalling their first encounter, he would have definitely pegged her as one.

Smugly shaking her head with downturned mouth, "Definitely not! A flash in the pan is impressive for only a moment then is gone, usually with a personal agenda already mapped out. The faithful, the dedicated, the ones who are always there – they are impressive. They are the ones who are too often overlooked and underappreciated. The ones who roll with whatever tide is coming in and gets it done. The ones who know it is more than teaching a student, it is educating a whole person and they know that sometimes that child is there every day to eat, or to feel safe, or needs just a little more tenderness. That's when things like algebra and the periodic table and the Magna Carte are completely unimportant."

Caroline is very decided in her answer and Seth guesses she has someone specific in mind for each 'flash in the pan' and each 'faithful'. He too remembers both types of teachers from his years in school and how he was often *that child*. He asks wanting to know where she fits.

"So, you are a member of the faithful?" as he serves the meal onto each of their plates.

"Heavens no!" is her response filled with laughter. Seth is startled by her answer and humor. "I am not even close to being a good enough teacher to be considered the faithful!" smiling bright, looking as young and lovely as she did earlier; laughter painting her with a completely different brush. Seth feels he could easily get washed away in the tide of Caroline Hatfield.

"To be the faithful, teaching often has to be your first priority – it is who you are. For me, it probably doesn't clear the top five!" Seeing disbelief on his face, she clarifies, "Don't get me wrong, I love teaching. There is no better place than Belfry, hands down, but at the end of the day, it's a job." Humor gone, Caroline becomes introspective, nostalgic. "Dad told us when were young, there was something important for us to remember. 'Your job is not your life. Your spouse, your children, your home – that's your life. Your job is just what you *do* to pay for that life.' I could be at Belfry for twenty more years, or if necessary, I could leave tomorrow... Life is short and can change in an instant. Being tied to a job was never that important to me."

The air seems to sizzle around them. That was a lot of information for Seth to take in and far more than Caroline intended on sharing. She breaks their silence in jest, "Whew! I didn't mean to preach you a sermon! I promise I won't take up offering!" child-like grin returns and she squeezes his hand.

Dazed by what she just said, he loosely laces their finger and asks quietly, not adding to her comments, "Would you like to pray?" looking at her with earnest.

Her heart tumbles all over the place and he closes his eyes. "Lord, I simply want to say, thank You...AMEN."

Caroline's nerves have quieted and she finally feels relaxed. "Seth, I'm sorry. I didn't mean to get on a soapbox," picking up her fork and knife ready to dive into her plate of steamed broccoli, carrots, and cauliflower, roasted potatoes, and grilled chicken.

"No need to apologize. I liked it. You are very..." looking for the right words, "self-assured. Not many people are like that," taking a bite of carrot and potato.

"No!" laughing in near embarrassment. "I'm weird and awkward and wildly insecure!" hiding behind her glass of sweet tea.

Nonplussed, "Yes, but we're all that way. You know who you are. That's what makes you different." Seth continues to eat as if that were an obvious observation.

Caroline appreciates the compliment. "Let's change gears."

With a mouthful of food, "Ok. Go ahead."

"How long have you lived here?"

"It was a year in February."

"And how long have you been in Williamson?"

"It was a year in February."

"Oh. Where were you before you came here?"

"A few places in Pennsylvania."

"So, what brings you to the writhing metropolis of Williamson? And remember, I like long stories, so don't leave anything out," eating a way too big bite of broccoli, grinning at her lack of ladylike behavior.

"Well, the main reason I came to Williamson was for a rank change," knowing she will continue to quiz him if she thinks he is leaving out details, Seth decides to give the full story.

What is about this girl that I feel like I can tell her anything? Like she really wants to hear my story and will evaluate me without judgement.

"Rank changes can take lots of time if positions do not come available or you are not in active combat. I had been enlisted for 14 years when I moved here. It was like I was stuck as a sergeant forever."

Caroline interrupts with a question, "So, Staff Sergeant is better?"

Liking her question and her interest, "Not exactly better, but higher rank. A few more responsibilities and more pay."

Smiling with raised eyebrows, "Then it is better!"

"Yeah, I guess so," chuckling, knowing money can make some things better.

"I interrupted. You said you were stuck as a sergeant. Why was that?"

"Well..." Getting another piece of chicken, he adds, "This is all pretty boring stuff. Are you sure you want to hear it?" Seth is skeptical, believing there is something more interesting they could be talking about.

"Yes! Of course, I do. It lets me know how you got to here – who you are and in this town...Go ahead! I'm listening," forking in another mouthful.

Seth decides to give her all the details, because she has a way of ferreting them out anyway. He feels like a faucet and whenever she wants him to talk; she has to just turn the handle and everything starts pouring out.

Releasing an exaggerated sigh followed by a short growl, "I was in JROTC in high school. My stepdad, Tim was the instructor. In fact, that is how he and my mom met. She got a job as the business clerk for the high school and they started dating not long after."

Caroline would like to hear all the details of that story and more about his parents, but decides to hold her questions. She wants to hear more about Seth right now.

"During my Junior year, we went to a retreat at Camp Dawson in Kingwood, WV and took a tour of WVU. When I got home, I was really excited and announced to my mom that I was joining the Army. Not quite the news she wanted to hear. She always knew that was an option for me, but when the time finally arrived for me to start making decisions, she was not thrilled. We compromised and filed for early enlistment with the Pennsylvania National Guard 28th Infantry Division in Holidaysburg. I completed basic training that summer, because I had already turned 17, but would return to school that fall and graduate as normal. Also, I would be in sort of semi-deferment of active duty until I finished college. I would still complete all the 'One weekend a month. Two weeks a year,'" mimicking an ad campaign, "but I would not be called upon unless necessary. So, Mom's plan was that college would serve as a diversion and any grand ideas about the Army would be out of my system."

"If you were in JROTC and already enlisted while in college, why didn't you come out as an officer? I thought that's how it worked?"

Seth is pleased she has enough knowledge to ask good questions and still be interested in what he has to say. "That is one option, but I decided not to go that route. I believed the best officers are not just educated, but made from experienced soldiers. I chose to stay as *enlisted* improving my rank, then I would go to OCS – Officer Candidate School – later."

Caroline is very impressed with his answer shining light on his character. She has finished eating and her arms are folded in front of her plate ready to gobble up anything else Seth will say. So instead of stopping there, he continues.

"I ended up staying at WVU a fifth year getting a double major."

"What in?"

"Political Science and Comparative Literature."

"Really? That's an interesting combination," she is a little surprised.

"It's no more interesting than biology and social studies!" answering with a mocking smile.

"You are correct. The Poli-Sci is believable, but the Comparative Literature is a bit of a stretch."

"To be honest…Political Science is because I considered going to Law School…The Literature is because this really hot girl was in front of me in line at Freshman Orientation. She registered for a poetry class, so I took it. Sadly, I never saw her again. I liked the class and took another in the Spring and before I knew it, I had a double major."

Caroline laughs at his explanation. "The hot girl sounds about right, but I'm still not convinced," looking at him with eyes filled with speculation and mirth.

Leaning back in his seat, he taps the fingers of both hands on the edge of the table. "Want me to prove it?" he challenges.

Resting her chin on the heel of an up-drawn hand, her eyes with their inky-black lashes begin to speak before her mouth does, in sultry tones, "If you think you can."

Seth is out of his chair and down the hall before she realizes what he is doing. He is gone for a few moments and returns carrying a picture frame. She assumes it is his diploma as he reaches it to her. Sitting down, Seth waits as Caroline reads.

Looking up after she is finished, "This is beautiful. What is it?" confused smile on her face knowing he does not just have framed poetry lying around his house.

"Comparative Literature. I wrote it," pleased he has trumped her and proud of his work.

"You wrote it?" she asks in disbelief as she looks back at the clean font of the print framed by a navy-blue matte. Before she has time to read it again, Seth begins to speak.

The day in which we first met,
I know my heart stopped for a moment.

Your eyes, the window to your soul,
are icy pools in which all of Neptune's great waters cannot compare.

Your laughter is as pure and gentle as the morning song of the sparrow.

Your voice can calm the raging sea
or comfort the hurt of a sorrowful child.

How I long to breech the chasm between us,
for my love, I know you not.

You are present in my thoughts and dreams,
then I awake, only to find you are not there.

You are always beyond the realm of my grasp;
in my sight, but never within reach.

I pray that during this lifelong journey,
Our paths will someday cross.

To find us bound for eternity,
Living the dream that once was.

Caroline cannot decide what has captivated her more – his voice, his words, or just the manner in which he is speaking, but she is moved. "Seth, that is…is so beautiful! Such talent!"

Seth is pleased by her admiration while modest enough for a faint color to rise in his cheeks. "Nah. It was just an assignment and you were convinced not to believe me!" he jabs at her as she hands back the frame.

Caroline is quick to defend, "I *believed* you! I was just meaning that it didn't seem to fit this picture I guess I have of you!" Her face is much pinker than Seth's fearful she has offended him, chalking up yet another blunder. "I could never write or say anything like that…that lyrical and haunting," looking at him again with intensity that makes him not want to look away, but also makes him feel like she is seeing so much more than

183

he would like to show. "My words come out sounding cold and intellectual; misinterpreted as arrogant, emotionless."

Remembering the initial picture, he had of her, and having those same assumptions, describing her with nearly the exact words, Seth begins to figure her out. "There is nothing wrong with intellectual and even arrogant at times, but anyone who would think you are cold and emotionless has not taken the time to try to know who you are."

Seth has seen this girl run the gamut of emotions in a few short days. Not a psycho witch that is screaming one minute and crying the next. Caroline feels very deeply, is moved by simple actions, recognizes important moments when you are still in them not after they are gone, but in order to keep herself in check from spilling all that out, she self-protects. She locks all that emotion away behind confidence and wit and poise, because it is a rare individual who can match her depth and if they do, would need as much strength as she is willing to give.

"How about I help you clean up?" Caroline brings them both back to reality.

Smiling at her offer knowing she is sincere and would probably find a way to make washing dishes fun, Seth declines. "No, there are just a few. I can get them later."

Standing, she picks up her plate, "I really don't mind. It won't take but a few minutes," and is reaching for her glass when Seth takes her hand.

"Caroline, no," he is firm and does not expect her to politely argue further. "I don't want to do dishes."

Unmoving, she bites her lips together, setting her plate back down. Tugging at her hand, he leads her from the table to the couch. He occupies the corner and pulls her next to him, so she does not try to scamper away. Caroline offers no resistance and tucks her feet under facing him with her elbow bent on the back cushions with his arm stretching out to meet her, toying with her sleeve or hand, not annoying or fidgeting, but certain his touch does not leave her.

"So why did you entitle it *My Beloved*? Did you have someone particular in mind?" she asks so straightforward there is no need to not proceed with honesty.

"Not really, but maybe I thought so a little then," wondering what she was going to ask next.

"So, what was the assignment? What made you write such stirring lines?"

Again, Caroline's genuine interest and ease at asking questions has him spilling so much information. "We had to choose one of the excerpts that was covered in class, there was about a hundred of them, and write a poem – prose or verse – that had the same essence as the original piece. I chose the *Song of Solomon*, because it was the closest to being like a poem to begin with. He wrote some pretty powerful stuff – risqué for the Bible!" teasing and a little shocked he found such *stirring lines* in scripture.

"It's not risqué. It is beautiful! I love it! Powerful lines are a dying art. No one talks that way anymore, so occasionally, someone should write them," her face lighting up as the back of her hand touches her forehead in a silent film swoon.

Seth goes on to further explain, "When I was doing my research, it was hard for me to quite understand the author – Solomon. One place I read depicted him as a misogynist and used his power to just increase the size of his harem and probably was captivated by the girl for just a moment before moving on to his next conquest. Another talked about how the girl was only a metaphor and that Solomon was actually talking to God. That was *really* hard for me to believe, because some of that stuff I don't think you hear preached on Sunday!" sucking his teeth with a very animated face like they should not be discussing this.

Caroline does not skirt the subject. "*I am my Beloved's and he is mine!* That is poetry!" swooning a little again, but then becoming more serious. "The first time I read it, I also thought it was a little shocking! I have since read it several times and even did a Small Group study on it. I think Solomon was talking about a specific woman, but also God. The poetry, the metaphor, is that Solomon – in all his wisdom – still did not have adequate words to describe his *Beloved* and was so swept away by her. So, if we can imagine the overwhelming flood that stimulates all the senses as Solomon talked about – that love you can only feel for another – is still surpassed by the love God has for us…That is powerful!"

Seth has always been so filled with doubts, always questioning, needing something more, but listening to Caroline, she is not spouting rehearsed verses drilled into her from childhood days of Sunday School or catechism. Like with most of her answers, she believes them with confidence. Seth looks at her with subtle dejection, "Yeah…but that doesn't make it any easier to believe."

Caroline's belief, her faith is not 'in your face' – cross around her neck, fish on her bumper, the only topic she can discuss. It is also something that is not compartmentalized; an aspect of her life she acknowledges only on Sunday. It is soft and gentle, like an essence or an aura that surrounds and envelopes her; seamlessly part of her life from which you cannot separate her into different entities. Her faith is who she is, not something she has. Seth is immediately pleased to finally meet someone with that conviction, but also afraid she will figure out he is woefully lacking in faith or the confidence to believe in much of anything.

Her face says she has many questions, but chooses to ask just one. "Have you ever met God?"

How wonderfully simple; like God was a friend that would stop by to sit on your porch swing and talk, drinking lemonade. Seth becomes nervous and uncomfortable. He cannot get further away from her, because he planned sitting this way so he could control – or at least lead – where the evening went. He is held prisoner by her simple question, but not threatened. He wants to answer, but is afraid the magical moments of the last two weeks will be lost in the honest admission of his disbelief. So, he chooses aversion. "We may not be friends any longer, if I told you all my thoughts on religion," feeling the heat rise in his chest, knowing he will not be able to explain to Caroline something he does not even understand.

In a very decided tone, she clarifies, "That's not what I asked…Meeting God is about a relationship. I'm not a fan of religion either."

Seth is able to answer hoping she will understand this is not something he wants to talk about – at least not yet. "Ok…Let's say, I've been *avoiding* Him."

Lips pursed and shaking her head, "Hmm, you can run for a long time, but eventually, you will tire." Leaning slightly closer to him, she lays her palm on his chest, "One day, I'll introduce you."

Before he can say he is not so sure about that, she pulls away and fires another question. "Have you ever been married?"

Laughing and shocked, "Goodness! You don't let up!" pinching her thigh until she squeals at his playfulness.

"Ouch!" swatting at his free hand that is now resting on her leg. "You obviously wanted to talk about something else, and I changed subjects! Sooo, have you been married?"

"No."

"Ever been close?"

"Not really."

"Why not? You seem like a real catch!" flirtatiously teasing and laughing in his face; not mocking and completely cute.

Near scowling, he offers, "Would *timing* be an acceptable answer?"

"Hmm…for now! But, I know what you mean. Timing is a big thing. Sometimes I feel like I am married to Belfry High School and that all aspects of my life are somehow connected to it. There are days when I would LOVE a divorce, or at least a trial separation!" laughing at her own joke behind a curled hand with glistening navy nails.

Seth has never enjoyed talking to anyone more, but is ready for conversation to end and for him to have a little more control over the evening, "Is there anything else you would like to interrogate me about?" as he takes a more possessive hold onto her arm while his other hand is enjoying the linen feel of her dress with the hem that falls just at her knees and is brushing up against his leg.

Tapping a single finger to her lips, she looks around the room to agitate him further loving – what did Sophie call it? Cat and Mouse? Ah, but who is the cat and who is the mouse? "Hmm…I really like your tables. Wheredjagetem?" intentionally being silly.

Cool confidence, Caroline is thrilled by the arrogance to his voice, "I made them."

"Really?" she asks before she realizes she again sounds like she is doubting him.

Disappointed he has opened another can and her questions will start worming out, "Yep! All of them including the cabinet and the table and chairs in the dining room."

Whipping her head around to again look at all the pieces, "Seth, they are so nice and the craftsmanship on the credenza is clean and modern and the corners are dovetailed!"

Pleased she is impressed with his work and if she knew how alluring it was for her to know what a dovetail even was much less appreciate its purpose, and that he finds her intellectual conversation *more* than stimulating and definitely not *emotionless*, this very good girl would have jumped off the couch! Unwilling for her to turn this into their very own episode of the *New Yankee Workshop*, he says, "I thought it was just a cabinet and are we seriously going to talk about tables?"

Innocently, she asks, "Why? What's wrong with that? I was just admiring your talents." Thinking he finally has the upper hand, Caroline cleverly, coyly, and with near masterful technique, changes the tone and direction of the conversation. "Do you have many more?

Seth's heart races and the fire returns to his chest, "Several." Knowing his answer is heavily laced with suggestions they will not explore this evening, *Thoroughbred* and *Kentucky Derby* flash through his mind.

"Really?" is Caroline's echoed response though now it holds no evidence of doubt.

"Want me to prove it?" Seth challenges, but he knows he must keep himself reigned in not wanting to be embarrassed if Caroline should have to nor get too far ahead and ruin something potentially wonderful, because he lacks control.

"If you think you can." Caroline's voice is teasing and seductive, but he waits.

Her lips smile wickedly for just an instant and one eyebrow raises. The gauntlet is thrown down! Grabbing her by the waist, Caroline shrieks with delight as Seth hauls her onto his lap.

"Now, young lady," whispered and husky, he is so close to her face, she can feel his breath on her skin. "No more questions."

"Yes, Mr. Garrett."

They smile against each other's lips and the rest of the evening is spent as mildly reckless teenagers with Caroline finding out he is in fact very talented and Seth is also particularly well pleased.

Yes, for two weeks exactly, Caroline is able to enjoy Seth all to herself… but Thursday arrives.

Chapter XV

"...you may be sure that your sin will find you out."
– Numbers 32:23 NIV

The bell rings Thursday afternoon and the hall music begins to play. Seniors file out, with a few lingering behind asking about scholarship information that is due at the Guidance Office on Monday.

"Ms. Hatfield, I have all of my application completed, but I need one more recommendation letter. You wrote me one in the fall for the WYMT Scholar. Could you just tweak that one for me?" Jordan Baisden asks. "Grr! Jordan! How long have you known about this scholarship? It is due *Monday* and you are asking for a Letter of Recommendation on *Thursday?*" Caroline grills him even though making the necessary changes to his letter will only take a few minutes. Besides, she does not mind – it is for Jordan Baisden.

During his sophomore year, he was barely above mediocre and a below average student making solid D's as he fondly put it. Towards the end of the Spring Semester, every teacher was assigned a group of students to conference with about their plans for the future and to see if they were on track to reach personal goals. Jordan was in Caroline's group. He was goofy and hilarious, encouraging everyone to watch cat videos, complaining *Hot Pockets* were not sold at lunch, or giving anyone who spoke to him ridiculous nicknames like 'General Monkey Brains' or 'Pocket-Protector Superhero'. His future was making it from one laugh to the next.

He comes in that day and sits in the student desk that is pulled over next to hers, making foolish small talk, Jordan says, "Alright, Ms. Hatfield, let's talk about my future!"

189

"Ok, let's," as Caroline opens his student file. "Jordan, if you could pick your dream job, what would it be?"

Confused and almost frustrated, he asks, "I thought we were supposed to talk about me going to Summer School again this year and how I'm not going to make it to college. What's this?"

Reassuring him, "We'll get there, but this is where I like to start. So, tell me – DREAM JOB – what would it be?" Caroline is eager to hear, because she has always liked Jordan despite his constant antics.

Jordan mellows and becomes contrite, even embarrassed as he looks away from Caroline and replies, "I don't know…You wouldn't believe me if I told you…or you'd laugh!"

Most students who did not want to talk would say just anything to get by or lie. Jordan obviously wanted to tell otherwise he would have used different tactics. Caroline is firm in her reassurance. "I will not laugh. Tell me. What would you like to be?"

Without hesitation, Jordan blurts out, "The president of the Atlanta Falcons!" and waits for Caroline's response to which he is surprised.

"Ok," and she writes on his form.

Disbelief and shock creep into his face and voice, "Ok?!? You mean you don't think that's stupid?"

Again, calm and collected, "Nope. It's a Dream Job, so you must dream big. I hope you do then I will move to Atlanta and you will hire me for some sweet position where I hang out with professional athletes and celebrities and make lots of money!" smiling like she was already plotting their success.

Jordan's face lights up with excitement, "So you think I can do it?"

"Not at all!"

Jordan's face flames and his anger rises, "I thought you said you wouldn't laugh!"

Leaning closer to him and taking on one of the many teacher voices that any skilled professional comes to master through the years, "Jordan, I'm not laughing at you. I'm being honest." He sits back with thin lips pressed together and graciously takes all the honesty she is ready to dish out to him. "Jordan, for two years, you have been a waste. Not as a person, but a student. You are one of the most popular kids at this school, everyone knows your name and is always talking to you. You won class president by a landslide two years in a row and whenever you walk into a room, you are a commanding presence! But," looking at him with only slight fierceness, "But, you waste all of your talent and energy at being a buffoon neglecting your intellect."

Knowing her scolding has been enough, Caroline changes tone to one of encouragement. "The reason I said that you will not be the president of the Atlanta Falcons is not because you can't, you will simply not be prepared. Guys who have those jobs oftentimes are former athletes, businessmen, or lawyers. You don't play any sports and your grades are definitely not getting you into law school."

Jordan bursts out in his own defense, "But I am their biggest fan! I know every stat for the last ten years and I never miss watching a game!" His face is near pleading as he attempts to convince Caroline of his merit.

Smiling, she moves in to comfort, "Jordan, I have no doubt that you are, but there are probably thousands just like you…Now, you want to be the president of the Atlanta Falcons. What do we have to do to get you there?"

Shocked again by her frankness and her apparent belief he could do it or at least try, Jordan decides to listen. "What do I have to do, Ms. Hatfield?"

The remainder of the hour, Caroline and Jordan discuss his academic future at Belfry High School, possible options for college, Jordan admitting his parents have already told him their funds are very limited on helping, encouraging him to get involved in more extracurricular activities, signing him up with a weekly after school tutor.

Their conversation comes towards its end and Jordan adds, "You said I should be a football player. I'm too fat and slow to play and doubt they would even take me as a junior," his dejection returning.

Caroline thinks and in a moment of genius, comes up with the perfect solution for Jordan. "How about you just join the athletic program? You could be an equipment manager! That way you are part of the team, but you don't have to be a player! What do you say?" Caroline is thrilled by her idea and hopes Jordan agrees.

"I can't just become a manger! What am I supposed to do?" His words are fussing, but Caroline knows his mind is interested and his heart has to be pounding a little harder.

Caroline does not want to argue and goes out on a limb for Jordan. Picking up her phone, she waits for the man on the other end to answer, "Coach Brewer, I have a student who would like to be an equipment manager...Yes, he is with me right now...Jordan Baisden...Ok. Thanks so much. I'll tell him," and she hangs up the phone. "Coach Brewer says for you to come to the complex and talk to him."

"Really?!?" Jordan is picking up his stuff and on his way to the door before Caroline can answer. "Thanks, Ms. Hatfield!"

The next day he comes in carrying two t-shirts, two polos, a hat, and mesh shorts telling her all about how he was the new equipment manager and that he was just in time for Spring Practice. At the door, Jordan calls back to her, "Thanks again, Ms. Hatfield!"

Now, two years later, Jordan Baisden is again asking for her help. It is with pride and privilege that she is honored to help him. He went on the be the equipment manager for the football, basketball, and baseball teams, his grades made a complete 180, and he will be offering the Student Address at Senior Banquet in a few weeks. Jordan is one of those reasons, as rare as they may occur, as to why Caroline loves being a teacher – the student. The student that works hard, shows they are deserving, knows what it means to want something and they go after it. The student that makes your heart sing, "This is why I teach!" Jordan is a portrait of redemption.

"I'm sorry Ms. Hatfield. I have been filling out so many, I got this one confused. I thought it asked for just a narrative and your number, because you were going to be called for a phone reference, but it wants a letter, too." Kind and mannerly, he gives her a sheepish smile.

"Jordan, not because you are just anyone...I'll have it ready in the morning."

Taking the hand of the sweetest girl Caroline has ever had in class, whom Jordan has been dating since before Christmas and will join him at Alice Lloyd College in the Fall, Jordan leaves, but offers one of his signature goofy statements, "I'll get you a box of *Hot Pockets* for your trouble!" and laughs down the hallway.

Caroline laughs as well, but his absence from the room leaves a pressure on her heart. *Jordan, there will never be another one like you!*

Before she has time to get lost in her thoughts, Nick enters and saunters over to the desk Jordan has just vacated. With exaggerated movements, he sits down, before he says anything. Continuing his little charade, Caroline finally asks, because she knows he wants something.

"Nicholas, is there something you want?" using a very teacher voice with him as well, ready for his own brand of antics.

He responds quickly, "Not much, Sissy. I'm just here to ask how you are doing."

Caroline just looks at him and flatly answers, "Fine. How are you?"

Becoming more theatrical, gesturing and animated face, "Oh I'm just fine! ...But are you sure you are just fine? Possibly *more* than fine?" steepling his hands, he leans his lips to his fingers.

Caroline refuses to be baited, "Ok. I'm more than fine. I'm good, maybe even great. Is that what you want to hear?" careful to not allow fear or ire enter her voice. She crosses her legs and swivels her chair to face more directly him, attempting a casually relaxed pose though she is confident Nick has used Sherlock Holms methods to find out about her recent secret activities.

"Really?" looking to her for confirmation, which he does not get. Nick knows his sister is not going to confess, but he does not mind. This little interrogation will be near torture for her and an absolute pleasure for him. Pouring on the theatrics, Nick adds melodrama to his voice laced with surprise and delighted shock. "Did you really say, 'Great'? This Spring weather must be good for you."

"It is. I have always loved Spring," flatter this time for effect.

"Yes, Spring is wonderful...But are you sure there is nothing else besides *Spring* in the air that is making the days GRRREAT?!?" devilish smile, illuminated eyes. Nick is patient and will allow Caroline to drag this on.

Without looking away and showing Nick the fighting side to her that he does not see enough, Caroline answers in coy notes, "Nicholas, I have no idea what you mean."

Jerking back in his chair and shaking a finger in her face, "You are lying!" ready to roar with laughter. He has her hooked and is going to reel her in.

Caroline remains poised. Nick will have to say the words, because she is not going to volunteer any information he may not already have. It would be just like Nick to only have an inkling of an idea and somehow get Caroline to answer all his questions revealing the truth. NOT THIS TIME!

"Nick! You're crazy! I'm not lying! I love Spring!" she shouts at him avoiding his other comments.

Nick leans in low on his desk, suggestion and doubt curling around each of his words. "You have been pleasantly…*preoccupied* for the last two weeks. For the last two weeks, you have been much slower in returning my messages and calls. For the last two weeks, you have been scarce at the house and when I have come down the hill looking for you, you are often not home. For the last two weeks, you have been more than a little mysterious and I have been on a secret quest to find out what is going on. The pieces came together slowly at first, then it dawned on me." He should have said, "Elementary, my dear Watson!" to take the character even further. "What happened two weeks ago? Why do I continue to meet a green Jeep? Never in the cove, but out in Forest Hills. Why is there so much student chatter that includes your name?" Leaning even closer to Caroline and whispering, "Don't lie to me sister, dear…You have a man!"

Unable to control the red flood that takes over her face, Caroline shouts denials, because Nick has caught her. "I do not! You are ridiculous!" Her foot falls to the floor and she spins away from him knowing her two weeks of secret dates and midnight phone calls, clandestine activities to keep suspicions down is over. Enjoying Seth all to herself is over. Whispering in a near defeated voice, she asks without looking at him, "How do you know?"

Roguish smile of victory is all over his face. "Weeelll, like I said the pieces came together slowly…But, what tipped me off was during homeroom this morning. Abigail Preston said she saw you Pikeville and you were with a tall, very attractive man. Being a 17-year-old girl, she naturally thought it was your boyfriend. So, you can imagine my surprise when I knew nothing about him…Have never met him, but you are gallivanting all over the county, apparently hiding him only from your family!" now looking hurt and disappointed.

"I've not been hiding him! I just wanted to keep him to myself…for a little while," Caroline smiles at her brother. He knows how she feels and appreciates her honesty.

"So, who is he? What's his name?" Nick is ready for Caroline to do the talking and fill in the gaps he is missing.

Caroline's face is puzzled, confused by his questions. "What do you mean who is he? It's Seth. Didn't you know that, already?"

Nick is equally as confused, "Seth? Seth who? I just figured it was someone you met at the college. One of those dorky professor-types. I don't know Seth."

Caroline's face scowls at her brother. He has always teased her about working at the college, eager to label her as a nerd or a lab rat. It does give her a thrill, however, to proudly explain it is Seth.

"No, you smart-aleck punk! Seth Garrett – the guy from the Armory. We had lunch with him a couple of weeks ago. You met him!"

Nick's roar is of shock and pleasure. "Caroline! That soldier who you acted like a maniac in front of at lunch? I would have never thought he would talk to you again! But good for you! It was so obvious you were attracted to him in the first moment."

She chooses to ignore his insult that is somehow wrapped in a minor compliment. She does not give all the details about the last two weeks – only the highlights. Nick would not appreciate her girly swoons or how she has analyzed the two weeks and has ridden on a cloud the whole time. When she finishes, Nick has been absorbed in her retelling.

"So, we have seen each other almost every day and I really enjoy him.'

"And that's all?" Nick probes to see if she is holding out.

"That's all. I really like him, too! But, that's all," Caroline beams and Nick quickly notes he has not seen his sister this happy in a while. He also mentally notes to question Darby if she has heard about Caroline's new romance and has kept it a secret from him.

"Great! Is he coming to dinner?"

"When? Tonight? With Mom and Dad? I doubt it!" frightened for the first time since she mentioned Seth to Nick.

"Caroline, it is not like you can keep hiding him. Students have seen you, I know about him, and didn't you say you have been together nearly every day?" Nick offers her sincere advice. "He's not in 10th grade, so he will begin to wonder why he has not met anyone in your life – especially when your entire family is in this town. Call him. Bring him to dinner tonight. It is just going to be me, Mom, and Dad. Darby has to work and Gran is with Alex until Saturday."

Caroline knows this would be the easiest way to introduce Seth without overwhelming him with the whole family all at once, but is still unsure. Nick recognizes her struggle and makes it easy for her.

"Well, I know he exists and that is going to be hard to keep to myself. Besides, I don't like hiding secrets from Mommy and how will her heart be broken that her only daughter and very best friend is not telling her about her new beau?"

Nick rises to leave after he drives that last nail into her coffin. At the door, he turns back to instruct her further, "Call him! I'll see you two at dinner," and he is down the hall expecting her to do exactly as he says.

Caroline knows he is right. Seth has even asked lots of questions about her family, he knows there are several, even hinting at meeting them. Caroline also knows her mother, who is her very best friend and with whom she shares everything, will be hurt if she keeps Seth a secret much longer.

Charlotte will be a hard sell. She will take time to warm up to Seth; not one of those mothers who adore a new boyfriend immediately. He will be under her magnifying glass for a while before she consents to come anywhere close to giving her blessing. Clay will quietly be in Charlotte's camp letting her decide when to fully welcome Seth. In the meantime, he will make Seth completely comfortable and close to overwhelmed with hospitality. He will be very interested in who *this boy* is and in a relaxed manly fashion, can interrogate him probably learning more than Caroline does.

Looking at her phone, Caroline knows it is time and dials. One ring – ANSWER! Two rings – DON'T PICK UP! Three rings – GO TO VOICEMAIL!

"Hello, Pretty Girl!" Seth's honey coated voice thrills her every time.

Feeling frisky, "Have I told you how much I like it when you say that?"

"Nope," smiling at her sweetness.

"Well, I do!" leaning back in her chair using one foot to swivel back and forth.

"Good! Because I like saying it," a little extra honey coating. "What do you have planned for us this evening?" mildly teasing, but so glad she called. Seth has also enjoyed Caroline all to himself these past two weeks, and even though greenlights have been everywhere, there is still hesitancy. He does not want to overwhelm her and then have her tire of him.

"That's what I was calling you about," nervousness ripples through him, but is quickly alleviated. "My parents invited me to dinner at their house tonight and I was wondering if you would like to join us?" As soon as those words leave her mouth, Caroline is a nervous as a cat and begins to rattle. In a saner moment, she would have accused herself of gobbling like Aunt Nadine. "If you don't want to that's fine! We can meet afterwards. Or, I don't have to go. It's just going to be them and Nick, the one you met at school. Really, you don't have to come, but I would like you to, but either way is ok." Caroline stops talking by putting her hand over her mouth convinced she has him confused as to what she really wants, but Seth is clear.

"Caroline, I would love to have dinner. I want to meet your parents. What time should I pick you up?" There is no balking, there is no apprehension that it is too soon to meet her parents, there is no awkward pause like he is thinking of an excuse not to come.

Caroline swallows hard before removing her hand from her mouth. "Around 6:00 will be fine."

"Then I will see you at 6:00, Pretty Girl. Bye!"

"Bye…" How would Marsha Brady describe Seth – just dreamy!

Taking a quick spin in her chair as a modified victory lap, Caroline giggles and taps her feet in excitement. Yes, this was going to be a rip-the-*Band-Aid*-off-moment when she walks in with Seth, but Nick will be there and he can act as a buffer. Thursday night dinner with her parents is usually more than casual, but Seth is joining them, so she rushes home.

I wonder if I should call Mom and give her a heads up? What if she has not planned for extra? What if she thinks the house is a wreck or she changed into mismatched comfy clothes with holes or paint stains? She will kill me! Maybe Nick will tell her…Hopefully, Nick will tell her.

Caroline does not take time to think about it or decide. She just goes home to get ready for Seth, who arrives at 5:57 shower clean and smelling delicious wearing a cotton button-up in the tiniest print in shades of blue, with cuffs turned exposing thick, strong wrists, dark, tailored jeans, and lace-up boots in dark brown distressed leather – fashionable and a touch of trendy. Opening the door to him, he takes her breath away how he can transform into so many characters so effortlessly with each more appealing than the last.

Seth's eyes take her all in from head to feet, then back again. Caroline's hair is a messy curled tumble across her shoulders and midway down her back that her hands are always in and where Seth would like to find his hands right now. Her thin navy blue sweater has a wide v-neck with four small, shiny buttons that look like they are marching their way to the hollows of her collar bone where a delicate silver disk is suspended on a silver chain bearing her monogramed initials. She is also wearing dark jeans – snug across her curves and angles, flared at the ankle showing three python straps just behind red shiny toes. Of all the colors of polish she wears, shocking red is his favorite.

Seth does not wait to be invited in, but comes through the door with his arms around her waist and his lips whispering on her neck, "I've changed my mind...I don't want to meet your parents...Because when they see the hunger in my eyes has nothing to do with dinner, they will throw me out and lock you in your room!"

Enjoying being swept away by him too much, Caroline giggles, "You wicked boy! What am I going to do with you?" her lips grazing the edge of his ear and temple as her hands circle his neck, two fingers slipping inside his collar loving the feel of his warm skin.

Still nuzzling her neck, Seth replies, "I could offer a few suggestions!"

Caroline squeals and exclaims, "Seth! Hush that!" smacking his shoulder. "Come on! We have to go. Besides, you have already put enough marks on my neck...My mother is bound to get suspicious!"

Gnawing on her even more, Caroline runs her fingers into his hair and gives his nape a none-too-gentle tug. "Seth Garrett! I told you to stop!"

Growling, he pulls away, obediently taking her hand, and leading her to his Jeep.

"Don't be nervous if my mother is quiet, because she probably will be. She's just sizing you up; not in a bad way, but she is. She won't rush over to meet you and hug and gush. My dad will do most of the talking and she will just be taking you all in." He thinks how Caroline's mother's evaluation of him may be very different than her daughter's. "Dad will ask lots of questions. He's not nosy, just very interested." Caroline does not seem nervous, but is giving him lots of play-by-play warnings.

Seth stops short of her door and asks, "Should I be worried?"

Caroline looks at him with complete certainty, "Not at all. Just giving you a heads-up."

Seth still does not move and asks in all seriousness, "Hey, are we just having dinner or am I *meeting* your parents?"

Caroline's eyes are wide, concerned for the first time this may be too early of a step in their very new relationship, so she answers honestly. "Is it ok if it is a little bit of both?"

Seth sighs feeling relieved and a whisper of anxiety that was not present two minutes ago. Smiling, his voice is deep and full of emotion in his simple reply, "Yes," and he opens her door.

Chapter XVI

"...firmly tied, fell in the blazing furnace." – Daniel 3:23 NIV

"CLAY! Caroline is here!" Charlotte calls to her husband as she sets the table making several trips from the kitchen.

"I'm ready!" Clay shouts back at his wife, tucking in the tail of his shirt following his extended bathroom visit. Charlotte scowls as she crosses in front of him and he gives her behind a playful whack of warning, "You had better watch your sassy self!" Walking to the front room, Clay looks out the double French doors and informs his wife, "It's not Caroline! It's some guy in a Jeep...Wait! It is Caroline...The guy is with her!" Turning to Charlotte, he asks, "Do you know who this is?"

Charlotte sets the bowl she is carrying on the table to join her husband looking out the door. Watching the tall, young man get out of the Jeep, he comes around and opens her door. Taking Caroline's hand, they start up the sidewalk towards the porch. Charlotte is mixed with feelings of shock, disbelief, and even dread.

"No, I don't know who he is, but they are obviously together," her mind reels and starts barking out orders. "Let them in. I have to go to the bathroom," walking back through the house, she shouts upstairs, "Nicholas! Get down here!" shutting herself behind her bedroom door.

In her bathroom, she brushes her teeth for the second time since coming home from work. Opening her makeup drawer, she hurriedly completes some touchups and runs damp hands through her messy pixie hair getting it to kick out in all the right places. Back in her room, she changes her shirt, because the one she is wearing still bears the grape jelly stain when one of her students dropped their toast at breakfast. Standing before the full-length mirror on the back of her door, Charlotte smooths her hands across her waist and hips, as pleased as she will be with her appearance, and begins to wonder.

Who is this guy? Why has Caroline not told me about him? How long have they been together?

Blinking back several thoughts and maybe a few tears, Charlotte opens her door as Nick bounds down the steps. Before he can get by her to join everyone in the living room, Charlotte grabs his arm and gives it a pinch, viciously whispering, "You are in big trouble, Mister!"

Nick squirms and laughs, "I'm not the one you should be talking to! Caroline is the one keeping secrets!"

She cannot quiz him now with Caroline and Seth just steps away, but Nick knows his mother will expect a full explanation; at least his version before either of them sleep tonight. When he makes it to the doorway of the living room, he turns and motions, silently mouthing, "Aren't you coming?" Pausing, he waits for Charlotte just out of the view of the doorway, then placing his hand respectfully on her back he leads her in to join the others, then abandons her.

"Seth! It's great to see you again! I'm glad you could make it for dinner!" Nick leaves his mother, and as if he and Seth are old friends, gives him a strong handshake and a pat on his back. He is intent on making him comfortable, because he already knows how happy his sister is. He also knows his mother will feel very awkward tonight – total stranger with *Caroline*. He is going to go out of his way to make this a good evening, even if he irritates his mother a little in the process; that will just be a bonus!

"It is good to see you as well! I am so glad I could join you all this evening," returning an equally as confident handshake. Seth is pleased that Nick is such a commanding presence in the room. It does not matter if you are a teenage or a full-grown adult, meeting a girl's parents is usually a nerve-racking event. Seth is also reminded how much he enjoyed Caroline's brother when they first met. These few moments are just additional confirmation of that day.

"Yes, me too. Besides, Caroline could not hide you away forever!" leaning in to tease his sister and letting her know he will be her ally this evening, "And she is not too good at keeping secrets." Letting go of Seth's hand, but keeping one on his shoulder to continue to guide him through

201

the evening, Nick continues to control the room. "Seth, I guess you have met our dad," nodding towards Clayton, Nick can already see his dad is well pleased, he turns to their mother – the hard sell. "Let me introduce you to our mother, Charlotte."

Charlotte has not been hovering at the doorway, but she is close. She had hoped Clay would come to her rescue or at least bring her into the conversation, but with that chatterbox Nick doing all the talking, she instantly feels out of place in her own home. Nick extends his arm to her invite her in to their impromptu circle of introductions. When she hesitates, Nick glares, only for her to see, jolting her back to reality and if by force of will, she moves towards the very tall and very attractive young man who moments earlier had a possessive hold on her daughter. Before she can speak, Seth does.

"It is very nice to meet you, Mrs. Hatfield. Thank-you for having me. The lunch Nick brought us at school was delicious, so I am very much looking forward to dinner." Seth shakes her hand with appropriate firmness and maintains strong eye contact until she speaks.

However, Charlotte is unable to respond. Her mind is running in fifty directions. She looks at Seth then glances at Clay wondering why he looks so composed, like this evening was planned instead of her daughter, her *only* daughter showing up with a man Charlotte has never met; one whom her daughter has failed to mention even exists!

I make lunch for Nick almost every Thursday. Which Thursday is Seth talking about? How long has Caroline been seeing this boy? When did Nick meet him?

She does not know what to say, because Seth's words sound like Charlie Brown's teacher. She again must be prompted to enter the conversation.

"Mom?"

Caroline's questioning voice reminds her she must speak and alerts her that she has obviously been standing dumbfounded for longer than comfortable, so she says the first thing that comes to mind.

"When was it you had lunch with Nick?" this would answer several questions at one time, completely forgetting that she has yet to exchange any simple pleasantry with Seth or even acknowledge introductions. Withdrawing her hand, she looks to him for answers.

Nick rolls his eyes at his mother, which she completely ignores while

Caroline's face is panicked disappointment. Clayton notices his wife's mild rudeness and does not become angry, but recognizes her tactics. Everyone – minus Charlotte – is pleased with Seth's unflustered and almost prepared response.

"That was two weeks ago today, ma'am. I met Caroline that day as well. I was at the high school with Cpt. Tyler giving a presentation for Career Assembly."

Charlotte is irked that his words do not seem the least rehearsed and is so comfortable saying them. It is like he knew she was fishing for information and was pleased to oblige her. Instead of relaxing, Charlotte probes further.

"Cpt. Tyler? Where do you work?"

"At the Armory in West End, ma'am. I'm in the West Virginia National Guard." Again, no hesitation, almost like he was ready to answer any question she may have for him.

Charlotte does not realize the scowl she has on her face as if she were dealing with something – no someone – very unpleasant. "No need for the ma'am. You can call me Charlotte. And how long have you been at the Armory?"

Cool and collected, "I have been in Williamson for a little over a year, but I have been in the National Guard for 15 years, but that has been in Pennsylvania, ma'am," unconscious of the ma'am, but force of habit. Seth does not allow his eyes to waver from Charlotte or look to Caroline for help. She told him her mother would be tough, so he was determined to win her over. He just had to figure out what strategy will work the best.

Charlotte has a coolness in her voice that is rimmed with ice, "So you are from Pennsylvania, then? Whereabouts?"

Seth's easy warmth is an interesting contrast to Charlotte's frost. "West central, from a small town in Blair County called Hollidaysburg just south of Altoona."

"Oh, I've never been there...And your parents. Are they still in Hollidaysburg?" Charlotte now feels uncertain as to why she continues to question this boy and why no one else is talking.

"My mother does, but my father is in Florida, just south of Kissimmee. They divorced when I was a child, ma'am."

Somehow, the ma'am suddenly stops bothering her and her heart warms with sympathy when he admits his parents are divorced. Unsure what to say next and wanting to retreat to the kitchen, Clay finally comes to her rescue – sort of.

"Well," Clay begins after an awkward silence and everyone waits for Charlotte to speak again. "Before Charlotte finishes with the third degree, I'll see if she needs any the help in the kitchen and we can continue this conversation at the dinner table."

"I can help, Dad," Caroline offers, because she knows her mother has as many questions and more for her, but would rather talk to in private.

"Thanks, Caroline. No need. I think everything is ready," Clay says, escorting his wife out of the room leaving Nick to settle the new couple in with what he hopes is more relaxed conversation. As soon as they are from earshot, Clay gently scolds his wife, though he has been with her long enough to know the bond she and Caroline share, he treads lightly and teases her.

"Charlotte, what's your problem? You act like Caroline has brought a terrorist over for dinner?" standing at the sink beside her pretending they actually have something to do, but in truth are in sidebar.

"What's *my* problem? What about Caroline? Showing up here with someone we have never met! We don't know him! He very well could be a terrorist!" glaring at her husband and not appreciating his humor at all nor lack of concern.

"You're right. We've never met him, but I would guess that's why he's here – so we can *meet* him. That's why we're having dinner – to find out. And if he in fact happens to be a terrorist, I will make him leave before dessert!" laughing at his wife's frustrated whispers and foolish accusations, but seeing the near sadness in her eyes.

Drawing her close to him, Clay again pats his wife's behind in comfort and consolation. "Charlotte, she's over 30…I think it's time she brings a boy home for dinner." Clayton Hatfield knows the struggle his wife is facing. He will never understand it, because those thoughts, those feelings are reserved only for mothers and they are the strongest between mothers and daughters. He leaves her to gather herself for Round 2 and calls the kids to dinner.

Clayton takes the seat at the head of the table; Charlotte and Nick are to his left with Seth and Caroline to his right. Everyone quiets and joins hands for prayer. Seth is becoming more adjusted with this custom, because Caroline always holds his hands while they pray. It was awkward and unfamiliar at first, but he is growing to like and expect it.

"Lord, we come to you tonight thankful for this meal and we ask that You bless it to our bodies. We are thankful for the ones who share our table. Lord, we thank You for our new friend, Seth. We ask that You bless his life and all he may face. We thank You for Your Son, our Savior and it is in His name we ask all these things...AMEN."

Clayton's hand gives Seth's a powerful squeeze and a feeling of approval, comradery, and peace rush through him. Caroline rubs her thumb across the back of his hand and quickly releases before her mother's hawk eyes see her touch lingering. And the meal proceeds.

"So," Clayton waits until everyone is finished passing bowls and platters before he begins his own interrogation of Seth. Just like Charlotte, he too wants to know who the striking young man accompanying his daughter really is, but he also does not want him to feel overly scrutinized. "Seth, you have been in Williamson for a little over a year, where were you before that?"

"Hollidaysburg and a few places in Pennsylvania. Williamson is my fourth unit assignment since I enlisted, sir."

Clayton smiles faintly at the *sir* knowing it is very military and knowing in anyone else, Charlotte would be impressed, but he is sure coming from Seth she is finding it irritating.

"Your fourth unit? Why have you made the transfers?" Clayton notices the young man has a very poised elegance about him. His manners, his speech, even the way he handles a fork and knife is graceful; not the least feminine, but confident and self-assured and he is already impressed.

Seth calmly steadies himself for the next round of questions. Not once does he look to Caroline for reassurance or Nick for confidence. This is a conversation mainly for parents. Caroline and Nick just happen to be members of the audience and only expected to listen.

"I went back and forth between full-time and part-time duty. I changed units as new positions came available with hopes of advancing." Taking a bite between questions, Seth continues to focus his attention on Clayton, because he knows there are more to follow.

Clayton gestures with his fork, "And you came to Williamson to for a rank change?"

"Yes, sir. I had been at a sergeant for a while and without a deployment it felt like I was stuck and not advancing. Coming here, I became Staff Sergeant to the Unit Captain." Seth's blood pressure begins to rise and takes a drink of his iced tea to cool his mind knowing where the next questions are headed and these are topics he and Caroline have yet to discuss.

"Then deployment was also in your plan when you chose to come to Williamson. Is that right?" Clayton pins him down, though he does not see Seth break, Clayton glances to Nick then Caroline who have been attentively listening and he notices each of them flinch to some degree.

Seth decides to be very open with Clayton for the simple fact that he is Caroline's father and is only inquiring with her best interest at heart. He sets down his glass and wipes his mouth ready to answer.

"Yes, sir. Deployment was a major factor as to why I chose to come to Williamson. We began our first stages of readiness in January." Seth has wanted to explain all of this to Caroline and answer her many questions and let her know he understands if this was more than she wants to take on, but the last two weeks with her have been dreamlike and he has not found the right time to spoil it with reality. That is no longer an option, because Clayton is voicing all the questions that are flooding the thoughts of the three other people at the table.

Clayton stops eating though fork and knife are in his hands, his elbows resting on the arms of his chair. "You have entered readiness." Sighing, his lips are set and he slowly nods his head. "When do you leave?"

When does he leave? What are they talking about? The National Guard works during floods and hurricanes and forest fires. Why are they talking about deployment?

Caroline's mind is frantic. She feels almost tricked and her parents and Nick are all in on the joke and everyone will start laughing soon, but as the conversation between Seth and her dad continues, she realizes this is not a joke.

Seth feels like he is betraying Caroline. Like he is revealing a lie she has had no idea about and she will be hurt. However, the respect he so quickly has formed for Clayton and knowing Caroline would not want him to point out she is unaware of these conditions, Seth continues honestly hoping Caroline gives him the opportunity to explain later.

"Preliminary readiness can last as much as six months, before we are alerted further. We still have transfers coming in and all of our squadrons are not full and that can take time; maybe 18 months."

Charlotte jumps in when she, like her daughter, begins to realize this boy will be going to war. "Seth, have you ever been deployed?"

Seth smiles tenderly, because Charlotte's tone and manner have changed dramatically. Her face indicates many of the same questions his own mother has. "No, I have not, ma'am, though I have tried. I had finished college after September 11th, and was in the middle of my second enlistment, but the unit I was in was not scheduled for deployment. When that enlistment ended, I planned to enter the full Army, but there were some paperwork issues about my years in service and rank, so I was advised to join the Guard full-time, gain some rank, then make a lateral transfer. I shuffled through three units, had over a dozen stateside assignments, but it seems like I was always missing deployment. West Virginia has historically sent more military support than most states, so when I saw their battalion was in que for deployment and readiness was soon, I took the position."

Apprehension and fear mix in Charlotte's voice, "Then you will be going to war?" Her eyes wide, she does not want to hear his answer. She does not want Caroline to hear his answer.

Quietly, he answers knowing this will be the first of many wounds Caroline will have to endure, "Yes, ma'am."

These revelations also captivate Nick, because he has been naïve and ignorant to the fact that Seth is a soldier and the country is involved in a war, conflict, incident – whatever you want to call it – and will be expected to fulfill his duty.

"Will you go to Iraq or Afghanistan?" Nick asks, sadness washing over him knowing his sister's happiness is now a little tainted.

Looking at Nick, seeing the sympathy and maybe even disappointment in his eyes, Seth feels like he has also betrayed him and again quietly answers, "Iraq."

"Son, that's a lot for you to expect my daughter to take on," though his tone is brusque, Clayton is neither accusing nor condemning.

Here is where it ends. Seth is going to wake up from this two-week dream. "Yes, sir. You are correct and I will have no bad feelings towards her if she chooses not to. Really, it is more than I should ask.

Clayton takes on a fatherly tone meant for Seth and Caroline. "Whatever she decides, we will support her and Seth, no matter what, you have our prayers," as he grasps Seth shoulder making him feel likewise approved and appreciated.

She sees it. Charlotte sees it. A quick moment shared between Caroline and Seth as her daughter places her hand on Seth's leg when he finishes talking with Clayton. Seth squeezes her hand under the table then looks at her for the first time since this discussion began and gets the reassurance he is looking for. A moment of tenderness and certainty. Neither of them are foolish children unaware of the world, blissfully ignoring that difficult times are sure to come. It is mature strength wrapped in the beginnings of love. It is new and fragile being tested for the first time, and in their silent exchange, each finds confidence in the other. Charlotte easily recognizes it, because she has shared the same with Clayton for years. She does not quite understand why, but something inside her begins to hurt.

Erasing the tension that has settled around them, Clayton changes the conversation, addressing Nick, and allowing Seth to finish eating. "Nicholas, I hope your schedule is free on Saturday. Marty and Alex will be here and that porch is coming off." Clayton looks at his youngest anticipating no objections.

"PORCH is written on my calendar in red. I wouldn't miss it, Daddy!" Nick resuming his normal teasing and silliness. He is more than ready to change the mood in the room.

"Seth, you wouldn't happen to be capable with a hammer and saw? I wouldn't mind a little more help on Saturday? We're taking off the porch and salvaging all the lumber to start the expansion of the living room. When it's all finished, I'm putting a wraparound porch that Charlotte has always wanted," winking at his wife silently acknowledging to her that they, too are on the same team.

"Yes, he is! You should see these tables and credenza he made!" Caroline has been near silent during the meal and proud to brag on her new beau.

Seth's smile is huge and meant only for Caroline as he touches her quickly, innocently, tenderly. Charlotte notices and is not as putout as she was earlier. She can easily see why her daughter is so taken by the striking young man and does not blame her for wanting to keep him a secret.

"I worked in construction for about two years with my uncle during and right after college, so I could probably hold boards for you and sweep up sawdust," he answers humbly not wanting to inflate his skill.

Clayton clapping him on the back, "Great! Then we will be happy to have you on Saturday. You'll be able to meet my oldest, Alex. He works in construction, so you will have lots to talk about."

A genuine smile for Clayton, Seth wishes he could shake his hand again to show him how much he appreciates how good he has made him feel, instead he replies, "It will be my pleasure to help, sir."

Adding his own humor, Clayton mocks his wife, "Charlie, I am fairly certain, Seth isn't a terrorist, so I think he can stay for dessert!" Everyone laughs knowing the interrogation is over and Seth has passed muster. Now, in their own relaxed way and at their own speed, it will be up to everyone to get to know Seth on personal level.

Seth has been a nomad most of his life never quite understanding how people can stay put in one place for so long. Now, he is learning…It is because they find a home; where they belong. Not necessarily a place, but a feeling; a person you want to travel life with. Tonight, Seth feels so comfortable and at home around this table for his first meal with this family, he sees why it is so easy once you find home, you never want to leave it…Maybe he has finally found his.

The evening concludes with Clayton and Charlotte along with Nick walking Caroline and Seth out. Clayton takes time to show the boys what he has planned for Saturday and where they will begin. This gives Charlotte and Caroline just a moment together.

Taking her hand, Charlotte whispers to her only daughter and best friend, "Caroline, I believe you have found yourself a very good boy," and hugs her daughter tight, with actions saying so many things where words fall short.

Caroline whispers in her mother's ear, "Yes, Mom, I believe I have!" kissing her cheek.

Resting a hand on her face, Charlotte tells her, "We will talk tomorrow," letting her know that she approves, but there is still much they must discuss.

The men rejoin them. Clayton and Nick shake Seth's hand then hug Caroline goodnight and Charlotte reacts completely out of character hugging Seth. Not a side hug that is forced and awkward, but a full hug – comfortable and relaxed.

"Seth, it was a pleasure meeting you and we look forward to having you on Saturday!"

"Thank-you, Charlotte. The pleasure was mine," and in the darkness, that surrounds them, Seth gives her hand a light squeeze winning another important point from Caroline's mother. Then he takes her daughter's hand, leading her down the steps and to her door before rounding the front of his Jeep, calling back to them, "Thank-you again for the wonderful dinner. Goodnight!" and they drive away.

Nick smiles as his dad drapes his arm over his mother's shoulders and walks in the house giving them a moment, though he knows they are just beginning to recap and analyze the evening. Clayton echoes Charlotte's earlier sentiments.

"I believe Caroline has found herself a very good boy."

"Yes...I believe she has..." Charlotte's voice has changed to a new tone; one of tender melancholy. The one she reserves for when she speaks intimately about her children.

Clayton does not push her for words knowing she has experienced much this evening. Instead, he stands there quietly with her, watching Seth's taillights fade in the distance. When they disappear, he hears her sigh. He pulls her to him chafing her shoulder.

"No worries, Momma. All will be well." Lacing their hands, Charlotte lets her very good boy take her in for the night.

———◦———

Seth walks Caroline to her porch stopping before he climbs the first step. Feeling the tug on her hand that he is not following her, she turns to see his hesitation.

"Aren't you coming in?" she cannot read his features in the dusky glow of twilight.

Instead of answering, he takes her other hand lifting them both to his lips. On the step and in her spiky shoes, she is almost eye level with

Seth though she can barely see the pained expression on his face before he begins.

"Caroline, your dad is right…This is a lot for you to take on…you have your own life to live…"

She drops his hands and takes hold of his face tracing his brow and jaw and chin. "You are never to say that to me again…I know what I am doing."

"I wasn't trying to deceive you…We just hadn't talked about deployment…I didn't want to mention it, because I was afraid it would spoil everything…"

Filled with tenderness and understanding, "Seth, I don't feel deceived and it hasn't ruined anything…You are in the military. Deployment is always a possibility."

"Yes, but Caroline, there is so much uncertainty in the coming months…Things could change at a moment's notice…Life could get very difficult for us…Deployments are hard on everyone," Seth is near pleading with her, ready to convince her she does not have to go any further.

Still calm and steady, "Seth, I realize that, but life is difficult and always uncertain. We are starting out already aware of many of the things that are going to be hard. Not many people are fortunate to have that knowledge."

Her hands are at his nape, his neck, his collar. His judgement could easily blur. Putting his hands on her hips, he shakes then steadies her, wanting her to know he is serious.

"Honest, I will understand if this is more than you bargained for. You can get out now with no hard feelings…Trust me, it's ok."

Her hands are on his face again holding his head so as not to break eye contact. The moon has come to full rise and illuminates their faces just enough. Caroline looks at him as the seconds tick by.

Her voice has lost its tenderness and is replaced by determination. "Seth Garrett, I told you not to say that to me again…I know what I am doing…You are here, now…I choose you without hesitation."

His arms are around her with force and his mouth crushes her like he wants to devour every morsel that she is. Moments pass as sense and reason begin to falter. His mouth pulls away, but his hold does not. She lays her head on his chest and he pants breathless in her ear, his chin grazing her cheek as he speaks.

"Caroline, thank-you…Thank-you for thinking of me." His voice is husky and emotional

Caroline wishes they could stay like this. She feels so warm and protected in his arms.

"Seth…"

"MmmHmm?"

Lifting her head, she hangs one arm around his neck while the other rests on his chest, her hand again on his face. As she talks, he kisses her fingertips.

"Seth, I wasn't trying to hide you from my family…I was just… enjoying you…I just wanted you all to myself for a while, before I had to share you with anyone…Is that ok?" Caroline asks, worried she may have hurt his feelings or made him think she did not want him to meet her family.

"Caroline, it is more than ok. I wanted you all to myself for a while, too…and I enjoy you more and more every time I am with you."

Sense and reason flee again and they allow it for a while.

"Caroline, if I don't leave now, I'm going to want to come inside."

"And Seth, I can't allow that."

"And I'm never going to insist that you do…Spend tomorrow with your mom and I will see you Saturday…" Seth lingers making no attempt to leave, neither does Caroline. They stand there holding on to each other knowing they are both entering unfamiliar waters and they are going somewhere neither has been before, but neither is scared and they feel safe knowing they are going there together.

"Spend tomorrow with your mother and I will see you Saturday."

"Yes, and I will miss you until then," kissing his jaw.

Seth pulls away before it becomes impossible to do so. Lifting her hand like a fair maiden to his lips, "Saturday."

"Saturday."

And he jogs down the sidewalk to get in his Jeep before he changes his mind.

So, as Spring begins to blossom around them, the first buds of love sprout and they look forward to Summer to nurture it and watch it grow.

Chapter XVII

"Humble yourselves before the Lord, and He will
lift you up..." – James 4:10 NIV

Caroline continues past her driveway on her way home Friday afternoon. Once leaving school, she has not taken time to call, because she is sure her mother is waiting on her to *talk*. Bright and warm Spring sun is shining through the trees on this cloudless day when Caroline parks beside her mother's car – the only one in the driveway. They will be alone in the house.

Caroline has no feelings of apprehension as she opens the door to the empty living room. She wants to talk with her mother. She wants to share everything about the last two weeks. Caroline wants Charlotte to be as excited as she is. Charlotte is her very best friend, who else would she want to talk to about Seth.

Caroline and Charlotte share a bond like no other and they have both always loved it. Charlotte never wanted sisters, because she always had Ruby. Caroline has felt the same, because she has Charlotte. Caroline has always enjoyed being the only girl and the only granddaughter. She knows she is *special* and relishes all its advantages. Alex and Nick, as well as Will, have teased her over the years that she is a petted princess, but they say it with no amount of jealousy. Charlotte and Gran do not love any of them less and all the children have been petted and taken care of, probably more than they should since they are all adults. It just happens that Charlotte and Caroline are also friends; something not all parents are fortunate to have.

"Mom?" Caroline calls to her mother.

"I'm in the kitchen, Caroline," she hears her mother yell back and goes to join her.

As the director of First Fruits Preschool at Williamson Wesleyan, Charlotte has Friday's off. When Alex is born, she leaves her job as a legal secretary to stay at home and raise their family which has always been her and Clayton's plan. Several years later, the coal market enters a slump as it is known for – feast or famine – and Clayton goes through a layoff that lasts longer than anticipated. By this time, Nick has entered kindergarten, and with the encouragement of the government's efforts to restructure a hurting and dislocated workforce, Clayton and Charlotte go to college.

Right after Clayton completes his degree; he is called back to work and is quickly moved into management positions. Many other workers sat idle during the layoff or viewed it as an extended vacation, for Clayton, it proved to be one of the best things that could have happened. Charlotte finishes a year later also with an Associate's of Business and Early Childhood Education. The church has wanted to expand their reach in the community providing Christ-centered education, and Charlotte was the natural choice.

So, Charlotte goes to work and is in the planning from the ground up. In three years, they have teachers in a two, three, and four-year-old class, a six-month waiting list for registration, and run the most successful preschool in the region. At first, Charlotte hated no longer being the stay at home mom, but the family quickly finds a new rhythm – the preschool operated on the same calendar as the kids, Monday through Thursday, they rode the bus home to Gran and Poppie's with Charlotte coming home about an hour later, Friday's off and they have the same holidays and snow days. The only change is when the kids are at school, Charlotte is at work and she is great at her job – organized, efficient, disciplined, tender, loving, and creative.

Coming into the kitchen, Caroline finds her mother closing the freezer door holding a container of ice cream.

"Would you like some? I've got hard chocolate and strawberries," Charlotte asks her daughter as she retrieves bowls and spoons.

Sitting in one of the stools at the island, Caroline agrees, "Yeah, that sounds really good."

The women chat about their day, the long week as the kids are gearing up for summer, state testing, and more idle conversation not avoiding what they are here to talk about, but letting the other know they are completely comfortable with whatever is going to be said.

"Where's dad?" Caroline asks as she drizzles hard chocolate all over her ice cream, toping it with strawberries and juice.

Charlotte coats her ice cream with chocolate opting for just a little juice and no berries and suggests, "Let's sit at the table. He and Nick went to pick up the lumber for tomorrow. Most of it is being delivered along with the trusses on Monday, but he had a few things he wanted extra. You just missed them. He said they would pick up pizzas for dinner. You can stay and eat if you want, but I wanted some ice cream now."

Charlotte makes an 'I don't care' face at Caroline, like she is not hiding that she is having dessert early. The running joke in the family is how Clayton is the Food Police and he fusses at Charlotte for being a 'junker'. She reminds him that she has always been this way and after almost 40 years together, he should be used to it by now.

"I think I will stay, because pizza sounds good and don't have anything planned for dinner."

Charlotte picks up on that point immediately and uses it as an opportunity to open discussion, "You don't have plans with Seth?" His name was so new, Charlotte is not yet accustomed to saying it even to Caroline.

Caroline does not have to force calm or relaxed in her voice, because she easily feels both when she responds, "No. I'll see him tomorrow." She takes another bite allowing her mother time to ask as many questions as she wants; and there will be many.

Charlotte's voice cracks a little, because this is all so new to her. She has gone through it with Alex and Nick, but there is no accurate way to describe it. With a daughter, it is just different. "You can invite him up here if you want."

Smiling tenderly at her mother, "Yeah, I know. I may call him later. We just didn't have anything planned," and Caroline continues to wait, letting Charlotte adjust the speed of the conversation.

"So, how long have you all had plans together?" Charlotte hopes it is not a long time, because then she will know Caroline has been keeping him from her, but if it is too short, she worries, because the attractive couple already appears very bonded with each other.

Charlotte's inquisitive face nearly telegraphs her thoughts, so Caroline answers honestly and saves her enthusiasm for a few minutes.

"We met two weeks ago when Cap. Tyler spoke at Career Assembly. James invited them to stay for lunch and they did." She debates if she should tell the full story and decides her mother will appreciate it. It also paints a better picture and Caroline has never been a fan of condensed versions.

"I met them that morning and we chatted some before the first session, but we didn't talk again until lunch. I was so together that morning, but then Nick was with us at lunch and I got all nuts and nervous, because Seth was seated next to me and was asking me questions. I started rattling and I think I even offended him. So, I was really surprised when I heard from him." Caroline rolls her eyes, because she knows her mother knows her well and her many struggles in social situations, particularly with men.

Charlotte's brow crinkles not wanting to seem too interested in the story, though she is, and wonders how Seth got in touch with Caroline. "Did he call the school to talk to you?"

Caroline's enthusiasm can no longer be contained, "He wrote me a letter and had Deaton Tyler deliver it to me at school!" Her face lights up as she tells her mother the story. "...and we have seen each other every day since."

Charlotte clinks her spoon into her bowl. "Wow! That's a story." Her enthusiasm does not match Caroline's, but many of her questions are answered. She decides a mother's honesty is necessary at this moment.

"So, you really like him?" same flat tone she used with Seth the night before.

Caroline's confidence and excitement do not diminish, but her words come a little harder to find. "It's just been two weeks...Things are still very new...But, I do really like him! Can you believe how nice looking he is?" Giddy and impish, the way you are supposed to act about new love.

Charlotte wants to quickly agree and comment on how tall he is and how refined and mature he seems, and how the word striking continues to come to mind, but she needs to hold on to some of her cards. Smiling slightly, "Caroline, you say things are new and it has only been two weeks, but you are not 17 and neither is Seth. Where your time together may be lacking in quantity, you've made up for it in quality. Anyone who would see you two for a minute would recognize it is already serious." Before she gets the chance to comment, Charlotte continues, "I will be honest, despite all of Seth's apparent good qualities, he is not who I would have chosen for you."

Caroline feels like she is 17 and her mom is telling her she does not approve of her prom date and she must choose again. She is hurt and shocked and maybe even a touch angry. "What?!?"

Charlotte sees she has upset her daughter and that is definitely not what she wants. There is a fine line a parent must walk between being supportive and giving wise guidance. So, she goes on to explain.

"Caroline, Seth seems like a wonderful young man, very much like what you have been waiting for…It's just that his situation is not ideal." Speaking firmly, she will say the things her daughter may not want to face now, but could be a hardship in the future. "Caroline, Seth is a solider and he *will* go to war. It doesn't matter if it is in 6 months or 18, he will go to war and when he does, he will have to leave you. I'm not saying you haven't thought of all of this. I'm not saying you and Seth haven't talked about all of this. I just want you to be aware it **IS** going to happen and do you realize what it can possibly do to you?"

Charlotte's hurt is the hurt all parents feel as they come to crossroads with their children. When they want to make decisions for them, but they cannot, so they must try to warn them of what is ahead, because they never want to see their child harmed. Charlotte knows in the best of situations, the coming months and possibly years are certain to be difficult even heartbreaking for her daughter and as mother, she wants to protect her at all costs.

Part of her knows Seth very well could be the boy for which she has prayed for Caroline, but part of her wishes they had never met. She knows her daughter is lonely, though she rarely admits it. She knows she feels like everyone else's life is moving ahead and she is stuck on an endless plateau. She knows that Caroline references her age more often and has teasingly commented her youth is slipping away, though her smile may be bright, her eyes reveal a sadness Charlotte wishes was not there, but is powerless to fix.

Caroline has never had the opportunity to have this conversation with her mother. She has never had the opportunity to say what she wants and mean it. She has never had the opportunity to share her heart in this way and be willing to love everything familiar and at the same time be so ready to look for happiness in someone completely new knowing it feels so right. She has never had the opportunity to dare to want more. And Seth, he is more…So much more.

Caroline reaches to take Charlotte's hand and as she does, her mother's eyes well with tears so touched by her daughter's words and wisdom. "Mom, I will be honest, Seth is so…unexpected…He is not what I had planned for, hoped for…He is so much more…"

For so long, Caroline has doubted she would ever be given the chance to share these moments with her mother. She has begun to condition herself, compartmentalizing thoughts and emotions, and accepting that some things are just not going to happen. But, now, it all seems different; feels so different, like what was so completely unexpected is happening and she has been holding her breath up to this point and now that Seth has arrived, she can finally breathe.

"You're right…We are very serious, because we're not 17 and because we both know who we are. We don't feel trapped or obligated to some timeline or boxes that we are required to check off…The last two weeks have been dreamlike and relaxed and so comfortable. Like I have found someone with whom I fit…No, I have not wanted to think about him leaving or going away…or even worse. I don't even want to consider that, but I had to. Seth has even tried to convince me this is more than I should take on. He even said I could bow out gracefully with no hard feelings…"

Squeezing her mom's hand a little harder, Caroline voices the honesty she rarely wants to admit. "Mom, I have been safe and cautious and looking ahead my whole life…I have taken so few risks and because life has been so blessed and everything I have ever wanted, it has been easy for me to never step out on faith…Even through all that care and careful planning, I have fallen short so often, though I have tried to always do what was right…I know any life with Seth appears to have so much uncertainty ahead," smiling her voice winsome and playfully nostalgic, "but I remember a story you have told so many times of when you saw a yellow moving van pull into the parking lot at church and a sweet boy – the new pastor's son, who you would later find out to be a little bit of a rascal and drove a motorcycle, climb down out of the passenger door and you said, 'That boy will be mine!'. At the time, he probably looked like a risk, too…Mom, Seth may be a risk, but one I am willing to take, because for once I would just like the opportunity to try…to try and find something wonderful…"

Caroline should be in tears, but she is not. As close as she and Charlotte are, there are things she holds onto all to herself and does not share with mother, because Charlotte has never had answers for her daughter's loneliness.

"Mom, I would really just like the opportunity to try and find happy that is all my own…Try to make someone else happy."

She could have said more like she was tired of being lonely and sad. That she was tired of watching others get what they want while she must plaster her face with happiness and excitement, then watch those same people become disappointed or unappreciative of what they have. How she hates that with every passing day she finds herself becoming more distant and emotionally self-protecting. That for too long she has wondered why no one has given her the opportunity to be happy with them. Why no one has ever found her quirky or interesting and their eyes are drawn to her from across the room, because something about her laughter or her behavior has dazzled him. She wants to know why she has been so apparently lacking in all qualities that are desirable and attention getting. Caroline just wants the opportunity to try, even if it all blows up in her face, she would like to try.

Charlotte sniffs and snorts and ungraciously wipes her nose on her shoulder. Caroline does not have to tell her all these things, because her mother's heart already knows them and she has asked herself and Clayton and God time and again why her daughter who is more beautiful and more amazing than any other she has ever met – why has she never had the opportunity to try. Why happiness and a life of love and adventure has evaded her.

Before they can speak further or dare to voice any of the thoughts traveling through their heads, Clayton and Nick come home, announcing their arrival by blaring the horn. Charlotte WHEWs and Caroline gives her a tight hug saying, "Mom, I'm so glad we could talk. I've been wanting to share Seth with you this whole time!" and they go out to meet them. As Clayton shuts the door on the truck and Nick hops down holding two pizza boxes and a smaller one on top, Seth's Jeep pulls in behind them.

Caroline looks at her mother and smiles then rushes down the steps to meet *her boy*.

"Hey stranger! What are you doing here?" Caroline smiles looking up into Seth's beautiful face.

His one hand finds her waist while the other rests on the top of his door he just closed. He does not pull her too close, because Seth respects he is in her parents' driveway. Caroline, however, does not seem to mind resting her arms on his chest and dancing her fingertips to his neck. He has not taken time to change and Caroline is thrilled, because how many people can boast someone who so looks the part of a hero showing up at their door for dinner...None that she can name off hand. SWOON!

Smiling at the face that is already burnt in his memory that distracts his days and blissfully haunts his nights. "Well, I was getting ready to leave the Armory and I get an *interesting* text from your brother."

"What did he say?"

Seth gives her a wonderfully wicked grin, "He said he got my number from Cleat and among other things, I was to be at dinner this evening." Knowing she is ready to begin her normal questioning, he does not allow it. "I might tell you later..." grinning at her mischievously, he wishes her family were not so nearby and he would tease her more with his lips without saying a word. Resisting the urge, "We had better go in, your dad is yelling for us," and before she can protest, Seth grabs her hand whisking her to the steps to be greeted by a smiling Charlotte and a hearty slap on the back by Clayton.

Chapter XVIII

*"And the streets of the city will be filled with boys
and girls at play." – Zechariah 8:5 NLT*

And so, the transition of welcoming Seth Garett into the lives of the Hatfield Family is relaxed and seamless. On Saturday, he is treated like one of boys as he is put to work alongside them while his talent and ability speak for itself and he quickly becomes a fixture at their dinner table, and even fills a spot in a pew with them most Sundays.

Seth also realizes how much this family enjoys each other and spends time together playing and having fun. Nick is eager to rekindle his childhood friendship with Cleat inviting he and Leanna with Seth, Caroline, and Darby out to dinner the next week. Seth and Caroline join Alex and Meghan a few days later at Hillbilly Days taking the boys to the parade and afterwards they fuss over who gets to sit with Seth on the carnival rides. The highlight of the day is when Seth wins a stuffed, plush pineapple wearing sunglasses which he gives to Sam, sealing a place in the little boy's heart.

The first weekend in May, Will challenges Seth and Caroline to a round of golf, but says he must be spotted a few points, because he will have Sophie on his team which is a disadvantage. Seth spends most of the day laughing at the pair as Will vainly coaches Sophie's very poor game, barks at her when she cannot find her ball, and calls her *Steve* indicating he wants her to bring his putter. Seth and Caroline come out on top, even with the spotted points and Will rehashes the day as Sophie and Caroline finish the dinner dishes.

"Sophie, if you would just keep your head down and slow your backswing, you would make much better contact with the ball!" Will, in very Will fashion, bellows to Sophie from the corner of the couch where he is recuperating from a hard day. Dessert bowl resting on his belly, he shouts again, "Sophie! Are there nuts in this crust? You know I hate nuts!" Angry face and accusing tone, Will takes his spoon to lift the edge of his pie to examine the bottom then timidly touches the end of the spoon again with his tongue certain he is going to be grossed out by the contents.

William Walter Dotson is Caroline's first cousin, is in between she and Alex in age, and has been raised so close with her, he is like a third brother. He is loud and boisterous, hilarious and ridiculous. If one did not know any better, they would mistake him for a large child adding humor to all situations, though he has his serious side. When he finds out Seth is from Holidaysburg, he tells him he has been there once, which is a surprise to everyone.

"It's part of the Pittsburgh Division. *N&S* has a car shop there. It's much smaller than the one here in Williamson, but still has several jobs. They were installing some new equipment and coming online with a system we've used in the Pocahontas Division for a while. So, I was sent there as part of the team to get them ready. It is a nice area; looks a lot like West Virginia, without the deep, narrow valleys. It seems they have more level land than we do."

"Yeah, it does and I know the place you are talking about. My best friend in middle school, his dad ran the shop, but he may be retired by now, because I haven't talked to him years," Seth recalls his hometown humored by the connection Will has made.

"Marcum Tucker," Will answers also humored by the connection.

"YES! That's his name! Eric Tucker's dad," Seth is almost delighted by this Six Degrees of Separation from his past.

"He hasn't retired, though he's been threatening for a few years. He is the best at what he does and there is not really anyone to replace him. I talk to him every month or so when one of our shops needs something."

Will then goes on to give volumes of information about the railroad, coal hauling, timed-freight, chemical transport, and derailments. Will's grandfather was a railroader retiring after 47 years and was dedicated to his core to the company. There was never anything else Will considered as a career, though his grandfather began as a brakeman and ended as an engineer, Will started as a conductor and with the help of his management degree, he quickly moved into administration. Just like his grandfather, he is railroad to the core. Now, feet stretched out on Caroline's coffee table, he continues to yell at Sophie.

"Sophie! Are these walnut or pecans? I can handle it if they're pecans, but not if they're walnuts," angry face still intact.

Sophie does not answer, but takes her place beside him eating her own pie with ice cream melting on top.

"What does it matter if you like how it tastes?"

Growling without looking at her picking at the crust with his spoon, "The point is, I hate walnuts!"

"Well, you're in luck – neither. The crust is graham cracker and toffee bits," speaking as she would to a five-year-old.

Without missing a beat or a bite, "Oh, good. I love toffee!"

Seth smiles and shakes his head at them for the umpteenth time today. Caroline sits close to him bringing them both pie and ice cream. Conversation flows easily and entertaining usually from something foolish Will says, is then scolded by Sophie, with Seth and Caroline laughing. After instructing Sophie to get him a second helping of pie, Will eats it and then asks Sophie to rub his belly.

"I am not rubbing your belly! You shouldn't eat so much!" fussing at him, Sophie nudges him with her elbow when his head lolls to the side and makes vomit faces at her.

"Well, then rub my feet, because they are killing me and it's your fault! If you'd learn to keep it in the fairway, I wouldn't have to walk every square inch of *Twisted Gun* looking for your ball!"

"My fault?!?" Sophie shouts back, pushing his head away and ignoring his dramatic moans. "I am pretty certain, you laid down a few *cough balls* today and I don't think the PGA has offered you a place on Tour, yet!"

"Fine! Put my bowl in the sink," he orders her as he stands and rubs his hands across his belly. "We gotta go. You know I love my bathroom best!" Will steps around Sophie and makes his way to the door. "Seth, when do you leave to Fort Campbell?" With his hand on the door, he is talking to Seth, but motioning for Sophie to hurry.

"Tomorrow morning. I'll be home Friday night or Saturday morning depending on what time the training ends," Seth answers walking over to Will to shake his hand and thank him for the day.

"That sounds good. You be safe driving and the next time we go to the *Gun*, I'll get someone better in my cart and we can have a real match!"

Will's words hit the mark and Sophie lands flogging him with her hands and words. He opens the door and the two spar all the way to Will's truck.

"Stop hitting me you no-talent wench!"

"Next time, I'll bring a lifejacket for your ball and the four iron you lost in the pond!"

Seth closes the door behind them shaking his head again. "Are they always like that?" coming back to his place beside Caroline thinking he would never call her a wench, but he is sure she would never act like one.

Sighing and rolling her eyes, "ALWAYS...since we were kids. They keep it somewhere between flirtation and fiasco, but I think they are really just best friends. At some point along the way, each of them have wanted more, but they have never been able to meet on the right page. I blame it on timing, so they take the easy road and stay friends."

Seth props one foot on the coffee table and half turns facing Caroline. She likes how his long legs are getting tan and he is beginning to take on the look of the coming summer. Raking a red nail up his shin and across his knee, he asks, "How is staying friends the *easy road*?"

Caroline's nail stops and she looks at him in disbelief; her face all crunched up like she cannot believe he asked such a question.

"Anything more than friendship takes work. As friends, they can keep it casual and enjoy it other only when it's convenient," looking at him, she should add, "Like duh!"

"But I thought we were friends..." baiting her, he turns a little closer.

Still confused by his questions, Caroline frowns thinking Seth does not understand what she is saying, "We are friends."

Finding her hand that is resting on his knee, he asks while kissing her hand, fingertips, palm, "Best friends?"

Realizing she has been lured into his trap, Caroline is happy to find herself caught in his web. Her words are silky as she answers, "I want us to be very best friends...But, I am also willing to put in the work for so much more...I have no plans for this to just be casual." Her voice is parts challenge and seduction and confidence letting Seth know she is not one to be trifled with.

He responds with his own challenge, seduction, and confidence. "That may be a lot of work...Do you think I'm worth it?"

Coming very close, Caroline whispers, "Oh, completely worth it!"

Seth's face is skeptical and in jest asks, "I wonder how I got this lucky?" Caroline's tone changes to one of dry sarcasm, "It has to be the Lord, because He is the only one to hand out blessings of this level."

Laughing in his face, she changes the mood to one of playful banter. Realizing she has changed direction and is teasing him, Seth grabs her and wrestles her back into the cushions.

"So, the smart mouth has decided to join us this evening!" glaring as he has her pinned.

"She's missed you and has wanted to come and visit!" laughing at him again not feeling the least threated by his playful attack.

"Well, I haven't missed her!" he growls holding her by her upper arms pushing her deeper into the couch.

Caroline giggles and struggles under his hold, but he does not let go. Kissing the tip of his nose, she goads further, "Yes, you have!" laughing at him again.

Their evening remains playful; they laugh about the day and discuss Will and Sophie. As Caroline walks him out for the night, she asks just as he steps off the porch, "Would you like to go to the Cabin with us?"

Many questions are written on his face and she tries to answer them. "The house we have at the lake? It's in Abingdon, VA on South Holston. We go every year over Memorial Day and since our last day of school is the Friday before, we are staying over through Tuesday...So, I was just wondering if you would like to go with us?"

Seth does not appear enthusiastic or even agreeable. A weekend away with Caroline sounds more than inviting, but a trip with a group is not his idea of a fun vacation. He tries to not sound uninterested, "Who will be going with *us*?" Seth stops on the sidewalk with Caroline on the bottom step. He knows he has flustered her and she begins to rattle off all the details.

"With us? Nick and Darby, Sophie, Will, and Carter. Alex and Meghan sometimes go, but they haven't mentioned it...It is our kick off to summer. We'll go on the lake and maybe do the Creeper Trail and just have fun. We never really make any plans...I would like you to come, but if you don't want to, that's ok, too. We just go every year and this year I want you to come with me."

When Caroline's face takes on her childlike innocence and she speaks with a voice that is genuine and pure; when her eyes are wide and bright and eager, it is like he is seeing something he has never noticed in anyone else before – something good and fine and true – he finds it very hard to deny her. Placing his hand on the post, he slides one foot on the step beside her, leaning in close. "I would rather go away with just you…" holding her with his eyes not breaking his gaze. Her response surprises him when he does not detect a note of flustration.

"I would too…and we will…eventually."

"Is that a promise?" leaning closer. His eyes never leaving her.

"Promise…eventually."

Seth chuckles knowing her answer has many meanings, but decides to press her no further. Never in his life has he allowed a woman to control the speed of a relationship, but with Caroline, it seems different. He does not feel like she is holding him back or dragging her feet through uncertainty. She yields the reigns to him often allowing him to lead, but with confidence, she could lead just as well and more importantly, be just as capable. Capable – that is one of his favorite qualities about her and how she pulls it off, he does not know. She is strong and independent and resourceful. There are few things that she cannot do or not willing to try, but at the same time, is not intimidated or insulted by his confidence, independence, and resourcefulness. She expects and depends on those things from him without being needy or patronizing. She is all parts woman and lady and girl – such an obvious combination yet so rarely found.

Caroline's arms circle his neck and buries her face as he lifts her off the step walking to his Jeep. Leaning against his door, he sets her down and she hugs him tight.

"What am I supposed to do with you gone all week?" she asks laying on his chest.

His hold is just as tight as he plays with her hair that falls down her back. "I hope you miss me."

Looking up, she smiles, her young smile that makes him think they are 17 and life and the world is just waiting stretched out before them.

From this angle, Seth looks stern. Caroline loves his stern face, because it makes his smiling face more of a surprise and appreciated when it appears.

"Seth," his name on her lips sends a flutter straight to his heart. "You give me hummingbirds."

His stern face hardens and he repositions without releasing her so he can see her better. "Hummingbirds? What?"

Smiling – young, girl, sweet innocence, "Yes, hummingbirds...When I am with you, hummingbirds are caged in my chest. Their wings beat against my ribs and like right now, when I am so close to you, they are flying all over the place with excitement...When you leave, they settle down, but they still hover...I guess I am trying to say, that I miss you as soon as you leave and I want to thank-you for hummingbirds...It has been a long time. I thought they had forgotten me...But now they are back."

Seth has never been described hummingbirds so clearly, so accurately. How does she know exactly what to say, because if he had the words Caroline does, he would have told her, she too has given him hummingbirds and he is thankful, because he was afraid they had forgotten him as well? Love should be hummingbirds.

Placing his hands gently on the sides of her face, he brushes her hair back from her forehead combing and recombing it behind her ears. Resting his thumbs on her cheeks, he kisses her eyebrow, her nose, her jaw, and before he kisses her lips, his mouth hovers and their eyes open as he says, "Caroline, thank-you for hummingbirds.

Chapter IXX

"If anyone thinks they are something when they are not,
they deceive themselves." – Galatians 6:3 NIV

A s Seth has hoped, Caroline misses him every day, when she can find the time. The final three weeks of school is a push – complete the last unit before semester exams, plan for fall curriculum changes, attend Senior Banquet – cry a little when Jordan Baisden gives the Senior Address – organize the remaining details for the Spring Tea, inventory books, collect locks, tag record cards, update transcripts, and maintain law and order with students who are wildly eager for summer vacation. Caroline misses Seth most in the evenings; in the time after school usually spent enjoying him more and more each day. In those hours, she tries to be productive, but she finds herself staring at the clock or picking up her phone waiting for him to call. Each night she is already be in bed before the phone rings.

Seth's week is busy as well. He has accompanied Cpt. Tyler as his personal aid to maintain and organize paperwork that will be distributed to the entire unit upon their return. Much of it deals with the legalities of going to the battlefield – insurance, disability, payroll, transfers, DNR orders, next of kin, statements of intent, and personal effects. It will not be until at least fall, possibly early winter before any of the men will begin making decisions about these grisly details, but Cpt. Tyler and Seth must be ready for implementation.

The last two days, Cpt. Tyler is in executive meetings and Seth has his own training to attend. Each morning is classroom work – PowerPoints, tests, endless handouts – and the afternoon is lab experience. The first morning, Seth enters a classroom with six long tables on either side of the room. At each seat is the notebook for the class, a stack of color coded handouts, and a DVD that will be shown to the men of his unit when he provides this training for them. Seth is one of the first to enter the room and he picks the middle seat at one of the middle rows, drops his backpack in the floor, and removes a red, blue, and black ink pen, a yellow highlighter, and an index card to serve as a straightedge.

Once he is settled, he opens the notebook. The title page has *Department of Defense* across the top and symbols of all the branches of the military below followed by the words 'Approved by the American College of Surgeons and the National Association of EMTs'. In bold blue letters is TCCC – Tactical Combat Casualty Care. Seth looks at the marker board in the front of the room. To its left is a projector screen and a podium is situated in the middle between the two. The marker board also reads 'Tactical Combat Casualty Care' in blue ink and listed underneath are the three points of the training (1) Care Under Fire (2) Tactical Field Care (3) Tactical Evacuation Care.

He flips through the notebook waiting for the instructor to arrive and one of the pages catches his eye – Battlefield Wound Care: How to Prevent Bleed Out. Scanning the page, he learns that *exsanguination* means 'the process of blood loss to the degree sufficient to cause death,' followed by a series of statistics about preventable loss of life due to hemorrhaging of the extremities. The next page has one statement, 'Do Not Get Shot While Assisting a Fellow Soldier!' Seth thinks how it seems comical that telling you to not get shot is a necessary instruction as opposed to common knowledge. The next pages detail hemorrhage control and wound dressing. The final pages of the section are diagrams explaining the types of tourniquet for arm, leg, and torso and how they can be applied to yourself or others.

Before he can read further, the instructor enters the room and the seats are filled. In a commanding voice, the Major who is also a doctor, begins his lecture.

"90% of all battlefield casualties…" and he proceeds to take them through the morning discussing the three points from the board, preventable death, common mistakes, procedures in safety, bleeding, airway obstruction, traumatic injury to the brain and spinal cord, CPR, and shock. In his final points, he encourages questions, leaving them with honest advice.

"Gentlemen, no matter how much training you have had, nothing will prepare you for combat. Leading up to that time, you will drown in hours of boredom to be washed away by moments of extreme terror. When casualties occur, and they will, it will take every ounce of your wit and calm to aid you in making the best decisions in a split second in hopes casualties do not result in death. Gentlemen, may God go with you!"

The Major closes his book and assumes attention. Every man in the room rises in unison and respect for the doctor who leaves the room ahead of them with his mind full and heart heavy as it is after every session he teaches.

How many of these boys will not make home from the battlefield?

This question has always plagued him – the paradox of war – and after 33 years of service, he is still uncertain if he can answer it.

That evening on the phone, Caroline has snuggled into her bed when Seth calls.

"Hello, Sweet Boy! I miss you! Tell me all about your day!"

Seth can feel her smile and carefree eagerness.

"No, Pretty Girl. I just had class all day, a meeting this evening, and I went to dinner with Cpt. Tyler and some other officers…I have waited to talk to you." Seth insists, because he wants to be lulled and comforted by her girlish chatter and has no plans to tell her about hemorrhaging or brain trauma.

He is relieved when she does not question him further and asks, "Will you be home tomorrow?"

For more than a year, Seth has never considered Williamson his home. It was just a means to an end; a transfer, a rank change, an opportunity. TEMPORARY. It is funny how so naturally and unexpectedly, Williamson is still not his home, because home is not a place, but a feeling. It is a feeling you share with another person and no matter where you are, they have become home…Quietly, unexpectedly, thankfully – Caroline has become home.

"No," not wanting to disappoint her, he adds, "but we will leave first thing Saturday morning. I will be home in plenty of time. When do you want me to pick you up?"

Caroline is giddy thinking about Saturday as she looks at the dress hanging on the door of her closet more than eager to wear it for Seth.

"Hmm, around 6:00 will be fine. Mom and Gran want to see us before we go."

Smiling at the thought of Ruby who winks at him and pats his hand when he sits beside her at dinner. He teases Caroline about who she loves more – Gran or Charlotte – referring to them as the Three Musketeers. He sees so much of Ruby and Charlotte in Caroline almost like they are the same person at three different stages of life and if Caroline should slowly become either of them over time, he has good things to look forward to.

"It's been a while since I went to prom…Am I supposed to buy a corsage that matches your dress or personality?" surprised at how excited he is about going; not really prom, but going with Caroline, proud to be seen with her, eager to see what she chooses to wear.

Caroline is more excited for Saturday than she was for either of her high school proms. She knows before they even arrive at the school, she is certain to have the date that turns the most heads.

Sorry girls! There is no teenager that will compare to Seth Garrett!

She is excited to be seen with him, proud to show him off, and just enjoy the night together.

"Well, you haven't seen my dress…So I guess, you had better go with my personality," giggling and giddy.

They discuss more of their day, talk of silliness, vent frustrations about bureaucracy and paperwork, deadlines that are approaching, but most importantly the moments they must wait until they are together. Fortunately, Saturday arrives and Seth makes it home with plenty of time to get ready and meet her. He takes care to be pressed and polished when he arrives in his tailored black suit, black vest cinched tight against his ribs, and black tie. His look is modern and sleek and completely male.

Walking up to her front door, Seth finds a note clothespinned to the ribbon on the boxwood wreath. Written in Caroline's bold, curvy hand, it reads,

> *Seth,*
> *I'm not quite ready. The door is open so come on in…I can't wait to see you.*
>
> *Caroline*

He does not knock or ring the doorbell, but enters as instructed and waits at the bottom of the stairway for her. A few minutes later, Caroline emerges from her room and pauses at the top of the steps to look at him and smile. Seth takes one step closer as his heart flipflops and his breath catches in his throat. Knowing he has never seen anyone more beautiful, his smile takes up his whole face indicating his overwhelming approval.

Caroline's heart flipflops as well. She just keeps thinking what a beautiful man Seth is wondering if you can describe men as beautiful. But Seth is, not just because of his obvious physical blessings, but his manner, his personality, his strength, and a heart of tenderness Caroline has seen in many forms. She makes her way gracefully down the steps like Scarlett on her way to the dashing, smiling Rhett. A grand descent that all girls – all women – dream about. Unhurried and timed just right as his eyes draw you closer to him. Eyes that are filled with happiness, appreciation, and desire. A moment when you feel more than dreamlike, surreal, and you wish you could capture it somehow to relive it over and over and over again. Breathing deeply, heart pounding with a smile that has no intention of fading, she makes her way to Seth…He is waiting and has been waiting for her, maybe his whole life.

Her strapless dress is banded at the top with a black satin cuff across her modest chest. The willowy black crepe falls to an a-line skirt and subtle high-low hemline puddled in the back and revealing her strappy red shoes laced around her ankles in the front. Her hair is up in some type of arrangement that Seth does not know the name for, but highlights all her best features adding a regalness to her neck and shoulders with tendrils falling at all the right places. Her makeup is natural with soft smoky eyes and lips that are lightly stained red. Diamond rhinestones earrings hanging on long silver hooks are her only jewelry. Meeting him, Caroline becomes self-conscious. Looking away, she laughs nervously behind a hand showing off her signature red nails.

Seth does not allow a moment of shyness, delicately taking her into his arms careful not to muss any part of her.

"Mmm, my Beautiful Girl," kissing her gently.

Caroline's face is on fire in part to his apparent appreciation of her, his touching words, and the fact that he is the most beautiful man she has ever seen. Smiling back, she returns the compliment.

"My Beautiful Boy."

They meet Nick and Darby at her parents' house. Gran is there as well beaming and happy wishing them all to have a good time. Seth did not buy Caroline a corsage, instead, he brought three bundles of Lilly of the Valley tied with ribbon for Caroline, Charlotte, and Ruby.

When Ruby takes her flowers, her cheeks match her name and she says to Caroline, "Patricia!" and they both laugh. Charlotte takes Caroline's flowers and offers to stop by her house and put them in water. On their way, Seth asks what Ruby meant by *Patricia*.

"That is the name of a book by Grace Livingston Hill that Gran and I have read dozens of times. It has to be one of our all-time favorites. In it, John Worth brings Patricia Prentiss Lilly of the Valley. How could you have ever known how much I love them?" smiling at the amazing man beside her who is quickly claiming every piece of her heart.

"You told me to bring you flowers that matched your personality, so I did. Beautiful, happy, graceful, lovely," kissing her hand between each word; the first of many times tonight.

The evening with Seth is magical as are the weeks that follow with Spring giving way to the coming Summer. The school year ends and Caroline attends graduation on the last Friday in May. She does not hide her emotions as Mr. Stowers, the principal, comes to the podium one last time.

"Before we declare you graduates, it is time we bestow one last honor. Some would even say it is the highest honor given to a member of the Senior Class. We as a faculty and staff believe this student is the embodiment of everything that represents the spirit and pride of Belfry High School. We believe this student is the example, the high mark to which all our students should aim and we look forward to seeing the mark they will place on our community. It is with great pleasure that I present the 2006 John Hunt Memorial Award to...Jordan Baisden!"

The class is on its feet in thunderous applause before Jordan even realizes his name has been called. On his way to the stage, shouts, whistles, and high-fives greet him. Jordan shakes hands with the administration and the superintendent, then turns to the class holding the plaque over his head and they roar again. He leaves the stage and instead of returning to his seat, he rushes to the section of chairs reserved for the faculty. Standing before Caroline, he says, "Thank-you Ms. Hatfield, I could not have done this without you!"

Jordan laughs at her tears as Caroline begins to sob taking the boy who she has been fortunate to call her own, even if just for a time, into a tight embrace. There is no need for words of pride, admiration, or even love. Caroline and Jordan know it is there, because they have for a season, traveled life together.

Many hugs and pictures, a few sad goodbyes; whimsy and melancholy meet eager expectation and apprehension about the unknown and another school year is over, another class has graduated. Caroline does not take time to ponder, because she has been on this road before and she, like the excited graduates, wonders where the next road will take her, because it has already brought her to Seth.

Rushing home, she sends him a text saying they will meet him in the morning around 10:00 and puts the final touches together for their trip to the Cabin. She started packing the day he agreed to go, but first she had to do some shopping and try on nearly everything in her wardrobe. She has checked the weather 50 times a day for the last week to make sure nothing catches her by surprise. Shoes, clothing, jewelry, accessories, bathing suits, beach towels, and oodles of other essentials she will not use, but would hate to be caught without just in case. At 12:18, she crawls into bed disappointed she has not gotten a call or text from Seth, but excited to go to sleep ready for tomorrow to begin.

Will and Carter have already picked up Sophie when they arrive at 9:30am pounding on Caroline's front door. True to form, he walks in bellowing.

"Caroline! Why don't you have the garage doors open? Carter's outside ready to load the *Waverunners*."

Caroline pops back in the kitchen from the garage and answers nicely, "The doors *are* open and all of my luggage is on the front porch, if you would like to get it for me," Caroline knows better than to carry anything to Will's SUV, because no matter where she puts it, it will be in the wrong place.

"Ok," is his simple reply as Sophie walks in the door and he begins to bark out orders to her. "Sophie, you be sure to go to the bathroom, because I am not stopping in Pikeville, because you can't hold your pee!"

going back out the door to load Caroline's luggage and help Carter with the trailer.

Growling and irritated, Sophie asks, "Are you sure we have to bring him?"

"Well, he goes every year…It would be hard to get rid of him now. Besides, when he's not fussing at one of us, he is pretty funny!" and Caroline laughs knowing a trip without Will would be boring.

Sulking, Sophie agrees, "I guess!" and without being told again, she makes one more trip to the bathroom.

Nick calls before he leaves and says he is on his way to get Darby and will meet them at Seth's. Caroline sends a text that they are on the way, she and Sophie climb in the middle row of Will's Yukon, and leave on their first adventure of the summer.

At the end of Forest Hills, Will turns left and Carter asks, "Where are you going?"

"To pick up Seth. He lives in Fairview."

Carter is confused, because he has not heard of Seth. "Who's Seth?" Will's face is also confused as he looks back at his friend pulling across the highway. "Seth Garett. Caroline's boyfriend…Haven't you met him?"

This is news to Carter. "No. I haven't met him." Considering if he should ask the next question, "How long have they been dating?"

Carter is instantly irritated wishing he had said nothing when Will shouts to the girls in the back, "Caroline! How long have you and Seth been dating?"

Her face shining as her voice sparkles with delight, Caroline is happy to answer, "A little over two months. We met the 23rd of March!" She and Sophie giggle like schoolgirls. "Why?"

Will answers for Carter. "Carter wanted to know where we were going and I told him we had to pick up Seth."

Carter says no more staring out the window as they chatter and laugh and tease like children on their way to what they hope is the best place ever. A few minutes later, Will pulls into Seth's driveway where Nick and Darby are waiting. Getting out, he wants to check the trailer, rushing Caroline to hurry.

"Caroline, get Seth and tell him we are READY!" walking to the back to check the cables and his break lights one last time before they leave town.

Running onto the porch, Caroline does not notice Seth's Jeep is not in the driveway as she knocks on the door. Peering through the screen, she sees the house is dark and jiggles the doorknob finding it locked. Coming back to the car, she reaches in her purse to check her phone. No message from Seth.

Seeing the disappointed confusion on her face, Sophie suggests, "Maybe he's at the Armory? I wonder if he thought we were meeting him there?"

Caroline tries not to sound worried, "I don't know…Maybe." After Will gets back in, Caroline says, "Will, swing by the Armory. Seth's not home, so he might be there," as she hurriedly sends him another text.

Upon reaching the Armory, there are three cars in the parking lot and none of them are Seth's. Caroline nervously gets out walking to the door feeling five sets of eyes on her. She is relieved when she pushes on the door finding it unlocked. Seth brought her here a few weeks ago to show her around and though it still feels very unfamiliar, she remembers Seth's office is in the main room just through the doors.

Looking to the left and right, the hallway on either side of her is darkened for the weekend, though she can hear a few voices in the distance and the sound of work being done or moving furniture. She decides to enter Seth's office, because the door is open and the lights are on. A man dressed in ACUs just like Seth is crouched in front of the copier fussing about a paper jam he is trying to fix. Caroline knocks on the door to get his attention.

Spinning on his heels, the man looks up, and once he sees Caroline, rises and asks, "Yes, ma'am. What can I do for you?"

His tag reads Parker. Caroline has never met him nor has she heard Seth mention him. She suddenly feels more nervous, like she is not supposed to be here, trespassing.

"I am looking for Seth Garett. I was supposed to meet him today." She hopes Parker does not want more of an explanation as to why and where they were to meet.

Smiling at her, he tries to help. "Ma'am, Seth is not here," scanning the huge marker board over the copier, Parker finds his name. "He's been on assignment since Thursday. He may not be back into the office until Monday…No, at least Tuesday, because Monday is a holiday."

Caroline's mind is reeling. Seth did not say anything about being gone and she talked to him on Thursday. She does not want to indicate to Parker this news has taken her by surprise, but she asks, "*Assignment?* What does that mean? Where has he gone?"

Without breaking protocol, especially to someone he does not know, Parker answers, "I don't know the details, ma'am, but he could be just about anywhere." Noticing this is not what Caroline wants to hear, he offers, "Ma'am, if you give me your name, I will leave Seth a note on his desk to contact you when he gets back."

Disappointed that he is unable to help, Parker waits for Caroline to speak. She is lost in her thoughts for a few moments and Parker prompts her, "Ma'am, there are a few other guys here. If you want, I could ask them if they know when Seth will be back."

Caroline blinks herself back to the present and responds, "No, that's ok. I will just call him." It is important for her to let him know that she knows Seth on a personal basis and not just some random girl who shows up where he works. "Thank-you for your help…have a nice weekend."

"Yes, you too, ma'am," and Parker watches her leave the office and join the others in the parking lot. "I sure would like a pretty girl with a pair of *Waverunners* to come pick me up at work!" Laughing, shaking his head at how lucky some guys are, he returns to his work on the copier wondering where Seth is and why he has not let this girl know he would be gone.

Caroline does not know what to do. Checking her phone, there are still no messages from Seth. She walks back to the others, knowing she must decide.

Should I wait for him? Did he forget about this weekend? Why did he not tell me he would be gone?

Her face has a faraway look; puzzled, trying to figure out what to do. Carter's window is down and he is relaxing an arm on the door. His words are quiet and smug, mocking Caroline without laughing.

"I guess your boy stood you up!" His grin bears his teeth sneering knowing her mind is all over the place.

Her voice is faraway, but her stare pins him down. "No, he's not like that…He would not do that." Climbing in beside Sophie, Caroline explains before anyone asks, "You can go ahead, Will. Seth is out of town on assignment and won't be back until Tuesday." Looking out the window, Caroline spends much of the trip in silence.

Will puts the car in gear, silently finding Sophie's eyes in the rearview mirror. Without having to say a word, Sophie mouths to him with raised eyebrows and shaking head, "I don't know."

Carter also spends much of the trip silent looking out the window feeling dark pleasure that *this* Seth has disappointed Caroline and will not be joining them this weekend. His sneer returns at the small victory.

"I'm going to go ahead and fill up here. It's cheaper than at the dock. Caroline, do you and Sophie have the grocery list?" Will asks as he pulls to the gas pumps at Food City in Abingdon. He was glad that by the Virginia state line, Caroline seems to have her thoughts sorted out and begins to join in the conversation. He harasses Sophie a little more than usual and is far more foolish in his comments trying to lighten the mood, even though he also wonders why Seth did not tell Caroline he would be gone.

'Yeah, we've got it. We'll just meet you inside,"

Caroline and Sophie get out stretching from traveling for three hours with no bathroom break per Will's mandate. Nick has pulled up at the pump beside Will and is filling up his truck and *Waverunner* as well. The plan is to pack the cooler and be on the water as soon as possible. Darby heads inside with the girls. As they are about to step on the sidewalk in front of the automatic doors, Caroline's phone rings.

"It's Seth!" Darby and Sophie gesture for her to answer.

"Hey, Pretty Girl!" Any disappointment she has felt flees at the sound of his voice.

Not wanting to sound pleading, Caroline asks, "Seth, where are you?!? We came by to pick you up and you haven't answered any of my messages." She hopes he has a good excuse, because she has looked forward to this trip for weeks.

"Where are you?" Seth avoids answering with a question of his own.

Caroline's disappointment turns to frustration. "What? I'm in Abingdon! We just pulled in at Food City." Rolling her eyes, she glares at the girls who are only hearing one side of the conversation, but are also getting aggravated at Seth.

"The Food City next to Little Caesar's?"

"Yes!"

"How far is Gray, TN from Abingdon?"

Caroline is so confused. She does not know where Seth is and he keeps asking meaningless questions. Not attempting to hide her frustration, she barks at him, "I don't know! About an hour I guess!"

"Really, I made it in 48 minutes."

Caroline whirls around to see Seth's Jeep coming across the parking lot. He pulls into the space nearest to Caroline and the girls and she goes to him at a run. His wide smile and open arms are waiting for her.

"I didn't know what to think when you weren't home. Then you didn't return my messages. I didn't know if I should leave without you…I didn't want to leave you!" Her hands are on his chest, his neck, his face like he is an apparition that may disappear.

"I know! I'm sorry. I should have told you. It was a last-minute trip and I thought I would make it back." Seth is wounded by the sounds of desperation in her voice.

"I don't care! You're here now!"

Unabashed, Caroline grabs his face kissing him passionately as if he has been gone for years not days. Seth does not hesitate to respond unfazed by the hoots and whistles of their onlookers.

"Give me a break! You're in public!" Will yells at out his window as he pulls up alongside them to park. Getting out, he and Nick greet Seth. "Glad you could make it, because Caroline's sad face would not have been good for our weekend!" Both of them giving him the male hug – part handshake, part backslaps, part chest bump. Will steps aside and says, "Seth, let me introduce you to my best friend and the final member our group, Carter MacGuire."

The two men shake hands, but the feeling of welcome and comradery is not shared. The few words exchanged are clipped and curt. Seth clinches Carter's hand a beat longer than customary and Carter, whose height matches Seth's, looks him in the eye with challenge. Before anyone else notices, Nick gives instructions.

"We can talk on the boat! Let's get the groceries and get on the water!"

They descend on Food City buying the remaining necessary items for their weekend and then are on their way to the Cabin. Pulling in the drive, Caroline is eager to show Seth her most favorite place.

The *Cabin* as the family fondly refers to it, is single story with a walkout basement with cedar siding and hunter green roof and trim. A large eat-in kitchen and living room are on the front facing the lake with access to the wraparound covered porch from the living room. Two matching bedrooms and a bathroom are in the rear. The basement has four large identical bedrooms, a bathroom, and a door leading out to a ground floor porch. A concrete path winds down from the porch to a concrete patio carved out of the bank at the water's edge. The patio is framed on either end with stonework planter boxes like what Seth has seen at all the Hatfield's homes. In front of each box is a wooden bench. At the center of the patio, concrete steps lead to a gangplank attached to the dock. On the right, three round metal café tables with four matching chairs around each. Striped umbrellas in red, yellow, and turquoise in each table are down and secured with bungee straps. A fire pit is to the left and to the far left a wooden bench built into the dock runs the length. Beyond the entertaining side of the dock, there are slips for two boats and three floating lifts on the end.

Standing next to Caroline, Seth takes in everything – the house, the view, the lake – and a calming and welcoming feeling passes over him. Looking at her he asks honestly, "How can you ever leave here?"

Caroline is so pleased by his question, "It is very difficult…Come on! Let's unpack and I will show you your room so we can go." Spiriting him away, she is eager to get to the water.

Vehicles are quickly unpacked and they head to the lake. Passing the sign welcoming them to *Sportsman Marina,* Seth offers to help Nick unload.

"Yeah, that'll be great. Get all the stuff out of the back and the girls can take it on down to the boat. When the tires are completely under, you can unfasten the straps and it will float off the trailer."

Everyone hops out and springs into action. Seth and Caroline have ridden with Nick and Darby to the marina and he loads everything out of the truck bed onto Caroline's dock cart as Darby hooks lifejackets over her arm. Sophie joins them to help and they have everything unloaded making their way to Caroline's pontoon. Nick circles the parking lot with the sound of gravel crunching under his tires as Seth walks down the ramp directing him as he backs up. Once Nick's *Waverunner* is secured to the nearest cleat, Seth stands thigh-deep in the water and waves for Will to come down the ramp.

Repeating the process to Will's trailer, Carter is across from him releasing the cables and says, "I got it."

"Ok. I'll just help with this one until Will parks," Seth says floating the first machine towards Nick's.

Carter is much more firm in his repeated insist, "No…I've got it."

Looking at Carter, Seth hears tension in his voice that his face does not reveal. Hesitating one, two heartbeats, his mind quickly fills with anger and he drops the tow rope allowing it to float. The cool water trickles from his shorts down his legs squishing noisily in wet flipflops as he walks back up the ramp to the parking lot. The heat in his chest subsides when he sees Caroline has rushed back to meet him after carrying supplies with the girls. Her cheeks are bright and she is a little breathless.

"Are you ready?"

"More than ready!" Reaching an arm around her waist and kissing her, he swings her off her feet and she shrieks with delight. Hand in hand, they walk down the gangplank to the covered slip where Caroline houses her boat.

Nick, Will, and Carter are circling just outside the no-wake zone waiting on Caroline to come around. She will not be able to match their speed, but they will all go up the lake together with the boys racing ahead. Jumping back and forth across the wake, the three become tricksters showing off for each other spurred by the cheers and shouts from the girls. They are tasting the first bites of summer freedom – bright sunshine, warm breezes, cool water. There are few things better in life.

Passing under Aven's Bridge, Caroline slows to idle speed and the boys circle the boat like raiders getting ready to attack a wagon train. Nick comes the closest whipping around sending a fantail spray over the edge of the boat showering the girls who also shriek with delighted laughter.

Will kills his engine and floats over grabbing on to the railing asking, "Who's first on the tube?"

"Me! But you have to promise to be nice." Sophie is already buckling her lifejacket before Will responds.

"Sophie, I will be good as gold! Just don't be a wimp!" Both laughing already absorbed in the joy of play.

Seth tosses Will the rope and he hooks it on as Darby and Caroline steady the tube. Sophie flops on her belly reminding Will to be nice and pushes away from the boat. Will just laughs, starts the engine, and takes up slack. When the rope is tight, he calls over his shoulder, "Ready?" Sophie responds, "READY!" and the *Waverunner* leaps forward with Sophie screaming.

As promised, Will takes her on what he would consider a mild ride. Sophie returns in one piece and the others take turns while Nick and Seth raise the bonnet under the powerful sun. Caroline is the last to ride and makes it all the way to the boat without bouncing off the tube. Climbing the ladder on the back of the pontoon, Darby notices her dry hair.

"How did you make it back without getting wet?" she asks knowing Will tries to knock everyone off.

"Skills baby!" Caroline prances for everyone as Will ties off on the side of the boat to join them getting the laughter and sarcastic comments she has hoped for.

Seth looks up at her from his relaxed pose and says, "We're at the lake. It should be a rule you have to get wet," And before she knows what is happening, Seth has her thrown over his shoulder like a fireman giving her behind three whacks. Everyone is cheering, Caroline screams, and in four long strides, Seth is at the front of the boat plunging them both in the water. Coming up wet and gasping, Caroline tries to wrestle him away from her, but is easily overpowered. Laughter, kisses, and lake water all run together as the others jump in to swim and play.

When Will asks Sophie for the tenth time if he is burning, Nick wants to know what Darby packed in the cooler and if she brought snacks, they all decide to climb aboard. Searching through bags and coolers, everyone finds something to eat as they drift along warmed by the late afternoon sun and each other's company.

Will gets up to find sunscreen for another application handing the bottle to Sophie roughly telling her, "Put this on my back!"

Yanking the bottle away, she says, "Will! Notice how nicely Seth asks Caroline to put on his sunscreen. You could take a lesson!"

Turning his back to her, he replies, "Fine! Next time, I'll ask Seth… Be gentle! I think I'm already burnt!" squealing and winching when the cold lotion touches his back.

"You are burnt! You always get burnt! By the time we go home, you will be one giant freckle!" Sophie fusses, but she is smiling.

Reaching in the cooler, Sophie grabs a chunk of ice running it between her palms to rinse her hands and Nick asks, "Soc, find me a couple packs of gummies and toss'em over."

Digging through one of the bags, Sophie comes out with three, firing them at Nick landing each on his belly. He opens the first pack, gobbling down several, then tosses the next three in the mouth of the waiting Will.

Seth laughs again at the easy playfulness they all share. Once Sophie returns to her seat, he asks, "Sophie, why do they call you *Soc*?"

Will and Nick snicker shouting, "JONATHAN CAMPBELL!" roaring laughter at her, choking a little on their gummies.

Seth grimaces asking Sophie again, "I don't understand. What's that mean?"

With the two 7th graders still laughing, Sophie snaps, "Shut up you two!" directing her attention to Seth, "We moved to Belfry when I was in the third grade around Thanksgiving and was placed in Mrs. Kirk's class. That was the first day I met Nick." Seth looks towards Nick who is making a foolish scared face as Sophie continues. "Mrs. Kirk introduces me to the class using my full name – Sophie O'Hara Cross. Jonathan Campbell immediately piped up and repeated my name – *Sophie O'Hara Cross* – *SOC*! Naturally, as an eight-year-old, I was embarrassed and nervous, because it was my first day. That afternoon on the playground, I was talking with some girls and he came over and was teasing me. I tried to explain him I was named for my grandmothers – *Josephine Cross* and *Vivian O'Hara*. The little insect that he was would not listen and he had to be squashed. So, in between his donkey laughs, I," looking at her waiting audience proud to tell her favorite part, "walked over and *socked* him in the nose four times…After that, the name sort of stuck!"

Seth smiles in disbelief, "I hear marking your territory is very important and you didn't waste any time…A fight on your first day at school. That's impressive."

Sophie's face becomes almost ashen as she corrects Seth. "There was no fight…His nose burst like a tomato and he rushed to Mrs. Kirk and told her he had a nosebleed and needed to see the nurse. He wasn't about to tell her I hit him. I was a little bit of celebrity there for a while at Varney

Grade School. I hit him four times and he never bothered me again...*And*, he never called me Soc." Wheeling around to Nick, Sophie asks, "Did you know he went to college to become a youth minister and works at a huge church in Marietta, GA?" shocked at the thought that something as impossible as that would have ever happened.

"I actually did," Nick confirms putting the last gummie in his mouth wadding up the packages and rising to get a bottle of water out of the cooler. "He sent me a friend request a few months ago to tell me about a young men's retreat their church does during Christmas break each year. He wants me to bring some boys down. It sounded really great and they have premium speakers, lots of them Christian athletes, workshops, and those teambuilding obstacle course things. I mentioned it to Coach and I think we are going to try to take a few guys down...You should go with us, Soc. He's not married and I'd say he would *love* to see you!" winking as he takes a gulp of his water.

Disgusted, Sophie declines, "Well, I would not *love* to see him. I'm pleased he has left his wayward path and found the Lord, but I am sure, buried inside, he is still a punk!" and they all laugh.

Seth leans over and pats her knee, "I will never call you Soc!"

Sophie's only response is one palm warming up the knuckles of her other hand as a playful warning to Seth.

"Seth! I believe it is your turn on the tube!" Will hops up letting everyone know that snack time is over and he is ready for more play.

"I'm ready!" Seth agrees buckling his lifejacket. He dives off the front of the boat surfacing about twenty feet out with a "Waahaha!" shaking the water out of his face. With a strong overhanded crawl, he comes to the boat grabbing Caroline's ankles acting like he is going to jerk her in. She squeals and he asks, "You wanna ride with me?"

Girlish grin, she answers, "Yes, but you can go alone first, then I'll go with you."

Grabbing the bottom railing, he pulls himself up to Caroline who has sat down on the edge dangling her feet in the water. Her eager lips are waiting for him, "Have fun!" Flopping back in the water, he winks at her and swims to the tube.

"Seth, hook it up to mine!" Carter shouts through cupped hands. "We've used Will's all day. We'll give his a rest." Carter's lifejacket is on and his leg is thrown over the edge before any objections. Seth brings the rope to Carter to hook on and he holds the front of the tube helping Seth climb on top. Carter's foot gently pushes Seth and the tube away from the intake and says quietly, "Hold on!" Seth has no time to decide if his words were spoken through gritted teeth, because the engine fires and he is jerked forward.

Carter's machine has more power than Will's and this late on a Saturday evening, the water is like glass as he continues to increase his speed. Whipping around, Carter doubles-back across his own wake bouncing Seth over the waves, but his size and weight keep him close the water. Veering left, Carter shoots behind a cabin cruiser and four rows of waves going airborne before the rope pulls tight yanking Seth forward causing his neck to jerk and his body to slide to the edge. He recovers pulling himself back to the middle as Carter turns to the right bringing Seth close to the boat thinking he will drop. When he does not, Carter opens the throttle to a dangerous speed zooming past the pontoon where the remaining five are standing watching the whole scene take place. Carter's waves rock them with Nick and Will's *Waverunners* lurching into the side of Caroline's boat.

Will angrily yells, "Slow down, idiot!"

Nick looks to Carter who is several hundred yards away and asks no one, "Why is he going so fast?"

Swinging wide around the point, Carter is able to bring Seth almost parallel alongside him. He looks over expecting Seth to be tired and maybe a little scared. Seeing neither, Carter hammers down again going straight towards the boat. When he is about 250 feet out, he looks back at Seth who is still confidently on the tube. Making a sudden 90° turn, the rope slingshots then snaps tight sending Seth skipping like a stone then tumbling and tumbling. The girls scream and Caroline covers her face ready to cry. Will and Nick heedless of lifejackets, dive over the edge and swim out to Seth. Darby and Sophie hold on to the *Waverunners* tied up to the side as Caroline starts the engine to pick up the boys who have arrived at Seth who is face down in the water.

Seth has a secure hold on the tube and when Carter makes his final run back to the boat, he was going to let go knowing neither of their egos was worth getting injured or killed over. A second too soon, Carter turns in the other direction and Seth is completely disoriented before he knows what is happening. Skimming across the water, he feels like his limbs are going in four different directions then face plants taking in a lungful of water. His mind is dazed and addled, pain shooting down his back and legs, hurting like he has just landed on concrete.

Nick reaches him first turning him on his back. Eyes closed, Seth is coughing and choking and can hear Nick's questions, but his mind is not quite ready for him to understand much less answer. Bringing a hand to his face, Seth wipes his mouth and opens his eyes. By this time, Will is here and he and Nick hold his floating body as the girls slowly pull up not wanting the wake to jostle him.

Caroline cannot see him, but knows something is wrong when Sophie gasps, "Oh! He's hurt!"

Seth is upright and talking with Nick and Will reassuring them he is fine when Caroline leans over the boat to see him. "Seth!" tears fill her throat and eyes as her hands cover her mouth.

Seth leans back and squints one eye closed letting her know he is okay, "I'm fine, Pretty Girl. It's just a nosebleed."

Nosebleed or not, Nick and Will float him to the ladder. Nick scrambles up the rungs leaning down, he grabs on to Seth's lifejacket and helps haul him out of the water as Will remains behind to steady him. Leading him to the nearest seat, Caroline with Sophie and Darby descend on him like mother hens fussing and clucking. Seth's injuries consist of just a nosebleed, but he is sure to feel sore in the morning. Caroline removes his lifejacket and is drying him off as Sophie brings paper towels and Darby a zipper bag of ice.

Staying her hands, Seth knows Caroline is very close to tears. Speaking gently to her, "Caroline, it's just a nosebleed. Really, I'm fine. See! It's already stopped," he tips his head back as if Caroline will want to examine his nostrils for any trickles of blood.

"That was a great ride! The best I've had in a long time. We'll do it again tomorrow!" Looking past Caroline, Seth says to Carter as he gets back on. This whole time, he was winding up the tow rope on the tube and securing it to the side of the boat seemingly uninterested in Seth's welfare.

Carter comes up short when he realizes Seth is talking to him and replies, "Yeah, tomorrow. Definitely."

Seth gives him a slight wink. Carter, the only one to notice it, has the fire inside him burn hot. No apologies are spoken. Nick and Will would like to have few choice words with Carter using lots of adult language, Darby and Sophie scowl at him wondering if he would have treated one of their boys the same way, and Caroline is ready to filet him like a fish. No one on the boat presses the subject and all realize this is between Seth and Carter. The moments pass, and everyone appears back to normal not wanting this event to spoil the rest of the weekend.

"Will, the fire needs to be lit on the dock!" Sophie reminds Will as he walks around in the kitchen in their way as the girls put away dinner dishes. She is getting everything for s'mores on a tray along with the popcorn popper.

Will stuffs two huge marshmallows in his mouth promising Sophie, "I'll do it as soon as I get out of the bathroom!"

Rolling her eyes in exasperation, "It'll never get lit if it's up to him!"

Nick is on all fours refilling the cooler in readiness for tomorrow. Laughing at Will and Sophie, he adds more cans of pop before wheeling it over to the freezer to dump in the ice.

"Don't worry, Sophie. I'll start the fire," Seth offers then asks, "Nick, where is everything?"

Still scooping ice, Nick directs him, "The wood box is downstairs on the bottom porch just outside the door. There is a wood bag hanging on the side so you won't have to make several trips. Matches are over there in the second drawer and there are a couple of newspapers in the living room. If it doesn't light, Dad may have some starter logs somewhere. I'll be down in a minute to help if you need me."

"Ok. Sounds good."

Seth turns to leave and Caroline gives him an air kiss. Finding everything just as Nick has told him, Seth walks down the steps with his supplies ready to start the fire. The evening has reached almost full dark, but he can see well enough remembering where everything was earlier when they came in for dinner. Setting the bag down, Seth crunches the newspapers into balls arranging them in the bottom of what looks like a huge cast iron pot about three feet wide and a foot deep perched on four legs. He places kindling around the paper teepee style then strikes the match watching the paper catch hearing the kindling crackle.

As he reaches to place the first log on the fire, Seth feels like he is being watched then senses movement at the far corner of the dock. Carter comes from the shadows letting Seth know he has been here the whole time.

Still hunkered down at the fire, Seth admits, "Whoa Carter! I didn't see you there," placing another piece of wood in the flames.

"What are you doing, Seth?" Carter's voice is quiet and even.

Without looking up, he answers, "I'm building a fire. Will wanted s'mores and popcorn, so everyone's coming down."

Carter acts like he did not hear him asking again, "What are you doing *here*, Seth?"

Believing Carter's question is filled with hidden meanings; Seth decides to be totally transparent. Standing, he dusts his palms on his thighs looking him in the eye with the same challenge Carter had earlier. "Well, Friend, I believe I'm taking advantage of your missed opportunity." There is no hint of smugness or sarcasm in his voice, just honest accuracy.

Both men's faces are partially lit from below by the flames that are growing in the fire creating an eeriness to their features. Carter takes one step closer to him like they are both alpha males seeking dominance in the herd. In the moments of silence other than the hiss of the fire, they realize only one of them is going to come out alive – metaphorically and possibly literally. They wait for the other to speak. Carter yields first.

"You are wrong…I've always been here…I've missed nothing." Cold and calculating, Carter looks at Seth his voice filled with arrogance.

Seth has no desire for any truthful or fabricated explanation Carter should choose to provide. Instead, he waits calming the urge for his fist to knock him backwards in the water. Carter speaks again.

"You with all your soldier boy charm has no idea…"

"Well, I guess that's why I'm here…I intend to find out."

Carter comes to stand before Seth. They are not toe-to-toe, but a few inches would bring them there. Seth clinches his teeth and his jaw hardens. Carter's voice comes out again quiet and even – cold, emotionless, arrogant.

"Like I said, you have no idea…and I've missed nothing."

His words are full of insults and mockery. Seth knows he is being laughed at, but without asking more questions, he cannot be completely sure of Carter's meanings. He just stands there looking at him and never in his life has he wanted to put his hands on someone's throat as he does now wanting to silence everything that is not being said.

Before either of them can act on the emotions that are simmering like lava inside them, laughter comes from the house and Will storms on the dock yelling, "S'mores!"

When the parade joins Seth and Carter, they all take places around the fire. Carter grabs Will's upper arm and slaps him on the back. "I'm going to pass on the s'mores, buddy. I have a patient in their second day of recovery and I need to call the hospital. Caroline that was a delicious meal. Thank-you so much. Goodnight, everybody." Carter is happy allowing his smile to rest on each of them except Seth. The friends who have known and loved him since childhood are comforted his sullenness has lifted and glad that it does return the entire trip. In fact, Carter's mood is nearly gleeful. The young man who has so recently joined their group is suspicious doubting the genuineness in his behavior since it seems to be flipped like a switch.

That night, the rest of the house is asleep and Caroline is laying on Seth's bed. They are curled on their sides quietly talking in the soft glow of the lamplight being serenaded by night sounds from his open window. Her fingertips trace the lines of his face to finally rest her hand on his neck. Closing her eyes, she sighs and tells him again, "I am so glad you're okay. What would I have done if you were hurt?" Looking at him, her face shows uncertain sorrow and fear creeping in around them like fog.

Seth is certain her mind has gone into the future and she is no longer meaning a bloody nose at the lake. He pulls her close, tenderly kissing her lips. "Caroline, I'm fine. I'll be okay."

Her arms are around him kissing him with the fierce passion of the afternoon; near desperation. Enjoying her so much, Seth is ready to be swept away, but his mind checks when his body does not want to, taking his mouth from her.

"Caroline, enough...It's time for bed."

Trailing kisses down his jaw and neck, she tells him, "I'm staying with you."

His better judgement weakens, but before it is all gone, he pulls away again. "No, Caroline. You're going upstairs…to your room," her eyes are wide with disappointment, but Seth is not swayed. He chooses to be the responsible one. "This is your grandmother's house and she would not be pleased if we stayed together…And…we have an audience; neither of us want that." Before she has a chance to argue or pout, Seth rolls off the bed and takes her hand leading her to the door. He kisses her goodnight and she goes upstairs.

Closing the door, he takes off his clothes thinking about how he has never asked a woman to leave his bed when she wanted to stay. Maturity or insanity – he is not sure which has arrived.

The young man in the other bedroom watches the light from Seth's room spill into the hall then grow smaller and disappear. He lays there with his hand wedged behind his head thinking about the day and how 16 hours ago everything was so different and he wonders if his reaction would have been different today if had succeeded in killing him. Not killing him, just eliminating.

Chapter XX

"Thank God for this gift too wonderful words."
— II Corinthians 9:15 NLT

Carter is the last to wake up Sunday morning and everyone is dressed for church. It stings him to see Seth is ready, waiting on Caroline and his tie coordinates with her dress, wondering how he is so prepared when the only luggage he carried in was a knapsack. Will wants to know if he is going with them and without answering, Carter rushes back downstairs to get dressed, though not eager to attend church.

Green Springs Presbyterian is a short drive from the Cabin. Walking across the parking lot Nick says, "Seth, ask Caroline why she called this *her church* as a kid," Nick smiles as his sister's cheeks pink.

Before Seth asks, Caroline answers not allowing her brother's teasing to bother her, "I said it was the church I was going to get married in, because it's old and has stained glass windows. Nick is just being silly!" hoping Seth does not get the wrong idea.

Smiling, he folds her hand in the crook of his arm leading her up the steps. Taking the bulletin and exchanging warm handshakes with the welcoming deacons, Seth and Caroline follow Will and Sophie into the sanctuary with Nick, Darby, and Carter behind. During the opening hymn, they rise with the congregation and Seth leans over to whisper holding the edge of her hymnal, "I think this would be a perfect church to get married in," then faces the choir and starts singing.

Caroline's heart nearly stops beating and hopes no one else has heard him. She can barely concentrate on the remainder of the service as she studies and admires the sanctuary and allows her mind to visualize, if only briefly, herself in a vintage white gown and an extralong veil meeting an eager, smiling, and strikingly handsome Seth at the end of the aisle. The picture forms so quickly in her head, she is startled when Seth takes her hand as the sermon begins.

There rest of the weekend is enjoyed by everyone; a truly perfect kickoff to summer - two and a half months of freedom and play and adventure. Those carefree days where thoughts of school are replaced by laughter, all shirts are sleeveless, sunglasses become a required accessory, and ice tea splashed with lemonade is the drink of the day. Summer when nighttime comes much later begging you to stay out on porch swings watching fireflies or sneaking in midnight swims as a relief from the heat you prayed for during the endless winter. Food is barbequed and eaten outdoors, rowdy children have grimy faces and bloody knees, the smell of cut grass and tinkling windchimes become the siren song luring you into the magic, whimsy, and delight of all things summer. Badminton and croquet are competitive sports and as the wind plays music through the trees, if you listen closely, you can almost hear Judy Garland and Van Johnson sing.

The third week of June, the Hatfield's as well as Ruby go the Cabin on Family Vacation and Seth Garrett joins them. He has become one of them so easily, it would be unusual if he was not there. Days are on the water with evenings spent in the fierce competition of Euchre tournaments. Partners change every round, points traveling with the player, and on the fourth night, Clayton, Meghan, and Seth share a three-way tie. During the first round, Clayton and Caroline beat Meghan and Nick leaving the final battle with Seth and Ruby. There is quite a bit of good-natured trash talking as both teams enter the barn.

"Gran, you know you are a better player than Caroline!" Alex encourages his grandmother.

"Dad, no pressure! It's just your title on the line!" Nick laughs reminding Clayton.

"Seth! Are you really going to try and beat Caroline?" Darby teases.

"He has no worries. She'll let him win!" Meghan goads.

"Don't listen to any of them Seth. We've got this!" Ruby assures him.

"Ruby! No talking across the table!" Clayton scolds his mother-in-law and everyone laughs.

"Mom, you can do it! You're the one who taught Clay!" Charlotte coaches getting a traitorous look from her husband.

Caroline deals and the face up card is a ten of diamonds and it makes it through without anyone calling it up. Flipping the card over and removing the burn pile, Seth is to her immediate left and calls trump – clubs. Glancing at her cards, Caroline looks across the table at her dad and neither of them break concentration. Caroline looks back at her cards. Having the left bar and the king of clubs, if she pays attention, she and Clayton should be able to set them.

Each team has won two by the fifth hand, and Seth leads with the ace of clubs. Clayton and Ruby are out of trump and throw off suit. Caroline holds the last card and looks at Seth like they are in a smoke-filled saloon and she is Maureen O'Hara at the high stakes table with John Wayne. She smiles and her eyes raise to Seth as she lays the Jack of Spades on the stack. Clayton lets out a whoop and starts dancing around the kitchen fist pumping. Her smile is wicked and enchanting and all Seth can do is shake his head with a lips pressed smile. The eager audience sends up a chorus of noise and commotion as Alex snatches up the burn pile finding the Jack of Clubs – the right bar.

Still shaking his head in disbelief, Seth comments to Caroline, "I was so certain you were trumped out and the ace would make it through."

Caroline leans just a little closer and responds, "Sweet boy, nothing is ever certain; there's always a gamble!" winking at him.

Before she delightfully mesmerizes him, he focuses his attention on Ruby. "Lovely Ruby, I should have been a more capable partner for you."

Coming to his side of the table, Ruby places her arm around his shoulder. Seated, Seth is almost Ruby's height standing. She comforts the boy saying, "I don't mind! I've let Clay win for years…It makes him feel good!" scrunching her face and laughing so like what he has seen from Caroline many times and the whole family laughs.

They all seem to move at once during this halftime of play. Darby's phone rings and she goes downstairs to talk, Ruby says she needs to get ready for bed, and Charlotte and Caroline offer to help Meghan get the boys bathed and in their pajamas, even though they whine that a lake bath should do. Nick and Alex begin to rifle for snacks and second helpings on dessert wanting to know if the girls are ready for another game while Clayton invites Seth onto the porch.

Leaning against the railing, Clayton pulls two cigars from his pocket offering one to Seth. When he hesitates, Clayton explains, "I gave these up a little over three years ago now, when I had an *episode*, but occasionally, I don't think they could hurt. Anyway, a guy at work had a baby, so we can say we're celebrating."

Reaching the cigars towards Seth, he takes one and the lighter. Bringing the flame close, his face is illuminated and Clayton notices this is not his first cigar. Handing the lighter back to Clayton for him to use, Seth takes a long draw, exhaling slowly; he feels nervous. He and Clayton chat about nothing in particular as they quietly smoke, each of them taking turns blowing rings.

Clayton asks, "Have you had a good vacation, son?"

Seth smiles and answers honestly, "Yes, I have, sir. It is so peaceful here. I can see why Caroline loves it so much. It makes you want to stay forever."

Inhaling, the coal on the end of his cigar glows orange, looking up at the starry sky, Clayton blows out smoke and agrees. "Yes...I felt the same way the first time Charlotte brought me here...I loved it so much, I decided then to stay forever...That was almost 40 years ago," looking right at Seth, their faces are almost unreadable under the dark sky, though the light glowing from the kitchen window brightens one eye, half a mouth.

For a heartbeat, Seth is uncertain of his meaning, but by the next heartbeat, the message is clear. "Yes, sir. That would be nice."

Taking one last draw, Clayton tosses his unfinished cigar over the banister. Seth has been facing him in a bouncer rocker and as Clayton moves towards the door, he grasps Seth's shoulder. With a few simple words, Clayton Hatfield gives his consent. "Yes, son. That would be very nice...Remember, you're always welcome," and he goes inside to join his sons for sweet treats before the next game begins.

Seth does not move until Clayton is securely behind the closed door. Rising, he looks out on the lake. He can faintly see the outline of the dock, though he can hear waves lapping against the sides and Caroline's pontoon that has been brought up from the marina for the week bobbing in the drift. Taking another puff, he tosses the cigar off the porch watching it land in the yard sending up sparks. Leaning on his forearms, he thinks about what Clayton has said – approval and welcome all in the same message. Seth has not expected this conversation, nor anticipated it, but now that it has taken place, a rush of excitement floods through him.

He hears the door open and Caroline comes to the porch looking for him. Turning to watch her over his shoulder, she joins him leaning on the railing linking her arm through his then lacing their hands.

"What are you doing out here? Sam sent me to find you, because he has two books he would like you to read, before he has to go to bed." Kissing his arm through his sleeve, she exclaims, "Yuck! You stink! What have you been doing?" sniffing him like a bloodhound.

"Talking with your dad and smoking."

"Smoking! What for?" standing up so she can see him better wearing a disgusted face.

Nonchalant, he answers, "He offered me a cigar, so I had to smoke it." Knowing she is about to take on her teacher voice and scold them both, he defends before she gets all fired up. "He has a guy at work who just had a baby. We smoked less than half in celebration."

Caroline says no more thinking Seth's voice is sad. Lacing their fingers tighter, his free hand smooths the back of hers then lifting their hands, he kisses her knuckles. Sensing his uneasiness and wondering what her dad may have said, she turns him to look at her. Touching his face, she asks, "Seth, what's wrong? Are you ok?" sadness and anxiety in her voice.

He covers her hand and closes his eyes. After a few moments, Caroline becomes worried and asks again, "Seth?"

"I love you!" his eyes are wide with passion and emotion. "I love you! You, this house, your family…everything is so much more than I could have ever hoped for…I love you so much, but I know I am not nearly enough –"

She silences his words with her lips, because she does not believe them nor does she want to hear them. Hands, lips – searching, seeking, words are inadequate at this moment when actions can say so much more. Pulling away, her heart is pounding and her head is overwhelmed with euphoria. Taking his face in her hands, she knows she must speak.

"Seth, you are so wrong…You aren't just enough, you are *more* than enough…My whole life I have been…waiting for you!"

This glorious revelation nearly bursts his heart and the hummingbirds in their chests come close to cracking ribs. He is home! After years of loneliness and discontent. After moving and moving and moving, always feeling displaced and unsettled. After unsuccessful and unhappy romances that left him hollow and empty, riddled with disappointment and insecurity. After coming close to accepting that some things in life were just not going to happen – Seth Garrett is at home in the arms of a beautiful school teacher who is so different than, yet completely perfect for him. Who is genuine and innocent and quirky and childlike. Who loves being happy and makes him happy and tells him she wants go with him as he meets God. The girl – the home he has looked for makes all the uncertainty of the future seem suddenly clear and possible. Seth loves Caroline and no matter what is ahead, he knows everything will be fine, because, he wants to travel life with her!

Diving in to taste her again, Caroline resists him. "Seth, you are so beautiful and wonderful…and I'm not young or beautiful…and I'll never be lean and I talk too much and I'm really attached to my family…and I'm silly and foolish and too optimistic…I am not a trophy and you deserve so much more!"

He can hear the tears enter her voice before his thumbs reach to dry them away. His words and his hands are firm as he shakes her head wanting her to open her eyes.

"Caroline…Caroline! Look at me! You are beautiful and wonderful and amazing…You are not a trophy…you are so much more. You are the prize! And, and I don't deserve you, but I never want to let you go!"

She lets the flood come as her arms are around him never wanting to let go either. Memories of sadness, loneliness, disappointment, and the cold that she has allowed to reside in her heart are forgotten in an instant and the fire of Seth's love and the opportunity to finally give her love to him, heals her brokenness and she is whole.

Seth holds her and lets her cry as long as she wants, because he feels close to crying as well. Overwhelmed and joyous, he lets the last few minutes just wash over him. Soon, Caroline's tears are no more and she looks up at Seth.

"My Sweet Boy…I love you! I love you so very much and I never want to let you go!" And the two just laugh in each other's face, holding on to one another, loving that life has brought them to now, to this moment with each other.

With love still bubbling inside, Seth reminds them both, "Sam is waiting for his stories."

Hand in hand, they go inside – from the darkness into the light knowing that everything has changed and from this point, nothing will ever be the same. Life, relationships, love reaches plateaus where emotion grows and deepens giving you strength to climb to the next summit. Seth and Caroline have just scaled the first pinnacle.

The Friday before 4th of July, Seth and Caroline decide to have a low-key evening at home with Seth agreeing to allow Caroline to choose the movies they will watch though he hopes to entice her with other diversions. Simple times together, making the effort to get to know one another is so important for them. Moments do not have to be complicated or expensive to be enjoyed. As long as they are together, that is all they need.

Thursday afternoon, Seth gets a phone call from his mother telling him they will be in town Friday evening and would like to stay with him until Sunday. He calls Caroline that evening and after some drawn out hemming and hawing, Caroline says, "Seth, I want to meet your family, but I think you need to spend Friday with them. We'll have an early dinner here on Saturday around 3:00. We'll eat out by the pool and if my parents happen to stop by around 7:00, that will work out quite nicely. How does that sound?"

"Ahhh, Pretty Girl, that sounds great. I've only been home a few times since I moved here and I haven't seen my family since Christmas. I would like some time with them first…Not that I don't want you to meet them. I do! I love you, so I definitely want them to meet you and I've told them about you and dinner at your house is perfect. I want your parents to stop, too…Caroline, this is big and you are the most important thing to me. I just want everything to go right…Do you understand? I haven't hurt your feelings, have I?"

Laughing to herself, it tickles her when Seth gets flustered, because it so rarely happens. She comforts her boy. "Seth, I love you and you are the most important thing in my life. I also have two brothers of my own, so I know a little about mothers and sons. I want to meet them and I want everything to work out just perfectly. This is a big weekend, so I understand," smiling again, she waits for her levelheaded boy to return.

"I'm so glad you understand. My mom and I...our relationship is different. I just need time with her first, then everything will be okay." Seth holds his breath until he is sure Caroline understands.

"Seth, that is fine. You need to see her; spend time with her without me and I won't bother you...I'll see you on Saturday around 3:00. If there is anything special that you want, let me know."

Seth knows Caroline understands. Knows she appreciates strong relationships with your parents. She is not needy or insecure and will be perfectly fine having to wait to see him for two days, not expecting him to call. Seth, however, is going to be the mess and will need to see her.

"No! Don't do that! Let's have lunch tomorrow and tomorrow night when they're all in bed, I will call you, because before I go to sleep, I want to hear your voice. I want you to tell me you love me and are excited to meet my family. And you'll let me explain that my brother and sister talk way too much and my mother will be sizing you up, asking you a million questions and that my dad will not be what you expect, but you will really like him...And..."

"Sweet Boy, I love you so very much! And I will love your family, because they are part of you. I get paid to listen to noisy teenagers, my mom interrogated you, and I know your dad will be wonderful...Rest well and be as glad as I am that they are coming."

Hanging up the phone, Seth wonders again how he is so fortunate to have Caroline in his life. He cannot wait until Saturday for them to meet her.

Caroline is pleased with her sun-bleached hair in its carefree mess secured low and to the side. And how her gauzy, racerback tank in clover green makes her hair look more blonde and eyes brighter highlighting her favorite features without drawing too much attention. She loves how the soft linen shorts cuffed at mid-thigh add the appearance of length to her legs and intensity to her tan. Finally, she loves how the strappy wedges fit around her ankle and show off her red toenails.

Taking the shortbread cookies, Seth's favorites, out of the oven to cool, she surveys the room to make sure everything is just right. The morning started out dreary to be followed by thunderstorms throughout the day and now has settled in to a steady shower. So, her plans of alfresco dining by the pool are out. Just the six of them will be at dinner and she has the dining room ready. Appetizers are on the coffee table and desert will be served on the screened porch when her parents join them. She has flowers at the center of the dining table and on the corner of the kitchen counter.

Everything is ready, so when she gets a message from Seth saying they are on the way, she lights three hazelnut candles and rushes to the bathroom one final time to check her appearance and deal with the nervous pees. Coming back down the steps, she hears Seth knock on the door, muffled chattering on the porch and his voice mildly scolding someone. With her hand on the door, she waits a few more beats not wanting to catch anyone off guard and to settle her our nerves.

I'm meeting Seth's family...I'm meeting Seth's family! Relax, don't talk too fast, be sure to let him introduce you to his mother first.

Opening the door, she is greeted by Seth who gives her a YIKES face as she steps aside letting everyone come in.

Timmy and Traci, Seth's 15-year-old twin siblings, are first in the door behind him. Quiet, but fidgeting, it is startling how much they look like Seth – same rich burnt brown hair, same striking blue eyes, they even share the angles of his face and jaw with slightly smaller versions of his nose. If they were seen together in the absence of their parents, it would be easy to mistake them as Seth's own children.

"Caroline, this is my brother and sister, Timmy and Traci."

The pair smile and in unison respond, "It's nice to meet you, ma'am." Caroline cannot decide if their words were rehearsed in the car or just the normal singsong speech of twins.

Stepping aside, Timothy Russell enters. He is a powerful looking man almost as tall as Seth and an equally commanding presence with the essence of military that after 24 years of active duty followed by almost as many years as a JROTC instructor, it is part of his being. When he speaks to Caroline, his smile is genuine and she feels relaxed and welcome.

"Caroline, we have heard nothing but good things about you and it is so nice we finally get to meet."

Tim does not quite hug, but squeezes her upper arm kissing her other cheek. Caroline takes a deep breath as Tim joins his children. She has only one person left to meet – his mother. Without waiting for introductions, Beverly Russell takes ahold of Caroline in an unexpected embrace and it is after a few moments of her chatter before Caroline responds likewise, because she is taken by surprise.

"CAROLINE! I am so happy to *finally* meet you! Seth talks about you all the time!" leaning out of the embrace, but holding her arms, Beverly exclaims, "You are beautiful! Very beautiful!" and she hugs her again holding her tight waffling her from side to side. "I am glad Seth has found such a wonderful girl!"

Surprised and shocked to say the least. Seth has made her a tad nervous about meeting his mother, knowing they are very close and share a very special relationship not too unlike what she shares with Charlotte. She now realizes his hesitation and inability to find the right words to describe his mother. She is warm and boisterous and chatty and even a little overwhelming, but in a matter of moments, she has made Caroline feel completely welcome.

Taking her by the hand and pulling her close, Beverly leads Caroline to her own couch as her family parts like the Red Sea to let them through, finding their own seats once she has Caroline secured beside her. Seth looks at his dad and they exchange raised-brow expressions settling in comfortably allowing Beverly to have control. Knee to knee, Beverly begins a pleasant interrogation of Caroline occasionally touching the girl's hair or face or clothing to emphasize her point.

"You are so beautiful…But so is my boy! I couldn't imagine you being anything less," grinning mischievously at Caroline pleased to provide the compliment.

"Your house is wonderful. Have you lived here long?"

Smiling, Caroline steels herself for many rapid-fire questions and provides plenty of details, because she senses that Beverly is not the kind of woman who will appreciate modest, nondescript answers.

"On the property, nearly my whole life, but I have only been in this house for about six years. My grandmother lives next door. You saw her house on the way in and my parents and younger brother live at the top of the hill."

"How many brothers do you have?" Beverly's face, mouth, and eyes are all smiling the entire time she questions and Caroline answers.

"I have two. Nick is my younger brother. He is a Special Education teacher at Belfry and my older brother, Alex, is a contractor and builder with a firm in Pikeville. His wife is an architect and designer. They have twins as well, Jackson and Jacob, and then there is sweet Sam." She looks at Seth and winks, because he is always teasing her about Sam and how he is her favorite. On their first meeting, the little boy informs him that he is five now and is Caroline's very best friend. In a very man-to man voice, the little boy wants no competition. Seth smiles back, so pleased with his beautiful girl and how his mother is happily gobbling her up.

"And you are a teacher?"

"Yes, ma'am. I teach history and Senior Studies at Belfry and Anatomy at the community college. Right next to where Seth works."

"Ahh, history is Timmy's favorite!" looking to her younger son whose face brightens when the attention is directed towards him.

The flood of questions continues and Seth allows his mother to commandeer Caroline for several minutes. Tim does not bring the conversation to a halt, because a wave like Beverly is not easily stopped, but he does get her to pause.

"Beverly, we are all excited to meet Caroline and we probably have a few questions of our own. She has also invited us here for dinner. How about we try to make ourselves useful and not overwhelm our hostess?"

Beverly scowls at her husband through thin lids, but does what he asks without arguing. She scurries Caroline into the kitchen insisting that she helps and soon everyone is seated in the dining room. Seth and his dad are at opposite ends of the table with their women to their lefts. Timmy captures the seat beside Caroline to the disappointment of his frowning sister. Once everyone is settled, he pipes up and offers, "I can pray, Caroline, if you like," his eagerness is evident and his enthusiasm is true.

Smiling at him, she responds sweetly. "That would be nice, Tim. We hold hands in my family, if that's ok." Caroline notices that Seth and his dad call him Tim, so she does likewise to not sound patronizing.

With the smile of a star struck teenage boy, Tim is happy to respond, "Sure! That's fine with me!" linking his hand with Caroline's, he prays, "Dear Lord, we are so glad You kept us safe in our travels. We appreciate everything You provide and how You bless us. We thank You for this food and being able to share it in Caroline's lovely home. And Lord, we thank You for Caroline; she seems very nice. I ask all these things in the name of

Jesus and pray we all find everlasting life...AMEN." He grips her fingers and smiles. Caroline is confident she has found a friend in Tim.

Conversation breaks out again, mainly directed at Caroline, but this time, Beverly gives everyone else a turn though she smiles brightly like everything Caroline says is just wonderful. Towards the end of the meal, Timmy proudly begins to tell Caroline the plans for the rest of their trip.

"We are leaving tomorrow to VMI. Do you know what that is?" excited to include her in his adventure.

"Yes – Virginia Military Institute. It's in Lexington, VA. I've been there before."

Timmy's eyes are wide with shock and pleasure. "You have! Why?"

Caroline knows she is about to reel the boy in and is happy to do it. "My uncle used to live near Lexington and we took a tour. In fact, I thought I would have liked to have gone to school there, but they didn't take girls at that time. Be sure to stop by Lee's Chapel just off the edge of campus. Robert E. Lee is buried there and so is his horse. Everything is impressive and beautiful. You will really enjoy it."

Timmy's mouth is open and he cannot seem to find the next words then they all tumble out. "I want to go to school there! Seth did too, but it was too expensive. I hope to get a scholarship. Did you want to be a cadet?" Answering with honesty, "Well, I guess so, but the main reason was because Stonewall Jackson was a professor there and he is my favorite character in history."

Timmy's face it astounded as everyone else at the table knows the thrill Caroline has just given him. "I LOVE Stonewall Jackson!" and he proceeds to share a history lesson with Caroline from Appomattox to Zion's Hill with her laughing and smiling at his interest and overwhelming enthusiasm. When he is finished and thoroughly impressed, Timmy looks to his older brother and declares, "Seth! Marry her!"

Seth's cool response does not indicate the heat that passes through his chest. "Just because she *loves* Stonewall Jackson?"

"That is reason enough!" looking at him dumbfounded.

Reaching, he takes her hand and smiles, "Well, ok!" Caroline blushes, Traci giggles, and Timmy pounds the table in confirmation.

The rain comes harder and the day becomes more relaxed, because Caroline feels she has now passed muster, which Seth accomplished months before. Clayton and Charlotte join them later for desert and there is easy conversation and an amicable blend of both families. By the time the day ends, everyone feels like old friends. Charlotte and Clayton walk home up the forest path and Caroline leads her guests to their car since the rain has finally stopped. As Tim taps the remote and the doors slide open for the kids to crawl in the minivan, Caroline tells them to wait and rushes back inside returning with a brown paper lunch bag.

"I brought each of you a lemon. When you visit Jackson's grave, you don't leave flowers, you drop lemons at the base of his statue, because he was always eating them."

"Because he suffered from dyspepsia!" Timmy eagerly adds.

Smiling at Seth's interesting and entertaining brother, "Yes, he did."

Hugs are given, Tim again confirms how nice it was to meet her, Beverly encourages her to visit soon, and before they reach the end of her driveway, Seth sends her a message, "Thank-you for today…I love you!"

Ahhh, SWOON!

Tim Russell organizes his crew and they leave Sunday morning on the next leg of their adventure. Seth stays home from church to see them off. After the others are loaded, bathroom breaks are finished, and Beverley gives him final instructions to bring Caroline home in a few weeks, Tim stays behind to speak to his eldest son.

"Caroline is a wonderful girl and so is her family. I know you have chosen well. Hold her in your hands and cherish her like diamonds and she will always sparkle for you!" Tim's hands brace Seth's shoulders speaking to him like a man and a father.

Shaking his head in agreement, Seth promises, "I will, Dad."

"Good boy!" and he brings him in a full embrace pounding his back. Kissing his neck, Tim adds, "I'll miss you! I love you, son."

"And I love you, too, Dad! Have a safe trip!"

Seth waves to them from the driveway with shouts from each of their windows. As Tim pulls onto the road, he beeps the horn three times, and they are gone. Seth stands with his arms crossed over his chest feeling lonely. He loves his family and there are days when he hates being so far from them, but he is here for a reason and today that reason is Caroline Hatfield and she will be here in a few minutes.

After dinner, they spend a lazy afternoon on the porch swing and

Caroline claims, "I know why you love me…I remind you of your mother!" laughing and teasing him.

Looking at her almost disgustedly, Seth disagrees, "What? I don't think so!"

"Yes!" Caroline continues, "We are both talkers and overly eager and perky. I remind you of her and that's why you like me so much!" she wants to irritate him, because she likes it when he gets growly and hateful when she teases him making her laughter even more fun.

"No – you chatter and my mom talks, too often *at* you and she can go on and on especially when she is railing on me about something. You are optimistic and enthusiastic. She is overwhelming and…and…uhh, excruciating at times!"

Smacking his arm, she scolds, "Don't say that about your mother! I think she's great!"

"I didn't say she wasn't great," Seth defends. "She is wonderful! But, she can drive me crazy at times…I think it's because it was just me and her for so long and then they didn't have kids for several years. Sometimes the line between parent and child gets blurred where we are also good friends and there is such a gap in age between me and the twins."

Caroline understands, "That makes sense." The teasing has left her voice. "Honestly, I really did like them. Timmy is hilarious and so eager; Traci is his lovely, quieter counterpart. It is like they have all of your qualities divided between them and they look so much like you!"

"Yeah, I know. I thought I was the only who sees that…They are so important to me. I guess where I was older when they were born, I feel like they are more my children than my brother and sister. Tim takes lots of energy and Traci is just good and pure and fine. *She* makes me think of you. I just hope she will one day have your confidence and security. She tends to be somewhat of a moth."

"Don't worry. She'll come into her own. Timmy has just found himself sooner and is louder about it. She will bloom before you know it." Leading Seth down a new path, Caroline says, "I really liked your dad as well. He seems like a man of high character."

Seth's face becomes one of tenderness as he begins to speak of the dad who raised him. "Tim wanted to adopt me, was ready to do it even before they got married, but it wasn't until I was about 12 that everything was in order. I was surprised when Dad came from Florida to meet with the lawyers to discuss it. He took me to McDonald's that morning and explained it the best he could. I was a kid, so I really didn't understand. We get to the office and he signs the adoption papers then is handed a second set," thinking back, Seth is no longer on the porch swing beside Caroline, but another place in time. "He explodes and starts yelling at my mom, 'TERMINATION OF RIGHTS! What's this? You just said this way Tim could take better care of him. You didn't say nothin' about terminating rights!' They start screaming and cursing, my mom is crying, Tim is angry, because this was news to him as well, and the whole situation was pretty nasty for a few weeks. I heard mom and Tim talking one night; he was hurt and angry with her. He said, 'Beverly, me adopting Seth is not a business transaction and I never agreed to Chuck not seeing him again.' You could tell he felt deceived like she had betrayed him and was only married to him for security. Like his army retirement and insurance were his most attractive features. A few days later he takes me fishing and tells me that no matter what, he loves me and I am his son and that he is glad that I am Chuck's son, too. From then on, I called him Dad, because he was – he is. But, Chuck is also Dad."

Caroline's eyes never leave him during the whole story. Both of Seth's hands hold one of hers tracing lines with his thumbs, because often his eyes skirt away from hers. Her other hand gently lifts his chin so he looks at her. His cheeks are a little flushed from embarrassment and Caroline truthfully comforts her boy.

"Seth, I think that is beautiful…You are not at fault for the decisions or behaviors of your parents. Chuck and Tim are both your dads and that just shows me, you have a greater capacity of love than most people. You shouldn't feel embarrassed…All of that happened a long time ago when their emotions were still raw…You were caught in the crossfire, but came out alive."

Shaking his head, his heart swells with love for her, but she does not have all the pieces. If she knew everything and took time to examine them, she would think differently, so very differently about him. "No, Caroline, there is so much more I could tell you. Things were a mess for a long time before Mom and Dad divorced and even after she and Tim got married and then when the twins were born. It was…"

She is in his arms kissing him, not wanting him to say anything else. She is unwilling for him to dig up old wounds after a wonderful weekend. Sighing heavily, they lean on each other's foreheads and as everyone does, because everyone has a past, they sit in silence wishing parts of it would go away.

Pulling away from him so she can look in his face with comfort, but conviction, Caroline lays both her hands on his chest and says, "Seth, I love you completely and without hesitation…Anything that happened in your life – before me – brought you to here, to this very moment. All the good and bad, happy and heartbreaking has made you the man that you are, the man I love," pushing against his chest, she continues, "Everything that you have locked inside here, I want to see it. I want you to tell me all about it. I am not frightened. I won't be shocked or disappointed. I won't run away…I love you!"

Seth holds her tight again and Caroline thinks he may crush her and she holds him right back. Seth must squeeze his eyes shut to blink back tears. He is not ready to tell her more, but knows he wants to, because Caroline makes him feel safe and loved.

"Stonewall Jackson…You named your dog Lemon, because of Stonewall Jackson," followed by a breathy laugh against her hair.

Chapter XXI

"There is no fear in love. But perfect love drives out all fear..." – I John 4:18 NIV

Fourth of July, Seth picks Caroline up before noon, because they have been invited to a cookout at the Tyler's where they will join several other couples from his Unit. As always, he is eager to see her and what she chooses to wear. Meeting him at the door, Caroline is in a navy blue strapless cotton dress covered in tiny white polka dots falling above her knee and strappy gladiator sandals. Her hair is up high in a neat, yet tumbled mess and secured with a red bandana headband. Nails and toes painted rich red with each ring finger white with a coat of red and blue glitter on top. Healthy diamond studs are in her ears twinkling in the sunshine causing him to wonder if they are real.

Kissing her hello, he says, "Well, don't you look festive!"

"The same could be said for you!" as she approvingly looks at his clothing holding his hand out wanting him to twirl.

Seth is also very festive and striking as always. His hair is shorter for summer and face is tan. His red polo shirt is tucked neatly into blue seersucker shorts cinched with a navy woven and brown leather nautical style belt. Long, tan legs stretch down to khaki canvas deck shoes. Looking at him, fireworks better than she saw the previous evening go off inside her and she thinks how they could be on the cover of a *Banana Republic* catalog.

Caroline walks to his Jeep with Seth behind her. Opening his door, he gets in beside her and says, "There is no way I am going to make it through a whole day without putting my hands on those red buttons trailing down your back," smiling at her wickedly and all boy.

267

"Seth, hush!" Caroline is embarrassed, but will never tell him she bought the dress simply for the buttons.

The afternoon at the Tyler's is very nice and Caroline is pleased Cleat and Leanna are on the guest list, so she can have an ally. They have only been married two years, so many of these functions are still new to Leanna as well, but she is familiar with most everyone there. This is a first for Caroline and she gets confused as to who belongs with whom when the men refer to each other by last name, but their wives use their first.

She circulates with Seth for much of the first hour. The food is set up on tables in the back yard with everyone eating casually when they want. Chairs and colorful umbrellas are scattered and people are seated talking. Cpt. Tyler and Deaton challenge Cleat and Seth to cornhole and Caroline is left with the women. Shannon, Cpt. Tyler's wife joins her, Leanna, and few others under one of the umbrellas. They chat and begin to share with Caroline the joys and pains of military life. Most of it is accompanied by laughter so as not to dishearten her too soon.

Seth watches her from across the yard and he is so pleased with her graceful, confidently relaxed ways. He knows she was nervous coming to an event like this, but found her calm poise as soon as they arrive. She is pleasant and cordial during introductions and is able to stand on her own very quickly in conversation. Though he would have been happy to stay by her side all afternoon, it is also important to him that she gets to know the other wives...Wives – Seth loves that Caroline is becoming a part of that group today and he hopes very soon she is a permanent member.

"Your girl is an impressive young lady, Seth," Cpt. Tyler interjects between tosses speaking as a friend, not as a superior.

"Thank-you, sir. I believe she is," Seth is proud to speak of Caroline, allowing the Captain to continue.

"My children have both enjoyed her. She is a tremendous teacher, if she can put up with Deaton and his boys. He reminded me she did her student teaching in his sixth-grade class. They have all had her at least one more time at the high school and he hopes to get her for Senior Seminar."

"I didn't know that sir. She did tell me she had Deaton in class," Seth waits on Deaton and Cleat to finish their turn listening to the Captain.

"It is a rare person who can take care of your children, help them in ways you can't, especially when you're gone," Cpt. Tyler's pinning glance is for just a moment, but Seth is aware of his meaning. "So, do you like her family? Has she met yours?"

Seth laughs as he describes the Hatfield's, "They are a Norman Rockwell painting hanging on the wall of a house in Mayberry. Sometimes I think that they can't be real, but…they are," looking to his captain for fatherly advice. "Sir, they have made me feel welcome from the first day, but there are days when I feel like I don't deserve them. Does that make sense?"

Thinking he has not understood his question, Cpt. Tyler gestures to the women pointing out his wife. "Do you see Shannon sitting with the others? When I look at her, I would like to think you feel the same when you look at Caroline…Son, you probably don't deserve them, just like I didn't deserve Shannon's family and all they have been and done for me these many years. Don't get discouraged, though, because that beautiful Caroline will make you worthy," saying no more, he picks up the bags off the ground tossing them back at the other board.

Cpt. Tyler and Shannon escort each of their guests out as everyone begins to trickle home. "Caroline, I would like to take you to lunch this week, if that would be ok."

"Yes, I would like that very much."

Caroline feels like she has joined a new club or sorority with Shannon as the last step leading to membership. Seth has already preempted her that Shannon takes a personal interest in any new wife or girlfriend that comes in the unit. She has been part of this longer than any of the other women and she knows support and encouragement is the only way to be successful.

"I will call you tomorrow and we will make plans," Shannon says squeezing Caroline's hand before Seth opens her door.

Once in the Jeep, Caroline kisses Seth's hand, she says, "Thank-you for today. I was very proud to be here with you."

"And I was proud having you with me."

"Did you bring your shorts? Because Sam called this morning and said you are supposed to go swimming with him this evening," grinning knowing Seth is almost as fond of her nephew as she is.

"Nope. We'll have to swing by the house." Seth has thrown back the top before they left the Tyler's taking Caroline on a windy ride back to his house. She told him she loves riding in the

Jeep with the wind blowing in her face and thinks it is a little scary when he drives fast, but exciting. Her hands keep coming back to her lap as the wind lifts her skirt. Seth finds it hard to keep his eyes on the road as they are drawn to those brief seconds when her thigh is exposed before Caroline captures the material forcing it back down.

Getting out, they walk onto the porch and Seth unlocks the door letting her enter first. The house is dark, but the sun coming through the windows lights their way. He pulls the door closed and she has made it only as far as the edge of the couch. He is behind her in two giant steps locking his arms around her waist while his lips find her neck. Seth turns her to face him as Caroline yields to madness and all sense of reason is quickly fading. The moral compass that has been a lifetime guide is slipping away from her reach even as her mind shouts with promises of virtue and holiness. With the remaining shreds of clarity, Caroline stammers, "Seth… Seth, wa…wait…"

Unable to finish her sentence, he stalls momentarily considering her face with labored breathing as the pieces of his mind come together understanding what she is saying. Grabbing her by the hand, he nearly drags her through the house. Roughly depositing her on the edge his bed and leaves the room.

In the bathroom, he plunders through every drawer and cabinet. Outside, the cloud cover thins and light streams through the window and he sees his reflection in the mirror. Leaves flap in the wind and it looks like a light is blinking on his face. In quick repeated scenes, he sees the man he was and the man he is easily blurring together. A few moments tick by and Seth is thinking more clearly. Gripping the edge of the sink, his shoulders slump and head falls. Disappointed in himself and the whole situation, decision made, he returns to his room.

Seth chafes at the thought of how different Caroline is from anyone else he has encountered and as he watches, her innocence becomes glaringly apparent.

Caroline is as he left her, obediently waiting for his return. He studies her for a moment. She is quietly picking at something on her skirt then rests her hands back on her lap lacing and relacing her fingers. She is not undressing or plotting her next move in seduction. She is waiting…just as she said.

The floor squeaks and she looks up at him, wide-eyed with several strands of hair pulled free by the wind spilling down on her shoulders. She makes such an inviting picture that Seth knows he will never forget this moment, this day, and he hesitates to move or speak.

He stands in the doorway as if intentionally keeping distance between them and Caroline waits. Their eyes hold each other, though both are silent. Seth wants to be gentle and hopes she understands.

"Caroline..." with his first word, her heart stops.

"Caroline..." with the second, his stops.

Her face is unreadable giving no indication of her thoughts and he wonders if her mind is a whirlwind like his. Is she torn between soul and body?

Slowly walking towards her, he finishes his thought. "I think we should wait...Now isn't the right time..."

Caroline's cheeks burn bright then almost as quickly, he watches the color fade from her face as she turns away from him and his heart sinks. Sitting beside her, Seth tries to explain for the second time why she will again not share his bed. "Caroline...I am not going to put you at risk... And this isn't the way I want it – a few minutes with you while your family is waiting on us to go swimming." She pulls further away as soon as he sits down. When she sniffs, and wipes her nose with the back of her hand, he knows she is crying and it kills him.

Idiot! You should have planned better!

Seth tries to console her, "Hey, hey, hey...Pretty Girl, don't cry. Please don't cry!"

But Caroline cannot help it. She is overwhelmed – guilt and conviction wash over her as she remembers person she is. Then disappointment, embarrassment, and rejection fall on top of her as she considers who she has so quickly become. She curls into his chest doubting he has ever used these lines on anyone before.

"Caroline, I love you and I want this with you, too. I want to take my time and enjoy you completely...And I am not going to put you at risk for something neither of us is ready for."

His hand rubs the skin on her back trying to sooth her where moments before he only wanted to entice. He is worried she does not understand as she continues to sniff and snub, refusing to look at him. Then suddenly she lifts her head and says, "Ok, Seth...Whatever you say." Turning her back to him, she does not even ask and he buttons her dress. He wipes her eyes and kisses her. No more words need to be said by either of them and they leave.

After hours in the pool and endless basket tosses, the little boys are called from the water and taken inside for baths. Sam is the first finished and runs back out to everyone. He is in shorty cotton pajamas that fit him like second skin – white covered in multi-colored cartoon dinosaurs. Rushing over to Seth, he demands, "Set! Smell me! I'm queen!"

Lifting the little boy to his lap, he sniffs then tickles him until Sam is cackling. Seth and Sam share a whispered conversation as Sam snuggles in his lap. Soon, the little boy quiets as he listens to a story. Seth crosses his ankle over his knee creating a nest for Sam cradling him in his arms. Sam's movements still, his breathing deepens, and a tiny hand rests on Seth's neck. He is warm and cuddly smelling like strawberry shampoo and Seth gets a lump in his throat.

Jackson and Jacob have come out finding rest on their Frinny and Poppy's laps. Caroline comes to the steps of her back porch and seeing Sam asleep on Seth's lap, she must gather herself quickly or else cry.

Alex and Meghan get ready to leave and the boys wake up. Immediately, Sam begs to be allowed to spend the night at 'Aunt Care-Wine's' and his parents agree. They leave, Clayton and Charlotte say goodnight, Nick and Darby walk Ruby home, and Sam asks Seth to piggyback him inside.

Dropping him on the bottom step, Seth says, "Good night, big man. I'll see you in a few days," and Sam walks up the steps with instructions from Caroline to brush his teeth.

Seth sighs heavily and Caroline falls onto his chest. He wishes there was some way to reassure her, because he knows that her head is filled with doubts. He does not know what to say that will take the look of sadness off her face. Instead, he just stands there holding her saying nothing.

Their moment of solace is disturbed when Sam shouts from the top of the stairs, "SET! Wanna sleep over, too? Care-Wine can make you a pallet on the floor!"

Seth leaves Caroline taking the steps two at a time reaching Sam in seconds scooping him up and the little boy cackles again. Carrying him to Caroline's bed that is already turned down, Seth tucks him in.

"Big man, that sounds like a good idea, but I didn't bring my toothbrush," Seth explains as Caroline walks in the door.

"Well, merember next time!" and that was all the answer Sam needs. He reaches up for kisses from Seth and Caroline then orders them it is time for prayers. Caroline kneels beside the bed and Seth joins her. Taking her hand, Sam begins to pray and Seth takes her other hand.

"Dear Ward, fank You for fun days and swimming pools and hotdogs. And fank You for Care-Wine and Set. I love them both. In Jesus name… AMEN."

Caroline tells Sam she will be back up after she tells Seth goodnight. Walking him to the porch, he reminds her, "I agree with Sam. I want a sleepover, soon. But, I don't want a pallet on the floor." To this teasing remark, she chuckles a little, but he cannot see her face in the dark. Kissing her with only their lips touching, he whispers, "I love you, Caroline."

"And I love you."

And Seth leaves for the night wishing he could somehow fast forward time and it be he and Caroline tucking their own little boy into bed.

Be patient! Thoroughbred…Kentucky Derby…Triple Crown!

Over the weeks of July, Seth and Caroline fall back into a comfortable routine, though nothing else is mentioned or planned for sleepovers. At the end of the month, Seth takes a few days off to go home. It is his parents' 23rd anniversary and they have a big party planned. Seth wanted to know why this year was so important, thinking 25 was the big year to which his mother informs, "We like to break with convention!"

Caroline has been invited to Holidaysburg for the weekend and very much wants to go, but is scheduled for a conference in Louisville. She has spent days trying to get anyone else to go in her place with no one agreeing. She even calls the conference to see if the school can get a refund and they tell her the refund window has closed. So, she and Seth are very disappointed.

Traci calls her and says she is excited about her coming and maybe they could go out as girls one day for lunch. Since their visit, Timmy and Traci have become Caroline's fast friends sending her friend requests and texting at least once a day. Seth tells her if they are pests, he will get them to stop and she fusses at him saying she enjoys them and he is pleased.

When they find out that Caroline will not be coming with him, they both whine and ask if there is no other way. Caroline promises she and Seth will come up for Labor Day and the twins reluctantly agree that is a decent consolation prize.

The morning she must leave for the conference is the morning Seth leaves to Pennsylvania. He invites her out breakfast and they meet at 34:Ate. Sitting at a bistro table on the patio, they both pick at their food and are distracted by their own thoughts. Checking his watch, Seth asks, "What time do you have to pick up Libby?"

"I told her I would be at her house around 11:00," Caroline answers her mind buzzing trying to think of any way she can to get out of going on this trip to be able to join Seth.

Standing, he pulls out his wallet laying money on the table, then reaches for her. "Well, I guess you had better go...And Mom said she would like it if I could make home for dinner."

They walk slowly to their cars, neither of them excited for trips they both wanted to take months ago, but have dramatically lost luster now that the time has arrived. A *Norfolk and Southern* train makes its way through the yard behind the parking lot as Seth kisses Caroline goodbye. She thinks how this fills like a 1940's movie and they are standing on the platform of a train station and the soundtrack of their lives just changes tone and melody.

Holding her face in his hands, Seth quietly confesses, "I've missed you these last few weeks...It has felt like you haven't been with me."

Caroline's face is sad and she confesses as well, "And I have felt like you haven't been with me either."

They have been together nearly every day, but they both know why they feel distant. There is a huge elephant in the room that neither of them want to talk about. Seth decides he has enough courage to say it.

"When we get home, how about we make plans to go away? Spend time with just each other and enjoy a completely new adventure," rubbing his hands down her arms, he waits to for her answer wondering if this has been on her mind as much as it has his.

Caroline does not answer and he sees her pulse beat in her neck. Looking at the ground, she sighs a few times and then is silent. Taking his hands, she kisses his palms and wrists and fingertips. Looking into his face, her eyes wide and almost tear filled, but she answers then smiles, "Seth, there is nothing I have ever wanted more."

Kissing her hands, Seth smiles in relief and eager expectation. Taking her into his arms, he holds her secure, but not tight – loving, comforting, safe. "Pretty Girl, and there is nothing I have wanted more than you."

They part that morning with a flood of emotions and the coming days provide them no opportunity to compartmentalize and examine, but they are certain that the roads that are now taking them apart will lead them back together.

Caroline arrives home late Sunday afternoon. Seth calls her when she has made it to Pikeville and says he will meet her at her house. He has left early that morning with the intention of arriving in Williamson before she does. He knocks on her door and does not wait for her to answer going in. As soon as he is inside, he starts calling for her and she rushes down the steps to meet him. His greeting is wordless as his lips quickly find hers and in one swift movement has her pinned against the wall with his hands and kisses coming fast and aggressive. As suddenly as the foray begins, it ends and Seth has her in his arms tight, in fierce desperation. Burying his face in her neck, he is panting and mumbling, repeating over and over, "Caroline, I love you…I love you so much."

Caroline realizes this is not passion in his voice, but sadness and possibly fear. She has never seen him this way and becomes a little worried. She tries to reassure him, "Seth, I love you, too," repeating it many times.

"Caroline, never forget…Never forget that I love you…No matter what happens."

Tears spring to her eyes, her voice is steady, ardent. "Yes, Seth…I will remember…I will never forget."

Seth begins shaking and Caroline's worry intensifies. "Sweet Boy! Is everything alright?" She knows he is overwhelmed and distressed, but does not know how to help him. She pulls away just enough to lead him to the couch, feeling as though she may have to carry him. Caroline sits down and he collapses wedging her in the corner laying on her chest with his arms tight around her back. Seth whimpers and is close to crying and Caroline panics, but remains quiet. She kisses his forehead raking her nails across his scalp and down his back.

"It's ok, Sweet Boy…I'm with you…I'm not going anywhere…I love you, Seth." Caroline continues these words in a soothing chant as he trembles without relaxing any of his hold.

"Don't leave me, Caroline…Please, don't leave me…"

"No, Seth…I won't leave you…I'm not going anywhere, Sweet Boy,"

"Don't leave…Please, don't leave…"

The hour grows late and only a few whispered phrases have been shared between them as Seth's body and grip relaxes. Caroline moves and he sits up. Taking his hand, she leads him upstairs to her room. Standing him at the end of her bed, taking hold of his hem, he lifts his arms like an obedient child as she removes his shirt followed by his shorts and she chuckles to herself when she sees his lime green boxer briefs; those she leaves on. She turns down the covers and he sits down. Kneeling before him, she removes his shoes and he instantly falls on the pillows tucking his feet under the blankets. Caroline goes to the bathroom, puts on the white eyelet nightgown that is hanging on the back of the door, and shakes down her hair. Coming out, she sees Seth is turned on his side facing her unblinking. Going to the windows, she closes the blinds against the remaining glow of the evening, darkening the room, and crawls into bed with him. Curling up behind him, Caroline rests her cheek between his shoulder blades and slides her hand around to his chest finding his clenched under his chin. Tenderly, she tries to link their fingers and his grip relaxes folding her hand with his. Quietly, she waits feeling his heartbeat beneath her arm.

Whispering against his skin, she says, "Sweet Boy, I am here…I am here with you…" and she waits.

Seth does not move and says nothing, but holds her hand rubbing it with his thumb. Several minutes pass and he rolls over to face her. Brushing her hair back from her face, he buries a hand in her hair and pulls her mouth to meet his. The kiss is long, but gentle – asking and telling nothing. Opening his eyes, he looks at Caroline. His voice is raspy and passionate certain to convince her of his truth, "Caroline, I love you… Really, I do…I love you more than you will ever know!"

Caroline has a wave of uneasiness followed by a sense of calm, answering truthfully. "Seth, I know you do and I love you, too."

Nothing else is said as they tuck themselves close to one another and soon both are asleep.

Seth is so hot. He is running and running. He looks and cannot find Caroline. Panting, his vision is blurred and he cannot tell where he is. He is confused and disoriented and so very thirsty. He hears the shrill blast of a train whistle in the distance. His legs and back are aching and his shirt is drenched with sweat. He tries to call for her, but his throat is raw and feels like it is full of sand.

Coughing, he is on the road that leads to Caroline's property passing the sign that reads *Sunlit Cove*. The trees are heavy with leaves making his way dark like he is in a forested tunnel. He sees Ruby's house and he thinks about going and asking her where Caroline is, but keeps running noticing the windows are dark. Taking the path through the woods, he sees the front door to Caroline's house is open. Stumbling up the steps, he rushes inside to find it empty – the furniture is gone and each room is an empty shell.

Trying to call her name again, Seth leans over the counter to rest, rubbing his back and legs, he sees it – the bundle of Lilly of the Valley he brought her for prom. Lifting the bundle from the mason jar vase, they are tied with a black ribbon. The house is silent, but he can hear voices in the backyard.

Seth tries to run, but is limping and his back hurts worse. He struggles to make it down the steps, but when he does, everyone is there. Mom, Dad – Tim and Chuck, Timmy, Traci; Clayton, Charlotte, Nick, Darby, and Will; Alex and Meghan holding the hands of Jackson and Jacob with Sam standing in front of them; Ruby and Marty and Nadine, and just beyond them Cpt. Tyler and Shannon with Cleat and Leanna…Caroline is nowhere. He looks in each of their faces wanting to ask them, but his raw throat clenches with unspilled tears and everyone just sadly shakes their heads – No.

Two dogs bark and he looks beyond the yard in the distance. Seth's heart leaps, because he can see a woman with blond hair playing with the dogs and he hobbles over the uneven ground working his arms to gain momentum clutching the Lilly of the Valley. He draws closer, but the woman keeps her back to him. He knows it is Caroline when Feather and Lemon rush over to greet him pawing at his legs, licking his hands, and whimpering. Seth is just steps away from her and she is almost within his grasp when the train whistles loud and long startling him. He looks back and everyone is gone. Falling, he is on all fours and the dogs are running around him and he begins to lose sight of Caroline. He tries to crawl to her as the ground under his hands turns to sand fading its way towards her and he finds his voice screaming, "RUN!"

The light is bright and intense, heat has overtaken him, his legs will no longer move, and his back feels broken. In his last struggle to reach her, Seth screams again and Caroline turns to face him, but it is not Caroline... All goes black.

Seth wakes up panting, sweating, and scared as he has never been. The shivers and whimpering has returned and Caroline awakens. Hearing his distress, she again tries to console him.

"I...I...lo – lov – love you...Run!"

"No, Sweet Boy! I am here...I'm not leaving...I love you, Seth...Don't leave me...My Sweet Boy."

Again, his body calms and he returns to sleep, their bodies woven together not in passion, but for comfort, protection. Caroline's sleep is deep the rest of the night and does not hear Seth leave just before dawn. She turns hoping to find him and he is gone, but a note is waiting on her nightstand. Picking it up, she reads Seth's simple words.

Pretty Girl...I am so sorry...I love you.

Jesus replied,
"You don't
understand
now, but someday
you will."
John 13:7

Chapter XXII

"You don't understand now what I am doing, but someday you will." – John 13:7 NLT

The heat of August is oppressive and close to unbearable as the start of a new school year approaches. Seth's mood, enthusiasm, and vigor of Spring has returned reassuring Caroline's heart. These final days of vacation are jammed packed with activity – a play Jenny Wiley, a hike to Castle Rock, a proper picnic with plaid blanket and wicker basket, dinners, game nights, pool volleyball tournaments, and for Seth's birthday, Caroline takes him to the Clay Center for an Oak Ridge Boys concert; every day is an adventure. Cleat and Leanna have joined the group always getting invites and it is like they are all back in high school. All their times together are filled with friendship and play. Seth has never been happier and neither has Caroline.

He has even come to tolerate if not appreciate Carter, whose stormy nature has not returned and though warmth is not felt between them, the frost stays hidden most days. Carter works longer hours than the rest of them and is called out often, so it is not unusual when he is absent from their fun.

A few weeks after their trip to the Cabin, Seth feels like it is safe enough to question Caroline about him without appearing too suspicious. He has come to her house for dinner and they are spending the afternoon in the pool. Lazing on the steps, Caroline is curled close as he laps water on her back.

"What's wrong with Carter's shoulder? It looks like it's been chewed on," Seth's voice is casual, but interested remembering the series of uneven scars across his shoulder and how they distort what at one time has been a *Superman* tattoo.

Sitting up, Caroline explains and he is so glad she does not know how to tell a short story.

"He had shoulder surgery in college."

Seth wants all the details, so he continues to lead her. "That must have been some injury, because the scars look terrible."

"It was actually…a pretty sad story, when you think about it," troubled, Caroline looks off into the past.

Seth's interest is piqued and encourages Caroline to tell him everything. Sitting up he asks, "Really? What happened?"

"Carter played baseball at WVU. Well, he's played baseball forever and got a scholarship to college. During Spring of his junior year, he was injured during a game. He leaped to catch a ball and his feet were tangled and landed on his shoulder. I remember Lucinda, that's Carter's grandmother and Gran's best friend, telling Gran that the doctors continued to refer to him as the '1% Scenario' – the 1% of patients who have all the complications. They said since his arm was extended it put his joint at an awkward angle, so when he hit the ground, it broke his collar bone, cracked his shoulder blade, and chipped his humerus. He also hyperextended a ligament and tore his labrum. His surgeon said he had seen all of those injuries, but it was rare for all of them to be in the same patient…That was just the beginning."

"The beginning? You mean that wasn't enough?"

Caroline continues after a sarcastic chuckle. "Carter has all kinds of allergies, medicines too, and antibiotics. His shoulder was not healing properly and it gets infected and he has to have an additional surgery opening him back up to clean everything out. That was supposed to do the trick then there was a mix up with his medications one night and he was given something he was allergic to and he went into anaphylactic shock. It was really bad for several days. He had to go on a ventilator and they were worried his body would not regulate and he wouldn't make it, but he did. His shoulder healed, but he was sick for a long time, lost all kinds of weight. It was a while before he was back to himself."

Wanting to know the rest of the story, Seth asks, "So what happened to baseball?"

"His dad had an army of therapists working with him and he was released to play that fall, but he was just not the same. He had not regained his weight and was about as lean as he is now. Even though it was not his throwing arm, he favored it for a long time. I think he was in more pain than he let on so he could get back to playing. He played his senior year, but his game had changed so much." Caroline's disappointed smile takes her back to days when her friend was struggling.

"What position did he play?" the picture of Carter as a happy boy playing baseball does not gel in his mind, but a arrogant college player waiting on the Major League fits him perfectly.

"He was big hitter and a skilled utility player – he could go just about anywhere from inning to inning if need be, but catcher was his favorite. He said, 'You got to see everything as it is happening.'" Caroline says in a voice parroting Carter.

"So, was there ever a chance he would have gone pro?"

Sad smile again, "Carter was scouted in high school; heavily scouted by D1 schools and the pros. He had always said he was going to college for at least two years. At the end of his sophomore year, he wanted to enter the draft, but that was the year of the strike, so he went back to school, then comes his injury, and by the time he is eligible his senior year, as much as they wanted to keep it quiet and show that he was as good as new, he was *damaged goods* and not worth the investment…Carter was a different player and the calls never came."

Seth has genuine sympathy for him – life being mapped out and then taking a tragic new course. "He didn't consider Minor League?"

"I don't really know why, but Minor League was never an option; more like – never a consideration. Carter's dad was very *influential* over him at that time. It was hard for Carter to make his own decisions and it caused lots of tension between them."

Caroline hesitates and Seth believes she does not want to tell the rest, but she continues. "Dr. MacGuire was very focused on Carter following a track that would be the most…" searching for the appropriate word, "profitable and Carter still wanted to play ball. He said he would have liked to coach or at least have a job in some aspect of baseball, but his dad thought differently…So, Carter goes into medicine, just like his dad, but instead of becoming a doctor, he's a surgical nurse with an orthopedic group in Pikeville. I think that was a little bit of rebellion against his dad, even though medical school would have been easy for him; everything is always easy for Carter…It's sad, because Dr. MacGuire's focus was for Carter to make money, which he has plenty. But, you've seen, he is not very happy and has been that way for a long time."

"So, they're rich?" Seth expected as much after his first visit to Carter and Will's apartment.

Caroline laughs, "Small town rich, I guess, with diversified interests. His granddad, Warren MacGuire, was my Poppy's best friend and they moved to Williamson together from Virginia. He began to dabble in commercial real estate, then it became a pretty large side business. Before Carter even finished college, he had started working with him. He is his only grandson, so when he died, Carter took control of the company. He has several properties, now. He even owns the building that he and Will live in."

Seth does not believe she is being untruthful, just very modest, because she has lived in a world, a family, where hard work pays off, so accumulating assets, even substantial assets, is the natural result. He can only imagine what 'several properties' could mean. Before he has time to think about it, Caroline splashes him in the face, swimming away laughing.

"You're going to pay for that!" Seth shouts.

She looks back at him with just her head bobbing at the surface. Giving him an evil grin, she dips below the water before he reaches her. A few seconds later, Seth feels her teeth nip his ankle and he squeals thrashing in the water trying to grab her only to have her surface behind him laughing at his failed attempts. Lunging, Caroline avoids his grasp pushing off the side and shooting past him like a fish – laughing when he misses her again.

Thrilled with frustration, Seth warns her when she comes up a third time, "Little girl, I know you think you are so very funny, but how many more laps down this pool do you think you can make before you tire?"

"SEVERAL!" Caroline yells zooming under the water and between his legs before he realizes she is so close. Jerking around, Caroline is right behind him and asks, voice filled with innuendo, "The question is – how long until *you* tire?"

Seth's laugh is male – all chest and face. The kind of laugh that women wait a lifetime to hear. The kind of laugh that invites and delights. The kind of laugh that comes from a man, never a boy. His voice also drips with innuendo like the water rolling down his face, dripping off his chin, creating small rivers that run and branch down his chest and across his skin. A voice filled with pleasant wickedness as he roughly takes ahold of her and she allows it without complaint.

"I…never…tire!" is his slow growling whisper and excitement spreads over her face. Thinking he is coming close for a delicious kiss, she waits for it, but at the last moment, he gives her body a jerk dunking her under the water.

Caroline comes up gasping and yelling looking for Seth. Wiping the water from her face, she scans the pool, but he has disappeared. YANK! He has her by the ankles and topples her in the water again. Grabbing and clawing she reaches for him under the water, but he quickly swims away. Surfacing with just his eyes above the water like a crocodile, she makes her stealthy journey to him – revenge on her face.

"I'm warning you! I don't tire and you are about to get more than you have bargained for!" Caroline is heedless of what he is saying and lurches for him. He catches her by the upper arms before she can reach him and he tosses her to the side like a ragdoll and she goes under the water again. Coming up, she is breathless and irritated he is beating her at her own game.

"Give up?"

"NEVER!" as she yells and is tossed aside again.

Caroline stays under the water longer than the previous times and when she comes up she keeps her back to Seth, no longer interested in play.

"Are you tapped out?" She does not turn around and slaps the water in his direction. Worried he has hurt her, he asks contrite, "Caroline?" When she still does not reply, Seth swims over to her and tries to turn her to face him. "Pretty Girl, are you ok?" and she just shakes her head. "Are you hurt? Did I hurt you? I'm sorry, I should not have played so rough."

Slowly turning towards him, Caroline's head is still down as he continues pleading. When he is again about to take her in his arms and console her, she pushes him hard and he falls backwards under the water with her on top pining him to the floor of the pool. Seth grabs hold of her waist picking them both up. As soon as they surface, she yells, "PSYCH!" in his face and laughs hysterically.

The two play and wrestle the rest of the afternoon like children, though both wonder how much longer they will be able to resist increasing desire.

The second Wednesday in August is Opening Day and students flood the halls once again for the start of a new school year; a fresh start. Caroline tells Seth she is always optimistic at the beginning of the year and excited about the newness of it all and that enthusiasm will last until at about February, when you are sick of winter and the end of the year is too far away. She even takes him on a shopping trip to buy schools supplies informing him that *Crayola* markers are the best, colored pencils destroy electric sharpeners, and you can never have enough clipboards and *Post Its*.

During the second full week of school, Seth leaves on Wednesday and does not return until Sunday from training. Caroline hates that he is gone, but the first few weeks of school are crazy and she can use the afternoons to prep and organize. He calls Sunday night when he gets home and says he has late meetings Monday and Tuesday, but wants to make her dinner Friday, to which she agrees. The next afternoon, Sophie stops by her room to chat.

"So, what do you and Sergeant Sexy have planned for this evening?" Sophie asks munching on her favorite snack – salted almonds and dried cranberries.

"Nothing. He has meetings this evening and tomorrow evening, but he's making me dinner on Friday," Caroline swoons and smiles at Sophie.

"Making dinner? Any special occasion?" popping another cranberry in her mouth.

"Other than he loves me and thinks I'm great? No. Just dinner and togetherness!"

Licking her thumb and forefinger, Sophie speculates, "Just dinner, you say…I bet he has BIGGER things on his mind!"

Caroline's face nearly catches on fire as she fusses at Sophie. "Sophie hush!"

Flapping a hand at her friend and frowning, she responds, "Please, Caroline! He's a guy – that is ALWAYS on his mind! I was meaning big things, like big *shiny* things!" Sophie's face lights up with eager anticipation.

Frowning as well, Caroline rationalizes, "Sophie, don't be silly! We have only been dating since Spring."

"And it is almost September! Come Caroline, I know you have thought about it! You've probably written his name and yours a thousand times, linking your initials in monogram. AND, you and I both know what you

285

will say when he asks. It's not like you two are 17. You've had more than enough time to decide if that is what you want."

Sophie is right; Caroline knows exactly what she will say if Seth should ask, but he is not going to ask. That would just be silly! They have been dating less than six months. That is just ridiculous! Or is it?

Over the next two days, Caroline thinks so much about Sophie's preposterous idea, but with each passing moment, it becomes less ridiculous and a hopeful possibility. Wednesday, she and Seth meet for dinner and nothing seems out of the ordinary other than he is tired from trips and meetings and seems a little distracted. Thursday morning, Tori and Lindsey burst in her classroom at the beginning of her planning period.

"I just can't stand that girl!" Tori is wound up as she walks through the door.

Looking up from the notes she is working on, Caroline asks, "Tori, what's wrong?

"Agh! It's that entitled freshman! You know the one – she looks like an angry, painted clown. I can't stand her!" Tori begins to rage as Lindsey takes the seat next to Caroline's desk. "I would like to scream in her face to MOVE when she and her group of mean girls stand in the middle of the hall!"

Caroline smiles with a good idea who she is referring to. Tori and Lindsey are two of her favorites. She had them as freshmen, sophomores, and now seniors. Tori is loud and laughing while Lindsey is quiet and questioning. They are opposites that complement each other perfectly and Caroline finds them both to be wonderful.

Changing routes dramatically, Tori's tone and demeanor are near pleasant. "Ms. Hatfield, what do you have planned this evening?"

Knowing Tori is getting ready to ask for a favor, Caroline asks, "What do you two want?"

Lindsey speaks up, "I don't want anything. It's Tori doing the asking."

Tori thins her lids at her best friend thinking she has thrown her under the bus and her plan is about to go awry. She decides questioning will help her tactics.

"Ms. Hatfield, you play golf, don't you?"

"Yes."

"At *Twisted Gun?*"

"Many times."

"Well, ya see...the golf team is having their first match this evening and I want to go."

Caroline plays it cagey, because she has a feeling Tori has ulterior motives that go far beyond school spirit.

"Then go."

"And I need to take pictures for the yearbook."

"Then go," Caroline repeats.

"See...I don't know where it is and I'm not sure I know what to do," stammering, Tori tries to get to her point.

"Wharncliff. Just get in the cart and don't talk."

"Yeah, I don't know where Wharncliff is and I'm not sure I can stay quiet...So, I was thinking..."

"Tori, what is you want?" Caroline tries to focus her conversation.

Tori blurts out what she has been holding back. "Would you go with me to the golf match?"

"Tori, that's nearly an hour drive away and no one goes to golf matches."

"I know, but I need to take pictures for the yearbook and I really want to go and I'll drive if you want or you can drive my car. I'll pay for the gas...Please?" Tori hopes the *please* will push her over the edge.

"Tori, I'm not dressed for a golf match."

"Couldn't you run home during lunch?" she suggests.

Scowling at her, "I could...Lindsey, why does Tori want to go to the golf match?"

Lindsey laughs and says, "I'll give you a hint – it has something to do with that angry, painted clown in the hallway and one of the boys on the team. She was talking to him and is unaware he is off limits..." Lindsey, with uncharacteristic spunk, gouges Tori, "WAIT! He's not off limits, because Tori is *too* chicken to talk to him," and Tori starts to rant again.

"Lindsey! That's not the truth!"

"So, you really are going all the way to *Wharncliff* just to watch the golf match?" Lindsey rolls her eyes knowing Tori is all talk and scared to death – of one boy in particular.

"Ms. Hatfield..."

"Tori, I don't have time to listen to this...especially, if I'm going

287

home during lunch to get clothes." Tori squeals and gives Caroline a slew of thank-yous. "You two meet me at my car after the bell, now get to class!"

"Thanks, Ms. Hatfield!" and the pair are gone.

Caroline picks up her phone and calls Seth. "Sweet Boy, I'm taking some lovesick teenagers to the golf match this afternoon."

"All the way at Twisted Gun?" Seth cannot believe she is going.

"Yes, all the way to Twisted Gun...I hate that I won't be able to see you, but this will just make me more excited to see you tomorrow!"

Laughing, he is flattered by her words, "That sounds good...I'll see you tomorrow then."

"Tomorrow...Love you!"

"Love you."

Only Tori is waiting when Caroline comes out of the school. "Where's Lindsey?'

"She had to work," Tori answers tossing her backpack in Caroline's back seat eager to get underway. "You didn't tell me you were going to get golf clothes to wear!"

Caroline looks down at her red polo with black and white varsity *B* stitched on the left chest and khaki shorts. She has twisted her hair up and claw clipped before putting on a charcoal grey visor with *Twisted Gun* stitched in red.

Laughing at Tori, she asks, "Tori, we are going to a golf course. What did you expect me to wear?"

"Well..." Tori is at a loss for words, something that so rarely happens, "Now, I don't look like a golf course...Do you have another visor?"

Caroline smiles and shakes her head walking to the rear of her vehicle and opens the gate finding two visors, she brings to Tori as they both get in and buckle up. Tori looks at them, trying them both on admiring herself in the mirror as Caroline pulls off campus. She cannot decide and asks Caroline, "Which do you like?" trying on another *Twisted Gun* – royal blue with white and one khaki and navy *Jonathan's Hope.*

"Tori, I like them both, because their mine. Either one looks fine on you."

"What's *Jonathan's Hope?*" she asks switching the hats again.

"It's a foundation to help children and their families who are battling cancer. I have a friend from college who is part of the foundation. They have a golf tournament every year to raise money and I've played in it and a visor is one of the gifts they give you."

Tori's face brightens, "Ooo, I'll wear that one!" and she spends the next few minutes trying to arrange her hair like Caroline, then gets frustrated, putting it in a side braid wearing her borrowed visor.

Caroline pulls in the drive-thru at Wendy's and asks, "Tori, what would like?"

"You don't have to buy me anything! I have money – I'll buy yours!" reaching in the back for her bag.

Caroline appreciates Tori's offer, but declines, "Tori, I've got this. Besides, I've been cooped up too much at school in the evenings; this will be a nice break."

Their food comes and Tori chatters almost the whole way to the course. Her bubbly behavior makes Caroline feel young and girly, like they are both in high school going to watch their favorite boys play. For a moment, it takes her back.

Finally arriving at the course, Tori is pleased, "I didn't think we would ever get here!"

Caroline knows what she is saying. The trip winds you through the twists and turns of narrow roads leading you to the top of a mountain only to wind you back down into the next valley with the roads getting tighter and tighter. The final assent doubles back and forth until you reach the summit; the world opens up and is huge.

Getting out, Tori is silent for the first time since they left school, "Wow!" and she makes a full turn taking in the whole scene. "Wow! This place is huge! I feel like we're in the sky!"

Caroline smiles, pleased she is introducing something completely new and impressive to Tori. "I know! I feel the same way when I'm here," also taking a moment to admire her surroundings. "It's amazing the good things you can do with land when you finish mining coal." This gets several questions from Tori to which Caroline must finally insist, "Tori, the teams are here. We should get a cart."

Tori sombers and she remembers they have come to the golf course for a reason and somewhere in the near distance, is a boy she is eager to see. Taking her to the clubhouse, Caroline pays for the cart and chats with the boy behind the counter. Walking back out on the porch, Tori pipes up, "He was cute!"

Laughing again at this sweet and silly girl, she decides to join her at being a schoolgirl, "If you think he's cute, you should see the golf pro – now, *he* is something to look at!" Smiling, Caroline gives her a look of pleased admiration.

Tori acts like someone has yelled SQUIRREL, whirling around to look for him. "Really?!? Where is he?"

Scolding, Caroline instructs, "Tori, get in the cart!" and they pull over to the practice green in the lineup behind the other parents as all the boys make their way from the driving range. Tug Valley is hosting the match and Belfry is joined by Mingo Central and River View. Tori is fidgeting asking Caroline lots of questions and Caroline reminds her to not talk or make noises when they hit and she settles down.

The coaches bring all the players in and gives them instructions dividing them into groups and everyone is ready for play. Austin Wilson, a senior at Belfry, has a big smile on his face and hustles over to Caroline.

"Hey, Ms. Hatfield! What are you doing here?" Austin asks as he hangs on the edge of her cart.

"Well, I's just wondering if you boys knew how to golf, so I thought I would come see it firsthand!" teasing the boy who is an impressive player.

"Ahhh, we hit it around as best we can!" and they both laugh. Tori is silent, but staring him wide-eyed.

"Hey, my dad's not here yet. Do you think you can cart me out to my first hole? Then you can go watch whoever you want," Austin smiles at Caroline, but she sees his eyes dart to Tori.

"Sure, we can! Hop on!" Caroline agrees and Tori looks frantic wondering how the three of them are going to fit in the cart, but Austin climbs on the back.

"I'm on number five. You can just cut across through nine if you want," Austin says leaning his head around to Tori's side, still only speaking to Caroline. He is gone in an instant and then pounds the roof of the cart letting Caroline know he is ready, startling Tori and she jumps. Caroline pats her knee, discovering why they have made the journey to *Twisted Gun* as a huge smile takes over her face thinking about her days in high school.

Caroline is the first to arrive stopping her cart several feet behind the tee and Austin jumps off coming again to Tori's side, but speaking to Caroline. "Thanks for the lift, Ms. Hatfield!" and he shrugs his bag on his shoulders walking to the tee box. Taking a few steps, he turns and says, "Tori, thanks for coming!" not waiting for reply, he stands his bag and begins his rituals of bending and stretching, putting on his glove, marking a ball, tees in his pocket, and selecting his club. The other players join in him in similar displays.

Tug Valley's coach arrives meeting the boys on the tee and they all shake hands. He walks back to the cart path and blasts an airhorn and Tori about jumps out of her skin. Caroline places her hand more firmly on the girl's knee, but does not have to remind her to be quiet as the boy in navy blue shorts, light blue polo, and a *Miners* hat steps up to tee off. His first swing sends his ball sailing down the fairway drawing a little and clipping the edge of a bunker. Tug Valley slices out of bounds and River View is short of the bottleneck forcing him into a long second shot.

Then Austin.

Austin has stood back watching the other three, arms crossed over his chest – concentrating. Their first hits reveal no emotions, no change in expression as he patiently waits his turn. Each boy has used a different club with each producing a different result. Though he took practice swings earlier, all his clubs are in his bag. It is a long par 4 that narrows in the middle and doglegs to the left. Caroline has heard talk around school that Austin is an aggressive player rarely taking safe shots. Pulling his driver from his bag, he addresses the ball with collected confidence. Poise and strength, Austin blasts it easily clearing the bunker. Watching it soar, he knows where it lands without seeing it hit the ground. Two of the other boys release a grunting sigh as they pick up their clubs and begin to walk the fairway to see Austin's drive is safe just short of the green. This first hole would be the indication of his dominance in his group over the next eight.

Following them to the green, Caroline suggests they at least watch some of the other groups to not look so obvious, reminding Tori she is supposed to take pictures for the yearbook. Tori agrees and as Caroline turns to go back to the other groups, she asks, "What's that?" pointing to a boxcar that looks like it has been sidetracked.

"It's boxcar from a train."

Huffing, Tori wants to say that she is not dumb, but asks, "Yeah, but what's it doing here?"

"Oh, it's bathroom. The one on the back nine is a caboose."

"Huh, that's pretty cool!" as Tori begins to think this golf thing may be interesting after all.

Chuckling at her young friend, Caroline agrees, "Yeah, I think so too!"

The girls watch every other group, but Caroline knows Tori prefers to follow the Ones though she does not ask and catches back up with Austin's group for the last four holes. The afternoon is beautiful, the breeze is just enough to keep you comfortable, and Caroline has enjoyed her evening with Tori. She is quiet when she needs to be, realizes you do not cheer or clap, whispers when she asks Caroline a question, wants to know why the other boys hit more times than Austin, and why he takes his glove on and off.

They are the last cart of spectators as they come down the fairway of #3 and Tori squeals in surprise, "That sand looks like a heart!" Tori swoons and says, "Ah...I found my heart at *Twisted Gun*!" Caroline laughs out loud enjoying the girl's foolishness.

The match ends and Tori snaps pictures as the teams are verifying their scorecards. When everyone is finished, she takes a picture of the group and everyone heads to their cars. Austin's dad has arrived and loads his son's clubs in his truck as he walks Caroline and Tori to their car.

"Thanks again, Ms. Hatfield, for coming. Maybe we can play sometime," bright-eyed, youthful, enthusiastic; Caroline remembers that feeling well.

"That would be nice, but you'd beat me to death!"

"Nah, I'd go easy on ya, and give ya lessons each hole!" They both laugh and Austin gives his total attention to Tori. "Hey, Tori, thanks for coming and if you didn't get enough pictures, we have a match on Monday and another here next Thursday...You can ride with me, if you want," the attractive young man looks to the nervous, squirrelly Tori for an answer and she flubs it.

"Well, I don't know...I do need some more shots...I will have to check...I think that would be ok..."

Caroline is close enough to her to pinch Tori's shoulder without being seen, getting her attention. "She would love it and it will save me the trip!" Caroline gives Austin the smile he is waiting for.

Smiling at Tori, though hers does not quite match his, Austin says, "Goodnight and you all drive safe," before he jogs over to his dad who is waiting for him.

Caroline uses this as a teachable moment that goes far beyond the classroom. "Tori, I am more nervous and squirrelly around boys than you are. AND let me tell you, it only gets worse as you get older…But, I would like to think, if someone as cool as Austin Wilson was interested in me, I would try to pull it together!"

"Really?!? Do you think he's interested?" Tori sits up like a birddog, shock and fear washing over her face.

It is in these moments Caroline likes to pretend if her student was actually her daughter, she would give good motherly advice. "Well, Tori, it has been a while since a boy asked me to watch him play ball…But, if he invited me *and* offered to drive me to the match, yes, the insecure, crazy girl in my head would think he was just being nice. BUT – the hopeful, excited girl in my head, would already be thinking about what I was going to wear."

Tori slumps in her seat chewing on this kernel for a few moments. Before they make it back out to the main road, Tori gets a text from Austin. Squealing with delight, Caroline is the outsider in the conversation, though Tori shares each message with her asking for help on her responses and the trip back to the high school holds a very different mood than earlier.

Seventh period Friday, a student worker brings her a sealed envelope and says she is to read it and respond. Opening it, there is one page folded inside. Realizing it is from Sophie, she laughs and says, "Tell Ms. Cross – Ha! Ha!" and she looks back at the cartoon drawing of a ring + a heart = a bunch of smiley face stickers. Caroline just laughs, but rushes out the door when the bell sounds to avoid being trapped by Sophie.

Coming to Seth's home still gives her a thrill and she is always excited to be there, but she refuses to allow Sophie's comments to make nests in her head and her stomach is surprisingly calm. Getting out of the car, she is confident as she walks up the steps in her red, strapless handkerchief dress with the cutouts along the hem. There is some relief in the heat, a faint whisper of the approaching fall, so Caroline has left hair down in bouncy curls.

Seth greets her at the door in khaki shorts and a turquoise short sleeve Henley stretched across his chest – striking as ever. His kiss lingers and he says, "I love your hair," threading his hand around her neck to her nape holding her away from him under long study like he is trying to memorize her face.

His hold relaxes and she responds saucily, "Thanks! I do, too," kissing a smile on his lips.

Caroline joins him in the kitchen and he asks her about the golf match. She chatters happily telling all about Tori and Austin. Seth chuckles as he makes his way around the room completing their dinner. They finish about the same time. Seth has everything arranged on serving trays and suggests they eat on the back deck. Helping him carry everything outside, the table is already set with candles and flowers. Caroline's heart catches in her throat and her pulse begins to race. Her hands tremble and she jostles the tray. Hearing the bowls clink, she is no longer stunned and her heart slows. Seth goes to the other side of the table and to lay out the food not noticing her pause.

Dinner is delicious with food, conversation, laughter, and company. They put everything back on the trays out of their way linking their hands across the table. The sun has dropped behind the trees putting them in the shade. Suddenly, Seth grows quiet and with downcast face, he studies their hands rubbing his thumbs over her fingers. He sits there in silence and the hummingbirds in her chest are flapping wildly. She waits allowing him to speak when his words are in order. Time seems to stretch on forever, but she is patient.

"Caroline."

Her heart leaps.

"Caroline."

She must press her lips together to keep from shouting YES!

Looking at her for the first time in several moments, Seth's face is sad. "We were informed Tuesday that we have entered the second phase of readiness…I've suspected it for a while, but it came official this week." Swallowing hard against his emotions, Seth is determined to remain calm so Caroline understands what he is telling her. "We deploy in January… if not sooner."

He gives her a few heartbeats to process this then removes his hands bringing his chair directly in front of her. "Caroline, you have known from the beginning, I would have to leave. It's just a little sooner than planned."

His voice changes – a switch has been flipped and he presents facts to her quickly and without emotion, like he has become all military and she is just another thing that needs to be taken care of. "The next few months will be a major task as the mobilization process begins. All our squads are full and we will complete final stateside training by the end of November. It is important I stay focused on all the responsibilities I have before me. I cannot afford to be distracted and my unit depends on me to give 110%. This is what I have planned for, trained for…This what I want."

Seth sits up straight no longer touching Caroline. His voice is not cold, but is robotic like he has pressed play on a recorded message and it will not stop until the end, not allowing her speak. Beyond his shoulder, she sees the sun has broken through the trees shining on the peaceful river as a pair of kayakers paddle by. The first leaf of autumn falls from a branch and Caroline watches its silent descent and she feels the thud as it crashes to the ground and with it her heart. Her eyes return to Seth as he continues.

"Please understand…I can no longer see you."

He continues to speak, but in her ears is a shrill ring like she is about to faint and everything around begins to blur. She pushes her chair away from him and legs make a loud noise raking across the deck, then catches on a board lurching her forward. She grabs the edge of the table and the arm of her chair coming to her feet and working herself down the steps as quickly as possible though her legs feel like licorice. Running her hand down the wall of the house, she is stable and her feet make it to the ground. Her throat begins to clinch, but she finds an ounce of sanity and strength to hold herself together not allowing him to see her cry.

Seth continues to speak and Caroline just walks. Walks away from him, from this house, from his voice that with every syllable is another arrow to her flesh with the final word mortal and deadly piercing her heart.

"I'm sorry, Caroline, but for me, Williamson has always been just… temporary."

Caroline stops at the edge of the house. One more step and she will enter the front yard out of his sight. The ice that she so expertly has packed around her heart for years returns with that last word to save her. The ice saves her, because she knows her heart is dying. You cannot hear these words without your heart dying. The cold ice preserves her heart, otherwise she knows it would have stopped beating.

Armed with the tiniest particle of resolve, Caroline turns to face him and humor flutters through her as she surveys the sad, yet grossly poetic moment. Seth has not followed her trying to explain, to bring her to reason, but stands on the edge of the deck allowing his words to drive her away completing the task he set out to do. Of the many words that have passed between them, in their final moments together, they share only silence.

One heartbeat…Tick-Tock…Two heartbeats…Tick-tock…Three heartbeats…

When nothing is said and shockingly nothing is crying out from her soul, screaming in her mind, Caroline turns and leaves him. There is no need to look back as she rounds the corner, there is no need to run, because he is not following her.

Seth waits until he hears her engine start then fade off in the distance. Only then, does he move – again robotic. He clears the table bringing the candles, flowers, and tablecloth inside. He washes the dishes and puts everything away. When he is finished, he locks the front door, drawing the shades on every window in the house and goes to his room. He turns his phone off and lays it face down on the dresser. Stuffing his hands in his pockets, his finger feels something round and hard, the metal warm being so close to his skin. Without looking at it, he takes it from his pocket and opens the top drawer finding a small, red leather box the same shade as Caroline's dress. Releasing the latch, Seth secures the delicate item in its velvet bed closing the box before he sees it. He then buries the box deep in the back corner of his drawer.

His body begins to tremble as he removes his clothes crawling into bed. He is exhausted; weak and spent. The pillows and sheets are a welcome cradle to his tired mind and body. Shivering, he curls on his side pulling the sheets to his chin. His thoughts are everywhere and his mind will not quiet though fatigue grips him.

She had to leave.
This had to end.
She cannot be part of this.

296

This is what I want.
She will never understand.
This has always been my plan.
She is hurt.
This is for the best.
She did not say a word, did not ask why.
This is what I want.
She did not cry.

Though he is quickly to sleep, his night is restless and filled with dreams. Dreams of Caroline. Caroline in her red dress. Caroline and her beautiful hair with her back to him walking out of his life.

Caroline is numb. Everything is surreal; a weird *Twilight Zone* moment. She is not conscious of her drive home, but somehow arrives safely. She drops everything at the front door locking it behind her and climbs the stairs. In her room, she walks out of her clothing littering it across the floor on her way to shut the blinds. Turning off her phone, she lays it face down on the dresser avoiding her reflection. Unplugging the phone beside her bed, she crawls under the sheets.

She does not move looking at the ceiling watching as the shadows lengthen and light completely fades from the room. Her soul feels as naked as her body – raw and hurting, every hair standing on end, every nerve being stimulated sending deep aching pain to through every fiber of her being. The weight of the last few moments, hours, weeks, months bear down upon her pressing deeper and deeper. She feels like she is being buried alive, the oxygen is quickly escaping and she is suffocating. Her throat and neck clinches. Her chest feels like it is going to burst. Her heart is pounding, pounding, pounding. The shrill ringing in her ears is near deafening. All this must stop else she will go mad or perish.

One tear.

One tear escapes.

One tear falls from the corner of her eye trailing down her temple and it is an overwhelming sensation when it splashes against her hairline. Seth's words were the first crack in the dam, now her whole body is shattered and pressure has built up behind. The one tear is quickly followed by many through the many cracks; the wall is breeched and the flood comes washing away and destroying everything in its path.

Turning to her side, drawing the sheets to her chin, Caroline cries for hours – sobbing, moaning, aching and gasping, wailing, and the barking cough – the only and best way to express the complete destruction of the heart. The death of a heart that is forced to continue living though you feel dead inside. Caroline is unaware when her anguish gives way to exhaustion and the darkness of the night parallels the darkness of her soul.

Well past noon the next day, she looks at her clock and in the bottom, right hand corner of the oversized digital face, she reads the date – 9/2/06. Strangely, she realizes – Summer is over, September has arrived and she has finally awoken from the dream to be living a nightmare.

About the Author

Frist time author, Sarah E. Kincaid is from eastern Kentucky, in the coalfields of Appalachia, where she is a high school teacher and the golf coach - which is hilarious, because it is not any indication of her skill. She loves adventures with her family, especially her 4 nieces and 4 nephews with many of her favorite memories being spent on the waters of South Holston Lake where the family has had a home for many years. She believes God has a wonderful story for everyone to tell and wants to show that Christ is in the ordinary parts of our lives making each day extra-ordinary.